A RELATIVE STRANGER

A RELATIVE STRANGER

BY MARGARET LUCKE

ST. MARTIN'S PRESS   NEW YORK

Production Editor: David Stanford Burr

Design by Judith A. Stagnitto

Library of Congress Cataloging-in-Publication Data

Lucke, Margaret
       A relative stranger / Margaret Lucke.
          p. cm.
      ISBN 0-312-06307-5
      I. Title.
      PS3562.U2547R4   1991
      813'.54—dc20   91-19913
                                              CIP

First Edition: November 1991

10 9 8 7 6 5 4 3 2 1

For my parents
Valerie Bohnert Harris and S. Henry Harris, Jr.
and of course for Charlie
with love

A RELATIVE STRANGER

ONE

The phone rang, jangling me out of a good sleep.

"Jessica Randolph?" said the voice at the other end.

"Yes . . . who is it?"

"This is your father."

"Roger?" But this was not Roger's deep, chuckly voice.

"No. Your real father."

"*What?*"

"Allen Fraser. Your real father."

I slammed down the receiver.

The phone trilled again. By this time Scruff was up and barking.

"Jessica, I must talk to you," he said when I answered.

"Look, whoever you are. It's one-thirty in the morning. I had a rough day. I'm in no mood for jokes. Now leave me alone."

I banged down the phone and tried to calm Scruff. Almost at once the ringing resumed. I pulled my pillow over my face and stared into it, counting. The phone rang twenty-two times before I finally yanked out the plug.

I pushed through the office door, past the little brass plaque that said PARKS & O'MEARA, INVESTIGATIONS.

"Hi, Jess. How'd it go this morning?" Claudia looked up from her keyboard and grinned. It's a nice habit she has. My first impression of Claudia McFarlane when she applied for her job two years ago was of a wide grin under a mop of unruly brown ringlets. She was fresh out of school but quickly made herself indispensable as receptionist, secretary and mother hen to Tyler Parks, O'Meara and me.

"It went fine. I'm sure we'll win." I'd spent the morning testifying in court. Our clients, two partners in a high-tech firm down on the Peninsula, were suing the third partner, who'd been selling microchips off the books and pocketing the cash. They'd hired Parks & O'Meara to catch him at it, and we'd succeeded.

"You don't seem real thrilled about it."

"I'm just tired. Last night I—well, I didn't get too much sleep. Besides, there was no question about Videau taking his buddies for a ride. We had him cold."

There was a pair of in-boxes on the table behind Claudia's desk. I didn't feel up to facing the letters and message slips heaped up in mine; instead I lifted the morning *Chronicle* from Tyler's. He didn't need it; he was at La Tavola, wooing a prospective client over veal piccata and sauvignon blanc. Marketing—you rarely see a detective doing it on TV, but it's like any other business: you have to bring in the customers if you're going to pay the bills.

P&O occupies two large, open rooms at the top of what once had been a whiskey warehouse on upper Sansome Street. A friend of Tyler's, an enterprising young architect, bought the building cheap some years ago, exposed the brick walls, added skylights, opened the roof to create an interior courtyard, and made his reputation. It's a pleasant location—convenient to downtown, yet lowscale and sunny. Now, unfortunately, high-rise developers are discovering the neighborhood.

I carried the paper, my leather satchel and my brown bag from Irma's Deli into the big office that Tyler and I share. Tyler's half holds our computer setup, every electronics catalog ever issued, and a museum-quality collection of chewing gum wrappers—every time he quits smoking, he tries to find a way to satisfy the oral cravings without gaining weight. His desktop is gradually being swallowed by a huge Boston fern. In the corner is a mound of blue blankets, high and soft, for his partner and best friend, O'Meara.

O'Meara padded over to greet me, wagging his copper-red tail. Or actually, to greet my lunch. Irish setters are hunters, and O'Meara is among the champs. He zeroed right in on the brown bag.

"Forget it, fella. Sneak some dog yummies out of Tyler's desk drawer. This is all mine."

Dogs never believe you when you say you're not going to feed them. O'Meara hovered by my desk, tongue at the ready, as I set out a picnic on my desk—chicken piroshki, some apple juice, one of Irma's irresistible chocolate chip cookies with pecans. The cookie made it a better deal than La Tavola any day. I promised myself ten extra laps in the pool to make up for the indulgence.

I skimmed over the newspaper while I ate. The Giants had been brave against Atlanta last night—about time they won one. The San Francisco police had no clues in the murder of the socialite whose body had been found in a Tenderloin alley after the Arts and Flowers Ball. The Middle East was boiling up again, but the president was expected to announce yet another peace plan soon. A shouting match broke out at a Planning Commission hearing between members of a tenants' group and an owner who wanted to turn their apartments into condos and them out into the street. Charlie Brown lost another round to the kite-eating tree.

One bit of good news in five items—there have been worse days.

I tossed O'Meara the last bite of piroshki, which I'd generously saved; it never hit the floor. Then I went out and scooped up my mail. In with the ads and memos and invoices to be okayed there were three pink telephone slips.

All of them from Allen Fraser.

"Claudia, these three calls."

"Oh yeah. That guy." She lifted her curly head from her work. "He sounded real eager to talk to you. I told him you wouldn't be in till this afternoon, but he called back twice anyway."

"What did he say?"

"Well, the first time he called smack on the dot of nine. I hadn't even hung up my jacket. I said you were expected around lunchtime and could I have you return the call. So he gave me his name and number. Then he called again about eleven. I said you still weren't in, could someone else help him. Tyler was here then. But he said no, he had to speak to you, he hoped maybe you'd got back early. The last time was maybe half an hour before you walked in."

"Damn him. How'd he find me here, anyway?"

"What's the matter, Jess? Who is this guy?"

"He says he's my father."

She looked puzzled. "I thought your dad's name was Roger."

"Roger's really my stepfather. He married my mother when I was thirteen. My father left when I was a baby. I don't know him at all. As far as I'm concerned, Roger's the only father I've got."

Claudia was wide-eyed. "And this is the first you've heard from your real father in all that time?"

I nodded. "If it's actually him."

"Wow. What are you going to say to him?"

"Nothing. I'm not going to call him back." I crushed the pink slips into a ball and flipped them into her wastebasket.

"He'll call you. He's already tried three times."

"Four. No, more than that." I told her about last night's calls. "For thirty years he's ignored me completely. Never a phone call, never a letter, no birthday cards or Christmas presents. So suddenly he's so eager to be in touch, he's got to do it in the middle of the night. Well, forget it. I've gotten along fine without him so far, thank you, and I can live without him for the rest of my life."

"If it was me I'd be curious about what he's like," Claudia said. When I didn't respond, she asked, "What do you want me to tell him?"

"Just that I'm not interested in speaking to him."

I headed into our combination kitchen-library-conference room, which is partitioned off by bookcases from the reception area and Claudia's desk, and made myself some tea. Back at my desk, I spread out my notes for my report on the Videau case. But I couldn't focus on it. I found myself doodling: a still life of my mug and my pencil holder, the cascading fronds of Tyler's fern, stick figures of a man and child holding hands.

The phone rang. My body tensed. My stomach twisted. I heard Claudia say, "Good afternoon, Parks and O'Meara." Pause. "Mr. Parks isn't in, Mr. Gardner. He should be back in twenty minutes or so. May I have him call you?"

My pounding heart calmed down, but my stomach refused to unknot.

I'd made no progress at all on the Videau report when Tyler returned from lunch, dressed for client-impressing in his one and only blue suit. He hates that suit; he never wears it unless it's absolutely necessary. It's ten years old and he was twenty pounds lighter when he bought it, but he'd find it agonizing to shop for another. His favorite attire is a beat-up pair of corduroys and an ancient, misshapen forest-green sweater that he's as attached to as a baby to its blanket. He goes into withdrawal whenever it has to go to the cleaners.

Now he shed his jacket and tie with the air of a condemned man being released from prison. He perched on the corner of my desk and rumpled the fur on O'Meara's neck while he tried to impress me with tales of his salesmanship. As he talked I became aware of the phone ringing, Claudia answering, the light on my extension winking as she put the call on hold. There was an almost interminable moment of waiting. Then she appeared in the office doorway, a little worried furrow between her brows.

"Jess, it's him. What do you want me to say?"

That twisted, knotted feeling grabbed me again.

"Tell him what I told you. I don't want to talk to him."

"Are you sure? I mean, this could be your only chance. You might regret it later."

"I'm sure. I don't want to talk to him."

"Well, if you're sure you're sure."

"Yes, damn it, I'm absolutely, positively sure."

"Well, okay. If it was me, though—"

"Claudia!"

"Okay!" She scooted back to deliver my message.

"What was that all about?" Tyler asked. "Some jerko pestering you for a blind date?"

"Not exactly." I told him the story briefly. He was my colleague, my employer, my good friend, but I found myself oddly reluctant to talk about this. It was as though having other people know about it might somehow make Allen Fraser more real, his claim on me more legitimate.

"I'm with Claudia," Tyler said when I finished. He patted his pockets for cigarettes, remembered he had quit again and unwrapped a stick of gum. Tyler has perfect looks for a private detective—just over average height, thick but not fat, brown hair just starting to thin out. He looks comfortable, trustworthy and unmemorable. "You oughta talk to him."

"What for? He never cared about me. He was never around when I needed him. Well, now I *don't* need him."

"But he's part of you, Jess. It's a chance to learn some more about who you are. If you don't find out what he wants, you'll always wonder."

Claudia returned, looking reproachful. "I told him. He sounded awfully disappointed."

"Think of it as an investigation." Tyler was getting all fired up. "You're a good detective, you like getting to the bottom of things. Answering questions and solving problems."

"There weren't any problems until he called. Damn, I wish I'd had my phone machine on last night."

"He'd still be calling here," Claudia pointed out.

I was up, restless, pacing from one side of the room to the other. O'Meara, thinking it was a game, trotted at my heels. "That's another thing. How'd he get this number, damn it?"

"Phone him, Jess," Tyler urged.

"I can't. I . . . I'd feel disloyal to Roger."

"He'll understand," Claudia said. "Just meeting your real father won't change things with Roger."

"Claudia, you don't get it. You grew up in a nice storybook family, mommy, daddy, kiddies, all sweetness and light. It's not like that for everybody." I wasn't being fair, but I didn't care. "Besides," I added, dropping back in my chair, "what about my mother?"

"Ah," said Tyler. "That's the real issue, isn't it. You can't hurt her now, you know. If this guy had turned up while she was still alive, it might be different."

"Anyway," said Claudia enthusiastically, "you don't have to like him or even see him again. This just lets you find out some things."

"Do what you think is best, Jess," Tyler said. "But maybe—just maybe—it would be good to hear his side of the story."

Two against one. Were they right? Would I always wonder? Damn it all anyway.

"Okay. You win. I'll call him."

"Hooray," said Claudia. They stood there, waiting.

"Well, I'm not going to do it with a goddamn audience. Scram. All of you."

They retreated, even O'Meara. I could hear a clatter of coffee mugs and a murmur of voices from the kitchen. I went out, fished one of the pink slips from Claudia's trashcan and uncrumpled it on my desk.

Allen Fraser. My tongue wrapped itself around those strange syllables but I didn't say them out loud. I walked over to the window. If you looked to the side of the new gray office cube across the street, then out past the freeway, you could see a blue patch of bay glimmering in the afternoon sun. Two white sailboats were scudding along in the spring wind. How did their owners get time off to go sailing on a Tuesday afternoon?

Allen Fraser. I turned back to the phone, picked it up, put it back down. Then I lifted the receiver again. They were right. Before he called, it didn't matter. But now, like it or not, he'd made himself part of my life, even if just for a moment. I had to play it out to the end. Come on, Jess. Breathe deep. One, two, three . . . and I dialed.

The number was for the posh Royal Pacific Hotel, downtown near Union Square. Something was doing a tap dance in my stomach as the operator connected me to his room. The call was answered on the first ring.

"Thank God," he said when I told him my name. "I was afraid you really wouldn't talk to me."

"I wasn't going to call back," I admitted. "Some friends talked me into it."

"I'm glad. Can we meet? How about dinner?"

"I can meet you for a drink after work. I'm busy later." I wasn't, but I didn't know how much time I'd want to spend with this man.

"Good." There was a note of relief in his voice. "I'll pick you up at your office."

I also wasn't sure how deeply I wanted him to invade my territory. "I'd rather come to your hotel. Seven o'clock?"

"Fine. I'll be in the lobby. I'll wear a white carnation so you'll recognize me." He gave a small, nervous laugh. "A fine thing for a man to have to say to his own daughter."

"All right. I'll look for a white carnation."

"Jessica, thank you. This is a life-saver for me. I do want to get to know you. But there's more than that. I need your help. Professionally, I mean." He took a deep breath. "You see, Jessica, I think I'm wanted for murder."

TWO The white carnation wasn't necessary. Allen Fraser was unmistakable. Tall and lean like me. Curly red hair like mine, though his was darker and thinner and a good bit shorter, with a touch of gray at the temples. He stood by a marble pillar near the reception desk, wearing a dove-gray suit and a paisley tie in warm red.

I pushed at my hair and tugged at my blazer to straighten it, and then felt annoyed with myself—why should I worry about making a good impression on this man? In my court-going clothes I looked as cool and professional as he did. I could pretend this was just another meeting with a potential client.

Sure I could.

How do you greet a father you've never seen before? An embrace was out of the question. A handshake somehow seemed too businesslike.

"Hello," I said. Good Lord, I didn't even know what to call him. Allen? Not Mr. Fraser. Certainly not Dad. Mom had always referred to him as "your father," and not with affection, either.

"Jessica." He reached out a tentative hand but quickly withdrew it and looked away. Of course. This would be awkward for him too.

"Let's go up to the Vista Room," he said.

"Fine."

We were the only people in the elevator, and we rode up thirty stories without a word. He stared at the flashing numbers over the door. I memorized the placards advertising the hotel's restaurants. Baron's Grill for the best in beef. The Cable Car Room, fine dining in an "old San Francisco" atmosphere. The Vista Room, cocktails in the clouds, jazz nightly at nine.

We settled into a pair of pink upholstered armchairs with a low table between us. Beyond us, through an expanse of plate glass, were North Beach, the Golden Gate and the gray Marin hills. The sun was dimming. Lights were winking on below.

"What will you have?" Allen Fraser asked. I pulled myself away from the view. The cocktail waitress stood by the table, pencil poised. I ordered a glass of chardonnay. He requested Glenfiddich on the rocks.

"Well, Jessica," he said as the waitress walked off. He couldn't decide what to do with his hands. They moved from his knees to the arms of the chair to his chin to his knees again. "Thank you for seeing me. I can understand why you might not want to." He smiled a little. It wasn't a bad smile. Sweet. Almost shy.

"I wasn't going to. The people at work convinced me I'd regret it if I didn't at least find out what you look like."

"And it turns out I look like you." The smile grew broader. The close resemblance seemed to please him. "You're a lovely young lady, Jessica. No tribute to the family relationship, of course."

I didn't know what to say to that. I turned back to the window. A container ship was sliding its nose under the Golden Gate Bridge, first step on a journey to Hong Kong or Japan.

The waitress brought our drinks, and Allen Fraser lifted his glass in a toast. "Here's to a new chapter in our relationship, Jessica. No, it's the first chapter really. I can't make up for the past, but I hope the future will be better between us." He looked at me nervously, expectantly.

I hesitated, then returned his salute with my glass. "To the future," I said; that should be ambiguous enough. We each took a ritual sip.

A moment of strained silence, which I finally broke. "You said you wanted to see me professionally. About a murder." How bizarre that murder should seem like the most comfortable, most impersonal subject to talk about.

"Yes. Which I didn't commit, as I assured you on the phone. Shall we . . . I mean, is that where we should begin?" He twirled the swizzler in his glass. His hands were squarish, with long tapering fingers. I spread my left hand in my lap and stole a look. More slender, but the same general shape. All on its own, my hand clenched itself into a fist.

"How to start, how to start," said Allen Fraser. "I asked for this meeting, yet now that you're here I don't know what to say." He fidgeted in the pink chair. "Jesus, I feel like a junior-high-school kid on his first date."

"Why *did* you want to see me all of a sudden? Why all the drama, the middle-of-the-night phone call and everything?"

"I'm sorry for that. I'd just found out about Debbie and I was upset. I didn't think about the time." He leaned toward me, looking earnest. "But the desire to see you wasn't sudden, Jessica. I've wanted to for a long time but I was afraid. Debbie's death—it's horrible, an awful thing. But . . . well, it gave me an excuse to call you. I thought maybe I could still get to know you, if not as your father then as a client."

"So why didn't you want to get to know me when I was a kid and needed you?" That wasn't what I'd meant to say. I tried to swallow the question with a sip of chardonnay and get the discussion back on a professional level. "Who's Debbie? How was she killed?"

But Allen Fraser wouldn't cooperate. "I did want to know you. Your mother wouldn't let me. She . . . I guess she had her reasons. She was a proud woman, you know."

Yes, she was a proud woman, my mother. Proud and independent and strong. She died two years ago, too young, of an illness that proved to be mercifully brief. A sudden sharp longing for her pierced me like a knife. I looked at the window. The sky was lilac and orange now, the distant hills deepening to purple. The container ship was clear of the bridge and steaming into the open sea.

"I'm sorry about your mother, Jessica." His voice was nearly a whisper.

"Why did you leave?" I asked, staring down into my glass.

He sipped his scotch, as if to fortify himself for the story. "We were much too young when we got married, your mother and I. If it hadn't been for you . . . we didn't have any money and I hated my job, hated the responsibility of it all. I . . . well, I guess I . . . took it out on Mary. Then someone else came along, and I let myself fall in love with her. She was a model, beautiful and glamorous and free. When she went to New York to try to further her career, I followed her."

"My mother was beautiful," I said sharply.

"Jessica, don't—"

"How come we weren't good enough for you? A home, a family—lots of people think that's highly desirable. But no—we weren't *glamorous!*"

"Please, Jessica."

I bit my lip and blinked to hold in the tears that stung my eyes. I set down my wineglass; I'd been ready to fling it at him. This afternoon I had promised myself I'd be calm, contained, controlled.

He leaned forward again, looking seriously at me. His eyes were gray, while mine are green in most lights. I was grateful for this small point of difference.

"I'm not proud of all that, you know. It's not a part of my life I feel good about."

"Did you marry her?" I asked, sinking deeper into my chair. "The model?"

"No. We lived together for about a year. By then I realized I'd made a mistake and Arlette had figured out I wasn't going to be much help to her career."

"Do you still live in New York?"

To my surprise he laughed, a rich, warm sound. His eyes crinkled at the corners and he seemed to relax a little. "We really don't know much about each other, do we? I should have brought a résumé. Or maybe a letter of introduction. I live in Manhattan. I never married Arlette or anyone else. I was a banker for a while, then a friend invited me to become his partner; we do personal financial planning."

"What's that?"

"You know. Setting up trusts and estate plans, counseling on investments, that sort of thing. We help our clients define their financial goals and get the maximum return on their resources."

"I see." It must be nice to need such services, I thought. My financial goal was to have enough at the first of each month to cover the rent.

"We operate pretty independently, really. We've each got our own clients. Brad's a bit of a loner. Doesn't quite trust me with his clients, I guess." He chuckled; it was apparently a joke. Then he turned somber. "Debbie is . . . was . . . his daughter."

"The murder," I said.

"Yes. Saturday night. She was—"

He broke off abruptly as the cocktail waitress appeared. We ordered fresh drinks. When she had gone to fetch them, he changed the subject again. "You know, I tried to come back once. To your mother, I mean. It was after Arlette and I broke up and I thought I had . . . well, had certain problems under control. I flew back here to see if Mary and I couldn't give it another try. But by then she'd finished her degree and had that librarian job. She said she'd gotten over me and I should get out of her life—get the hell out, to be precise."

"She never told me about that."

"You were about four then. I took Mary out to a fancy restaurant and a nightclub—made a big occasion of popping the question. I came to that little house in Oakland to pick her up, and you and I played with your toys on the living room floor while Mary finished getting ready. I brought you a doll. That was the last time I saw you. Look."

From his jacket's inside pocket he pulled out a dog-eared snapshot: a small flame-haired child in a yellow T-shirt, clutching a clown doll and staring solemnly at the camera. A vague, unwelcome memory teased at the edge of my mind.

His gaze was focused on something distant, way beyond my shoulder. "It was the last time I saw Mary too. She made it quite clear that we were completely, totally, irrevocably finished. I kept trying to tell her I'd changed, but . . . I'd no idea I'd hurt her so badly. I should have known, of course. There were a lot of things I should have known back then." He looked back at me, gray eyes full of pain. "But I didn't want to make things worse, so I did what she asked and stayed out of your lives. I sent money for a while, but she quit cashing the checks, so I stopped sending them."

"I didn't know you'd sent money." In fact, my mother had told me very little about my father. I must have asked questions when I was small, but I figured out early on that she didn't like talking about him. My mother in those days always hovered at the edge of sadness. She kissed me often, helped me with my homework and apologized for not baking cookies like my friend Gina's mom. Each night she came home from work tired and silent. Not until she met Roger did her eyes lose their distant gaze, her face soften, her laughter start to flow.

Our new drinks arrived. I started to prompt him. "Your partner's daughter. What happened on Saturday night?" But I had an even more burning question. "How did you know I'm an investigator, anyway? How did you find me?"

"I have a friend here in town who stayed close to you and Mary, too. He's kept me posted—Jack Emerich."

Uncle Jack! A spy in our midst all those years. He'd always show up on holidays and family occasions with presents and treats. For a while, when I was eight or nine, I had campaigned to get my mother to marry him so he could be my daddy, but nothing had come of it. Even after she'd married Roger, though, Uncle Jack had come around regularly to join us for Saturday night supper or to take me and my little brothers, as they came along, to places like the county fair. I'd had lunch with him only two weeks ago, the traitor. Never once could I remember his mentioning my father to me.

"So you know all about me then." I felt angry. Betrayed. Suddenly I was at a distinct disadvantage here.

"Not nearly all. And certainly not enough. Look, Jessica, all this time you've blamed me for not being interested in you. All right, I deserved it. But then it's not fair to get mad because I've turned out to be more interested than you thought. Give me a chance."

"I *am* giving you a chance. That's why I'm sitting here."

"And there's so much I don't know." He tried out the shy smile again. "This detective business, for instance. How did you ever get involved in that? I thought you were going to be an artist."

Maybe Uncle Jack hadn't given everything away after all. "I am an artist. But that's not a very reliable way to buy groceries. When I graduated from the Art Institute I wanted to earn money but still paint, so I answered an ad for a part-time job as receptionist at Parks and O'Meara. Tyler had just started the agency then. I began helping on cases and found myself fascinated by investigative work, and good at it too. Finally I decided to get my own license. By then the business had grown and we could afford to hire someone else as receptionist full-time."

"So you gave up on art?"

"Not at all. In fact I'm going to be in the Ars Nova show at the Hammerwood Gallery." I said this proudly; it was a coup. Muriel Gittelsohn, Hammerwood's owner, holds the show annually to showcase the most promising local artists. It's highly competitive; only six artists are selected each year. The day I learned I'd been chosen was one of the most exciting days of my life.

"I'd like to see your work," Allen Fraser said.

"The opening reception's on Sunday. I'll get you an invitation."

An odd look—disappointment?—crossed his face. Maybe he was angling to be asked home to see my studio. It was far too soon for that.

"Yes. Well, I'll be sure to come if I'm still in town."

No! I wanted to scream and shake him. You don't get it! If you cared about me you'd make a point of being there. Muriel Gittelsohn is the most powerful gallery owner in town, renowned for her unerring eye, her prescience about who will make it. This show could be the best thing that's ever happened to me.

But I said nothing. The sky was dark now. Lights sparkled in the city below us and on the distant hills. The illumination in the lounge was low to keep reflections from blotting out the view. A waitress moved about the room, lighting glass-globed candles on the low tables. Allen Fraser and I sat, avoiding each other's eyes, sipping our drinks.

At last I broke the painful silence: "Tell me about this murder you didn't commit."

THREE Allen Fraser glanced around the room—a little furtively, as if all at once he realized it wasn't the best idea to be overheard discussing a killing in which he was involved. There were other people in the room, chatting and laughing over their drinks, but none seated nearby. On the bandstand the piano stood soundless, waiting for nine o'clock.

"You probably saw the news reports," he said as he turned back to me. He looked older suddenly, grayer, slacker. "Deborah Collington. Some wino found her body in an alley Sunday morning. She'd been strangled. The night before she'd gone to a dance, an arts benefit, and she was still dressed up in her green silk gown. But a valuable necklace she was wearing, diamonds and emeralds—the necklace was missing."

I'd read the story in the paper. "The police think she might have been robbed and killed by a man she met at the Arts and Flowers Ball. They were seen leaving together. The media have been calling him the Mystery Stranger."

"That's right." He studied the scotch and melting ice in his glass, then set it down and studied me, as if trying to decide what to say. His voice was bleak when he spoke again. "Jessica, I'm their Stranger."

My reactions tumbled in so fast I couldn't sort out which ones made sense, which were unjustified. Shock, sympathy, rage, wariness, fear. Calm down, Jess—this makes him the prime suspect, all right, but it doesn't mean he's really guilty of . . . of anything. Hear the man out.

"If you didn't kill her," I asked, "why haven't you gone to the police?"

"I, uh . . . well, I'm afraid that would make them even more suspicious. You see, I've got the necklace."

Rule number one for conducting an investigation—be objective. Gather the facts and don't make judgments until you've got them all—or at least a reasonable number. I willed myself not to get up and run away.

"Maybe you'd better tell me what happened."

"As I said, Debbie . . . was . . . my partner's daughter. You know, for a long time I envied Brad. He seemed to have a perfect family life, the kind you see on TV ads but no one really has. Sweet wife, two nice kids. All the things I'd thrown away, like a fool." He offered a rueful smile.

"Go on."

As Deborah grew up, he explained, she had started having problems. She ran around with a wild crowd, stayed out all night, was probably into drugs. She and her father had fought constantly. Bradford Collington had a bit of a temper and his daughter always knew just what to do to provoke it. Finally she dropped out of college and ran off to San Francisco with a boyfriend.

Her father flew out to drag her home. He was appalled when he found her: living in a filthy room, grubbing away at a waitressing job in some dive, the boyfriend lying around stoned beyond coherence. Yet she refused to go back. Brad Collington was furious, but there was nothing he could do; after all, she was twenty years old. That was the last her family had heard from her for about four years.

Then the Collingtons received a wedding announcement. Their Debbie had married an older man, someone with lots of money, good business connections. Her father was pleased—she seemed to be settling down at last. But the marriage broke up and Deborah hadn't been in touch with her parents since.

Allen Fraser told his story well. He maintained good eye contact. His expression was open and forthright. His gestures looked thoughtful and controlled, the hands that made them looked strong.

What did I think of this man? I'd never seen him before—at least, not within memory—yet he seemed somehow familiar. Or was I imagining that—wishing it, dreading it? There was a sprinkle of freckles across his forehead, a small scar by his nose, a mole near the corner of his left eye.

I had freckles too.

I had to force myself to pay attention to what he was saying. I broke in: "You say Deborah and her family weren't in contact. Yet you took her to the Arts and Flowers Ball."

"I met her there. I came out here to meet with an important client who just moved to Palo Alto. Brad asked if I would be willing to sound Debbie out about a reconciliation. When I got in on Saturday I phoned to ask if I could see her. She said she was going to a dance that evening and I could join her if I wanted. Her date had the flu so she had an extra ticket. She left it for me at the door."

"And afterward you went off together."

"That's right. We couldn't really talk there. The music was loud, and people kept coming up to say hello to Debbie. So we left and drove around for a while. I convinced her that her father was sincere about wanting to get back on good terms, and she agreed to call him. She gave me the necklace to take back to him—sort of a gesture of good faith."

That made no sense at all. "But why would she give away something so valuable? The paper said it's worth six figures."

"It seemed odd to me too. I didn't want to take it but she insisted. We made a swap, the jewelry for my tie. She said that made it even—they were both neckwear, they were the same colors. The tie was emerald green."

"I'm sorry," I stood up and reached for my satchel. "You did fine up to here, but this just doesn't ring true."

"I swear it. Hear me out—please."

I wanted to leave. I wanted to stay. "Nothing but the truth," I commanded, sitting down again.

He nodded agreement as he continued his story. "When she gave me the necklace she seemed—well, amused by the whole thing. Like for some reason it struck her as delightfully funny. Debbie's always been prone to extravagant gestures. I remember one time, she must have been nine or ten, she invited all the neighborhood kids home for ice cream. Isabel, her mother, was frantic—here were about twenty kids standing in her kitchen. Of course there wasn't a drop of ice cream in the house and Debbie was wailing away because she'd *promised*."

"What did her mother do?"

"Went out and got ice cream. The kids got their treat and Debbie got her way, as usual."

I nodded, but I was still skeptical. Ice cream was one thing. A hundred-thousand-dollar necklace was quite another. "So she gave you the necklace. For the moment I'll buy that. Then what happened?"

"I took her back to her apartment. I didn't go in, but I walked her to the door and watched her go inside. So I know she was home safe."

"Which means she must have gone out again."

"That's right."

"The question is why, and where, and with whom, if anyone."

"That's what I need you to find out."

"No. You should take your story to the police. Let them do the investigating."

"Come on. I have the necklace and no alibi. I've got to have something better than that before I talk to them."

He was right—it wouldn't look good to the police. For that matter, it didn't look good to me. Father or not, I had no basis for judging this man's honesty. True, he had a certain charm, but a lot of liars are charming.

"I don't understand why you waited so long to call me," I said.

"I phoned as soon as I learned what happened. I was out walking on Sunday, exploring the city. Yesterday I was with my client all day. I didn't see the news until I picked up a paper at the airport to read on the red-eye home."

"Why didn't you just hop on your plane? You'd be home free."

"It never occurred to me. She was my partner's daughter." His voice quavered, and his eyes took on a wet sheen, like tears. "Brad's going to be devastated. He really wanted to straighten things out between them. And now . . ."

He polished off his scotch in a quick gulp. When he looked at me again he was in control. No tears had fallen. "I may have been the last person to see Debbie alive, and I was seeing her on Brad's behalf. I owe it to all of us to find out what happened. I couldn't live with myself if I ran."

Lifting the empty glass he signaled for the waitress. "Another for you, Jessica?" he asked. I shook my head. I felt befuddled enough already, although not from the wine.

"Besides," he continued, "I talked to people at the party, told them my name. Sooner or later I'd be found. I'd rather learn now what happened and not worry forever about being tracked down."

He reached across the table and grasped both my hands. "Jessica, will you take me on?"

"It's homicide. I'd have to check with the police, keep them informed." I pulled my hands away. "I don't think I'm the right one for this case. Tyler—Tyler Parks, he's my boss—sometimes he does criminal defense work for a lawyer friend. But most of what I do is corporate—embezzlement, industrial espionage, employee theft. Tyler's on a case right now, Meridian Insurance, but I'm sure—"

"Please, Jessica." He cut into my babbling. I didn't know what to say. We stared at each other for a tense moment.

Allen Fraser stood up. He faced the plate glass, gazing through his reflection into the darkness. When he spoke he wasn't addressing me. "Oh, shit. I knew this was a bad idea."

Rule number two—don't get emotionally involved with your clients. This man claimed to be my father. Whatever that meant, whatever it would come to mean if we got to know each other, there was emotional involvement here.

I had decided to turn him down. Which is why I was amazed to hear myself say, "Okay, I'll take the case."

He turned around, his face bright as the sun emerging from clouds. He moved toward me, looking as though he wanted to seal the arrangement with a hug.

I warded him off—let's keep this very businesslike. "Now, here's P and O's policy on fees and expenses. . . ."

FOUR When I arrived home everything was the same—yet everything seemed different. I wandered through the flat, looking at the familiar rooms and objects as if through new eyes. Allen Fraser's eyes. What if I had invited him back here—how would he have responded to this place? If he'd stayed around while I was growing up, would I have turned out the same? Would I still be living here, doing what I do? Art had been my mother's passion. Though she'd never had the time and energy to really pursue it, she had shared her love for it with me and had always encouraged my efforts. Wherever my red hair might have come from, the art had surely come from her—hadn't it?

"Hey, Scruff, get down, kiddo." The dog had leaped up, planting his front paws against my skirt and giving one sharp bark to announce that it was past time for his dinner and a walk. I gave him a grateful pat, because he'd interrupted the crazy circles my mind was turning.

I would have to call Roger and tell him about Allen Fraser. Tell my father that my father had appeared. But not right now. Thank goodness for Scruff—a good excuse to put it off.

Scruff was just past puppyhood. I had acquired him in the settlement of a paternity suit. Once O'Meara had disappeared for a couple of days. Tyler was distraught, but the dog wasn't contrite when he returned; if anything, he seemed smugger than usual. Some weeks later we found out why: an irate neighbor appeared at Tyler's door with a carton full of puppies. She announced that since Tyler's dog was responsible for doing such a horrible thing to her sweet, innocent Maisie, then Tyler could just deal with the consequences himself. Oh yes, *and* pay the vet bills. Reasoning with her proved as effective as arguing with a steamroller, and Tyler became foster dad to four hungry, squirming pups.

Claudia managed to distribute three of them among her assorted siblings and cousins. Tyler didn't precisely make my taking the last foundling a condition of my continued employment, but there were hints. I wanted to give him to Keith and Teddy, my little brothers, but Roger is allergic to canines. He endures the cat, two rabbits, a pair of gerbils and a tankful of fish, but a dog is out of the question.

I was reluctant to take him myself. I wasn't sure keeping a dog in the city would be such a good idea, especially with the strange hours my work requires. But it had been lonely in the flat since Dan had gone—more peaceful, yes, but lonely. Scruff—amber-colored, long-haired, smart and eager—has proved a fine companion.

I went into the bedroom to exchange my skirt and blazer for a paint-dappled sweatshirt and jeans. In the jacket pocket I discovered the snapshot of the solemn child with the red braids and clown doll. The doll had been named Crazy. Crazy the Clown with his lopsided, never-ending grin.

So that's who he was! That's where Crazy had come from! The dim, long-buried memory that had teased me surged forth. Bewilderment at receiving a present when it wasn't Christmas or my birthday. A big, strange, scary man who kept trying to make me laugh. And late that night, after the scary man had gone, a hollow feeling of despair as I gripped Crazy tightly and listened while my mother cried and cried. The night when Allen Fraser had come back, momentarily, into our lives.

Filled with an emotion that resembled rage, I grabbed the pooper-scooper gear. Scruff and I set out on our usual evening circuit, down Shrader to Haight Street, over to Cole, up Cole to Frederick, back to Shrader and home. After several months of this route, Scruff had

many well-marked spots to monitor. Tonight he insisted on checking out each one, and he strained at his leash and whined as I tugged
him along.

"Hey, move along, kiddo. It's chilly and damp out here." The
wind had picked up, blowing fog in from the ocean, unusual for
April. I wished it would clear my head, blow away my jumbled
feelings about Allen Fraser. But his shadow pursued me every step
of the way.

Home is near the corner of Shrader and Waller, a block south of
the sixties hippie haven of Haight Street and a block east of Golden
Gate Park. The neighborhood has moved quite a bit upscale in the
years since I came here, but it's still colorful and offbeat.

My flat is in the middle of a stack of three in a small, slightly
seedy Edwardian building. Dan and I discovered it while we were
still at the Art Institute. I try to remember only the early part of the
years we shared it, when the pleasures of making love and making
art together were fresh and exhilarating. Dan sang while he worked,
cooked my favorite strawberry waffles on Sunday mornings, made
my body feel depths of sensation it had never known were possible.
I loved his playfulness and high spirits; I'd had little enough of those
in my life up until then.

But exuberance like that needs a measure of responsibility to
balance it if a relationship is to work. And fairness, too—while Dan
thought certain rules applied to me, he could not believe they were
also meant for him.

Dan moved in and out several times before I kicked him out for
good, but I've never left. This place meets my two essential require-
ments. First, it has a sun porch at the back which makes a bright and
pleasant studio. And it has incredibly cheap rent. Mrs. Fiorelli, my
landlady and downstairs neighbor, has lived here for forty-three
years and she's managed to lose touch with the crazy state of the
housing market. Not that she cares. She's the most generous woman
I've ever met. She takes in foster children, at times it seems by the
dozens, and she tends to look on her tenants in the same light—
bigger kids but still in need of her velvet heart and iron hand. The

25

only difference is that the children call her Aunt Rosa, while the tenants call her Mrs. F.

Something thudded against the back of her door as Scruff and I climbed the front stoop, followed by a series of bangings and shrieks and squeals. The kids were staging World War III again—they do so regularly and with glee. It's the only drawback to living here.

Back upstairs, I fixed Scruff a gourmet meal of canned dog food and kibbles. He thanked me with a wave of his plumey tail and devoured the whole thing in about ten-and-a-half seconds. For dessert I gave him his favorite treat, a chunk of Swiss cheese. I filled his water dish and put the teakettle on for me.

The whole time I tried to avoid thinking about the call I should make to Roger. What would he say? For seventeen years he had been my father. I used his last name. He would always be my father in the ways that counted.

For thirteen years before that, I'd had no father at all.

I knew Roger well. I loved him; he loved me. There was no reason for my palms to be sweaty, for my heart to pound, as I made this call.

"In a way I'm glad," he said when I'd told him the news, although the gladness didn't come through in his voice. He has a friendly bass voice; usually there is laughter submerged in it. But not now. "People should know about their background. Remember when you'd hit those moody patches in high school? I was always scared you'd say the hell with us and run off to find him. You know, on the theory that whatever your real dad was like, he had to be a better deal than your mom and me. But thank goodness, you never did."

"No. Having you come along after all that time seemed like the best deal to me."

But I felt a pang of guilt as I said that. I hadn't thought of it in years, but I *had* schemed to search out my father once. I must have been sixteen because my brother Keith had just been born. My moody patch, as Roger so kindly called it, had felt like a black pit. I could think of only one way to climb out of it: to leave this new family that seemed to have no connection with me and find one of my own. For weeks I skipped movies and bought only doughnuts for lunch. I put aside my allowance and baby-sitting earnings toward a bus ticket to New York—the expense of a plane was beyond dreaming about. How had I known where to find him?—I must have picked up on talk of him somewhere along the line. But then I went to the library to find his address in the New York phone books. No listing for an Allen Fraser in any of them. I called a few Frasers at random but that proved fruitless and I soon gave it up.

"Jess? You still there?"

"Yes, I'm here, Roger."

"Good, good." He gave a deep sigh. "Well, you're a sensible girl. I'm sure you'll handle this fine. Just remember, whatever happens, we're still your family. The boys and me, that is. Which reminds me"—he sounded glad to change the subject—"Keith's birthday dinner on Friday. God, fourteen already, can you believe it? You'll still come, won't you? Even with all this happening?"

"Of course. I wouldn't miss it."

"Good. Seven o'clock. His friend Benjamin will be there too. They want to go to a movie afterward."

"Okay. I'll make sure I'm on time."

I also tried calling Uncle Jack Emerich, that traitor. But there was no answer.

Roger's mention of dinner reminded me that I should eat something. Two glasses of wine wasn't much of a meal. Allen Fraser had invited me to join him at the Baron's Grill, but I pleaded my fictitious previous engagement.

I made a toasted-cheese-and-tomato sandwich and took that and my tea to the round oak table in the bay window of my living room. I also brought the newspapers from the past couple of days. The fine points of a murder make great suppertime reading: calming, good for the digestion.

Monday's paper had the bare details: the discovery of Deborah Collington's body, still clad in the finery she'd worn to the Arts and Flowers Ball, the fact that she'd been seen leaving the dance with a tall, fiftyish man whom no one seemed to know, the disappearance of the emerald-and-diamond necklace.

An obituary in the same edition gave a sedate recital of Deborah's life. Born in New York City, raised on Long Island, attended a posh-sounding prep school. Arrived in San Francisco eight years ago, worked as a cocktail waitress, clerked in various stylish boutiques. Married George Sanmarco, a dealer in investment gems, four years ago and divorced him two years later, when she opened a high-fashion shop of her own. Survived by her father, Bradford Hudson Collington, her mother, Isabel Mayhew Collington, and her brother, Bradford Hudson Collington, Jr., all of New York. The family requested that in lieu of flowers, donations be made to the Bay Area Arts Council, an organization that made grants to local arts groups and had sponsored the fateful party.

The obituary was accompanied by a bland studio photograph, perhaps a wedding portrait, of a passively pretty young woman— blond hair, forced smile, expressionless eyes. She might have been anyone.

This morning's paper was more interesting. On page three Nicholas Gardino, the homicide inspector in charge of the case, admitted that there were no new leads and asked anyone with information about the Mystery Stranger to contact the police.

Below that was an interview with Lois Whittlesey Putnam, society grande dame and head of the Bay Area Arts Council. I'd met her once or twice; as I read I could imagine her imperious gestures, her breathy voice. How dreadful that such a tragedy could mar the festive occasion. How dismaying that a patron of the arts, even a stranger, could be connected with such a despicable act as murder. She confessed to being introduced to the mystery man herself, but given the nature of the event and her role as chairperson—such whirling excitement, so many details to attend to, so many people to greet—she couldn't recall the man's name. She called upon the police to marshal all possible resources to solve the case quickly. I bet Nick Gardino had loved reading that part.

She also announced that the Arts Council was offering a thou-

sand-dollar reward for the identity of the Mystery Stranger. For a
moment I was tempted. Turn Allen Fraser in and be done with this
mess.

I poured a fresh mug of tea and settled on the sofa to continue
my reading. Scruff curled up next to me with a comfortable sigh and
rested his head on my knee. Underneath us a truce had been declared
in World War III; bedtime is strictly enforced at Mrs. F's.

Back in the features section I found the best article yet. It was
headlined A WILD, EXTRAVAGANT LIFE AND A MYSTERIOUS, VIOLENT
DEATH—that ought to pull in the soap opera crowd.

The story centered around the scandal caused by Deborah's brief
marriage. George Sanmarco had long been married when he met
Deborah, who was half his age. They began an intense and very
public affair, much to the anguish of his wife, Lucia. She fought
bitterly when George divorced her to wed his young lover. After
losing the battle she attempted suicide and spent several months at
a swank private hospital.

George and Deborah, meanwhile, lived extravagantly. Their parties became legend in Pacific Heights. Deborah seemed to have a
charmed life: an adoring husband, far more money than people like
me can imagine how to spend.

But it wasn't enough. Deborah began being seen around town
with other men. She and George were observed to be quarreling a
lot. One night at a very elegant restaurant they had a famous fight,
complete with screaming, slapping, and the flying of a plateful of
veau à la crème. The fracas made the gossip columns and caused the
restaurant to ban the pair.

Finally the charmed couple split up, though the settlement he
gave her was rumored to be worth millions. Deborah opened Bumblebee, still one of Union Street's trendiest boutiques, and began
dabbling in theater, while George quietly remarried a triumphant
Lucia. Deborah went through several escorts before becoming engaged, just a month or two ago, to Peter Brockway, an entrepreneur
with a video production company. There was much speculation at

the end of the article about the identity of the Mystery Stranger, but no guess that was close to accurate.

The pictures that accompanied this article had much more life to them than the vapid obituary photo. There was a shot of Deborah playing Lady Macbeth—that was a role she must have relished. Another showed the beaming bride and her husband as they left their wedding reception in a shower of confetti; next to it, positioned to suggest that she was watching the festivities with disapproval, was a portrait of Lucia Sanmarco, thin, dark, pinchlipped.

A candid shot showed Sanmarco and Deborah on a yacht with several other people, champagne glasses raised in a celebratory toast. It must have been taken on a rare warm day on the bay, for Deborah was wearing a bare-shouldered dress.

But it was the final image that was truly remarkable. It might have been taken the day of the party on the yacht; both photos were attributed to the same photographer. In this one, Deborah's backlit head nearly filled the frame. It was thrown back and slightly to one side; she appeared to be laughing. The long blond hair, wind-tossed, glinting in the sun, surrounded her face like a wild fiery halo, while her eyes seemed to project a light of their own from within. How could anyone who looked so alive, so loving of life, ever be dead?

Even in the grainy newspaper reproduction it was a magical photo. I took my sketchbook from my satchel and wrote down the photographer's name: Kit Cormier.

I clipped out the articles, jotted more notes and put them all in a file folder. Then I headed to my sun porch studio. The half-done painting on my easel gave me a wordless challenge; I wanted to complete it by the weekend for the Hammerwood show. Bright yellows. Azures, tans and deep blues. It was an abstract arrangement inspired by the sunshiny morning beach. Too dark to work on it now, I decided, though it probably would have been fine if I'd turned on the overhead fixtures with their daylight fluorescent tubes.

Instead, I would finish inking in the pen-and-ink drawing I was doing for my brother Keith's birthday: an illustration of Merlin and the Knights of the Round Table—the King Arthur tales had recently caught his fancy. I put on a John Coltrane tape to drown out the rattle of the wind and lowered the bamboo blinds to block out the blackness that pushed against the window glass. When I switched on the lamp over the drawing table, the small focused pool of light threw large shadows into the corners of the room.

Long after midnight Coltrane was still blowing away on his mournful sax and I was still staring down at the paper on which I'd made no mark at all.

FIVE   My first call in the morning was to the homicide detail of the San Francisco police. Nick Gardino wasn't in. I felt a rush of relief at the reprieve. I hadn't yet concocted a tale that would satisfactorily explain my involvement in the Collington homicide. Worse, I hated having to make up a story. Professionalism demanded that as the very first thing, I should tell Gardino I knew the identity of the Mystery Stranger.

Next I called Claudia, to tell her I wouldn't be in today.

"So what happened last night, Jess?" she asked eagerly. "With your father, I mean. What's he like?"

"He's, well . . . I don't know." I'd been all set to tell her, but when the question came I found myself choking on the words. "He's nice enough, I guess. You know, it's funny—he looks like me. I didn't expect that."

"I bet you end up liking him. It'll work out fine." Claudia belonged to a large, warm, exuberant Irish-Italian family. The conflicts that flared up among the McFarlanes and the Minottis were heated and noisy, but they were quickly settled with hugs all around. "After all," she continued, "blood's thicker than water."

"There's too much blood in this situation. You know the Collington murder? Deborah Collington was his partner's daughter. Tell Tyler I've got a new assignment, okay? And set up a case file and billing record." I gave her a few more details, but I didn't mention the necklace or Mystery Stranger.

"So you're going to see him again?"

"Yes. This afternoon, in fact." We were going to Deborah's funeral. I was already dressed in my charcoal-gray suit, the closest thing I owned to black.

Allen Fraser was attending against my advice. "Are you crazy?" I'd said when he asked me to accompany him. "Someone's sure to spot you as the Mystery Stranger."

"I'll wear a disguise," he promised. "But I have to go. For Brad. What kind of friend would I be if I wasn't there?"

A friend who's not in jail, I thought, but I didn't say that.

My third call was to that traitor, my false uncle, Jack Emerich. I could feel anger bubbling up as I punched out his number. I didn't like the feeling.

"Are you free for lunch, Jack? I need to talk to you."

"I'd love to see you, sweetheart, but today's real tight. Tax season, you know."

"Income taxes had to be filed last week."

"True, but for an accountant that means everything else has been on hold since January. Next week looks better. How about Tuesday?"

"It's important, Jack. Isn't there any time before two you could squeeze me in? Just for a couple of minutes?"

"What's it about?"

"I'd rather tell you in person."

"Well, if it's that crucial—tell you what, sugar, pick up some roast beef sandwiches and be here at noon. We'll picnic in my office and you can tell me what's on your mind."

The last call was to Lauren Cassidy, editor of *Artspaper*, a monthly tabloid that covers the local cultural scene—music from opera to rock, the visual arts, theater and dance, film, literature, the whole works. It's a nonprofit enterprise, one of the Bay Area Arts Council's beneficiaries. Lauren and I met a couple of years ago at a gallery opening. We got into an energetic argument on the merits of abstract expressionism versus neorealism, debating enthusiastically until the rest of the guests were long gone and the owner, ready to lock up, kicked us out. We've been great friends ever since.

"Lauren, it's Jess. May I come over? I want to talk to you about the Arts and Flowers Ball. You were there, right?"

"Of course, weren't you? No, I guess I didn't see you."

"The tickets were about a hundred dollars more than I can afford. The ball's for rich patrons, not starving artists."

"I got in free as working press. We'll run a story in the next issue. That way the great Lois Whittlesey Putnam won't ax us off her funding list."

"So can you spare me a few minutes?"

"Sure. I'm about to go bug-eyed proofreading galleys. I'll be glad for an excuse to take a break."

The *Artspaper* office is in a shabby loft building on Folsom Street, above a dry-cleaning plant. A few blocks to the northeast, new highrises are pushing their way out of downtown into the territory below Market Street. Over to the southwest, the old brick warehouses are being rehabbed and filled with antiques wholesalers and interior-design showrooms. Here, though, the neighbors are still the small blue-collar businesses that have been around for decades— plumbing-supply dealers, body shops, an ice-cream factory.

The scarred street door and narrow dun-colored stairway don't prepare you properly for the *Artspaper* office. The big windows and skylights aren't too grimy to let in lots of light, and the place glows with color, thanks to Lauren's hobby. A marvelous assemblage of posters announces gallery shows, new plays, ballet performances and museum exhibits. Lauren has been collecting them for years. A decade of San Francisco arts is documented on the walls.

When I arrived the office looked as though she'd been collecting papers, too, for almost as long. There were papers scattered all over the two heavy old-fashioned wooden desks. Papers heaped on chairs, stacked in towers on the floor, pinned on top of other papers on the big bulletin board. Invoices, press releases, manuscripts, letters, sketches, torn sheets with handwritten scribbles, back issues of the tabloid. In one corner stood a pair of beat-up olive-drab file cabinets whose bulging drawers wouldn't quite close. I've never understood how Lauren can find anything, but she always seems to know right where to put her hands on whatever she needs.

Lauren was alone in the office, sitting in a small cleared space on her desk and talking on the phone. She was wearing jeans and western-style boots and a plaid shirt with the sleeves rolled up to her elbows. Her light brown hair, straight as a ruler, was hooked behind her ears; it fell nearly to her waist. Long strips of typeset copy—the galleys for the next issue—curled on the desktop beside her.

"I don't care," she was telling the phone. "It's got to be at the typesetter tonight. You're costing me overtime. If the story's not on my desk by five o'clock it's not in the paper. And no kill fee." She hung up without saying goodbye.

"I swear," she said to me, "everyone has such super reasons why they can't get their articles in on time. Too bad I can't use the same excuses on the advertisers when the May issue doesn't hit the stands until August." She slid off the desk. "Want some coffee?"

"Do you have any tea?"

"Nope, but you'll like this. Special blend—it's absolute nectar. And there's real cream in the fridge."

She poured the nectar and cream into thick white stoneware mugs and handed me one. "Have a seat." Motioning me into her desk chair, the only surface in the big room with no papers on it, she settled herself back onto her desk.

"So what do you want to know about the Arts and Flowers Ball?" she asked. "It was the usual society crowd in the usual tuxes and thousand-dollar designer gowns, dancing and drinking as usual. Lois pretty much has it down to a formula by now. The food, I'll have to give her credit, was superb."

"Did you see Deborah Collington there?"

"Good Lord, Jess, are you investigating that one? How come? It's not your regular sort of thing."

How should I answer? Lauren and I were close, but I just wasn't ready to spread the word that my long-lost father had suddenly dropped into my life to announce he was wanted for murder. "Some relatives of mine in New York are friends of the Collingtons. She'd been out of touch with her family and they asked me to find out what her life was like. Maybe it will help them reconcile themselves to what happened." That rationale didn't sound too bad. I'd have to try it out on Nick Gardino.

"Trying to find that Mystery Stranger the reporters are so in love with?"

I edged away from that one. "No one knows if this so-called stranger was involved in her death. Maybe he took her home and she went out again later for some reason."

"Or maybe she took *him* home and then got mugged by a street thug."

"Or maybe any of a number of scenarios." I sipped from my mug while I tried to think of another one. "You're right. The coffee's good."

"Told you so." She took a long drink of her own and sighed with contentment. "You know, I'm not sure how much I can help you. I talked to Deborah briefly at the ball—I interviewed her once, so I knew her slightly. But she didn't say anything that seems significant. No 'by the way, I'm meeting the mayor at the bus station at three A.M.' or anything like that."

"What sort of mood was she in? Happy? Apprehensive?"

"She wasn't having premonitions of death, if that's what you mean. If anything she was more exuberant than usual. That might have been alcohol—she'd had a bit too much. Nearly fell off her high heels at one point."

"Was she with the Mystery Stranger when you talked to her?"

"No, she was by herself. She was supposed to come with her fiancé, Peter Brockway, but he had the flu, she said. I saw the mystery man later, but just from a distance. Good-looking guy—I can see where she might have wanted to leave Peter home if she knew this other fellow would be there. He was probably twice her age, but so was Sanmarco, so that might have been a plus in her book."

"What did he look like, the Mystery Stranger?" The critical question.

"Tall, slender. Looked like he keeps himself fit. Red hair, but darkish—a lot like the color of yours, Jess."

I nodded. That was Allen Fraser, all right.

"You're empty," said Lauren. "Have some more." She did the honors with the pot.

"What about the Sanmarcos?" I asked. "Were they there?"

"No. Lucia used to be on the Arts Council board, but she dropped out of sight when her divorce got messy. They say she went a bit wacko—tried to kill herself and spent time in some hospital." She shook her head sympathetically. "Poor woman. Now that she's got George back, I think she tries to keep him away from places Deborah might be."

"Did you notice if Deborah spent much time with anyone else that night, besides the Stranger? Someone she might have met later, or talked to about her plans?"

Lauren twisted a strand of her long brown hair as she thought. "Let's see. She danced with Evan Krausgill quite a bit. He does PR for Pacific Playhouse. I wouldn't have been interested in meeting him later, but she might have been. There's no accounting for taste."

"Pacific Playhouse. Wasn't Deborah was involved with them too?"

"Yeah, she did Lady Macbeth for them last fall."

"Was she any good?"

"Quite good. I guess it came naturally—she was pretty theatrical in real life. That necklace, for instance, was very dramatic, although frankly I preferred her ring myself."

"The papers didn't say anything about a ring." Neither had Allen Fraser.

"It was exquisite—gold with an emerald set off-center and three small diamonds to the side. It reminded me of one my grandmother had, although Grammy's was probably glass."

"Why would she risk wearing such expensive jewelry to the ball? She was asking for trouble."

"Oh, it's not that surprising. There's always lots of impressive baubles at these fancy benefits. The insurance companies must throw fits, but really, how often do you get to show off a fortune in jewels if you happen to own one?"

"I suppose. I don't know what people do with that kind of jewelry. Mom and Roger gave me a string of cultured pearls for my eighteenth birthday, but I don't think that counts."

"Nope. My topaz pendant doesn't count either. You know, Jess," she said thoughtfully, "the mystery man might have gone there looking for something to steal. If so, he sure picked a winner."

"Most people were in couples. He couldn't have counted on enticing some lone woman away."

"Maybe he had a gun hidden under his jacket. He could have picked his victims, followed them out and mugged them on the way home." She slid off the desk and slunk across the room, fingers pointing ahead of her, like a person skulking along, gun in hand. "That happened last year, remember? After the opera's Winter Masquerade. Guy in a harlequin suit came up behind this man and his wife as they left and got away with fifty thousand bucks' worth of goodies. Deborah just made it easier, being alone." She came back and picked up her mug, discovering it empty. "Another refill?"

"No thanks," I said, getting up. "I should go. I don't want to keep you from the pleasures of proofreading."

Lauren grimaced at the galleys beside her. "Gee, you're all heart."

"I appreciate the information." I headed for the stairs.

"Hope it proves useful, what little I had. By the way, how's the Ars Nova show at Hammerwood coming? Ready for your big break into the art world?"

"It's just a little break. But don't think I'm not thrilled to have it. You know, it scares me a little. The other people in the show are really good."

"So are you," Lauren said matter-of-factly.

I smiled, then sighed. "I've got one more painting I really want to finish. I didn't count on having the distraction of my, uh . . . of this case."

"Just holler if I can help with anything."

"Thanks." At the top of the stairs a thought struck me. "Lauren, do you know a photographer named Kit Cormier?"

"I've heard of him. He's good, but he's not really part of the art scene. He does advertising and corporate work mostly, assignments for magazines, things like that. Why, is he involved in this?"

"He took some photos of Deborah that were in the paper. Maybe I should talk to him. Where's your phone book?"

"Right there." She pointed to the other desk, which was awash in a sea of papers.

SIX Kit Cormier's listing showed an address on South Park, a little grassy oval hidden in the heart of the industrial district. I had read somewhere that its developer, back in the 1850s, had envisioned its becoming the city's premier residential address, but to his misfortune the smart set had moved to Nob Hill instead. The park was ringed now with boardinghouses, artists' studios and a warehouse or two. In the center, incongruously, there was an elaborate play structure constructed of burly wooden poles. As I drove in a couple of shaggy-haired boys were on it, playing King of the Mountain.

I found the number I was looking for on a two-story building with peeling tan paint. There was a curtained storefront on the first level, probably an apartment above. Kit Cormier's business card was taped beside the buzzer.

My ring was answered by a pair of amazingly blue eyes, the color of a clear winter-morning sky. Then I noticed the gorgeous man who went with the eyes: mid-thirties, soft curling brown hair, well-trimmed beard. Perhaps six feet tall, with wide square shoulders in a denim workshirt.

"Well, hello." He smiled.

I tried to regain my composure long enough to introduce myself.

"A private detective? For real?" His smile widened. "I don't think I've ever met one before. What can I do for you?"

His expression turned thoughtful when I mentioned Deborah Collington's name. "What a horrible thing. And the media are pursuing it with such awful glee. But why come to me?"

"Those pictures you took. The ones in yesterday's *Chronicle*."

"But they weren't—" He gave me a puzzled look and then grinned again. I hoped I wasn't salivating too obviously. "Sure, come on in."

I did, and there directly in front of me was a huge blowup, larger than life-size, of that incredible picture of Deborah Collington, sun-rimmed, laughing, alive. I was filled with admiration—and despite myself, with disappointment.

"You see I have a special interest in this case," Kit Cormier said.

I swallowed hard. "It's a wonderful photo."

"Thanks. Sometimes you get lucky. Manage to click the shutter at exactly the right moment."

"Did you know her well?" I thought of the newspaper account, with its innuendos about the men parading in and out of Deborah's life.

"Not really," he said. "I have that up because it's one of the best shots I've ever taken. I like to remind myself that miracles happen."

I felt a tension release inside me. It annoyed me that it had even been there—what claim did I think I had after a two-minute acquaintance?

The old storefront had been converted into a studio and an office and a sort of sitting area, casual and comfortable-looking. Soft jazz tinkled from a stereo. There was a whiff of darkroom chemicals in the air.

The walls were a patchwork of pinned-up photos, samples of his commercial work: formal portraits, still-life arrangements of baked goods or electronics gear, interior shots of expensively furnished homes. They were excellent, though none was as arresting as the picture of Deborah Collington. Kit looked pleased when I admired them, though he made polite disclaimers.

I glanced around for more personal photos—a wife perhaps, a girlfriend. But I didn't see any. Good.

"You took both pictures in the *Chronicle* on the same day, didn't you?" I said. "That portrait and the party on the boat."

"Yep. Quite a bash. It was about three years ago. I was covering a big international jewelry show that was in town, for *Bay Breeze* magazine. You know, that local high-society rag."

I nodded. I'd seen issues of it from time to time.

"Well, this party was part of the festivities. She was Deborah Sanmarco then. Her husband was big in gem circles. They seemed to be good friends of the boat's owner too."

"Whose boat was it?"

"It belonged to a South American guy up for the show. A gem exporter, specializes in emeralds I think. That's right—the boat was called the *Esmeralda*. Huge sailboat, very handsome."

"Do you know his name?"

He glanced away, thinking, then looked back at me with those blue, blue eyes. "I should remember, but I can't. But that's all ancient history. It doesn't have anything to do with her murder, does it?"

"Probably not. At this point I have no idea what will turn out to be important."

"I should have a copy of the magazine on file if that'll help. Have a seat and I'll look." He rummaged in a file cabinet, then poked around in some cartons on the floor, while I admired his fluid, easy way of moving and the fit of his Levi's.

"Here it is." He handed me an old *Bay Breeze*. Wonderful—no wedding ring.

The whole issue had been devoted to the gem exposition; the pages glowed with jewel colors. Diamonds, rubies, sapphires, emeralds, pearls. Necklaces, tiaras, bracelets, earrings. There were pictures of people at the convention center, people at buffet tables—and people on the yacht.

As Kit had said, it was immense for a sailboat, though small for the crowd of people swarming over it. The shot of the champagne toast was there, and the extraordinary closeup of Deborah Collington, and photos of what appeared to be drunken revelry. One focused on the captain and host, a sun-darkened man with thick black hair and mustache and a heavy shelf of brow over arctic eyes. He was smiling genially in the photo, but you could tell those eyes were what counted. The caption said he was from Colombia, where the world's finest emeralds are found. His name was Guillermo Reyes.

"Looks like everyone was having a good time."

"Yeah," Kit said somewhat scornfully. "Lots of booze, plenty of coke."

"Cocaine?"

"I didn't mean cola," he shrugged. "It turns up all the time at these do's. Don't care for the stuff myself." A look of pain flickered across his face and vanished. I wondered what caused it but didn't dare ask.

I made a couple of notes on my sketchpad, as much for form's sake as anything. Kit was right—it was hard to see how a three-year-old party could have any bearing on Deborah's death. But it did give me more insight into the kind of life she'd led.

"Thank you." I stood up reluctantly and held out the magazine. "You've been very helpful."

Our fingers touched as he took it from me. "You're not leaving already? I was just getting ready to trot out my wit and charm."

He'd already done that, of course. What, I wondered, was the right word to describe his eyes? Cornflower. Azure. Cobalt. The color changed with the angle of light, with shifts in his expression. No word I could think of captured the essence of that blue.

I gave him my P&O card and what I hoped was a charming smile. Then, on second thought, I also handed him the business card I used in art circles. That one had my home number on it.

Kit looked delighted. "An artist as well as a detective. No wonder you're such a brilliant critic of photographs. Tell me about your paintings."

I made a couple of brief, hesitant remarks. I always found it hard to talk about my artwork. It brought people too close to some private inner core. Whatever might be there to be stated, I hoped I managed to say it in the paintings themselves.

But Kit knew the right questions to ask, and he seemed genuinely interested in the answers. I found myself babbling away about the language of color and line, about my Art Institute days, about the frustration of trying to cram painting time into my schedule.

"Wow," he said when I mentioned the Ars Nova show. "Congratulations. That's a real coup."

"The opening reception is on Sunday afternoon," I said casually.

"A chance to meet and greet the artists. You know, I just may find an excuse to be there."

"That would be nice." I tried to make my voice just warm enough—not remote, not too eager.

"Or—if you wouldn't mind—I might come up with an excuse to be in touch sooner."

I smiled into his blue eyes. "Oh, I hardly think I'd mind." Any reason or none at all would do.

As I finally turned to depart I spotted it on the edge of a nearby shelf—the photo I'd been worriedly looking for. A small, leather-framed picture of a young woman, delicate and lovely, her heart-shaped face framed by coffee-colored curls. *Love, Sara,* said the inscription. Damn, damn, damn.

On my way to Jack Emerich's office I stopped at Irma's Deli to pick up sandwiches. I gave myself a stern lecture on will power and self-discipline, then told Irma to put in two chocolate chip cookies, the ones with pecans.

Jack's accounting firm is near the top of a new glass-and-granite highrise in the Financial District. On the walls of his reception area are three abstract paintings—two by widely shown artists with good and growing reputations and one by me. It was part of my senior project at the Art Institute and I've always figured Jack bought it out of kindness. But I still feel a thrill whenever I walk in and see it hanging there.

The receptionist said Jack was tied up in a meeting. While I waited I rehearsed what I was going to say. I wanted to be tactful, to not become angry. Just get some questions answered and let Jack know how I felt about his deceit. It occurred to me that he and Allen Fraser both made their livings managing other people's money. Perhaps that was one of the points in common that had kept their long-distance friendship alive all these years.

Three men came in from the inner corridor. The tallest one, the one with the least hair and the most laugh lines, was Jack. When the other two left, Jack turned to me.

"Hi there, sugar. Come on back."

In his office I distributed the lunches while we made small talk: the Giants' chances (poor to none, even this early in the season), the weather (oddly foggy for spring), my little brother Teddy's softball exploits (he'd pitched his first no-hitter last week). Finally Jack asked, "To what do I owe the great honor of your company today, Jess?"

My throat was dry. I was twisting the crumpled brown bag from Irma's in my hands. But I tried to keep my gaze and voice steady. "I met an interesting man last night. I'd like some advice about him."

"A new boyfriend? Is it someone your old Uncle Jack would approve of?"

"His name is Allen Fraser."

Jack lowered the sandwich he'd been about to bite. I could see the shock in his eyes.

"Allen—you saw Allen? He called you?"

I nodded.

"I had a drink with him Sunday, but he didn't mention getting in touch with you."

"He said you told him where I was."

"Well, I've kept him up to date. Allen's always been interested, honey—in how you are and what you're doing."

"Why did he wait thirty years to see me, if he's so damn interested?" I was already slipping from my careful script.

Jack slid a hand over his gleaming bald head.

"Ah, Jess. Things aren't always what they seem. When you were a kid, your mother wouldn't let him. She . . . well, she had her reasons, sweetheart. Allen was . . . let's just say he hurt Mary badly and she was afraid he'd hurt you too."

"She wouldn't let him? He was the one who walked out."

"Jess, how much did Mary tell you about your father, why they split up?"

"Not much," I admitted. "Almost nothing, really. Just that he left us. I could tell she was angry about it, always. But sometimes she seemed . . . well, glad I guess, too."

"She had her reasons," he repeated. He picked up his sandwich again, as if the subject was closed.

"What reasons? Tell me."

"All that was a long time ago, Jess. Why not put it behind you and give Allen a chance?"

"So Mom wouldn't let him see me when I was a kid. Well, I haven't been a kid for ages, damn it. What's his excuse for ignoring me lately?"

"I think he was scared of getting the door slammed in his face. He asked me if you ever asked about him and I had to say no."

"I didn't even know you knew him." I could hear my voice getting shrill. "How could you do it? Betray us like that? I thought you were on our side."

Jack looked stricken, a wounded look in his warm hazel eyes. "Oh, Jess. Of course I was on your side. And on his too. You were all my friends, even if—" He gave his smooth head another polish. "You never seemed curious about him, Jess. If you had, I might have brought it up. This way was kinder to Mary. I was very fond of your mother, you know."

"Yes, I know." I was very fond of her too. Maybe that's why I'd never let myself think of my father too much—to keep from opening that deep hurt in her again. Or perhaps it was to keep from finding a deep hurt in me.

I leaned back in my chair, my fists clenched on the padded arms. Calm down, Jess. Breathe deep.

"Tell me," I asked, "what happened between them?"

Jack ate in silence for a moment. He appeared to be weighing what to say. Staring past my shoulder, he finally spoke. "Allen had a lot of romantic notions about what being an adult would be like, and he got upset when the reality turned out to be quite different.

He . . . he took a lot of his frustration out on Mary. They were just kids then, they wouldn't have even got married if it hadn't been for—" He shot me a quick glance and looked away again. "Anyway, someone came along who seemed to fit Allen's fantasy better. Unfortunately he couldn't resist."

"Arlette."

"He told you about her?"

"Just a little." At least the stories jibed. Even though I felt like half the story had been left out.

"When Arlette left him, Allen finally began to grow up. Realized he had a problem, started going to a shrink. He tried to get back together with your mother, you know. But she wasn't having any— leopard and his spots, she said. I can't say I blame her."

"He said he sent money. But she wouldn't cash the checks."

"That sounds like both of them." He looked down at his desk and focused on the chocolate-chip cookie. He took a big bite, seeming grateful for the distraction. "Umm, delicious."

"Irma's secret recipe. The best in town."

"You're not eating yours."

"No. I'll save it for later." My sandwich was untouched too.

Jack gave me a long thoughtful look. "How do you really feel about this, Jess? Allen's showing up out of the blue."

"I don't know." I could feel tears forming and I tried to blink them back. "I'm all mixed up. I was always proud of not needing my father. Now I'm furious at him for showing up and disrupting everything, and I'm also furious that he didn't do it ages ago. I'm curious about him but I don't want to be curious. I feel like I'm betraying my mother and being ungrateful to Roger."

The tears were there for real now. Jack came around the desk and laid a hand gently on my bent head.

"You want me to talk to him, sweetheart?"

"No!" I said sharply. "Don't say a word. I'll handle things." I dabbed at my wet face with a napkin. "I'm going to be seeing a lot of him for a while." I gave Jack a brief sketch of the murder case.

He looked upset. "Oh, Lord, sugar, are you sure you want to take this on?"

"No." I struggled to put on a smile. "But I said I would. If I do it, things will get resolved one way or the other. If I don't, they'll always feel incomplete." I started to gather up the lunch wrappings. "You're busy. And I need to get to a funeral."

"Are you okay, honey? Tell me the truth."

I nodded. "Jack," I asked, "can I trust him?"

"Ah, Jess. He's an honest man, I'm sure of that. I can't think—no, he's no murderer. But I guess he really doesn't have a good record on emotional relationships." Jack gave me a quick peck on the forehead, then put his arm around my shoulder to guide me to the door. "I hope you can trust him, honey. I sure hope so."

SEVEN Fog slid over the coastal hills and thickened into drizzle as it reached Colma. The dampness sharpened the pungent smell of pine and eucalyptus. I hugged the jacket of my charcoal gray suit close against the chill.

The world was reduced to the green of lawn and the gray of mist and tombstones. The people who milled around were somberly attired, adding plenty of commotion but no color to the scene. At the center of the throng was a brown dirt hole and brown wooden casket, slick with varnish and rain.

Deborah Collington was being laid to rest.

Years ago, when real estate fever made land in the city too valuable to waste on the dead, many of the cemeteries in San Francisco were relocated to this little Peninsula town. Over time the honor paid to the dead grew less and less elaborate. In the oldest section of Pines of Peace Memorial Park, the monuments included hefty granite obelisks, weeping angels carved in marble, and Greek temples that looked like miniatures of the banks downtown. As you moved into the newer areas the stones became simpler and smaller, until here you had nothing but little plaques set flush with the earth so they wouldn't obstruct the lawnmowers.

On this day the deceased was receiving no real honor at all. Although the newspapers had said the service was private, several hundred people were swarming around, showing off their mourning clothes and jockeying for the best views. Some were Deborah's friends and colleagues, but lots of them were thrill-seekers—nothing like a murder victim's funeral for a little vicarious charge. Business people, housewives with strollers, high school kids who'd cut afternoon classes. They were poking each other, pointing to Deborah's family. A buzz of whispers and murmurs accompanied the minister's words. There were three TV news crews. I kept looking around for the balloon man and the hot dog vendor.

I recognized George Sanmarco from his photos in the paper. He stood by himself at the edge of the crowd, his head lowered, his hands buried in his pockets. As I watched, a sandy-haired man in a tan trenchcoat approached and said something to him. Sanmarco's reply seemed to be short and sharp, though I was too far away to hear it. The tan man raised a fist as if to strike him, but didn't. Scowling, he wheeled and stalked off.

Another loner was a compact man with a dark mustache and a navy blue suit, who was watching the proceedings from under one of the pine trees that gave the cemetery its name. Nick Gardino, the homicide inspector in charge of the case.

Deborah's parents were standing in the drizzle at the edge of their daughter's grave. Brad Collington was a handsome man, with well-chiseled features and abundant silver hair; he could have been the anchorman for the newscast that would show all the video footage being shot here today. But there was a sag to his face and a slump to his shoulders that I suspected weren't normally there. Dressed in black silk, veiled head bowed, Isabel looked small and delicate beside her husband. They leaned together with arms linked, and he clutched her hand tightly in both of his. It was hard to tell who was supporting whom.

Young Bradford, their son, kept himself a few steps apart from his parents. He was three or four inches taller than his father, and stringy—I bet he got sick of being asked how the weather was up there. Or whether he played basketball. The answer to that one was probably no; he lacked an athlete's natural grace. He had blotchy skin and thick rain-spattered glasses, which must have added to his feelings of awkwardness. He was a freshman in college, Allen Fraser had told me. When his sister left home he'd been in fifth grade.

Allen Fraser and I stood together, facing the Collingtons across the grave. I was trying to keep him away from them—all eyes were focused on them, and he'd be noticed if he were too close. He had worn the promised disguise: a dark gray fedora to cover his red hair. He'd kept it on throughout the service at the chapel, which right there made him look suspicious. Brad had suggested it, he said. I hoped their firm's financial judgment was better than that.

The brief graveside ceremony came to an end. The casket was lowered into the ground and a ritual handful of soggy soil was tossed in. The gesture broke the crowd's spell. The murmurings became full-voiced conversations, the fidgeting became purposeful movement. With the show over, the gawkers started drifting toward the long line of waiting cars. Engines roared to life. The TV people began packing up their gear. People closed in around Deborah's family to offer them sympathy or gape at their grief.

Nick Gardino was heading in our direction. I separated myself from the others and moved to meet him. No point in letting him get too close to Allen Fraser and that silly hat.

Gardino nodded in greeting. "Well, well, if it isn't Ms. Randolph of the distinguished firm of Parks and O'Meara. Tell me, what would bring a private investigator to a party like this?"

I couldn't put it off any longer. I tested out the tale I'd told Lauren. "I tried to call you this morning, Nick. I have relatives in New York who are friends of the Collingtons. The family wasn't close, and they regret that now. I agreed to help them learn about their daughter's life out here. They think it will help them deal with their grief."

"I see. A family matter."

"That's right. How is your investigation going? Any idea what really happened?"

"You just said you were checking out her life, not her death."

"You can't blame me for a little professional curiosity, Nick. It's hard to get out of the habit of asking questions."

His smile showed even white teeth. "I know how it is. I'll even be nice and give you an answer, which is no. We really don't have much. She died early Sunday, probably sometime between two and six. There was nothing in the alley where she was found to indicate she'd been killed there, so we presume she was killed somewhere else and dumped there later."

A microphone was thrust in his face. "Channel Six News, Inspector. What can you tell our viewers about the progress of this case? Were you expecting the murderer to show up here at the funeral?"

Gardino's eyes narrowed; his mouth became set in a hard line. "No comment," he muttered, stepping away from the newscaster, the mike, the cameras, the whole entourage. "Goddamn pests." I trotted along beside him, confident he didn't mean me.

"Where do you suppose Deborah went after the Arts and Flowers Ball?" I asked him. "Could she have gone home and then gone out again later?"

"She could have gone to the moon and back for all I know." He stopped, sighed deeply, turned to face me. "But there were no signs that she'd been back to her flat. And if she was going out at two in the morning to buy a Sunday paper, why wouldn't she change clothes? She was still all gussied up when the body was found. Long silk dress, little flat dancing shoes. Except her jewelry and purse were missing."

"Her purse too?"

"Yeah. Green silk thing, matched the dress. A postal worker found it in a mailbox a few blocks away—purse snatchers do that a lot. The shift supervisor recognized her name from the TV and turned it in. Still had her driver's license in it and some other stuff, lipstick, hairbrush. No cash, though."

"So the motive was robbery."

"Looks like it. There was no indication of sexual assault, which is the other thing likely to happen to young ladies who wander out alone in the wee hours."

"Inspector Gardino." He was stopped in his tracks by the breathy voice and the firm touch of a tiny black leather glove on his sleeve. Though Lois Whittlesey Putnam was under five feet, she gave the impression of being twice that tall. Her hair had been artfully colored to match her coat of autumn-haze mink; both hair and fur glistened with fine droplets of mist.

"I assume you have better news for me than you did the last time we spoke," she said. "The publicity about this dreadful murder has been just devastating for the Arts Council. We must get it cleared up quickly. You can't believe—"

"Nothing new to report, Mrs. Putnam," Gardino said gruffly. "Now if you'll excuse me." He turned away, and she stalked off in a huff, hunching her coat around her.

His turning meant that he was looking straight at me. "Christ, Jess, you still here?"

"Just one more question, Nick. What about this Mystery Stranger the media keeps yammering about? Do you think he did it?"

"I have no frigging idea who did it. That's the whole problem. But whoever the Stranger is, he knows a hell of a lot more than I do about what happened after Deborah left that party. I sure want to hear his story."

"Yes, well . . . good luck finding him." I glanced back over my shoulder. Allen Fraser and Brad Collington were having a discussion with a young bearded man who wore a plaid sportshirt and carried a notebook and pen. I didn't see Lois Whittlesey Putnam anywhere; I prayed that she hadn't spotted Allen and made a connection with the man she'd met at the dance. "Thanks for letting me ask questions," I said to Gardino. "I'd better go pay my respects now."

Gardino was starting toward the Collingtons, too.

"Look, Jess," he said, "if your, ah, professional curiosity gets the better of you, you will let me know what you learn, won't you?"

"Of course," I said, crossing my fingers. Fortunately my hand was in my jacket pocket.

"Good. It always works out better when there's mutual cooperation, don't you agree?" He gave a little salute and hiked off toward the parking lot. Was there a veiled warning in his comment? Parks & O'Meara had a firm policy of working with, not against, the police. But this was different—it was a family matter. Wasn't it? Did a father you didn't meet until you were thirty count as family? Was he worth the risk of keeping secrets from the police?

Damn Allen Fraser anyway.

I reached the group of New Yorkers just in time to see the conversation with the young reporter erupt into an argument.

"Vultures!" Brad Collington was yelling. "All of you! You've got no respect for decent people."

"Cripes, Mr. Collington—" The kid, his face plump and pimpled, didn't look much older than Collington's boy. Even the beard didn't help.

"You leeches invade my Debbie's funeral, you print lies about her, you upset my wife with your terrible questions. What's it like to have your daughter murdered? Jesus Christ!"

"Brad," said Isabel softly, but he ignored her. Their son had wandered off, apparently pretending he wasn't with these people.

"Has anyone in your family ever been murdered?" Collington trembled with his anger. His face purpled; a vein pulsed in his temple. "Have you ever had anyone close to you die? Answer me, damn it."

"No sir," whispered the kid.

"This is what I think of your story!" Collington grabbed the notebook away from the reporter, ripped out the scribbled pages and tore them to bits. The scraps fluttered down onto the damp green grass and freshly turned brown earth. A smattering of applause burst from the onlookers who had gathered.

"Come on, Brad," said Allen Fraser, laying a hand on his partner's shoulder. "Let him be."

"Tomorrow you'll be back," Brad said. Something like a sob choked his voice. The notebook tumbled from his hand. "You'll hang around Debbie's apartment until I come out and you'll hound me some more. Your kind never knows when to give up. There's no humanity in you."

"Is that where you're staying, Mr. Collington?" the reporter asked. "Her apartment?" He plucked his notebook out of the wet grass and wiped it on his jeans. He had more guts than I'd given him credit for.

The rain on Brad's face looked a lot like tears. His wife took his arm. "Come along, dear. It's time to go." Gently she led him away, across the lawn, over the plaques that memorialized other people's loved ones. Young Bradford trailed several paces behind.

The reporter started to follow, but Allen Fraser stopped him, saying, "Hey. Show a little mercy."

The young man gaped after the retreating family. "I'm just doing my job."

Allen nodded, acknowledging and dismissing him at the same time. Then he turned to me and held out his hand. "Jessica? Ready?"

I felt wet, chilled, drained of energy, more than ready to leave. I fell into step beside him. But I didn't take the proffered hand.

EIGHT

Brad Collington stared into the glass that had held his third martini. "I made a fool of myself," he said.

"Don't be silly, dear," said Isabel. "That reporter was much too pushy. He deserved it and more." She had changed into a soft dress of cerulean blue. Freed from the black silk, she was a pretty, youthful-looking woman, with no gray in her fluff of brunette hair. Her eyes reflected the blue of her dress, but they weren't nearly as brilliant as Kit Cormier's.

"Yeah. He's lucky you didn't deck him," said Bradford, their son, slouching in his chair.

The five of us were seated around a table at Harbor Lights, a Fisherman's Wharf restaurant that specialized in low lights and high prices. We were only up to the salad course, but it was already clear that this would not be a cheery meal.

I hadn't really wanted to come. The unfinished work in my studio tugged at my mind—the drawing for Keith's birthday, that last painting for the Ars Nova show. But the more insight I had into Deborah, the more likely I'd be to find out what had happened last Saturday night. Spending time with her family might help. Besides, this dinner gave me another chance to observe Allen Fraser—and getting to know this man, my father, might give me insight into me.

The tuxedoed waiter was delivering dishes to the next table.

Collington caught his eye and raised the martini glass. The waiter came over.

"Another, sir?"

"Yes, please," said Brad. "Anyone else?"

"Don't you think you've had enough, dear?" said Isabel. "You want to be able to taste your dinner."

"No, I don't. Allen? Jessica?"

We both shook our heads. Collington looked coaxingly from one of us to the other. When we didn't respond, he set down the glass with a frown.

"Maybe you're right. Cancel it," he told the waiter.

"Yes, sir." The waiter cleared the empty glass and the salad plates and went off.

Collington mustered a sort of smile and aimed it in my direction. "You're getting a terrible impression of your father's partner, Jessica. I'm not at my best right now."

"Of course not. I couldn't expect you to be."

He reached for the vanished glass and seemed surprised when it wasn't there. With a sigh, he settled for water. "It's ironic, you know. I lose my daughter, yet because of that Allen finds his." He snorted; it might have been an attempt at a laugh. "Glad something good is coming out of this."

"So am I," said Allen Fraser, ignoring the sarcastic edge in Collington's voice. He draped an arm across my shoulders; they tightened involuntarily under his touch. "I'm just sorry it took such a tragedy to make me do what I should have done long ago."

Some people are good at saying the right words whether they mean them or not. I looked at Allen Fraser—were his eyes sincere? But he was facing away from me, toward Brad Collington. After a moment he removed his arm. I felt my shoulders relax.

"I'm sorry, too, that it happened this way," I said. I was referring to far more than Deborah's death.

"Debbie was close to your age, Jessica," said Isabel. "Did you know her at all?"

"No, we never met."

"And you're both interested in the arts. I wish I'd been able to see her on the stage, just once. She didn't take up the theater until after she moved out here, you know."

"I've heard she was very good," I said, glad of my conversation with Lauren. Debbie's mother looked pleased.

"You may not have seen her on stage," said young Bradford, "but you sure saw her put on plenty of melodramas. That's all I ever remember her doing."

"This is no time to be disrespectful of your sister, young man," warned his father. The boy shrugged and reached for another sourdough roll.

The waiter appeared with four plates of grilled salmon and herbed rice, plus a cup of shrimp bisque for Isabel. That and the salad were all she had ordered.

"Are you sure that will be enough?" asked Collington as the waiter placed the cup in front of her.

"I can't eat today," she said. "I've had no appetite at all since Debbie . . . since I found out what happened."

"You quit eating and Dad started drinking," her son said.

"Bradford, I'm warning you," said Collington.

The salmon was moist and flaky and tender, but I didn't have much appetite either.

"Brad told me about the mission he gave you, Allen—to intercede with Debbie for us," Isabel said. "He had such great hopes. He wanted to surprise me with the good news that we were . . . going to get our daughter back." She dipped her head and blinked. A single tear escaped onto her cheek. "Instead I had such horrible news for him when he got home Sunday night."

"You were away when the word came?" I asked.

"Yeah," Collington said. "One of my clients was annoyed because an investment I recommended didn't do as well as he'd hoped. I went up to Boston over the weekend to try to smooth his ruffled feathers. When I got home, the police had already contacted Isabel. I felt rotten that she had to face the blow alone."

"Braddy was with me." She patted the boy's hand. "He was a great comfort."

"Yeah, I'm sure," said Collington. His son glared at him.

Isabel's eyes darted between them. She gave a small sigh and squeezed Bradford's hand before turning to me. "Allen says you're a detective, Jessica. You're going to try to find out what happened for us."

"Yes. I told him it was a job for the police, but he wants me to look into it too."

"Do you have any ideas yet?" asked Collington, leaning toward me.

"No. Allen says he left her safe at home. If that's so, the first step is to find out why she went out again, still in her party clothes."

"But you have no idea why?" he persisted.

"Not yet."

"Who cares anyway?" said Deborah's brother.

"Bradford!" His father's tone was sharp.

"Now, Braddy, you don't mean that," said his mother in a softer voice.

"Sure I do. Finding out what happened isn't going to bring her back. You never liked her anyway, you weren't even speaking to her. You feel guilty because you drove her away, and now you're angry because she's dead and there's nothing you can do to stop feeling guilty."

"Goddamn it!" Collington slammed his hand against the table. Dishes jumped. Water sloshed from full goblets. People at nearby tables turned to stare.

He rose and leaned across the table toward his son. "You shut your insolent mouth. You don't know the first thing about it."

"Brad," warned Isabel. She tugged him back into his seat. This ordeal might have robbed her of her appetite, but she was clearly bearing up better than her husband, who was now slumped in his chair, rubbing a hand across his eyes.

"Oh Christ," he muttered.

Isabel reached over and smoothed a strand of silver hair back from his brow. "Are you sure we should go away and leave you?"

"I'll be fine." He brushed her away. "Plenty of things to keep me busy."

Isabel gave him a long look. She started to say something more but decided against it. Instead she picked up a spoon and stirred her cooling soup.

"Where are you going?" Allen asked her.

"They're flying home tomorrow," Collington answered for her. "I don't want Bradford to miss any more classes than he has to." The boy scowled, as though the prospect of classes didn't please him. His father went on, "I'm remaining here—someone has to start wrapping up Debbie's affairs. The police said I could use her apartment. They don't need it sealed, or whatever, for their investigation."

"Why don't I stay there with you?" suggested Allen. "I want to be here anyway, in case I can assist Jessica with her investigation." He gave me a smile. "It'll give us a chance to get know each other."

Collington frowned. "But the office. Someone's got to keep things running."

"Martha can handle it for a while. Our secretary," he appended for me.

Isabel looked relieved. "That would be a good idea, Allen. Thank you."

I had the feeling Collington was going to protest further, but he surprised me. "Oh, all right," he muttered.

"Have you moved into the apartment yet?" I asked.

"No, I'll go over there tomorrow after I take these two to the airport. Why?"

"I'd like to see it before things get disturbed. I doubt I'll spot anything the police missed, but it might help to have a look."

"Let's go over there tonight," Allen proposed. "No time like the present."

Collington looked weary, as if all he wanted to do was go to sleep. Or have that fourth martini. "Now?"

"Oh please, dear," Isabel broke in. "It'll be my only chance to see where Debbie lived."

"But, Izzy—oh, what the hell."

The waiter appeared to clear our plates. They were nearly as full as when he'd brought them.

I would have preferred to search Deborah's flat alone. That way I could do a thorough job without the risk of raising too much curiosity if I found something, or of offending family sensibilities and being told to quit. But there was no getting rid of them; all five of us trooped over to Deborah's place on a tree-lined block of Clay Street. The house was a queenly Victorian painted in five tones of blue and gray. It had been carved into condominiums, one to each floor. Deborah's was on top.

Inside, the intricately carved mantels and moldings of the period remained intact, but Deborah's taste had clearly been more contemporary. The front and back parlors, outfitted now as living room and dining room, were done up in black and white. The starkness was softened with an occasional splash of mauve or rose or celadon in a pillow here, a vase or picture mat there.

The artworks on the walls were mostly Art Deco prints. But one piece arrested my eye: a large painting hanging over the black lacquered credenza in the dining room. It reminded me of an explosion in a genetics lab—a huge double helix twisting, fragmenting into a jumble of acid colors. Orange and chartreuse, magenta and saffron. And of course Deborah's favorite black. It looked like Gerard Duplisea's work—yes, there was his spiky signature. His stuff always gave me headaches, but someone liked it; he was commanding top dollar right now. And more power to him, I thought with a sigh. Anyone who could make good money at art—

"The artist-detective is at work, eh," Allen Fraser said, chuckling. He seemed excited at the prospect of watching me in action. I kept a close eye on him. He was looking around with evident curiosity, as though seeing the place for the first time. I couldn't detect any flicker of recognition.

The flat looked like Deborah had just stepped out for an hour or so, fully expecting to be back soon. The police might have checked the place out, but they certainly hadn't neatened it up. Saturday's newspaper was scattered over the living room floor. A gray wedge-heeled sandal peeked out from under a chair. A magazine was splayed open on the coffee table, next to the remote control for the TV. Beside them was a not-quite-empty coffee cup; flecks of mold floated on the liquid's oily surface.

The things strewn around must have been left from early Saturday. Surely if Deborah had settled down after the ball to read, she'd have thrown on a comfy old robe, not lounged around in green silk.

Isabel wandered reverently around the room as if she were in a museum, staring at the pictures and touching the bric-a-brac, trying to get to know her wayward daughter through the possessions she'd left behind. She made a face when she reached the Duplisea painting.

"Do you think she really liked that? I didn't expect Debbie's home to be like this. So cold and barren. She was always such a . . . a ruffly child. Lace petticoats and hairbows and dolls."

"Ruffly? Not Debbie," objected Collington. "Her problem was that she wasn't feminine enough. She always was too independent and headstrong."

"That's not true!" Isabel rushed to her daughter's defense, although to me the accusation didn't require one.

"We all have unexpected tastes," Allen Fraser said placatingly. "That's what makes us interesting."

"That's right," I said, hoping to generate a few smiles. "Look at my dog Scruff. He'll do anything for a chunk of Swiss cheese." The crack didn't succeed at relieving the gloom.

Collington stood morosely in the archway between the parlors, arms across his chest. "So what is it you want to do?" he asked. "Lift up the floorboards? Slit open the cushions? Empty the drawers onto the carpet?"

Isabel spun toward him, looking shocked at the thought of such desecration. Young Bradford, who'd sunk into the sofa and taken on an air of profound boredom, said, "You've been watching too many cop shows, Dad."

"Don't be smart," his father snapped. "I never look at that garbage. You're the TV addict in this family."

"Yeah. Think I'll get me a fix right now." He picked up the remote control. Magically a deodorant commercial appeared in our midst. Collington gave the kid a disgusted look.

"I just want to look around," I told him. "See if anything might hint at why Deborah went out again Saturday night. There's nothing hidden or missing so far as we know, so there's no need to tear the place apart."

"The police think the necklace is missing and they didn't rip things up," Isabel pointed out.

"That's another thing," I said. "How are you going to explain to the police that you've got the necklace?" Allen Fraser had told me he'd given it to Brad, just as Debbie wanted.

Collington frowned. "Why tell the police anything?"

"They're assuming that the necklace was stolen and Deborah was killed by whoever took it," I said. "They should know they're wrong, so they can begin exploring other possibilities."

"But wouldn't that get Allen in trouble?"

"He's already in trouble because he didn't come forward right away. He'll just be in deeper the longer he waits."

"Brad," Isabel called; she had drifted toward the back of the flat. "Brad, come look at this."

I followed Collington and Allen Fraser down the hall. Two bedrooms opened off it. One, quite tiny, had been set up as an office—perhaps this was the business headquarters of Bumblebee boutique. An imposing ebony desk took up most of the space. There were neat stacks of magazines on shelves and a single tidy pile of papers on the desk. Deborah had lacked Lauren's talent for creative clutter.

Isabel was in the other room, Deborah's bedroom, looking at a display of framed photos on the wall. Deborah was the subject of all of them—it was as though she'd set up a little shrine to herself.

I recognized the Lady Macbeth shot from the newspaper and the magnificent picture by Kit Cormier.

As the men joined Isabel in front of this gallery, I ducked back into the office. The papers on the desk were invoices, ad proofs, sales reports—nothing likely to send her out on the street after midnight on a Sunday morning. There was a leather-bound appointment calendar with entries jotted neatly in purple ink. I flipped to last Saturday's page; the only entry read *Arts and Flowers Ball*. The day before had a notation that said *Pacific Playhouse, E.K., 3 P.M.* and another, more cryptic, that said simply *C-Day*. There was nothing marked for the Sunday she had died. On Monday she'd had a meeting with a real estate agent.

I fished my sketchbook out of my satchel and copied down all the entries for the two weeks surrounding her death, although the rest of them were uninteresting: some business appointments, some dates with Peter—her fiancé Peter Brockway, no doubt.

"Finding clues?" Young Bradford was in the doorway, his long, gawky body angled against the frame. Another commercial must have come on.

"Not really. There may not be any here to find." I closed the sketchbook. "Tell me about your sister."

He shrugged. "I suppose I should feel sad about all this but I don't really. I hardly even knew her. When she left home I was just a little kid. Ever since then they've kept me, well, sort of under lock and key. Like they're afraid if they let me do anything at all, I'll take off too."

I riffled through the stacks of magazines. *Vogue, Harper's Bazaar, Retail Store News.*

"Are you really a detective?" the kid asked.

"Yes, really." I looked up.

"Allen says you're an artist too."

"That's right."

"How'd you get them to let you do things like that?" His eyes shifted away, as if he were embarrassed by the question.

"You don't get someone to let you. You decide what you want to do and then let yourself."

"I'm an econ major." He grimaced. "Dad says it's a good background. He wants me to go into law. Or business, like him."

"Is that what you want?"

"I hate it!" The boy pounded his fist into the doorjamb, an echo of his father at the restaurant. I was amazed and delighted by his sudden fire.

"I want to be a musician." The words came tumbling out, faster and faster. "I'm an ace on the keyboard. In high school a bunch of us had a band, we played dances and stuff. We even talked about cutting a record. Now I'm jamming with some guys at college, we're trying to get some gigs, and—"

"What does your father think about that?" I was sorry as soon as I'd said it. The flame in him died as quickly as it had blazed forth.

"He thinks it stinks. Nothing's worthwhile if it doesn't pay a zillion dollars a year. That's what *he* says." The kid kicked at the floor. "What a bummer. Maybe I should run away like Debbie."

"Why don't you?"

He looked at me wide-eyed, like the small child he still was in many ways. "How could I? I don't have any money. I gotta finish school."

"You just said you hate school. Look, Bradford. Or Braddy— what do you like to be called?"

"Bradford is *his* name. My middle name's Hudson, so my friends started calling me Hud."

I kept myself from chuckling. "Okay, Hud. The thing is, you have to decide what you want to do more—be a musician or please your father."

"Yeah." His shoulders drooped. "Allen seems real proud of you."

"Does he? He has no right to. Whatever I've accomplished, it has nothing to do with him." The kid looked puzzled—he didn't know what I meant. "Come on," I said. "Let's see what they're doing in the other room."

They were still looking at photographs. They'd moved from the ones on the wall to a collection of silver-framed snapshots on a bedside table. The bed was unmade, a tumble of black satin sheets and black velvet spread. Across it was draped a mauve silk caftan— probably Deborah's idea of a comfy old robe.

On the other side of the bed was another table, with a phone, a lamp and a pad and pencil. I walked around the bed to take a look, but the pages of the pad were all blank. There was a pair of stiletto-heeled green pumps on the floor, half-hidden by the drooping black bedspread. I eased out the drawer. It was nearly empty except for a gun, a Beretta pistol. A woman living alone, she had probably deluded herself that it offered protection.

The dresser on the far wall showed the same signs of casual disarray I'd seen everywhere but in the little office. Its top was littered with balled-up pantyhose and crumpled Kleenex, and several items of jewelry had been left carelessly lying there. Gardino had had good cops searching the place; they'd resisted the temptation. There was a wide silver-and-onyx bracelet, earrings of hammered gold, a strand of pearls . . .

And the ring. Right there was the ring Lauren had admired at the dance, with its off-center emerald of deep jungle green and the three fiery diamonds to the side. It was a beautiful ring, an exquisite ring, a ring that proved Deborah had indeed come home on Saturday night. Allen Fraser had been right. He'd been telling the truth.

There was something else Lauren had said. About shoes—that's right. About how Deborah had been tipsy enough at one point to fall off her high-heeled shoes. Yet Nick Gardino had told me she was wearing flat-soled dancing slippers when her body was found.

The green shoes were by the bed. By the phone. I sat down at that spot.

Perhaps the phone is ringing as Deborah comes in. Or she decides to call someone. She would sit right here as she's talking, and it would be the most natural thing to kick off her shoes. Then something is said that makes her decide to go out. But not in these shoes. She's been on her feet in them all evening, and they look like torture. Yet it's urgent enough that she doesn't take time to change her dress—and safe enough, she thinks, that she doesn't take the gun.

Whom had she talked to? And what about?

But the important thing right this minute was that she'd really come home that night. He'd been telling the truth. I looked at Allen Fraser, standing with his friends across the room. They were facing away from me, their three heads—one red, one silver, one brunette—bent over Deborah's photos.

Allen reached to pick up another silver frame, and a new thought jolted me: whoever took Deborah's purse that night would have her keys. And he would have been able to put back the ring and change the shoes to suggest that she had returned home from the ball. To fake it. It would have been risky and complicated but it could have been done.

NINE In the morning the fog had retreated and the air was fresh with spring. I strolled with Scruff through the pleasant rosy light to Golden Gate Park. At this early hour we shared the park with two species of its native wildlife. Homo Joggus was out in force along Kennedy Drive, trying to get fit enough to face another day of paper-pushing in the Financial District. Homo Derelictus was rolling up its bedrolls beneath the bushes and ambling toward Haight Street to panhandle coins for coffee.

Scruff and I paused to admire the conservatory, a charming, extravagant confection of Victorian glass. In front of it beds of tulips, bright yellow and crimson, were beginning to bloom. Scruff barked at a pair of romping squirrels and yanked at his leash. I unhooked him and let him run. The squirrels made a great game of teasing him and scampering out of reach.

The first tricycles and strollers appeared, with kids aboard and mothers or nannies trailing behind. What a life, I thought—a whole carefree day in the park. What a temptation. Let the police discover what happened to Deborah Collington. Let Allen Fraser go back to New York where I'd never have to think about him again. If only it could be that easy.

But of course it couldn't be.

I dropped Scruff off at home, picked up my swimsuit and headed for the Arguello swim center. I find swimming a much more satisfactory form of exercise than jogging. No shin splints, no exhaust fumes to inhale. After a few laps, my body and mind get into a soothing rhythm and the way is clear for all sorts of answers and insights to come floating in. I do some of my best thinking in the pool.

Except on mornings like this. There was so much traffic in the water, I might as well have been on the freeway. We swam in a loop, up one lane, down the next. The soft, bulky man in front of me lumbered along like a farm machine, while the woman behind me was as impatient as a Porsche at full throttle. I tried to sort out the events of the last few days as I churned through the water, but that proved impossible. Things tumbled through my mind, willy-nilly: Debbie, Debbie, home to bed, go out again and end up dead . . . father, father, who's got the father? . . . hey, watch it, fella, that's my ear you just kicked . . . god, those eyes, so blue, magical blue . . . oops, keep away from that thrashing foot . . . use that blue in a painting, gotta get that painting done . . . what is a father, any-way? . . . no, I can't speed up; yell at that turkey in front of me . . . murdered, strangled, dumped in an alley . . . maybe he'll call; please, let him call . . . but he's taken, the girl with coffee-colored hair . . . Debbie, Debbie, home to bed . . . why did she go out again? . . . who? . . . what? . . . why?

At least I could feel virtuous about getting the exercise. To reward myself I stopped on the way home for blueberry muffins, which I washed down with tea while I perused my wardrobe. A couple of the people I wanted to see today were business types and they'd probably respond better if I looked businesslike too.

I put on yesterday's charcoal gray with a fresh shirt of cream-colored silk and studied the effect. Businesslike, yes, but boring. Since my first stop would be Pacific Playhouse I livened things up with a big theatrical scarf in a swirly pattern of gold, rust and blue. That was better—now I was ready for anything.

Sure I was. Another little rhyme jumped, unbidden and unwelcome, into my mind: *Jess, oh Jess, go back to bed, help out your father and end up . . .*

Gulls were squalling as I got out of my little Toyota, and the breeze was flavored with brine. Pacific Playhouse was located in a converted church in the Richmond District, just four blocks from the beach. It was an odd neighbor amidst the rows of pastel stucco houses.

The car parked ahead of mine seemed out of place too: a snazzy Jaguar XKE convertible in British Racing Green, old but in handsome shape. It had vanity plates that said: EVNZGR8.

The Jag made my Toyota look sadder and shabbier than usual. Although I lavish affection on my car, I haven't been able to make up for the abuse it suffered in its youth at the hands of its previous owner. Dan never understood that you have to treat with respect the things that are important to you, like relationships and cars. I rescued the Toyota by buying it from him one of the times he was desperate for cash; he believed it would compromise his artistic integrity to keep a steady job. Roger had been good enough to lend me the money. Rescuing myself had been harder.

I patted the Toyota's hood to reassure it that my head wouldn't be turned by the sleek green machine in front of it. Then I walked up to the theater.

I found the office on the second floor of what had been the Sunday school wing. On the door hung a poster for the upcoming production: Lorca's *Blood Wedding*. It was an elegant design—an umber silhouette of a rampaging horse on a background the tan of a Spanish landscape. The lettering spilled down the side in a splash of dark red. I knew Lauren would love it.

The big open room reminded me of the *Artspaper* space: second-hand desks and cabinets, piles of papers, an air of clutter barely contained. At a table in the corner people were chattering as they stuffed envelopes. Fabric samples were draped over another table: two women were feeling them, holding them up to the light, making notes on a sheaf of sketches. Someone was totting up figures on a calculator; someone else was talking on the phone. Close to the doorway a very young woman with a short brushy haircut was battling an ancient typewriter and losing.

"Oh phoo!" She whacked at the keys in irritation, rolled the paper up and slathered on some white correction goop. As she was blowing it dry, I asked her if Evan Krausgill was around.

"Evan? Oh yeah, sure, that's him." She jerked a thumb toward the man on the phone.

There was a carton of the *Blood Wedding* posters on the floor by his desk. While he finished his call, I lifted the top one so I could examine it more closely. The initials E.K. appeared as a signature along the curve of the horse's neck.

"Great poster," I said as he hung up the phone and stood to greet me.

"Thanks." He lowered his eyes and batted the lids in exaggerated modesty. "Designed it all by myself."

Evan Krausgill had slick black hair and a little black mustache and teeth too white to be believed. He was on the small side; even with the two-inch heels on his shiny black boots he was no taller than I was. He was well built, though, in the way that suggests lots of time on the Nautilus machines. He had dressed with full attention to the artistic and expensive detail: the single diamond stud earring, the plum-colored silk ascot arranged just so, the carefully fitted European-cut trousers.

"What can I do for you?" Evan asked. "No, don't tell me, let me guess. You're as wealthy as you are beautiful and you want to give us a check for fifty thousand bucks."

"Not quite."

"Forty thousand? We're not greedy."

"I'm Jess Randolph. I'm a private investigator looking into Deborah Collington's death."

He quickly put on an attitude of mourning. They should have had this guy on stage instead of in the office. "Alas, poor Deborah. Does this mean the police have given up already?"

"I'm sure the police are doing fine. I'm working for her family. She was estranged from them, you know. They want the murder solved, of course, but they're also curious about her life. Who was she, what was she like?" With each telling, this rationale for my involvement got easier to deliver. I was beginning to believe it myself.

"Evan, phone for you," announced the typist. "And you said you'd look over this press release. I'm not gonna—"

"Take a message, Candy." He grabbed my arm. "Come on, let's go down to the auditorium. We can talk better there."

Evan gave me the two-cent tour along the way. "The second floor here has the office and costume shop and dressing rooms. We made the first floor into another shop where we build scenery and props." He unlocked the door leading into the nave of the church.

The pews had been replaced by theater seats covered with worn red plush. We sat in the first row, facing what had once been the chancel and was now the stage, bare except for a card table and some steel folding chairs. Behind them the wall was covered with a huge white scrim. The pointed arch of a stained-glass window peeked over the scrim's top edge.

"We were lucky to get this building," Evan said. "We'll be even luckier to keep it. We've been able to rent it cheap since the congregation moved to fancy digs, but we keep hearing rumors that they're going to tear the old church down and slap up some condos."

"That would be a disaster. Where would you go?" Affordable spaces for artists and cultural groups are almost nonexistent in this city.

"Beats me, babe. If only you had that fifty thou."

"Is that what you do here—raise money?"

"Yeah, that's part of my job. Not the easy part, either. I also handle publicity. I do my humble best to get us good notices and pull in the paying public."

Suddenly the white scrim was awash in an amber glow.

"Tech crew's working on lights," Evan explained. "We're doing a lot with lights for this production. We'll substitute some Spanishy wooden furniture for that stuff on stage, and that's it. Very poetic play, *Blood Wedding*. Doesn't need a set, just plenty of atmosphere.

It's full of passion." He bared all those white teeth in a grin. Passion was apparently one of his favorite things.

"Was Deborah cast in this show?"

"No. Too bad, though. I mean, I'm sorry about what happened and all, but the media attention has really boosted our advance ticket sales. We open next weekend. If only Deb had been cast as the Bride, we'd probably sell out the run."

I grimaced inwardly. Never pass up a chance for publicity, no matter how gruesome. "I guess she was in a lot of your shows. Lady Macbeth last fall—"

"Yeah, that was superb. *Magnifique*, even." He kissed his fingertips in the classic Gallic gesture of approval. "She only did a couple of shows a year. She wasn't like some of our people. For a lot of them, acting is their whole life; it's as important as breathing. For Deb it was more of an ego thing. She got off on the attention and applause, but she had other things going, too, like her business, that Bumblebee place."

The amber light behind the stage faded and magenta came up in its place.

"Did you know her well?" I asked.

"Oh, Deb and I had our little frolics." He cocked his eyebrows into a leer that left little doubt about the nature of those frolics.

"I heard you were dancing with her at the Arts and Flowers Ball."

"Yeah, I tried to dance with all the beautiful women there. Since she was one of the most beautiful, I spent quite a bit of time with her. You must not have been there or I would have danced with you too."

"No, I wasn't there."

"Too bad. An opportunity wasted. We'll have to make up for lost time." He rested a hand on my knee. His heavy gold ring with its square-cut purple stone was impressive. But his nails were ragged and chewed, out of sync with his artfully constructed image.

I shifted my leg out of reach. "Maybe later," I said, not meaning it. "Right now I'm working. Did you make plans to see Deborah after the ball?"

"Funny, the cops asked me that too. Is someone going around saying I bumped her off?"

"Not that I know of. Did you?"

The white teeth flashed as Evan laughed. "That's how I like my women—direct and to the point. What would you do if I said 'Sure, I killed her'?" This time the hand on my knee didn't linger, just gave me a friendly pat.

"I'd tell the police."

"But I didn't, of course. I didn't see her after the ball, either. I wanted to. As soon as I realized she was there alone I made all sorts of lovely plans. Champagne and some, uh, other refreshments I had available. Soft music. Soft bed. Hard—well, you know." Again he did his little act with the eyebrows. "But she said no."

"Why did she turn you down?" I could think of several reasons why I would have, but I wasn't Deborah.

He lifted his arms in a helpless, what-can-you-do gesture. "I couldn't believe it either. She just said 'Sorry, Evan, I'm busy later.' She kept peering around like she was looking for someone, so I figured she had something going."

"No clue as to who she was waiting for?"

He shook his head. "It must have been that Mystery Stranger I heard all the fuss about on the news. At the time, I guessed it was her fiancé."

"Peter Brockway?"

"The same. But he never showed up."

"Deborah told someone he had the flu."

"Oh, really? He was here on Friday for our board of directors meeting and he was the picture of health. He's on our board, you know. Deb got him involved. I must say he's been something of a disappointment."

"Why is that?"

"Well, there are two qualifications that get you invited to join the board of a nonprofit group. Either you've got money or some sort of useful expertise. Now, Peter's not an accountant or lawyer who could give us pro bona service, and he doesn't know diddly about theater. He pretends he has a background in film, but his company just makes motivational tapes or something. So his credential was cash."

"And he hasn't come through."

"From what I hear, doll"—Evan leaned forward eagerly, conspiratorially; the white teeth were only inches from my face—"Brockway's company is in deep shit. I think the real reason he didn't show Saturday night is he flat-out couldn't afford the ticket."

"Where did you hear this?"

"Oh, around." He waved his hand vaguely at the stage. The scrim glowed with a deep sapphire blue.

"Around where?"

"Come to dinner with me tonight and I'll tell you."

"I'm busy tonight." Now if it had been Kit Cormier asking . . .

"Tomorrow then. I've got some great stuff you can have for dessert. A special treat."

I shuddered to think what that might be. "I can't. My boss has a strict policy about not going out socially with anyone involved in a case." That's one advantage to working with a firm of investigators instead of solo. It's amazing how many people will accept company policy as an excuse.

"I'm not involved."

"You're involved enough for the rule to apply. If you weren't I wouldn't be here."

"What a pity. Oh well, you'll solve it soon, won't you? Then we can have our fun."

Two could play his little game. "Maybe. If you tell me about Brockway's financial problems."

"Well, if you must know, I heard him fighting with Deb on Friday. She'd stopped by to bring over some, uh, some items she'd ordered for our costume people, through her boutique. She must have forgotten about the board meeting; I got the impression she was surprised to see Peter here."

"I saw her appointment calendar. She had a three o'clock meeting here that afternoon. With E.K."

His eyes glittered for an instant; then he made his expression carefully blank.

"Those are your initials," I pointed out.

"Me? Well, there's no other E.K. here, but she sure didn't have a date with me. I saw her in passing; we nodded hello. Nothing more."

"I see. Tell me about this fight with Peter Brockway."

He relaxed a bit, as if relieved to have the attention deflected away from him. My guess was that he felt that way rarely. "They were talking on the stairs when I started down from the office. He said he had to have the money that day, right now, or he'd lose his business, and she said too eff-ing bad." He grinned. "Or words to that effect."

"He was asking her for money?"

"Yeah. She wasn't giving him any, either. Of course, that was in character; she much preferred *getting* money. It's more blessed to receive than to give, that's our Deb." He clapped a hand over his mouth. "Whoops—mustn't speak ill of the dead. But I'll tell you, old Petie'd have a tough time hanging onto her if he was down the tubes financially."

"And they sounded angry?"

"He was livid. She seemed to be enjoying herself. She rather liked playing games with people."

"Did they know you heard them?"

"I, uh . . . no, I stopped at the top of the stairs till they were gone. It didn't sound like they wanted to be interrupted." He had the grace to look embarrassed, and covered it by glancing at his watch. "Oh shit, I gotta dash, doll, much as I'd rather stay and talk to you. I set up an interview for the *Blood Wedding* director on that KCQY radio noon call-in show. Sure we can't do dinner?"

"Positive. Where is Brockway's office, do you know? I think I should see him next."

"His company's called Success Videos. Very cute. The girl upstairs can give you the address." He stood and grabbed my hand to help me up.

"One more thing," I said. "May I have a poster? A friend of mine collects them. I know she'd love this one."

For the first time Evan's smile looked genuine. Pride in his artistry; a feeling I could relate to. It felt odd to have something in common with him.

"Of course. I'm honored. Help yourself when you go up. And listen, babe, why don't you give me your phone number."

I handed him only my P&O card. No home number for this fellow. "Call me if you think of anything about Deborah I should know."

"And if I want to talk about you?" He tried gazing soulfully into my eyes.

"I'm not a very interesting subject," I told him, pulling away.

As we left the theater the scrim behind the stage was burning with an intense, bloody red.

I laid the poster carefully on the back seat and climbed into my car. I turned the key in the ignition; the engine coughed and sputtered and died. The Toyota was feeling sulky and jealous because of the fancy Jaguar in front of it.

"It's okay, kid," I assured it. "I wouldn't trade you in on something showy and pretentious like that. You're honest and reliable and my favorite car in the world." That made it feel better; on the next try the engine began to purr.

As I pulled out of the space my eye was caught by the Jag's license plate. EVNZGR8. In a flash it made sense—*Evan iz great.* His job with Pacific Playhouse, he said, was to bring in money. Obviously some of it, from somewhere, stuck to him—look at his car, his jewelry, his costly clothes. And his friendship with Deborah Collington, who had expensive tastes. Surely the theater couldn't afford to pay him nearly that much.

TEN Success Videos, Inc., according to its glossy brochure, produced how-to videotapes for busy, ambitious executives. How to cope with stress, how to manage time, how to get your career on the fast track while lounging in front of your VCR.

I read the brochure four times while I waited to see Peter Brockway. His photo appeared on the second page: the sandy-haired man who had exchanged angry words with George Sanmarco at the funeral. This portrait showed him as the very image of the successful corporate president, guaranteed to inspire investor confidence—the self-assured smile, the forthright gaze at the camera, the boyish good looks. A touch more gray at the temples might have been nice, to convey an impression of seasoned experience, but perhaps that wasn't important. After all, this was the edge of Silicon Valley, a land of brash and youthful entrepreneurs.

I'd driven straight down here from Pacific Playhouse. Success Videos was next to the freeway in San Mateo in a brand-new office park. Just a few months ago this had been a salt marsh, with herons and egrets and breeding grounds for fish. Now workers were painting stripes on the parking lot and tamping earth around some straggly young junipers at the front door. The elegant teak-trimmed lobby still smelled of fresh-sawn wood.

Brockway had the whole third floor. His reception area—cool and sleek and clean-lined—was done in shades of gray, ranging from fog through mouse to charcoal. The chairs were upholstered in burgundy cotton, and that tone was repeated in the subtle pattern of the carpet. It all looked very tasteful, very expensive. If Success Videos had money troubles, they must have come up after the lease was signed and the decorator hired.

When I arrived the receptionist was leafing through a copy of *Cosmopolitan*. She looked like she belonged on its cover, as though Brockway did his hiring through a modeling agency. Halo of black curls, perfect cheekbones in an oval face—I found myself itching to sketch her. TINA MARGOLIS said the chrome nameplate on her desk.

At first she was reluctant to announce me. He's busy, she said; you need an appointment, she said. But when I mentioned Deborah Collington, her eyes widened. She punched nervously at buttons on a console with a magenta-tipped finger, cupped her hand over her mouth and mumbled something into her headset. Then she told me to take a seat and wait.

By now I'd been waiting for half an hour. The brochure wasn't fascinating enough for a fifth reading, so I tucked it into my satchel and leaned back in my chair. I squinted to make the sharp edges go out of focus and concentrated on the interplay of gray and burgundy. How would it look on canvas? It was a little too monochromatic for me, but with that winey red to liven up the neutral tones, maybe—

"Ms. Randolph," said a male voice, and I was vaguely aware that I was hearing it for the second time. I opened my eyes and sat up; there was Peter Brockway. Tina Margolis was still reading her magazine, which surprised me; I'd have thought that when the boss appeared she'd suddenly bustle with letters to type or papers to file.

Brockway didn't seem to care, though. He pumped my hand briskly and flashed the self-assured smile of the brochure photo. He came from the casual school of executive attire—a dress shirt with collar open, sleeves rolled up.

"Welcome to Success Videos."

"Thanks. You have a very impressive setup."

He led me down the corridor. "When I was a kid, I dreamed of being a Hollywood director. My dad kept telling me, be practical, go to business school. This way I've got the best of both worlds."

More burgundy and gray in his office. One wall displayed a line of poster-sized photos. "Samples of your work?"

"Those are stills from my first Success Videos production. I was a one-man show then, did everything myself. You can see how far I've come." He swept his arm in an expansive arc, taking in the whole third floor, the glossy lobby and probably a Mercedes or BMW in the parking lot. PTRZGR8, the license plate would say. *Peter iz great.*

"Business is good, then," I remarked casually.

The publicity-shot smile dissolved. "Well, it's a challenge, making it all work. Sometimes I'd rather be back behind the camera than here in the office. But really, I can't imagine doing anything else."

Brockway sat behind a massive desk and motioned me into a low armchair on the other side. A bit of psychological gamesmanship— make the other person look up to you, keep her at a distance.

"Tina said you're a private detective. You want to talk about Deborah." He raked his fingers through his thick thatch of hair. There was gray in it after all, I noticed, and dark smudges under his eyes. The brochure photo must have been taken on a good day. Or perhaps the interior designer had worked on him, graying him up so he'd match the decor.

Now, don't be rude, Jess, I told myself. The man's fiancée was murdered; he has a right to look haggard.

"That's right," I said. I gave him my tale about being hired by the Collingtons to look into Deborah's life and death.

"I met them at the funeral. We exchanged condolences. There didn't seem to be much·more to say. Deborah wasn't close to them, you know."

"I know. They regret that now. That's why they want to know all they can—to help them deal with the pain of losing her."

"The pain—oh God yes. Tell me about the pain." All vestiges of the upbeat public-relations image were gone.

"Will you tell me about your relationship?" I asked gently. "As a favor to her parents. How did you meet?"

"It was, oh, about a year ago. I stopped in her shop to buy a birthday present for my girlfriend. Deborah waited on me. She had a great laugh, a great body, all that blond hair—just beautiful." He looked beyond me, eyes soft, remembering. "On impulse I asked her out to dinner. She accepted and that was it. I never did give the other girl that birthday gift."

"And you were planning to get married."

"Yes. As soon as . . . see, I had a business deal brewing. I wanted that out of the way first. So I could go off on my honeymoon with a light heart." He laughed, but bitterly.

"Was she a good businesswoman?"

"Well, her shop was really just a hobby. Of course, it didn't much matter. The settlement she got from her ex-husband was enough to keep her comfortable."

A small woman with huge glasses appeared in the doorway. "Sorry to interrupt, Peter," she said, "but I'm editing the *Art of Negotiation* tape and I need to know how you want to handle that interview with the Stanford professor."

"Soon as I'm free here," he replied, waving her away.

"What do you know about the divorce settlement?" I asked when the woman was gone.

"Why? Her old man afraid George is going to screw him over?"

"Don't tell me, if I'm prying," I said, and then I quietly waited. Two of us could play little psychological games. The silence grew heavy.

"Hell, I don't know the details," Brockway said finally. "Only that it was very generous. Seed money for the boutique. Payments on her condo. Monthly alimony, I never knew how much. Tons of jewelry, but that's George's business, he could get it cheap. That damn necklace, the one she was wearing the night she . . . she died." He ran a hand along his collar, as if he expected to find the necklace there. "It belonged to George's first wife. Deborah admired it and asked him for it, and damned if he didn't talk Lucia into giving it up."

He narrowed his eyes at me. "If you find out what happened to her—on Saturday, I mean, the . . . the murder—does that mean you'll find the necklace too?"

"I don't know. The two things might not even be connected." No sense in tipping him off that I knew where the necklace was. "Sanmarco must be pretty wealthy to give her all that and not miss it. Or maybe he was still in love with her."

"Hardly. The divorce was his idea."

"Because she was playing around?"

He glared at me. "Lots of reasons. Deborah had a wild streak when she was younger, but she'd settled down by the time I met her."

"Of course," I murmured.

"Deborah had—well, speak about the art of negotiation. She knew how to get herself a good deal and she got one from George."

"Both sides usually get something when a deal is struck. What was in it for him?"

"How should I know?" He frowned. "Look, you should be asking him all these questions. Now, if you'll—"

"Excuse me." This time the person at the door was a man, middle-aged, soft and paunchy, with a pale round face. He had wire-rimmed glasses pushed up over his thinning hair. "Pete, we've got a problem with Peregrine Video Stores. I called to find out why they haven't paid this past-due invoice and their payables people are giving me a first-class runaround."

"Peregrine?" Brockway pulled his brows together, as though he were trying to recall the account.

"Yeah. It's real strange, Pete. I don't like it."

Brockway gave an exasperated sigh. "I'm busy right now, Len."

The man pursed his lips, making a small round O of disapproval in the larger O of his face. "Okay, boss. Just trying to keep the cash flowing."

"I appreciate that, Len, really," Brockway said. "Look, give me the invoice, and I'll check into it."

"Okay. Thanks." Len handed Brockway a paper and left the room.

Without giving it a glance, Brockway stuffed it in his top desk drawer.

"One thing about owning a business," he grumbled. "No matter how good your employees are, you end up taking care of all the problems yourself. Next someone will be bringing me a broken camera to fix." He pushed back his chair and stood up. "Have I given you enough? I need to get back to work."

I didn't move, except to lean forward slightly, looking, I hoped, earnest and sincere. "I'm really grateful for your time, Mr. Brockway. And Deborah's parents are, too—you don't know how much this means to them. Can you tell me anything that might shed light on what happened Saturday night?"

His face was a slammed gate. "Nothing. I didn't see her at all that day."

"Something she said in a phone call, maybe. Or something that happened before Saturday."

"What's your point? I thought she was killed by some wacko after that dance. A mugger after her necklace, or some pervert. That Mystery Stranger."

"There's some evidence she went home after the ball, talked to someone on the phone, and then went out again."

"What evidence?" Brockway dropped back into his chair and began drumming his fingers. "I know nothing about it."

"She didn't call you Saturday night?"

"Of course not. What are you driving at?"

"I heard you and Deborah had an argument the day before, at the Pacific Playhouse."

"Who told you that?" he demanded. "I bet it was that little creep Krausgill."

"Why do you call him a creep?"

"It would be just like him to eavesdrop. He was always pestering Deborah. He had the hots for her so bad he could hardly keep himself inside his pants when she was around."

"What did you fight about?"

"Didn't the little bastard tell you that too?"

I didn't say anything. I just waited, keeping my gaze locked on his. His fingers tap-tap-tapped on the desktop.

He broke away first. "It was nothing. A petty little disagreement that blew out of proportion. Deborah had a pretty good temper, you know. I guess I do too. I told her the hell with the dance, I'd find someone more congenial to spend the evening with. So I didn't see her at all on Saturday." He was twisting a paper clip, bending and unbending it without looking. "I should have gone. If I'd gone with her to the dance, it never would have happened. She'd never have—oh, Jesus."

"She told people you weren't there because you had the flu."

"Did she," he said flatly. "I guess she didn't want anyone knowing I might prefer another woman's company to hers, even for one night."

"And did you find someone more congenial?"

"You never give up, do you. Yeah, I found someone. You could say it was a very congenial evening."

"Who was she?"

"That's none of your business. Or the Collingtons' either. Anyway, she couldn't give me much of an alibi. We stayed in my apartment all evening, watching the VCR. That's what you detectives always want, isn't it? Alibis?"

I decided to give it one more try. "What did you argue about? Please tell me, it might help her parents to understand—"

"I did tell you: nothing. Every couple has little spats. Don't go looking for a murder motive there."

"I never suggested you killed her."

"Then why are you badgering me this way?"

"I don't mean to badger you."

His fingers rumpled his thick hair. "Oh Lord. This is such a hellish time for me. I loved that woman. You can tell her parents that much—I really loved her. It tears me up, thinking if she hadn't . . . if we hadn't had that blowup . . . if I'd gone with her to the dance . . ."

Brockway dropped his head into his hands, pushing fingers hard against his temples. We observed a moment of silence. His face was pinched when he looked up.

"Did you know her?" he asked. I shook my head.

"She was so beautiful. So beautiful. She grabbed onto life with both hands. If I ever get near the bastard that killed her—"

His telephone buzzed. Tina Margolis's disembodied voice floated into the room. "Peter, call on line one for you."

Brockway didn't have to pick up the handset to respond. "Take a message, Tina. I'll call back."

"It's George Sanmarco," came the reply. "He said you'd want to talk to him."

"Oh shit." The company president picked up the receiver and punched a button. "George!" he boomed in a voice that probably sounded hearty to someone who couldn't see his face. "This is a pleasant surprise."

He fluttered his hand at me. The gesture obviously meant *get out of here.* As I headed for the door he asked the caller, "What can I do for you?"

I couldn't hear the reply, of course, but whatever it was, Brockway wasn't expecting to like it. Before the phone rang, he had looked sorrowful and drawn. Talking to George Sanmarco, what he looked was scared.

ELEVEN

Back in the city, I decided to check in at the P&O office. My box contained two pink message slips. One from my father Roger Randolph. One from my father Allen Fraser.

Tyler and O'Meara were the only ones there. No blue suit today—Tyler was slouching comfortably in faded jeans and a floppy turquoise sweater. He was poking at his computer keyboard, making numbers dance around the screen.

"You will be delighted to know," he announced, "that my state-of-the-art cash flow projections indicate that we will indeed make payroll this week."

"That is good news," I agreed. O'Meara sauntered over to check out my skirt and shoes for a telltale aroma of Scruff. He hates it that my affections and loyalties are divided, even though his rival is his own son. I scratched his handsome auburn ears; usually that's enough to make him forgive me.

"Wanna join me for lunch?" Tyler held out a chocolate chip cookie.

"What's this?" I asked. "You've graduated from chewing gum? You don't watch out, pretty soon you'll be mainlining cheesecake and mocha truffles."

"A fate worse than death. I suppose I could take up smoking again."

"No, no, please. Eat cookies, dozens if you like."

"See, Claudia's sisters—or cousins, or both, she's got so many I can never keep 'em straight. Anyway, they came and kidnapped her for lunch. They kept talking about what they were in the mood to eat. Pasta con le vongole, roast beef sandwiches with potato salad, enchiladas with guacamole and sour cream." He had the expression of an angel describing heaven. "What's a guy supposed to do?"

"Go over to Irma's for a fix. Well, you won't tempt me," I said virtuously.

"Halfsies?" He broke the cookie in two. "You'd be saving me from myself. I've already had three."

"Well, since you insist." I took a piece. After all, I reasoned, I'd earned it by swimming this morning. O'Meara pawed my knee hopefully but I was mean and didn't share.

"Thanks." Tyler licked crumbs from his fingers. "Hey, let me show you our new toy."

The abundant fronds of the Boston fern on his desk had been shoved aside to make room for a box. Like so many boxes delivered to P&O before, this one bore the logo of Tyler's favorite electronic-supply mail-order house.

"Uh-oh, more gadgets. You sure we can afford payroll?"

"Be respectful. This kind of stuff is what keeps us on the cutting edge of the private-eye profession. It's a high-tech age, you gotta keep a high-tech perspective to survive. Just look at this beauty."

He lifted out a cylindrical object.

"A mini-telescope?" I guessed. "Some sort of binoculars? But it's only for one eye—that makes it a monocular."

"A night-vision viewer," he said proudly. "We can conduct surveillance practically in pitch blackness and actually see what's going on." He launched into a rapturous description of light intensification and diopter ranges and objective lenses. When he realized my eyes were glazing over he broke off, asking, "So how's it going?"

"I'm not sure." Back to work—I sat down at my desk with a sigh. "I've talked to two of the men in Deborah Collington's life—one of them doesn't have enough money and the other one seems to have too much. So what does that mean? She probably went out for a breath of air and had the bad luck to run into a psychopath in a foul mood."

"I meant with your father."

"Oh, him." I arranged the message slips on the desktop, side by side. Roger Randolph. Allen Fraser. Until I was thirteen years old, my name was Jessica Fraser. How strange that sounded now.

"Wanna tell your big brother Ty about it? I listen well."

I looked up at him, startled. I hadn't thought about it before, but we *were* sort of a family, Tyler and Claudia and me. And of course O'Meara. We had good times and serious times and silly squabbles. We teased each other and made each other laugh. We shared the details of our lives—likes and dislikes, triumphs and failures, hopes and fears. And most important, I absolutely would be there if Tyler or Claudia needed me, and I knew they would be there for me.

Tyler was regarding me with a mixture of warmth and concern. "Well? My rates are cheap."

But sometimes you have to deal with it—whatever it is—on your own. "Thanks, Tyler. But . . . not yet."

Roger's message didn't require a return call. The fame of Irma's Deli had spread—Keith had requested one of Irma's special double-fudge tortes for his birthday cake and Roger wanted me to order it and pick it up. That was easy.

What was hard was dialing the number on Allen Fraser's slip. I prayed for no answer.

But in vain. There was no hello, just a gruff "Mr. Collington is not taking calls from the press."

"Allen?"

"Oh, it's you, Jessica, good. I'm with Brad at his daughter's place. He has a plan he wants to tell you about. Can you come over? Soon—he has an appointment later with Deborah's lawyer to go over her estate." I agreed, with reluctance, to be there shortly.

I cradled the receiver and stared toward the window. When I first came to Parks & O'Meara, I could sit at this desk and see sky, clouds, an occasional gliding gull. Now I get to admire the sharp granite edge of the new highrise across the street.

Tyler interrupted my train of non-thought. "Client called this morning, by the way. About the Videau case."

"Videau?" I jerked my attention back.

"Yeah, that case you just spent six weeks working on, remember? Microchips? Embezzlement? Partners at each other's throats? Some guys just don't know how to make a partnership work, do they, old buddy," he said to O'Meara. Then back to me: "He wondered when he'd get a copy of his final report."

Oh, yes, that—the report on the case that had taken me to court Tuesday morning, the one I hadn't been able to concentrate on that afternoon because of Allen Fraser's calls. One more item to add to my list of unfinished projects, along with Keith's birthday present and the last painting for the Ars Nova show.

Tyler waited. He was my boss again—although there was no inquiry in his tone, I knew he was asking a question. Or issuing an order.

"He can have it as soon as I've written it. I'll do it at home tonight." My attempts at a draft still littered my desk. I stuffed them into my satchel as I left for Clay Street and Deborah's flat.

"Imagine—my little Debbie wearing baubles like this." Brad Collington held Deborah's necklace up to the window. The sunlight winked and sparkled off the jewels. It made the rich green of the emeralds glow and set the diamonds' fire to dancing.

Collington's eyes were reddened and sunken, and the lines in his forehead seemed more deeply etched than they had been yesterday. "Oh God, poor Debbie. Remember what a sweet kid she was, Allen? Back in the roller-skate days, before she . . . before it got all messed up?"

The three of us were sitting in Deborah's black-and-white living room. The men had moved in. Blankets and pillows were mounded on the sofa, where one of them would be sleeping, and a suitcase of lustrous tan leather stood upright on the floor. There were drinks on the coffee table—tea for me, coffee for Allen Fraser, a martini for Collington. Through the wide opening into the dining room I could see the Gerard Duplisea painting with its sour-colored coils and twists.

"Of course I remember," Allen Fraser assured him. He had been morose and mostly silent since I arrived.

"I still think of her as nine years old. Ponytails and skinned knees. If only I could turn back the clock."

"Let Jessica try that on," Allen Fraser suggested.

Collington looked at him in bewilderment. "What?"

"Let her wear the necklace. You can imagine what it would have looked like on Debbie."

"But I—oh hell, why not." He handed the beautiful object to me.

Emeralds and diamonds. I clasped the jewels around my neck. I was surprised that just touching them didn't make my fingers tingle and burn.

We went back to Deborah's bedroom so I could see the effect in a mirror. I slipped off my scarf and shrugged out of my jacket. My ivory blouse was all wrong—too sedate, too businesslike. "I need Cinderella's magic gown."

"Here, try this." Allen Fraser shook a pillow out of its green satin case. The bedclothes had been black yesterday; Collington must have put on fresh ones.

I undid my top buttons and turned the shirt collar inside. Then I draped myself with the pillowcase, arranging it smoothly under the necklace.

"That's it," said Allen. "Beautiful."

Savor this moment, Jess, I told my reflection. You may never again get to see what you look like wearing a fortune in jewels. The necklace was gold, shaped in a deep, curved V, like the wings of a flying bird in a child's drawing. Round diamonds alternated with square-cut emeralds along the wings. At the point where they joined, there hung a pendant, pear-shaped, as big as an old-fashioned silver dollar. The large teardrop diamond in the center was ringed first with emeralds, then with more diamonds. The deep green of the satin and the emeralds flattered my skin and red hair. I felt exceedingly gorgeous. I fervently wished that Kit Cormier were here.

"I can see why Deborah loved this," I murmured, running my fingers along the stones. I wondered how Lucia Sanmarco had felt about giving it up—and why she had done so. Surely not because of her warm regard for the woman who stole her husband.

"It looks wonderful on you, Jessica," Allen Fraser said. His face had brightened with a gleam of—what? Paternal pride? I turned away abruptly.

Collington's expression mixed grief, wonder, weariness. "Debbie would have looked stunning. God, if only—"

"I'll take it," I said. "Five dollars. You might even talk me up to ten." They chuckled, which is what I'd hoped for; it broke a funny tension that had been building.

I unlatched the necklace and handed it back. I wasn't sure how long you could wear something like that before being infected with terminal materialism, and given the state of my finances it would do me no good to find out.

"Have you told the police yet, Allen?" I asked. "About how Deborah gave you the necklace?"

The two men exchanged glances. Allen wouldn't quite look at me as he said, "Umm . . . that's the plan Brad has. I thought he should tell you about it."

"Come, I'll show you. I've already set it in motion." Collington led us back to the living room, where he nested the necklace in its tissue-lined box on the coffee table. Then he handed me a torn manila envelope and a sheet of white paper.

"I called that cop, the one who's heading up the police investigation," he went on. "What's his name—Gardner."

"Gardino," I corrected him.

"Whatever," he said. "I told him this package was waiting on the doorstep when I got back from taking my wife and boy to the airport. That asshole reporter had a story in this morning's paper announcing to the whole world where I'm staying, so anybody could have left it here."

I picked up the white paper, balancing its edges carefully against my fingertips, and read it: *I'm sorry. I never would have done it if I knew it would hurt so bad. I can't bring her back to life but maybe it will make us both feel better if I give you this.* It was inexpertly typed, with words xxx-ed out and misspellings here and there. The label on the envelope said simply: BRADFORD COLLINGTON.

"You made this up?" I asked incredulously.

"There's a copy shop nearby. You can rent a typewriter by the hour," Collington said. "Since there's no handwriting to match up, the police won't know I did it."

"But there will be fingerprints. Especially on that shiny label."

"The cops would expect my prints. It was addressed to me and I opened it."

"They'd also expect the prints of whoever typed the note and put the package together. And those won't be there."

"The person could have been wearing gloves," Allen Fraser suggested.

"Ever tried typing with gloves on?" I asked. "I can't go along with this. It's not just illegal to deceive the police, it's dumb."

"This won't affect their investigation. It just explains why I have the necklace without involving Allen."

"No, it doesn't. Why won't Gardino just conclude that the Mystery Stranger had an attack of remorse? It doesn't let Allen off the hook at all."

Collington was pacing restlessly across Deborah's shaggy white rug. "I don't see the problem. So the cops do figure out Allen's the Mystery Stranger. He can say he left Debbie at home safe and sound, necklace and all. It's almost true. This way he's got a plausible story and I don't have to hide the fact that I've got the necklace."

"If this is the way your mind works, I'm surprised you don't hide it. You could claim the insurance and have both."

He jerked to a halt. "Good God, Jessica, murder's not awful enough? You want me to commit fraud over my daughter's death?"

"This harebrained scheme isn't fraud?" I fought to keep from shouting. "If Gardino finds out I knew about this deception, I'll be in deep trouble. I'm already obstructing justice, just knowing that Allen is the Mystery Stranger and not telling the cops. It could mean the end of my license. And maybe Tyler's. I'm jeopardizing the whole firm."

I turned to Allen Fraser. "Can't you talk him out of this lunacy?"

He was slumped in a chair, reading Collington's clever note for perhaps the tenth time. "I thought this might work. But you're right, it still looks suspicious. It could have been me who left the package." He looked up worriedly. "I don't want you to get in trouble, Jessica."

"Tell Gardino the truth. It will only get worse the longer you wait."

"What do you want me to do?" Collington exploded. "Let Allen get blamed? I'd rather—God, I'd rather just have it go unsolved."

"You don't mean that, Brad." Allen Fraser sounded shocked. "You'd never rest easy."

"It was some random mugger—it has to have been. The police are never going to find him anyway."

"Buck up," Allen encouraged him. "Jessica's hard at work. If the police don't solve it, she will."

"Thanks for the vote of confidence." I hoped I wasn't overdoing the ironic tone.

Collington's gaze seared me; his eyes were like hot coals in his ashy face. "Right. Miss Nancy Drew. What have you found out so far?"

I swallowed a sharp retort and gave them a quick sketch of my talks with Krausgill and Brockway. "Next I'm going to try to see George Sanmarco."

"Sanmarco!" Collington fumed. "What for? His connection with Debbie ended two years ago."

"I think Deborah went out again that night because of a phone call. I have to check—"

"What good do you think you're doing?" Collington grabbed my shoulders. "You can't bring her back, damn it. You can't—"

"I'm trying to learn the truth." I yanked back; his fingers dug in. "To help Allen. Your idiot scheme—"

He started to shake me. "It was some street thug, some psycho, it had to be . . . the police said—"

"Brad! Stop!" Allen Fraser yelled.

I chopped at Collington's arms, breaking free. He sank heavily onto the sofa, angling into the pile of blankets. "Oh Lord," he moaned. "Jessica . . . I don't . . ."

"Phone Gardino back, Brad. Call off this plot of yours."

"I can't." He struggled to sit up. "He's got cops on the way already. They should be along any minute."

"Damn. I'd better not be here when they arrive." I picked up the necklace and wiped it off with the edge of a blanket; I'd also better not have my prints on the jewelry. "When Gardino discovers this is a hoax, I don't want him to have the slightest suspicion I know anything about it. Allen, please, do us all a favor. Tell the police the truth."

"I . . . I can't, Jessica. It's too late—Brad has this thing all set up. Think what a mess it'll create if we change our story now. And if it works, we'll all win out."

His expression was pained; his voice was pleading. No father of mine could be so stupid where the police were concerned.

Suddenly I couldn't stand to be in the room with them. "I'd better wash my teacup. Don't want the cops wondering who else was here." I stalked out, leaving them there.

The sound of hot water splashing from the kitchen tap was soothing. So was the warmth on my hands. As I set the cup and saucer in the dish drainer, I sensed a presence behind me and turned to face Allen Fraser.

"I'm sorry Brad was rough with you," he said. "Don't think too harshly of him. He's not himself right now. Deborah was his daughter, after all." He cocked his head, regarding me with his shy smile. "I'd be the same way, you know, if something happened to you."

"Come off it." I wiped my hands with a paper towel. "You don't even know me. We're strangers."

"In a way. But that blood tie, Jessica—it's the strongest tie there is."

"Is it really?"

"Of course it is."

"Well, I'm certainly glad it pulled you back after thirty years."

"Goddamn it, Jessica, give me a chance. You want me to feel guilty about abandoning you, fine, I feel guilty as hell." He ripped another towel off the roll and plucked the cup from the drainer.

"I feel guilty about Deborah too," he said. "No, not because I killed her. But I really wanted to be the one to get her and Brad back together. I'd ruined one father-daughter relationship—maybe I could help mend another one." He was rubbing the cup hard, as if trying to remove the twining-leaf pattern and make it pure white.

"As atonement? Don't bother."

"Of course not. Nothing can do that. I realize that much, Jessica."

"Jess," I corrected him. He looked puzzled. "Never mind," I said.

"I keep thinking, if only I'd brought Deborah home sooner, or later, or if I'd come inside—I could have stopped it from happening. She'd still be alive."

"You can't blame yourself. Not for her death. Unless you did murder her."

Allen Fraser gave me a bleak look. "But there must be something I could have done differently, that would have changed the pattern of events. It tears me up, thinking about it."

"Sure. You could have stayed in California way back when. Then you wouldn't even know the Collingtons."

He swiped at the cup again. The handle snapped off. Sighing, he dumped the pieces into the trash can.

"You don't understand," he said. "I'm guilty of so many things. Years ago there were people I . . . mistreated—"

He touched a stray wisp of my hair, so close to the color of his. "When you were born, Mary talked about how you looked like me. I never could see it, then. You were so tiny, so unformed. How was I supposed to know?" His eyes locked on mine. I stared steadily back.

"You have her eyes, though," he said. "She had such lovely eyes."

I broke away, losing the game. "How dare you talk about my mother's eyes? What right do you have?"

He looked as though I'd slapped him. He started to say something sharp in reply; I could see him tense up, ready for battle. But he stopped himself.

"Jessica, could Brad's plan really get you in trouble?"

"If the police find out I know about it. I should go straight from here to Gardino's office. Tell him everything."

His gray eyes darkened. "Please don't. Let's give the scheme a try. If it doesn't work, I promise we won't let on that you were involved. But it just might work."

Resign, an inner voice kept urging. Tell him you're quitting this case. But I couldn't make myself say the words out loud.

I gathered up my things and left. Outside I was glad I hadn't put my jacket back on. The sun was warm, the air sweet-scented. Across the street, scarlet rhododendron blooms blazed against a slate-blue house. At the corner, a police car pulled into Clay Street. I turned and headed in the opposite direction, even though it meant walking all the way around the block to reach my car.

TWELVE

Her name was *Sweet Lucy* and she was a beauty— over thirty feet long and freshly painted in white and a blue that nearly matched the sky. Her aluminum mast rose tall, gleaming like silver in the midafternoon sun. She rocked gently in place in the east harbor of the San Francisco Marina.

George Sanmarco puttered about, moving from deck to dock and back again, unloading gear, encasing the furled sails in blue covers. At the shore end of the pier there was a locked metal gate to keep out riffraff, thieves and private detectives. I sat on a bench and waited, doodling boats in my sketchbook to pass the time.

After leaving Deborah's place I had stopped at Sanmarco's office, where I learned from a chatty secretary that he was one of those lucky people who could leave work to go sailing on a sunny afternoon. No need to wait for the weekend, when the bay, if this weather held, would be so jammed with boats that you could use them as steppingstones to cross the water.

Sweet Lucy belonged to his firm and he often took clients out. But today, his talkative employee explained, he'd wanted to go off by himself for a while. His ex-wife had just died—was murdered in fact, wasn't that awful? So she could certainly understand if her boss needed time alone. He was supposed to check in by phone around three o'clock; he'd be back from his sail by then. She obligingly wrote down the name of the boat and its mooring place. I had arrived at the marina at two-thirty, just as Sanmarco was maneuvering *Sweet Lucy* in toward her slip.

Finally he finished his boatkeeping chores and came striding along the dock. He was not a tall man, but the purposeful way he moved conveyed an impression of height. He was built like a smokestack—a cylindrical body, round and thick, straight and solid. His hair, what was left of it, blended the colors of ashes and soot. He was wearing Top-Siders, chinos, a maroon knit shirt. A heavy gold chain nestled in the chest hair that peeked above his open collar. Each hand had a fat gold ring.

When he reached land, I was there to greet him. Behind us, the gate clanged shut.

"Mr. Sanmarco, my name is Jess Randolph. I'm an investigator. I'd like to talk to you about Deborah Collington."

"I keep telling you people. I have nothing to say to the media." He moved around me and kept going.

I fell into step with him. "I'm not media. I'm working for Deborah's parents."

"Sure you are."

"Girl Scout's honor." I held up my right hand, three middle fingers extended.

His pace didn't falter. "Collington wants to know something, he can ask me himself."

"Just give me a few minutes. It would mean a lot to them in their grief." I held out one of my P&O cards.

"Grief," he snorted. He dropped the card into his windbreaker pocket. "What the hell does Collington want with a private detective? Cops aren't good enough?" He didn't pause for an answer.

I gave him one anyway, trotting along beside him as I recited the public-consumption version of the reason for my involvement. "So you see how important it is to her family to learn about Deborah's life."

"Hell, you hang on tighter than a pit bull." Sanmarco stopped so abruptly I almost crashed into him. He gave me a speculative look. "So Brad Collington was out to patch things up with his daughter."

"He was hoping to. But unfortunately—"

"Yes. Unfortunately." His gaze flickered over me, from shoes to hairline, with a slight, annoying pause at bust level. He glanced at his watch; it was a heavy, gold-banded model with enough buttons and dials to handle a missile launch. "Tell you what, I'm expecting a phone call at home in a few minutes. It's close by. Come with me, maybe I can think of something to say about Deborah to keep her old man happy."

He took off across the Marina Green without looking to see if I was keeping up. School was out for the day, and yells and laughter punctuated the drone of traffic on the boulevard beyond. Kids were running on the grass, sailing Frisbees and playing ball. Three small Asian boys were struggling to launch a rainbow-hued kite with a dragon's face and a long, streamered tail.

Sanmarco's home turned out to be a vast penthouse on top of a Spanish-style building on Beach Street. The elevator panel had no button for the top floor; instead there was a slot into which he inserted a key. The elevator opened directly into his foyer. It was a space larger than my living room, with a marble-tiled floor and arches that led off in various directions.

"Lucia!" Sanmarco's voice boomed. The word bounced against the tiles, but there was no response. "Lu-cia!" he called again, frowning.

He ushered me into a blue-and-ivory living room. It showed an interior designer's cold, expensive touch: a patterned Chinese rug, fragile bits of antique furniture arranged just so, like pieces on a stage set. The whole north wall was glass; sliding doors led to a narrow terrace overlooking the bay. Above the fireplace was a large oil portrait of a brooding black-haired woman wearing a diamond choker and a sapphire-blue gown.

The few personal items in the room should have made it seem more homey, but they merely looked out of place. There was a fat navy-blue chair whose frayed cushions bore the imprint of San-marco's bulk, and a pipe rack and tobacco can on the table beside it.

"Guess my wife's not home," Sanmarco said. He leered a little. "Probably just as well." The phone rang, and he gave a little nod of satisfaction; we'd made it in time. "Excuse me—got to take care of that call."

While he was gone I gazed out the glass doors, pleased to see the dragon kite dancing at last on the breeze. I tried to pick *Sweet Lucy* out of the crowd of sailboats in the marina but I couldn't be sure which one she was. Sanmarco could spot her in a second, I'd bet.

From the depths of the apartment came the murmur of his voice on the phone. I tiptoed into the foyer where I might hear better.

"Hell, Guillermo," Sanmarco was saying. "Don't yell at *me*. That was my money you got paid with. I'm out a lot of bucks thanks to her."

There was silence while the caller replied. When Sanmarco spoke again he'd lowered his voice; I couldn't distinguish his words. A moment later he hung up. I scooted back into the living room, but he didn't return right away. I heard more muttering; apparently he was making the promised call to his office.

I moved to the fireplace to study the portrait. The artist had been much influenced by the Impressionists. The woman in the painting seemed not quite solid, as if she were a trick of light and shadow. One hand was touching the diamond necklace as if she couldn't believe she was really wearing such a thing.

Sanmarco appeared with a tray bearing heavy glass mugs and two bottles of beer. "Hope this is okay," he said as he poured, "since my wife's not here to make coffee."

He handed me a foaming mug and settled his barrellike body into the comfortable chair. I sat on the sofa, the only other piece of furniture that looked as if it wouldn't break under a little weight.

"So what is it Collington's chasing after?" Sanmarco asked.

"Information about his daughter, like I said. A chance to get to know her, even though it's too late."

"I can't tell you much." He leaned back, crossing his legs, sipping on his beer. But he didn't look relaxed. His eyes were sharp, watchful. "I hadn't seen Deborah lately. It's no secret we didn't part on the best of terms."

"Yet you gave her a very generous settlement."

He shrugged. "Collington ought to be glad someone was generous to her. He sure messed up his chance."

"What do you mean?" I opened my satchel and took out my sketchbook and pen.

"You know," Sanmarco said, "I actually felt sorry for the girl at first. When she came to California she'd more or less run away from home. She had no family support, financial or emotional. And the kid she came out here with was bad news, heavy into dope. He spent all their money on it. Deborah was hungry a lot. She lived in a squalid little dump full of rats and roaches. Tell her old man about that. It always terrified her, the thought of getting trapped in that kind of life again."

"So you rescued her from this boyfriend?"

"Hell no, he was long gone when I met her. As it turned out, she wasn't the type to stay with one man for long. But the others who followed were similar. She decided I was a good bargain—solvent and sober. Also, Daddy would approve of me."

"Her father? I thought she was rebelling against her family."

"Sure, in a way. She wanted to thumb her nose at him but she wanted his approval at the same time, you know? Hell, I was the same way with my old man. You must have been too. Everybody is."

I stiffened with indignation. "Not me. I never—" Or wait—was it true? Did I—? I mentally grabbed my shoulders and gave myself a shake. Not here, Jess, not now.

Sanmarco was rolling on, thank goodness, ignoring me. "Afterward, I realized that was part of my appeal. She could prove something to Daddy by catching me."

"How did you meet her? You obviously weren't traveling in the same circles."

"A colleague of mine introduced us. Guillermo Reyes."

"From Colombia. A wholesaler of emeralds."

Sanmarco gave me a piercing look.

"The photos in the newspaper," I reminded him.

"Oh yeah. Well, Guillermo comes here a lot on business. He has a yacht, real jewel of a boat. He sails it up from Buenaventura a couple times a year and lives on it while he's here. Deborah was a cocktail waitress at this yacht club he belongs to and they'd become friends. God, she was a wonder—beautiful, passionate. I was bored with my life then, kind of restless—I guess you could say I was vulnerable to her charm."

"It doesn't sound like she had any business background," I said. "How come you set her up with the Bumblebee boutique?"

"Why not? She had a good head for business. Besides, Lucia's old man staked me when I got started. It made me feel good, passing the favor along."

"You were divorcing her. Odd time for favors."

He swigged down some beer. "Oh hell, I did it to keep her out of my hair. The whole time we were married she kept wanting to mess around in my gem business, but frankly she just got in the way. I didn't want my company tied up in the divorce so I gave her one of her own."

"I heard you paid for her flat, too."

"So what? My financial arrangements with Deborah aren't Collington's affair." Sanmarco thumped down the now-empty mug. "You know, I learned a lot being married to his daughter. The main thing was that being married to her wasn't such a hot idea. I'd had it good before but didn't know it."

"Meaning your wife Lucia?"

"Yeah." He gave a deep sigh. "Meaning Lucia."

"You did win her back."

"*Win* isn't the right word. Lucia had . . . difficulties while we were apart. Well, I'm sure you've heard about that. We're still living with those problems. Every damn day." He gave me a crooked, self-mocking smile as he selected a pipe from the rack beside him. "Ms. Randolph, here's the sum total of the wisdom I've gained about life: Once something good is gone you can never get it back."

I watched as he went through an elaborate ritual of filling and lighting the pipe. The sudden smell of tobacco, at once sweet and acrid, filled the room. Sanmarco's hands were broad, his gold-ringed fingers stubby.

"Tell me about Collington." He was watching me intently now. "You say he'd gotten in touch with Deborah?"

"Not directly." I needed to be cautious in what I said next, so I wouldn't give away anything that might hurt Allen Fraser. "His business partner was planning to visit San Francisco. Brad asked Allen to talk to Deborah and sound her out about a reconciliation. Apparently she was willing, but before she and her father could get together—"

"She was killed." Smoke curled past his face. "Her parents seemed pleased when we got married. I thought they might get friendly again. We saw Collington a few times when he came to town on business. Things always seemed strained between them, though. It was like he never forgave her for getting out from under his thumb."

Sanmarco's gaze stayed fixed on mine as he sucked on his pipe. "But I got along okay with him. He even sent me a couple of clients, people he did financial planning for who wanted to invest in gems. Well, I'm sure he's told you about our business dealings."

"Of course." This was news to me; Collington hadn't said a word. "But I didn't exactly understand what he was describing. What are investment gems anyway?"

"Simply the best kind of wealth you can have." He brightened with the change of topic. "Safe, portable, inflation-proof. You can carry a million dollars in your pocket—you sure as hell can't do that with real estate. Or currency or even gold. Not only that, gems are valuable anywhere in the world."

"You mean expensive jewelry?" I thought of Deborah's extravagant necklace, of all the rich baubles that Lauren said had been flaunted at the Arts and Flowers Ball.

"No, no." He was warming to his subject. "That stuff is just vanity; it's for showing off. Most jewelers don't know shit about gems. They stick a little gold around the stone and push the price up out of sight. Hardly a sound investment. Wait, I'll show you."

He left the room, returning a moment later with a satin pouch and a towel. He spread the towel on the coffee table between us and emptied the pouch. A handful of green stones rained out, each about the size of my pinkie fingernail.

"Emeralds," he said with satisfaction. "Unset, as you see. They're beautiful, but not for themselves—green stones, so what. Their beauty is in the wealth they represent."

"How can you keep such things at home? Don't they belong at your office in a vault?"

"I just got these today. A new shipment from Reyes. Since I was going to be out on the boat and my girl might be on her lunch break I had them sent here so Lucia could sign for them." He frowned. "I didn't know she was going out today."

"How can you say they're not beautiful?" Perhaps it was the lingering effect of modeling Deborah's necklace, but to me these stones seemed alluring, magical. I reached out to touch one. When Sanmarco didn't object I picked it up. A small beveled rectangle of deep jungle green—the color, I imagined, of the rain forests in its homeland, Colombia.

"And what precisely do you do with these?" I asked.

"I'm a broker. I buy and sell little treasures like this for people. Collington's been kind enough to recommend me to his clients from time to time."

I couldn't resist asking, "Do you work with his partner too? Allen Fraser?"

"His partner? Can't say I have."

"How does someone who wants to buy gems—" I paused; how do they know they can trust you is what I wanted to ask. But I needed to put it more tactfully. "How can they be sure of what they're getting?"

"Because of this." He handed me a piece of paper. "Any reliable broker has his stones certificated by an independent institute. There are two or three in this country. You get a registration number for the stone and all the information about grading and quality that you need for an appraisal. The institute doesn't buy or sell and it doesn't get any cut of your deal, so the certificate is totally reliable."

I looked at the paper. It sounded like it had to do with clothing or furniture or lamps, being full of words like *girdle thickness* and *table diameter* and *ultraviolet fluorescence*.

"You've bought jewelry too, despite what you say," I commented. "That necklace of Deborah's, for instance. I understand it was Lucia's originally. I'm surprised she gave it up."

"Yeah, well, women like that kind of thing. Deborah fancied the necklace, and Lucia decided it was a small price to pay to get her out of our lives." He shook his head sadly. "I'm sorry it's gone, though. I hope the son of a bitch who snuffed her for it realizes he got a real prize."

"Actually, it's turned up," I said. There was no reason not to tell him. The news would blare from every TV in town in a couple of hours.

"It has?" He sat upright, suddenly alert.

I told him Collington's carefully fabricated tale. It sounded no better than it had when Brad first explained it.

"So Collington's got it." There was a subtle change in his expression, a new wariness. He hid it quickly by bending to relight his pipe. "Very interesting."

"You seem pleased by the news."

He gestured with the pipe, brushing off the subject. "It's a good piece of jewelry. I'm glad it hasn't vanished."

"When did you last see Deborah?" I asked him.

"Playing detective in earnest now? I told you, she and I weren't friends. But I hope I've given you something helpful for her father." He stood up, obviously expecting me to do the same.

"Is Evan Krausgill one of your clients?" I asked as I rose. I was remembering the diamond in Evan's ear, the purple stone on his finger.

"Krausgill? Never heard of him."

"How about Peter Brockway?"

He frowned. "Deborah's latest. No, I barely know him."

"I was in his office this morning when you called him. What was that about?"

"If you were there you should know. I was just giving my condolences."

Wrong—Brockway's look of fear hadn't resulted from an offer of sympathy. "You had no business dealings with him?"

"I told you, no. As far as I know all his money has been sunk into that video—"

He broke off as sounds came from the foyer: the hiss of the elevator door, the click of high heels on the tiles. A woman appeared in the archway, carrying shopping bags from I. Magnin and Saks. The black-haired woman of the portrait.

"Oh, George, you're home already? I was—" She stopped abruptly; the shopping bags slid to the floor. She had come in far enough to spot me, and she obviously didn't like what she saw. "Who are you? What are you doing here?"

Quickly Sanmarco was at her side. "Now, Lucia, don't get upset. This is Ms. Randolph, she—"

"You promised, George. You said never again." Her voice quavered as her eyes darted from the beer mugs to the emeralds to me.

"Lucia, please. You know what your doctor says." He put an arm around her and tried to draw her close, but she held her thin body as rigid as an iron rod.

Then, in a flash, she twisted free. Scooping up a handful of emeralds, she flung them at my eyes.

"You! Get out!"

"Hey!" I tried to duck. Some of the stones struck me before scattering onto the rug. I stood there a second, stunned.

"You better go, Ms. Randolph." Sanmarco had clamped his hands to his wife's trembling shoulders.

"But I—thanks for the information, Mr. Sanmarco." I walked past two pairs of glaring eyes and punched the elevator button. The lift was still there; the doors slid open and I stepped in. Before they shut again I heard Lucia's voice rise into a thin, keening wail.

"You'll pay, George! I'll make you pay!"

THIRTEEN

Union Street was nearby, so I decided to have a look at Bumblebee. As I retrieved my car from the marina lot, I thought about the boutique's late proprietor. Good head for business or not, it seemed odd that Deborah had persuaded Sanmarco to give her the startup capital when he clearly didn't feel kindly toward her.

Even stranger was Sanmarco's return to Lucia. He may have considered Deborah a bad bargain, but was either he or his wife better off living in the ruins of a shattered marriage? Why did Lucia accept him again? Did she really think things could return to the way they had been before Deborah invaded her life? Sanmarco was right: Once something was gone in a relationship you could never get it back. Especially when that something was trust.

However, that could be a hard, painful lesson to learn. I knew—I had taken much too long to learn it myself with Dan. After each small deception, each broken promise, he would plead for forgiveness, yet somehow make me feel that the transgression was my fault. Finally I realized that the bliss of reconciliation demanded too high a price in self-respect. The time came when I no longer would take him back.

And my mother—she had reached that point, too, with Allen Fraser. What had happened between them? How many times had it taken before—

Suddenly I felt flushed, hot with anger. How dare she die before she answered my questions—before I even knew I had questions to ask!

Then, abruptly, the anger was drowned in a wave of guilt. I had no right to be angry. My mother hadn't wanted to die. She had fought it hard. Grief was appropriate; everyone told me I'd handled it well; it had been two years, after all. I had come to terms with my mother's death. Hadn't I? A scintilla of anger still flickered, nagging at me, taunting me. Could it have been there all along?

Parking was tight as always around Union Street. Finally on a side street I got lucky. A Volkswagen beetle pulled out of a space between two driveways and I pulled in, centering the Toyota carefully so that it didn't block either driveway by more than a few inches. I muttered a brief prayer to the parking god that neither resident would get irked and have the car towed. Getting out, I surprised myself by slamming the door shut. I patted the fender in apology and tried to shove the last of the anger way into the deepest, coolest recesses of my mind.

As I walked toward Bumblebee I passed the Hammerwood Gallery. In less than forty-eight hours my unfinished painting was due to be delivered here along with five of its fellows. Sunday morning I'd join the other artists in helping Muriel Gittelsohn and her assistant hang the show, and by this time that afternoon the opening reception would be in full swing. My moment of stardom.

Could Lauren Cassidy be right about my breaking into the art world? People who counted paid attention to the Ars Nova show—critics, gallery owners, buyers whom others looked to as trendsetters. I could count on Lauren to give me a nice mention in *Artspaper*. What would the rest of them think? It shouldn't matter, I told myself. The important thing was doing work that satisfied *me*. But I cared about this show more than I was willing to let on to anyone—probably even myself.

Glancing in the window, I could see Muriel Gittelsohn's assistant, Darlene Chong, doing paperwork at the desk in the rear. Muriel herself, tall and aristocratic in her trademark black, was showing a painting to a potential buyer. I started to go in to say hello but changed my mind. How's it going, they'd ask. Ready for the big day? And I'd have to say—

Damn it anyway. Of all the times for Allen Fraser to drop back into my life. I stomped on toward Deborah's shop. At the corner a man was loading the latest edition of the *Examiner* into a vending box. The police reporter was on her toes. In two-inch letters the headline yelled: MURDER NECKLACE RETURNED.

A gold neon bumblebee, wings spread, hung in the shop window instead of a sign. The interior was painted black—a true Deborah touch. A bold stripe of gold zigzagged around the room, and a second neon bee, three times the size of the one in the window, glowed against the back wall.

I riffled through a rackful of shirts and dresses. The fashions were all designed for women who were under twenty-five, weighed less than 110 and earned over fifty thousand dollars a year. No wonder I had never been in here.

"May I help you?" The sales clerk glided up as I was savoring a beautiful blouse of teal-blue batiste and wondering how many more years I'd have to work in order to afford it. The clerk was taller than me but very thin—she'd have no trouble fitting into the goodies this place sold. Her lips were painted red in the manner once called beestung. No beehive hairdo, though; she was too trendy for that. She had a short angular haircut with the tips colored lime green. A gold pin shaped like the bumblebee logo had alighted on the shoulder of her black silk dress.

"That's an excellent blouse," she assured me. "A real classic, it'll stay in style forever. Ucciello's a super designer."

"I'm not here to buy, unfortunately." With reluctance I replaced the wonderful shirt on the rack. I introduced myself, explaining how I was looking into Deborah's life for her parents. "I half expected you to be closed today."

"We shut down yesterday for the funeral, but otherwise we've stayed open. I wasn't sure what to do at first, but Deborah's lawyer said to keep things going as usual. For now at least." She looked worried. I realized she was very young, perhaps no more than twenty.

"Are you the store manager?"

"Only since February. I don't know what to do about paying the bills or buying more stock or anything. She handled all that stuff."

"She didn't train you to do those things?"

"No. She didn't seem all that interested. I was afraid she was thinking of closing the place down."

"Really? Why did—wait," I said, catching a glimpse of two figures outside the window. "Here comes someone who might be able to answer your questions."

There was a bing-bong from the announcement chime as Brad Collington pushed through the door. Allen Fraser followed, removing his fedora, his ludicrous disguise. I wondered if he'd worn it for the cops who came to get the necklace.

"Jessica! What a pleasant surprise!"

His gray eyes sparkled. He seemed genuinely delighted to see me, even though we'd parted company less than three hours before. Collington barely nodded a greeting; he was preoccupied with looking around the shop, as if the answers to his daughter's life and death might be written on the walls.

"What are you doing here?" he finally demanded.

"Investigating. The job you and Allen asked me to do." I turned to the young woman. "This is Mr. Collington, Deborah's father. Brad, this is the store manager—"

"Wendy Hartnett." She stepped forward, extending a hand. Collington touched it briefly. His lips pursed in apparent distaste as he took in the jagged green hair.

Wendy ignored that. "I'm keeping things running for now," she told him, "but I was wondering what's going to happen to the store now that Ms. Collington—oh. I'm sorry. She was your daughter. I should have . . . I mean, let me offer my sympathy."

"Thank you. I appreciate it." Collington smoothed over her awkwardness, mustering a grace I hadn't seen him display before. It was good to know he had it in him. "I'm sure you're doing a fine job. We'll be selling the business soon and—"

Wendy's face fell. "Selling! But what will I—"

"We have to put the estate in order, you see. I'll talk to the lawyer. Perhaps something can be worked out so you can help with the transition."

"Maybe Bradford won't want to sell," Allen Fraser said softly.

"Of course he will," Collington replied.

"He might want to run it himself."

"Don't be ridiculous. He's got years of school left. He can't run a dress shop three thousand miles away from home."

"It's his company now, Brad. It's his decision to make."

Wendy looked bewildered. "Bradford?"

Collington just scowled, so Allen Fraser explained. "He just saw Deborah's lawyer. She left everything to her brother, including this." He gestured at the black walls and gold bees.

"He'll have to sell," Collington said firmly. "He's only eighteen, for Chrissake. He can use the money for law school, or to start a real business, or whatever he wants to do."

Which is to be a musician, I thought. This might buy the kid a way to follow his dream. He'd have money. All he'd need was the courage to face his father with the news.

"Well, until you do sell it," said Wendy tentatively, "maybe I could . . . see, I made a list of questions, as I thought of things? Would you mind going over them with me?"

"Sure," Collington agreed. "It will be helpful for me to know what's going on. I don't want to do anything . . . hasty." He shot a look at Allen.

Wendy picked up a legal pad from the sales counter. As she and Collington talked, I studied the counter itself. Black lacquered sides, a top of dark, gold-veined marble—it had obviously been custom designed. I wandered behind it. The others, engrossed in their conversation, ignored me.

From the front the counter mirrored the store's sleek image. But the back was all business: a complex of cubbyholes containing sales-slip blanks, a credit-card whacker, glossy plastic bags stamped with the logo in gold. In the lower right corner was the only closed compartment. It appeared solid—no drawer pulls or handle, nothing to open it with. That seemed odd. I ran my fingers over its face, then along the edges, then in the kickspace between the bottom shelf and the floor. Suddenly the front panel popped open—I had triggered a tiny springlatch. Built into the compartment was a small combination-lock safe.

"Find something interesting?"

The voice made me jump. Allen Fraser loomed over the counter, watching me. I stood up, nudging the panel shut with my toe.

"No. Hang-tags for the dresses. A box of rubber bands. That sort of thing." Why did this man's most casual questions feel like prying?

Collington and Wendy finished their discussion. "Thanks," she said. "I feel better, having some idea what's happening."

"My pleasure," said Collington. "Come on, Allen. Let's go."

Allen put his hat back on. "Say, Jessica, we're planning to find someplace to have dinner and then see a movie. A comedy, I hope. We need to get our minds off all this . . . this stress and strain. Why don't you join us?"

He smiled softly and made a small gesture, open-palmed, welcoming. I thought of all those questions I would never be able to ask my mother. Suddenly I felt very tired. "I can't. I've got work to do at home." And I want to paint, I added to myself. I'm going to paint.

"Are you sure?"

"I'm sure. Thanks for the invitation."

Collington was the first to reach the door, but instead of going out, he turned and stared back into the room. A succession of expressions crossed his face—bewilderment, pride, sorrow?—and he said quietly, "Look at this, Allen. Who would have ever thought that Debbie could have—" His voice caught. Abruptly he wheeled around and thrust himself through the door. Allen Fraser watched him leave.

"Well, Jessica. At least you and I have a second chance."

I didn't reply. He was about to say something else but changed his mind and went to catch up with his partner and friend.

The incomplete painting sat on my easel. Citron and ocher and aquamarine. Paint, I ordered myself. You know you want to finish it by Saturday. But the colors in my head were wrong: charcoal gray and burgundy, midnight black and deep, deep emerald green. They laid themselves thickly over the hues of sun and shore. My fingers found it impossible to pick up a brush. Daylight faded; the studio filled with shadows as I sat there.

Dan would not have liked this painting. For a time I thought this handsome and talented man was helping me with my work, and I was grateful. But as my skill grew and my eye became surer, it bothered him, and I began to get angry. He was trying to control my painting, to push aside my vision and squeeze his own onto the canvas by way of my brush.

With a sigh I got up at last, refilled my tea mug and put on a Wynton Marsalis tape to drown out the bumps and thumps from the kids playing downstairs. On my bay-window table I arranged my notes and drafts for the Videau report. Scruff stretched and yawned and curled himself at my feet.

It would be easier to write than to paint, I decided, to deal with facts and figures instead of colors and emotions and scraps of impressions all jumbled together in my mind. I like it when a case is finished, just as I like it when a painting is done. In each situation, some truth has been discovered, some sort of order achieved. To me, that's the heart of both art and detection: finding some bit of underlying logic that helps to explain what this crazy world is all about.

My first thought when the phone rang was of Kit Cormier. He'd been just beneath the surface of my thoughts all day. Those blue, blue eyes, those strong-looking shoulders, that soft, curly beard that invited nuzzling. Wouldn't it be wonderful if—but there was that photograph. The coffee-haired girl. *Love, Sara.*

The response to my hopeful hello was: "Jess? Evan here. You remember, Evan Krausgill."

Damn. How did he get this number? I purposely gave him the card with only the P&O phone.

"What's up, Evan? Did you think of something to tell me about Deborah Collington?"

"What? Deborah?" He laughed; I pictured all those white teeth. "Oh, no, nothing like that. I mean, I'm sorry about Deb. I liked her a lot and all that. But hey, life is for the living, right? You said you couldn't do dinner, but I thought maybe I'd drop by your place, bring a bottle of wine. We can get better acquainted."

No-o, thank you. "Sorry. I have a project I have to finish tonight."

"That's okay. I happen to be free tomorrow evening."

"I have a dinner date tomorrow." No point in mentioning that it was with my brothers and my father . . . or rather, my stepfather. Goddamn it, why did life have to be so confusing? "Look, Evan," I said, more brusquely than I meant to, "I told you, it's policy. I don't get involved with people connected to a case I'm working on." Sure I do, I thought, as Allen Fraser flashed into my mind. Not the kind of involvement Evan had in mind, but . . .

"Oh." For a second he sounded disappointed. "Well, hey, a case doesn't go on forever, right? I'll keep trying, and when you've got it solved, we'll pick up where we left off."

Pick up where we left off? This guy had a very active imagination. I maneuvered him off the phone and tried to concentrate again on the games Videau had been playing with his partners' money. Within the past thirty-six hours I'd met the most attractive man I'd seen in a long time and one of the least attractive. Just my luck that the wrong one would call.

Maybe I should just take the initiative and call Kit myself. I could come up with some excuse. For that matter, why did I need an excuse? Hi there, I really enjoyed meeting you, wouldn't you like to go out with me? If Sara was an issue, he'd just tell me no. So simple really. So why couldn't I pick up the phone?

I didn't have to. It rang again, making my heart leap. Surely this was Kit. My thoughts had telepathed to South Park, creating a sudden urge in his mind to phone me. "Hello," I said eagerly.

The voice was low, steady, muffled. "Quit nosing around about Deborah Collington. There's nothing in it for you but trouble."

"What? Who is this?"

"You heard me. She's dead now. Don't let the same thing happen to you. Or that nice dog of yours."

"What? Scruff?"

"Just think how pretty he'd look, all bashed in and bloody. Think how *you'd* look."

"Hey, wait a minute—"

But the caller had hung up. He—or she?—was gone so quickly I hadn't had a chance to pinpoint anything familiar about the voice. It had been disguised, but there was something in its cadence . . . I tried to conjure the sound and rhythm of Allen Fraser's speech. No, it couldn't be Allen. It just couldn't.

Jess, oh Jess, go back to bed, help out your father and end up dead.

Scruff whined, sensing my anxiety. I gave his silky fur a lavish rubbing. "It's okay, kiddo. We'll protect each other." I could hear the tremor in my voice.

Where I lived was no secret. Anyone could have staked out my flat, observed Scruff and me as we came and went. I could feel eyes on me right now. Watching. Waiting in the darkness.

I brewed more tea. I gave Scruff a treat, a chunk of Swiss cheese. I walked through my apartment twice, checking the window locks, flipping on every single light. Finally, I made myself turn back to the report.

At midnight I gave up. I was nearly finished, but I just couldn't focus any longer. The words swam on the papers, the papers swam on the tabletop.

I needed a good calming soak. I ran a steamy, jasmine-scented tub and settled in with a book, a fat new fantasy-espionage-romance-adventure novel, just out in paperback, twenty-three weeks on the bestseller list, guaranteed to let you escape from your own hum-drum troubles. The warmth of the water seeped into my muscles and bones, I began to feel myself loosen up, I got to the critical moment when Sergei sneaks into the bed of the voluptuous but traitorous Clotilde . . .

. . . when once again the phone sounded. Something knotted in my stomach. I wouldn't respond; let the caller make his damn threats to my answering machine.

A second ring. Scruff was barking furiously at the ringing monster. I yelled at him to shush but he refused. I imagined a dozen kids waking and whimpering downstairs.

A third ring. I found I couldn't resist knowing. If I could draw the caller into conversation, maybe I'd hear something that would identify him or her. I rose up dripping and hurried into the hall, grabbing the receiver on the fourth ring.

"Jessica?" I recognized the voice. This time, it was definitely Allen Fraser.

"Do you know what time it is?" I shifted my feet; everywhere I stepped I left a little puddle. "You're making a bad habit of these late-night calls."

"I know. But this is an emergency. We just got back and found it like this. Brad called the police, but please—I'd really be grateful if you'd come over too."

"You found what like what?"

"Oh, Jesus. Sorry. I guess I'm rattled. It's Deborah's place. Someone broke in while we were gone and tore it apart. It's been totally ransacked."

FOURTEEN

The bar of lights on the police car sent pulses of red and blue across the Victorian face of Deborah's building. Neighbors huddled in knots under the bottle-brush trees, maintaining a careful distance, whispering and pointing. As I started up the steps I felt a hand on my shoulder and turned. The man who had tapped me had pale eyes, a snowy beard and a shiny bare head that reflected the lights, blue-red-blue-red. I was standing one stair above him and he barely came to my shoulder, so I stepped down. Now he was nose-high, a slightly more comfortable level.

"You going in there?" he asked, angling his head toward Deborah's doorway.

"Yes," I told him.

"What's going on?"

"I don't know exactly. There was a break-in."

"That's where that woman lived who got murdered, isn't it?" I nodded and so did he; he already knew it. "She sure has created a lot of excitement for this neighborhood lately. You a policewoman?"

"No, I'm . . . uh, a friend of the family."

"Oh. Well, I'm sorry it happened. She seemed like a nice lady."

"Did you know her?" I asked.

"Can't say I did really. Saw her go in and out, said hello on the street a time or two when I was out taking my constitutional. I walk twenty blocks every day, rain or shine. It's what keeps me fit." He flexed his arm and stood up straighter to show me how fit he was.

"Was there excitement around here the night she was killed?"

"Just getting herself murdered was uproar enough. Edith has been jabbering on about it all week." He indicated an elderly woman leaning on a cane in front of a Tudor-style house across the street. "Course the lady wasn't murdered here. Down in the Tenderloin, the TV said, after that dance."

"Did you see anything odd around here that night?"

"Well, Edith and me, we weren't home most of the evening." He caressed his beard, apparently an aid to thinking. "Only peculiar thing was the man in the car, and that didn't have anything to do with her."

"What car?" I asked. "Tell me about it."

"I wouldn't have even noticed except he was parked in my spot. Well, it's a hydrant really, got a red curb so you won't park there. But I always do because it's right in front of my house. Edith doesn't walk so good anymore so I like to park close. They don't patrol this block much, so I hardly ever get a ticket. Kind of got to thinking of it as my private space."

"But someone else was parked there last Saturday night," I said, directing him back to the point.

"That's right. We get back from visiting some friends over in the Sunset and it's real late and we're tired, and damn if somebody isn't in our space. And the driver hasn't even gone anywhere, he's just sitting there in the dark, all slouched down with his hat over his face. I double-parked and walked Edith to the door, and then I had to go clear to Walnut to find a place to leave the car. The guy was still there when I got home."

"What time was this?"

"Maybe about one o'clock? Edith and me, we don't usually stay out so late, but we had a friendly little poker game going and I was winning. Always hate to break up a lucky streak."

"Can you describe the man?"

"No. It was dark and I didn't care what he looked like. Why's it matter? The lady wasn't killed around here."

"It seems strange, though, that he was here the same night. Didn't you wonder what he was doing, sitting in the car like that?"

"I reckoned he was waiting for someone. A woman got out of a cab just then, at the corner. I thought maybe he was meeting her. But she went up and rang someone's bell across the street." He tugged at his beard again. "Come to think of it, it was this place she came to."

"Deborah Collington's? Did you tell the police?"

"How was I supposed to know the lady was off getting herself killed? Anyway, no one answered; the woman just wandered off again. Never thought about it again till now."

"What did she look like?"

"Can't recall." He was working the beard hard now. He glanced at the police car, which was still pulsing blue-red. "The peculiar thing was, I got up about two-thirty to, uh, well never mind why, just say I got up. And just for the sake of being curious I peeked out the window and the car was still there. I did wonder then if maybe I should call the police."

"But you didn't."

"No. He wasn't disturbing anything really, and he was gone in the morning so I had my space back."

"What about the car?"

"Oh, a real nice buggy." He nodded in approval. "Big American car, Ford I think. Not one of those little Japanese things. Blue maybe? Hard to tell for sure in the dark."

Blue Ford. Driven by a man with a hat. Allen Fraser wore a hat. "Thanks for telling me about it."

"Say now, you find out anything, come let us know. Edith is fair to bursting with curiosity about it all. Jerome Argyle's the name. I live right over there. If that little green Dodge is parked by the hydrant you know I'm home."

■　　■　　■

Ransacked was one good word for the flat. *Plundered* would have described it also.

Drawers had been emptied onto the shaggy white rugs. Cushions had been ripped open and their stuffing yanked out; bits of feathers and cotton fluff drifted about the room. The Art Deco prints had been abandoned in a heap of broken frames, torn matboard and shattered glass. I looked for Gerard Duplisea's exploding double helix, but it was gone.

This damage hadn't been done by a see-what-looks-good, grab-it-and-run thief. Whoever broke in had been hunting for something specific.

The necklace, of course. The media had announced to the world that the valuable jewelry had been left like a foundling on Deborah's doorstep. At least ten thousand people must have found themselves wrestling with the temptation of such easy treasure. It was no surprise that someone had succumbed.

But this prowler had also been looking for something more. You couldn't hide a diamond-and-emerald necklace behind a print in a picture frame. The place looked like Deborah's father must have imagined it would when I was done searching it the other night.

Allen Fraser and Brad Collington were in the living room, talking to a pair of uniformed policemen, a tall black man and his shorter, stockier Hispanic partner. Allen's face was ashen; Collington's was red, contorted with anger.

"How do I know if anything's missing?" Collington blustered. "I set foot in this place for the first time yesterday. I don't know what's supposed to be here. You searched the place after my daughter was killed—you tell me what's gone."

Allen spotted me and hurried over. He looked weary and drawn. "Jessica. Thank God."

"Tell me what happened."

"Just what I said on the phone. We went out to dinner and a movie, then Brad insisted on stopping for a couple of drinks." He looked over at his friend, now slumped onto the remains of Deborah's black leather chair. The two cops had moved on to another room. "I'm worried about him. He's under so much tension."

"So are you," I pointed out. "Being the prime suspect in a murder case is bound to put you under a little stress."

"But I'm not—no, you're right." He sighed, then went on. "There was no sign of a problem when we first got here. The front door was locked, everything seemed normal. Then we got to the top of the stairs and found this." The sweep of his arms took in the whole debacle.

"You're not wearing your disguise," I said, referring to the silly hat.

"No. I decided that was foolish. I'm getting tired of the game, Jessica. If they spot me, they spot me."

"But you're still not going to volunteer."

He hesitated just a moment before he said, "No."

The destruction was as bad in the rest of the flat. Deborah's tiny office looked as though it had been ravaged by a typhoon. Papers and file folders were strewn everywhere. The metal drawers of the file cabinet had been wrenched out of shape when the intruder had forced the lock. In the bedroom the mattress had been slashed, the bureau drawers dumped, the dresser top swept clean, the fashionable silks and woolens from the closet heaped on the floor. Deborah's gun had slid between the nightstand and bed, overlooked by the thief. But no matter how much I picked through the jumble of sweaters and scarves and lingerie, I could find none of the jewelry. No silver-and-onyx bracelet, no gold earrings, no pearls. No gorgeous ring with an off-center emerald and three diamonds to the side.

Collington and Allen had gone into the kitchen, where the two policemen were examining the open back door. It led to a narrow porch and a flight of stairs down to the garden. This room had been attacked too: Silverware and utensils were scattered on the floor, cabinet doors hung open, dishes had been smashed. Even the refrigerator had been raided, the intruder flinging out butter and orange juice cans and wilted leftover salad in his zeal.

Collington made the introductions. The tall black cop was Humphreys; he had a jovial grin and a solid handshake. The smaller one, with a serious expression and steady brown eyes, was Gonsalves.

"This is definitely the mode of entry," Humphreys announced. "See—fresh gouge marks around the latch where he tried to spring it. Probably used a screwdriver. When that didn't work, the man got smart. Smashed the window and reached in." A few jagged edges were all that was left of the pane in the door. Shards of glass littered the white linoleum.

"Well, well, look who's here," said a voice from the hallway door. Nick Gardino, in jeans and a corduroy jacket, leaned against the doorframe. Of course he would have been summoned to this one. He looked tired and rumpled, as if he'd been in bed when the call came. "Still comforting the bereaved, Jess? Passing along the sympathy of your New York relatives?"

"That's right," I replied with what I hoped was a bright smile. "Mr. Collington and, uh, his friend called me and I came over to help out if I could. What are you doing here? It's a break-and-enter, not a homicide."

"No," he agreed. "But by the merest coincidence, it's the residence of a recent homicide victim. Naturally I was curious." He stepped over a box of frozen manicotti to shake Collington's hand. "Sorry this had to add to your troubles."

Then Gardino turned to Allen Fraser. I felt myself tense up. I'd known this had to happen sooner or later.

"I don't believe I've had the pleasure. Nicholas Gardino, San Francisco police. I'm in charge of the homicide investigation involving Mr. Collington's daughter."

Allen cleared his throat, glanced at me fleetingly, held out his hand to Gardino. But Collington jumped in before he could speak.

"This is Allen Fraser, my business partner. He's helping me get Deborah's affairs in order."

"I see." Gardino looked at Allen speculatively. "From New York? Good of you to come all this way to lend a hand."

"Yes, well . . . it's the least I could do." Allen was clearly flustered.

Gardino studied him in silence. Allen started to fidget. I moved closer to him, protectively. Realizing what I'd done, I stepped away again.

"You were in New York last Saturday night, I presume," said Gardino.

Tell him the truth, I coached Allen silently. He's figured it out, tell him the truth.

"Yes, well," said Allen, "as it happens I was here. On business. Uh, meeting with a client in Palo Alto."

"On Saturday night?" asked Gardino skeptically.

"On Monday actually. I came out a couple of days early." Now that it was inevitable, Allen seemed to be regaining his composure. Good.

"I see," said Gardino.

"What are you doing?" Collington burst in, not being helpful. "You can't possibly think that Allen—"

"The reason I'm asking, Mr. Fraser"—Gardino cut cleanly through Collington's protest—"is that you bear a striking resemblance to the descriptions we have of the Mystery Stranger who left the Arts and Flowers Ball with Ms. Collington the night she was murdered."

Allen reached up as if to pull down the hat he wasn't wearing and hide his face. He gave Gardino a small, rueful smile. "Yes, I suppose I do. There's a good reason for that."

Gardino nodded; suspicion confirmed. "Better come with me. We have some talking to do."

"Leave him alone," protested Collington. "He's got nothing to do with this. I know it. He can't possibly. Some mugger, some punk, some goddamn drug fiend grabbed my daughter. If you people were competent at all, you'd have nailed him by now."

"I appreciate your concern, Mr. Collington," Gardino said wearily. "We're doing the best we can. And doing our best requires that we talk to anyone who might have valuable information. The Mystery Stranger may be perfectly innocent, but he knows more than we do about what happened to your daughter after she left the dance. I'm also eager to learn why Mr. Fraser hasn't come to the police when he knows he could be helpful to us. Shall we, Mr. Fraser?"

"Nick, it's late." I stood beside Allen; no step backward this time. "Almost two o'clock. Surely you can talk to him in the morning."

"I'd rather do it now. No telling where he might be in the morning."

"He'll be at the Hall of Justice, in your office. First thing, whatever time you name."

"What makes you so sure, Jess?"

Allen's hand was on my shoulder. He gave me a little squeeze that said thanks.

I glanced up at him and pulled in a deep breath. I was going out on a limb now. "I guarantee it. You can have my license pulled if he's not there." ·

Gardino looked from Allen to me, from me to Allen. I saw the reaction register on his face as he took it in: the height, the leanness, the shape of the chins, the red hair.

"I should have known," he muttered. He watched us for a moment, rubbing a corner of his mustache. Then he made up his mind. "Okay, Jess. I'll take you up on your offer. Both parts of it," he warned. "Make sure he's there at eight-thirty sharp. Good night, gentlemen. I'll see you tomorrow, Fraser."

"I appreciate that, Jessica. Really," Allen said when Gardino was gone.

"Just don't disappoint me," I told him. He'd had thirty years to learn something about keeping commitments; I hoped by now he'd mastered the lesson. "I'm going to call Tyler. He has a lawyer friend who may not throttle him for phoning at this hour and insisting he meet us at dawn on the Hall of Justice steps. Then we can start cleaning up this mess."

FIFTEEN Allen Fraser was silent as we lurched through the rush hour traffic toward the Hall of Justice. He had said "Good morning" politely enough when I picked him up at Deborah's flat, but then he had dropped into the passenger seat, where he sat motionless, staring straight ahead. He looked bleary: his gray eyes were rimmed with darker gray shadows, and his well-cut blue suit seemed to bag on a suddenly shrunken frame. Some of it might be fatigue. But I suspected most of it was fear. He was on his way at last to talk to the police.

The fatigue was easily explained. I was exhausted myself—we'd been up most of the night trying to create a semblance of order in the flat. I'd put Allen to work in the kitchen and Brad in the living room so that I could tackle Deborah's office. I had to fight Collington for the privilege; at first he insisted on going through the morass of papers himself. I argued that I would be more likely to recognize anything that might have a bearing on the murder. His purposes— understanding her life, settling her estate—would be more easily served if I sorted the documents first. Allen took my side and eventually Collington gave in.

So I spent the predawn hours searching through file drawers and organizing a floorful of papers into orderly stacks. They reflected a wide range of interests: reviews of her Lady Macbeth performance, clippings of sailing articles, brochures from fashion manufacturers, worksheets from a course of Spanish lessons. Her business records looked straightforward, but if I was reading them right, Bumblebee was making little money. That surprised me. The most intriguing thing I found was a clipped-out cartoon with numbers jotted on it. Checking out what I hoped they meant was high on today's agenda.

But first I had to deliver Allen Fraser safely into the hands of the lawyer, so that together they could face Nick Gardino.

I turned the corner into Bryant Street. "Almost there," I told him.

"How well do you know this guy Gardino?" It was his first comment since getting in the car.

"I can't say we're friends. Tyler sometimes investigates criminal cases for the lawyer you're about to meet. So P and O deals with Gardino from time to time."

"What's the best way of handling him?"

His putting it that way irritated me. "To the best of my knowledge, Nick Gardino is smart, tough and honest. My advice is to tell him the truth."

"But the truth makes me look—yes, yes, I know," he said, catching the expression on my face. "Honesty is the best policy. Believe it or not, I agree with that."

"Do you?" I said quietly.

He sat up straighter. "Of course I do. How can you—no, of course not. You still don't know me well enough to be sure. Yet you've taken a big risk for me anyway, haven't you?"

I took a deep breath and let it out slowly. "Yeah, I guess I have."

"Listen, Jessica." His voice was soft and sad. "I'll be truly sorry if you get into trouble over this. That wasn't my intention. I know I haven't got the right—"

"No, you don't." A white blaze of anger erupted from nowhere. "You have no right to ask anything of me. You come waltzing back into my life after all this time expecting me to help solve your problems. Where were you when I had problems? Or when my mother did?"

"Jessica, I explained to you. I tried to get back together with Mary—"

"I should be flying high this week. Feeling ecstatic, painting up a blue streak. Don't you realize?—this show coming up is maybe the best thing that's happened to me. But I'm so muddled I can't even lift a brush. You've ruined it. I hate it that you've taken this week away from me."

"Oh Lord, I'm sorry I—"

"Don't you see? This is worse than if you were a total stranger. Then we'd have a clean-cut, professional relationship. Now there's all this father-daughter crap mixed up in it, all these emotions and expectations and . . . and garbage."

"Calm down, Jessica, I—"

"But you're not my father, damn it. You made that choice a long time ago. I don't know who the hell you are."

"And you don't care. Is that what you're saying?"

I dodged around a double-parked beer truck, then stole a glance at him. His eyes were wet. Tears? Good. He had tears coming.

I made myself relax my grip on the steering wheel. What was happening to my self-control, to the containment and discipline I took such pride in? I felt disgusted with myself, and annoyed at feeling disgusted.

"No, I'm not saying that. Frankly, it would be easier if I felt that way."

We had reached the great gray block that was the Hall of Justice building. It was eight-fifteen. I pulled into the loading zone in front, jerked up the emergency brake and turned to face this man who called himself my father.

"Look," I said. "You agreed that honesty is the best policy. If you have not been telling me the absolute truth about . . . about any part of this, I need to know it right now."

"Jessica!" He looked stricken. "I swear to you. Every word I've said—"

"Did you kill her?"

His body stiffened. "How can you say that? How can you possibly imagine—" But he stopped himself in the middle of the theatrics. "Oh, Jessica. I feel like I know you so well. Jack Emerich did a great job of keeping me up to date. I heard about your Girl Scout badges, your prom night, your graduations. The time you won the blue ribbon in that art show. I keep forgetting that to you I'm . . . worse than a stranger."

"And this break-in last night. You didn't stage that?"

"Jesus, what is this? Why would I do something crazy like that? If you don't believe me, ask Brad. We were together all evening. Except once when he went to the men's room—I'd scarcely have time to rush to the apartment, wreak all that havoc and return before he got back."

"I have to ask," I told him. "It's my job."

"Oh shit. Why did I ever—" He slumped down, looking toward his shoes. "I've got a hell of a long way to go to prove myself to you, don't I?"

A tap on my window saved me from having to answer. Stuart Weingarten, the lawyer Tyler had called, was standing beside the car, gesturing at the back door. I pulled up the lock and Stuart climbed in. He was a short, wiry man in his mid-thirties, whose well-trimmed brown curls were making a determined retreat from his forehead. His blue suit and white shirt were professional and proper, but the knot of his yellow tie was loose and the hazel eyes behind the owlish horn-rims hinted at mischief.

"Morning, folks," he said. "Jess, we've got a minute; why don't you take us for a little drive while you fill me in. Tyler wasn't too coherent when he called last night. Either that or I'm not real good at listening at two A.M." He thrust a hand toward Allen between the bucket seats. "I take it you're the client. I'm Stuart Weingarten."

Allen grasped the lawyer's hand and introduced himself. I let him tell his own story while I circled the block once, twice, three times. It was the same tale he'd given me. At least he could tell it consistently.

When I pulled up again in front of the Hall of Justice, they had just enough time to make it to Gardino's office.

"This is it. Let's go," said Stuart. Allen sighed deeply, then got out of the car, with Stuart following. I sat there feeling glum as I watched them cross the sidewalk. Allen's steps were slow, his shoulders sagging. When they reached the steps he glanced back at me. I lifted my hand in a little wave, then made a circle of my thumb and forefinger as a gesture of encouragement: It will be okay. I wasn't at all sure that was true, but it seemed to help. Allen gave me a wan smile, then squared his shoulders and proceeded through the big front doors.

"This meeting can now come to order," Tyler announced. He plopped a bag from Irma's Deli onto the table. The rest of us became alert, especially O'Meara; we all knew the bag was full of almond croissants. Everyone in an office has official duties, and one of Tyler's most important ones is to pick up the goodies for our weekly staff meetings.

We were gathered in the P&O kitchen, which is also our library and, on Friday mornings, our conference room. The meetings were Claudia's idea. "You guys are never here," she complained a couple of months after she started work. "How can I manage the office if I don't know where you are or what you're doing? What the heck goes on around here, anyway?" Since then, they've become a cherished tradition. Sometimes it's the only time all week that we manage to catch up with one another.

O'Meara laid his beautiful russet head on Claudia's lap and gazed up with soulful eyes; he knows a soft touch when he sees one. Claudia fed him bits of pastry as she told me about some calls I'd asked her to make.

"I reached the real estate lady, Jess—the one in Deborah's calendar? She was supposed to look at the condo on Monday morning. Apparently Deborah was thinking of selling it."

"I wonder why. Even if her shop wasn't making money, she didn't have to worry about her home. Sanmarco had paid for it." I put it aside to think about later. "What about Pacific Playhouse? The costume director?"

"Right. I asked her if Deborah had brought anything by for the costume department last Friday, like you said. She told me no—

130

Deborah ordered stuff for them once or twice but not in a long while. Nothing for this show certainly."

"So Evan Krausgill lied about why Deborah was at the theater that day." I started to reach for a second croissant but refrained, mentally slapping my wrist. Swimming yesterday did not excuse indulgence today.

"A question answered?" Tyler asked.

"No, more of them raised. There's too damn many questions lately and no answers at all." I slouched down into my chair. O'Meara padded over to offer me consolation and, incidentally, to lick off any traces of butter that might be on my fingers.

"I've got a question too," Tyler said. "Which is: Did you finish the report on the Videau case?"

"Damn it, Tyler, you know what kind of night I had. I called you in the middle of it."

"Yeah, I know."

"It's just that—look, it's almost done. I'll have it ready Monday, okay? I promise."

"Monday. I guess that'll have to do." He gave me an odd look as he pushed away from the table. "Well, back to work. The Meridian Insurance scam awaits."

"Jess," said Claudia, laying a gentle hand on my arm, "if I can help . . ."

"Thanks." I gave her a bright smile and went into the other room. As I reached my desk I realized I had the last of the croissants in my hand. Oh hell, why not? My spirits needed a lift.

When I finished chomping I called Lauren Cassidy to entice her away from her *Artspaper* desk for a little sleuthing adventure later in the morning, offering the *Blood Wedding* poster as a bribe. Next I phoned Hammerwood Gallery. Muriel Gittelsohn seemed to be plugged into everything that happened in the local art world. She was out so I asked her assistant, Darlene Chong, to let me know if they were approached by someone acting suspiciously eager to unload a valuable painting—for instance, the Gerard Duplisea work stolen from Deborah's flat last night.

While I had the phone book out I looked up Evan Krausgill's listing. The address shown was in Pacific Heights, not far from Deborah's place. It was a neighborhood in keeping with the Jaguar and the diamond ear stud and the license plate—*Evan iz great*. But not with his paycheck from a struggling nonprofit theater. It didn't make sense.

Of course nothing anymore seemed to make sense.

I slammed the phone book shut. Tyler was perched on the edge of my desk, unwrapping a stick of gum. "Want one?" He held out the pack; I shook my head no. "Did Stuart show up this morning? Everything went okay?"

"Stuart was there. I don't know how it went. They're probably still talking to Gardino."

"And you? You're okay?"

"I'm fine. Tyler, what is this?"

"Well, I couldn't help noticing this case has been kinda hard on you. I mean, that's to be expected, it being your father and all. And the way the media's pushing. That Mrs. Putnam from the Arts Council was on TV again last night."

"You're up to something, Tyler. Get to the point."

"Well, I was thinking it might be a good idea if I took over this case, since—"

"No!" I jumped up. "No. Absolutely not."

"Hear me out, Jess. It would be best for everyone—"

"It's mine, Tyler. Don't you see, I have to do it."

"That's what I mean, Jess. You can't keep yourself objective, detached, under the circumstances."

Claudia poked her head through the doorway. "Hey, sorry to interrupt. But there's a guy here to see you, Jess. Says his name's Leonard Hoffmeyer."

I told her I'd be right there. But first I turned back to Tyler.

"Goddamn it, don't you dare take this case away from me."

SIXTEEN

Leonard Hoffmeyer—the name rang no bell. But the man it belonged to looked vaguely familiar: pudgy, moon-faced, glasses with wire frames. Where had I seen him before?

As I came into the reception area he stood, fumbling with a battered briefcase. His green plaid jacket and red knit tie made him look like an overstuffed Christmas-tree ball. He stuck out a soft hand and let me squeeze it.

"Ms. Randolph. Oh good. I was afraid you wouldn't be here. I hope this isn't an intrusion."

It was hard to tell at this point. "Not at all," I said. "What can I do for you?"

He peered at me intently, as though trying to decide if he could trust me. I must have passed inspection because he gave a little nod. "I found your card on Pete's desk. You know, Peter Brockway? You came to see him yesterday."

"Of course, that's why I recognize you. You work for him—you came into his office while I was there."

"I . . . used to work for him. He fired me yesterday afternoon." Hoffmeyer's chin quivered; his voice was full of hurt and surprise. "Can you believe it? He . . . he . . ."

"Is that why you're here? Because he fired you?"

"Your card said you're a private investigator?"

"That's right."

"Well, what I want to know is"—he licked his lips nervously—"are you working for Pete or are you investigating him?"

"Why do you ask?"

"I thought . . . well, I thought maybe the venture capital people hired you to check him out. If that's so—" He glanced around. Claudia was at her desk, her curly brown head bent over her work. Hoffmeyer put his back toward her and whispered, "If that's so, I've got some information you might be interested in."

"Fine. Would you like some coffee? Or tea?"

Hoffmeyer looked relieved. "Oh, coffee would be swell. Cream and sugar. Three sugars."

When I came back with his mug Hoffmeyer was waiting with a bewildered look, the briefcase clutched tightly against his chest. I led him into the office. Tyler was fiddling at the computer. Hoffmeyer shifted my visitor chair to make sure he was facing the other way. Apparently it was okay to tell me his secret but not to have my colleagues overhear. He sat down and with great care placed the briefcase between his feet.

"What is the information you have?" I asked, pushing the steaming mug toward him.

"You're not working for Pete? You won't tell him I came here?" He grasped the mug with both plump hands, as if it were some sort of life preserver.

"I'm not working for either party you mentioned. What I saw Brockway about doesn't concern venture capitalists. Is he trying to find investors for Success Videos?"

"Oh, trying desperately." Hoffmeyer leaned forward, whispering conspiratorially. "He'll go under if he doesn't get money darn quick."

"The firm looked quite prosperous to me."

"That's the trouble. Up until three months ago we were in a warehouse in Daly City. It was fine by me, the rent was cheap, we could make money there. But it wasn't good enough for Pete. Didn't fit his snazzy image. We're selling success, he said, we gotta look like success. What crap." His eyes grew round, making him look slightly frightened. "Oh gee, I'm sorry, Ms. Randolph."

"I've heard much worse. Go on."

He swallowed some of the sweet coffee. It seemed to console him, just a little. "See, Pete was about to sign a huge distribution contract, thought he was the hottest thing since buttered toast. He was going to be a very rich man. We all were, what with the bonuses he promised and all." His voice trailed away. He stared down into the mug as if it held a vision of Pete's dreams, of his own dreams that now wouldn't come true.

"But it didn't turn out that way?" I prodded.

He sighed and shook his head. "Pete started spending like crazy, like the money was already in the bank, you know? Hired people, bought lots of equipment, committed us to all that fancy new space. Then the distributor backed out, decided there wasn't enough of a market after all. Pete said okay, someone else would come along and give us an even better deal. But no one did. Not only that, sales slowed way down. All of a sudden we couldn't pay the bills. That's why he started courting Investech."

"Who?"

"The venture capital people. Pete's got to convince them the company's got lots of potential, so they'll come in and save his neck. They were supposed to conclude the deal on Monday, but for some reason they put it off."

"But why did he fire you? Is he cutting back the staff to save costs?"

"No, no, he . . . he did it because I was catching on to him." Hoffmeyer set down the mug. This was a solemn pronouncement: "It's dirty pool, Ms. Randolph. It really is. I didn't know Pete was like that."

"What's happening, precisely?"

"About six weeks ago—right when Pete first talked to Investech?—we had several large orders come in. But we haven't been paid for any of them. One of my duties is, uh,"—he gulped visibly—"or *was*, I should say, to keep track of accounts receivable.

135

When the money didn't show up, I checked the files. In each case there was a note in Pete's handwriting, saying he'd talked to the customer and we could expect payment by a certain date. That struck me as odd. Pete doesn't usually interfere in my work like that. But he's the boss, we've been having money problems, I know he's worried. So I didn't think too much about it.

"Well, the date was last Friday. It came and went, and still no money. Things were really tight, Ms. Randolph; I was afraid we wouldn't make payroll. So I called the companies in question. And guess what I found out."

"Tell me."

"The first one was Peregrine Video Stores. They're a good customer, always paid promptly before. But this time, they claimed they never even placed the order. The purchase order number we showed wasn't in the sequence they use. So I went to ask Pete about it. That's when you were there. I didn't mean to interrupt your meeting."

"That's all right," I assured him.

"Pete just took the invoice and said he'd follow up himself. Well, you saw what happened. That wasn't like him. It made me wonder, so I called the other companies. Same thing. No order, no merchandise delivered, no invoice received, nothing."

"Did you ask Brockway about the others?" I asked.

"Yeah," Hoffmeyer said mournfully. "Yesterday, at the end of the day. He got really steamed, told me to mind my own business. I explained I was minding my business, it was my job to follow up on unpaid invoices. So he screamed at me. Actually screamed, Ms. Randolph, can you imagine? He said . . . he said it wasn't my job any longer and I could just clear out."

Hoffmeyer's voice trembled. His eyes were brimming. "I was totally stunned," he told the coffee mug he held in his lap. "Five years I've been with Pete, practically since the day he started. How could he do this to me?" The tears began to slide down his face. He shoved his glasses aside with a doughy fist to wipe the dampness away.

"I asked who would do his books," he went on. "He said he'd show Tina, the receptionist, how. Tina! She can't even answer the phone. He'll be bankrupt in hell before she figures out how to turn on the calculator."

"It sounds like he might go bankrupt anyway. Perhaps you're well out of there."

He shook his head forlornly. "What am I going to do? Pete was my friend. Darn it, darn it, I thought he was my friend."

The light blinked on my phone, then held steady as Claudia answered the call. Word of Allen Fraser's ordeal? I almost excused myself to check. But no, it was too soon to hear.

Hoffmeyer was wiping his tear-streaked glasses with the end of his red knit tie.

"What do you think Brockway was up to?" I asked. "What was so secret and serious about those invoices that he had to fire you?"

He put his glasses back on. The eyes behind them were a soft and watery blue. "It's obvious. Pete made up the sales. He's inflating the sales figures so Investech will think the firm is doing much better than it is. It's fraud, pure and simple."

"But won't Investech wonder when the invoices never get paid?"

Hoffmeyer shrugged helplessly. "Pete must think he can cover them somehow. A personal loan or something, I don't know. What I can't figure out is, the inventory records show those videos got shipped someplace. Where could they have gone?"

"Do you have copies of these invoices?"

"Right here." He brightened at this show of interest. Tugging the worn briefcase onto his knees, he popped open the latches. A sheaf of papers in a bulldog clip was the only thing inside. Hoffmeyer handed the bundle to me. "You'll give them to the Investech people?" he asked eagerly.

I leafed through the invoices. They represented hefty orders: each one listed multiple cartons of titles from the Success Videos line. The amounts billed ranged from four thousand to almost ten thousand dollars—a total of nearly fifty thousand dollars. Not a bad sum for a cash-starved business to collect in a single day. I wondered why

Brockway had thought the money would all come through on that particular Friday. And where he thought it would come from.

"I'm not working for Investech," I reminded Hoffmeyer.

His disappointment was palpable as he snatched the papers back. "Maybe I better keep this, then. It's only fair to give them the information. If you won't, I guess I should do it."

"May I make copies? They may be helpful to the case I'm working on."

"Be my guest." A little smile tugged at the corners of his mouth, relief mixed with satisfaction. Fairness to Investech wasn't his only motivation. Peter Brockway was going to regret this firing.

As I made the copies another phone call came in. Through the doorway I could see Claudia scowling as she talked.

When I was done Hoffmeyer tucked the invoices back into his briefcase, snapped it shut and patted the lid.

"What's your case about?" he asked.

I was surprised he hadn't inquired sooner. Apparently his need to strike back at his erstwhile employer was too great for him to worry about how.

"It concerns Deborah Collington."

"Oh, her." A dark look crossed his pale moon face. "Don't get me wrong, I'm sorry she's dead, but I never liked her much. She wasn't good for Pete. Oh, she was pretty, I'll grant you, and bright. But, darn, if she wasn't a manipulative little bi—I mean, woman. Poor Pete. He's really had a rough time lately." Then, remembering, he added, "Not that I care. He deserves it after what he's done."

"Was he upset about Deborah's murder?"

"He was upset about Deborah, period. They were on the outs, you know. Fighting all the time. Of course Tina's not much better." He grabbed the briefcase handle and stood up.

I rose too. "What did they fight about?"

"I don't know. Pete didn't talk to me much about his private life." He scratched his fat cheek thoughtfully. "I think she was seeing another man. Last week I heard him yelling on the phone about 'your damn buddy, Gilberto.' Some Mexican name like that."

"Guillermo?" Guillermo Reyes had introduced Sanmarco and Deborah. Had he been still on her string? I thought about the photos of the *Esmeralda* and its swarthy, frost-eyed captain. That reminded me of where I'd seen them: Kit Cormier's studio. Come on, Kit—if only you'd phone. Perhaps one of the calls Claudia had just answered . . . the first one, not the one that made her glower.

"Guillermo, that was it." Hoffmeyer's voice dragged my attention back. "Well, I better go, take this stuff to Investech. Then I guess I . . . I'll have to go to the unemployment office."

"Thank you for coming to see me," I told him. "I appreciate the information."

His laugh was small and bitter. "It's the least I can do for Pete."

I walked him to the main door. He held out his hand for a limp shake and looked around despondently. "I don't suppose you people need a good bookkeeper?"

As the door shut behind Hoffmeyer, Claudia came up, a pair of pink phone message slips in her hand and a worried look on her face.

"That lady who ran the Arts and Flowers Ball called. Lois Whittlesey Putnam? When I said you were in a meeting and couldn't talk right now, she got real rude."

"I'm sorry, Claudia. I can see she upset you."

"Oh, that didn't bother me. I can handle rude. This other one, though—be careful, okay, Jess?"

She handed me the paper: *Lay off Deborah Collington. Every dog will have his day—to die. And so will you.*

"I wrote down the exact words."

"No name?"

"On something like that? Are you kidding?"

"What was the voice like?"

"Muffled. Far-away sounding. I couldn't really tell."

My mysterious caller from last night. I tried to ignore the little grue that flickered up my spine. *Jess, oh Jess, go back to bed, help out your father and . . .*

"What does it mean?" Claudia fretted. "O'Meara—"

"No, not O'Meara." Not Scruff either. Last night, before going to

Deborah's ravaged flat, I had awakened Mrs. Fiorelli and placed him in her custody. "Look, Claudia, don't mention this to Tyler, okay?"

Claudia frowned. "Jess, maybe Tyler's right. Maybe he should take over—"

"Forget about it. You know how a case like this attracts loonies. Someone just got a cheap little thrill." I balled up the paper and tossed it into the wastebasket by her desk. Two points.

SEVENTEEN

"Here's the plan," I said to Lauren Cassidy. We were standing in front of a Japanese restaurant on Union Street, next door to the Bumblebee boutique. A fish wholesaler's truck was double-parked in front of us. A burly man in khaki coveralls unloaded crates of silvery tuna and green-shelled shrimp, nested in ice. He stacked them onto a handtruck and trundled them toward the restaurant door.

"I hope it includes lunch," said Lauren, eyeing the seafood. "Sashimi. Sushi. Shrimp tempura, perhaps."

"Later. It's barely past eleven." I explained my idea: "What I want you to do is create a diversion. The shop's not likely to be busy at this hour, so I'm hoping only one salesclerk will be there. Just keep her occupied while I check and see if I'm right." I fingered the paper in my jacket pocket.

I'd found it last night on the floor of Deborah's office: a cartoon about the fashion business, probably clipped from one of her trade journals. A hole at the top suggested that it had been pinned to the bulletin board above the big ebony desk. On the back, a tiny row of figures and letters had been written with precision in purple ink: *16L-12R-6L.* I hadn't found a safe anywhere in the apartment; my bet—my hope—was that this was the combination to the one built into the sales counter at the boutique.

Lauren laughed. "It can't work. Look at me—the clerk will never believe I'm a real customer. I didn't know I was going to need my cloak-and-dagger clothes today." She was wearing her typical day-at-the-*Artspaper*-office outfit: jeans and scuffed leather boots, a burgundy turtleneck and a fringed suede jacket she must have had since high school. Her straight brown hair streamed loose down her back. Lauren can be quite elegant when she has advance warning that elegance is appropriate. Otherwise she tends to wear whatever is handy and comfortable. I'd come prepared myself, in a cream-and-tan skirt, a coral-colored scarf and a camelhair blazer.

"Claim to be a recent convert to trendiness," I suggested. "Ask lots of questions, try on everything that might possibly fit, demand help in the dressing room. Just keep the clerk distracted. If you can't resist spending money, there's a wonderful teal blue shirt on the rack closest to the door. Feel free to buy it for my birthday."

"Your birthday's not until August."

"That's only four months away."

"It'll take me longer than that to save up for anything this place sells. You did promise this little expedition wouldn't cost me."

"It won't," I assured her. "Unless you find something irresistible. Let's go."

The man in khaki wheeled his empty handtruck back across the sidewalk and tossed it into his truck. Lauren glanced wistfully at the restaurant door, then followed me into Bumblebee.

"My, my, how arty," she murmured as we penetrated the black and neon interior. We were in luck. Wendy the manager was alone behind the counter. She greeted us with a smile and a toss of her hair, today tipped with hot pink. She was wearing black again—a silk suit with a pencil-thin skirt and a boxy double-breasted jacket whose shoulderpads would have made a linebacker envious. The gold bumblebee pin rode high on her lapel.

"Oh hi," she said, coming around the end of the counter. "You're the detective, aren't you? Jess Randolph? I'm glad you came back. Any news yet? About what they're going to do with the shop?"

"No news," I told her. "I'm here because I liked the store so much

I wanted to show it to my friend. She's thinking of revamping her wardrobe."

"Gee, that's super," said Wendy, turning to Lauren. Her smile decayed into a look of confusion as she took in the jeans and the worn western-style fringe. "Uh, what sort of things are you looking for?"

"Oh, just give me some suggestions," Lauren said breezily. "As you see, I need all the help I can get." Wendy laughed, and soon they were involved in an intricate discussion of silk charmeuse and crepe de Chine, the precise shade of red that was in this season, the merits of Calvin Klein and Maurice Ucciello. Lauren can surprise me sometimes.

They traveled around the store while I leaned against the counter, awaiting my moment. With Lauren's encouragement, Wendy pulled clothes off the racks. Dresses, jackets, blouses. She held up one garment to Lauren's shoulders and then another, as she chattered about the effects of olive or plum or mustard on her coloring. Finally, each with a full armload, they disappeared into the dressing room. Now, I thought. Just pray that no customer comes waltzing in, setting off the trip-chime to summon Wendy back.

Quickly I slid behind the counter. I zipped my fingers along the bottom edge—good! There was the trigger. The panel popped open, revealing the small black safe. I caught my breath as I pulled the cartoon from my pocket. A twist of the dial: left, right, left again. The tumblers clicked. And the door eased open to reveal . . .

. . . a plastic sandwich bag stuffed fat with white powder . . .

. . . a folded piece of paper . . .

. . . a flat green velvet box . . .

. . . and inside the box an exquisite necklace, green and white stones in a setting of gold. A necklace in the shape of a deep, curved V, like the wings of a flying bird in a child's drawing. A necklace with a jeweled teardrop pendant, silver dollar-sized, dangling from the point of the V.

It was the one Deborah Collington had worn to the Arts and

Flowers Ball. The very one that had been clasped around my own throat yesterday afternoon.

Except it couldn't be. That necklace was in the hands of the police.

I stared at it for a long moment. Even in this dim light the stones gleamed as though from an inner fire.

Setting the case on the floor, I picked up the plastic bag. It was taped shut. I started to reach into my satchel for the Swiss army knife I always carry. But no, I decided. I could guess what the bag contained, and it would do no good to scatter that substance about the shop or to have traces of it on me. I used my scarf to wipe the bag clean as I returned it to the safe.

The piece of paper was a sheet of embossed stationery with a company name in Spanish and an address in Buenavista, Colombia. The name Guillermo Reyes, as president, was printed under the address. A note was scrawled on the sheet:

> *Deborah, mi querida, I hope this serves the purpose you had*
> *in mind. It gives me great pleasure to present it to you. Amor*
> *a ti, G.*

Emeralds and cocaine. Two of Colombia's prime exports. I wondered which of the items in the safe the note referred to.

There was a murmur of voices. "Jess!" Lauren called from the dressing room. They were coming back. I slammed shut the safe and the secret panel and started to skitter around the end of the counter.

"Wait till you see this great stuff, Jess," Lauren's voice sang out.

My knee struck the jewelry case I'd left lying on the floor. Too late to put it back—I jammed it into my satchel and scampered behind a rack of cocktail dresses. As Lauren and Wendy emerged I was admiring a display of cashmere sweaters, soft as kisses and much more expensive.

Wendy headed for the counter with a bundle of tried-on clothes. Lauren, behind her, lifted her eyebrows in inquiry. I nodded; she grinned and gave me a thumb's-up sign.

"Cash or charge?" asked Wendy. She had taken two silk skirts from the pile and was starting to fold them. Lauren rummaged in her pocketbook. Was she yielding to temptation after all?

"Oh no," Lauren moaned. "You won't believe this. I left my checkbook in my other purse."

"What about a credit card?" Wendy asked.

"I can't. I ran them up way past the limit, so I cut them into bits." She looked woefully at Wendy. "This is awful. I can't get the skirts after all. And they're *so* luscious."

"I could hold them for you," the manager suggested. "Put them on layaway?"

"No, I'd better not. I hardly ever get to this part of town. There's no telling when I could come back to pick them up." Lauren heaved a huge sigh of regret. "Hey, maybe you could lend me the funds, Jess? They're a bargain, less than two hundred dollars each." She looked at me; laughter danced in her eyes.

"If I had any money I'd buy myself that teal blouse. Come on. Time to get back to work."

"Damn," Lauren muttered. "Well, thanks anyway, Wendy. You've been great."

"Please come back sometime," Wendy said. Her smile faded. "If we're still here, that is. Jess, you're sure Deborah's father hasn't decided anything? I told the other employees not to come in since I didn't know how they were going to get paid."

Or how she was going to get paid either. I tried to encourage her. "I know Mr. Collington appreciates the work you're doing. He'll keep you posted."

"I'm sure he will," she said, although she didn't look sure at all.

Out on the sidewalk I asked Lauren, "When did you take the acting lessons?"

"I figured she'd be more willing to spend time with me if I seemed like a serious customer. Did it work? Did you find anything?"

"Yes. It's very strange, though."

She swerved toward the door of the Japanese restaurant. "Good. You can tell me about it over lunch."

"Oh, no," I said, grabbing at her fringe. "Come on, we're going downtown."

Friedberg's Fine Jewelers was a San Francisco legend. Abraham Friedberg had sailed from Europe to California at the time of the Gold Rush, carrying his initial stock of gems around Cape Horn in his spare socks. Rumor had it that he'd acquired his inventory by stealing it from his employer, a German baron, but that had never been proved, and he might well have concocted the tale himself to enhance his stature in the eyes of his new rough-and-tumble neighbors. He opened up shop in a canvas tent, married a charming young prostitute and founded one of the city's most prominent and respectable families.

The firm's present store was on Post Street in one of the first buildings to rise from the ashes of the 1906 earthquake and fire. The thick beige carpet was a recent addition, but the rest of the interior looked much as it must have when the place was new. Heavy wood paneling, carved and pilastered and burnished to a coppery gleam. Plaster cherubs cavorting across the high ceiling with ivy garlands and baskets of fruit. A massive hanging chandelier with hundreds, maybe thousands, of dust-covered crystals.

Nothing in the old mahogany display cases rivaled Deborah's necklace for lavishness. Friedberg's pieces bespoke quiet elegance, fine breeding, excellent taste, and the kind of wealth that doesn't bother to ask *how much?*. Lauren paused in front of a pair of earrings, delicate oval sapphires suspended from gold posts. "Make you a deal," she whispered. "I'll get you the blouse for your birthday if you'll buy me those for mine."

A fresh-faced young man in a blue blazer and gray slacks snapped to attention as we came in. What height the fellow had seemed all to be in his scrawny neck. His Adam's apple vied for prominence with the Windsor knot of his tie. His cheek was scabbed where he had cut himself shaving off what no doubt was peach fuzz. When he took a good look at Lauren's jacket he relaxed. There was obviously no money here.

He grew respectful again as I explained my mission and showed him the contents of the green velvet box. His eyes widened; he ran a nervous finger around the inside of his collar. Murmuring, "I'd better get Mr. Friedberg," he disappeared into a back office.

The man he was escorting when he returned looked like another of the store's original fixtures. Mr. Friedberg's pink head, with its tiny wisps of white hair, barely reached the young man's chin. His gait was slow and unsteady; he leaned into the clerk's guiding hand on his elbow. He wore a black suit, a stiff white shirt and a black string tie. His eyes, also black, blazed with fierce alertness under shaggy white brows.

"Ah," the old man said as I told him what I wanted. He lifted the necklace from its box and held it up with surprisingly steady hands. "Ah," he said again.

He regarded it with a soft, loving look. "A most impressive piece. Very beautiful." Reverently he arranged it on the satin lining of its box, then turned his sharp eyes on me. "A private detective is here, Joseph tells me. I was expecting . . . who? Sherlock Holmes, maybe. You do not look like Sherlock Holmes, young lady." He shook his pink head sadly. A female private investigator—what was the world coming to?

"And you," he said, addressing Lauren. "You are a detective too?"

"I'm Dr. Watson," Lauren replied.

"A doctor? Oh yes, I see." He smiled. "Dr. Watson. That is Sherlock Holmes's friend, Joseph."

"Yes, Gramp, I know," the young man assured him.

"You want this appraised, you say?" Mr. Friedberg said. "Right now? Why so urgent?"

"You could say it's a matter of life and death. This necklace is evidence in a murder case." Evidence that I should have left in place. That I should—but knew I wouldn't, not yet—tell Gardino about.

He pursed his lips and looked away. Murder had no place in his ordered world of beautiful objects.

"That woman from the Arts and Flowers Ball," guessed Joseph, his interest perking up.

"That's right."

"She was wearing a necklace which disappeared, wasn't she? Is this the one?" He reached for the box, his Adam's apple bobbling with his excitement. His grandfather gently slapped his hand away.

"I don't know," I said truthfully.

"How do you come to have it, young lady?" asked old Mr. Friedberg sternly.

I gave him a look that I hoped was both enigmatic and charming. "I can't tell you. Not until the investigation is completed."

"Why do you come to me?"

"Because Friedberg's has an excellent reputation. You're the best."

"Yes, that is so." He nodded his approval.

I had a sudden inspiration. "Someone suggested I take it to another jeweler. George Sanmarco."

The black eyes flared. "Sanmarco. Pah. He is no jeweler. He deals in gems for investment. That is quite a different matter. The investors, they have no regard for beauty. There is a whole world in the stones they never see. Mystery. Love. Magic. All they see is money." He regarded me closely from beneath his thick white brows. "I have met George Sanmarco and I have heard things about him. Once or twice people have brought me stones to appraise, stones he had sold them, and they were not what he represented them to be. Take my advice, young lady: Keep away from Mr. Sanmarco."

"Wasn't he married to the woman who got killed?" asked Joseph avidly. I told him yes.

"The more reason it is better you have brought this to me," said Mr. Friedberg. "You would not get an honest answer from him if he is involved in your case. Perhaps you would not get one anyway."

He lifted the necklace again. "To appraise this will take time. So many stones, and each one must be examined. When they are in a setting it is hard to tell their value. The mounting can hide flaws, chips, imperfections."

"I don't need it fully appraised," I told him. "Just a rough idea. Is it valuable, or a fake, or what? But I need to know quickly."

"I could perhaps do a spot check," he mused. "Look at stones here and there, at random. This one, for instance, the big pendeloque." He laid a fingertip on the teardrop diamond in the center of the pendant.

"The what?" said Lauren.

"Such a cut, this pear shape, it is sometimes called a pendeloque," he explained. "This stone looks fine to my eye, but these days, the fakes are more and more sophisticated and my eye, I am sad to admit it, grows weaker. We shall see what we see under the loupe."

"Then you'll do it?" I asked.

"Yes, young lady. I will do it for you. Right now, as you wish."

"But Gramp," said Joseph. "It's your lunchtime. Remember what the doctors said: Eating at regular hours makes your medication work better."

"Pah. Doctors. I will do it right after lunch, then. Joseph, give the private detective a receipt for her necklace." The old man stroked one of the diamond-and-emerald wings. "Ah, yes, very beautiful. Come back at two o'clock, young lady. I will have it for you then."

Lunch for Lauren and me turned out to be sliced turkey on rye instead of shrimp tempura. We ate at a clattery coffee shop mobbed with suburban shoppers and Financial District secretaries. Not only did I give Laurent the *Blood Wedding* poster to thank her for her help, I also paid for her sandwich and coffee. Or rather, Allen Fraser did; the meal would go on his expense tab along with Mr. Friedberg's fee. He was just lucky I didn't express my gratitude by buying her silk skirts and sapphire earrings.

"I talked to your friend this morning. Lois Whittlesey Putnam," I said as we sat down. I had returned the call before leaving the office to meet Lauren.

"Lois doesn't have friends; she has money," Lauren replied. "She thinks they're the same thing, though. What did you talk about? Did she tell you that the Arts Council is going to give my humble tabloid a zillion-dollar grant?"

"Don't you wish. No, she found out somehow that I'm working on the Collington case. Gave me strict orders to solve it right away so the specter of murder won't be hanging over the Council's fundraising campaign. She told me about all the business she can throw my way if I do what she asks, by putting word out to the mayor and all her other influential buddies."

"Dear Lois. Are you going to be a good girl and go nab the culprit this afternoon? I'll take that pickle if you don't want it."

"If only it were that easy," I said. While we ate I gave her a rough sketch of the case to date, finishing with Leonard Hoffmeyer's visit. "After he left I called the companies shown on the invoices. He was right—every one of them insisted they hadn't placed any such order. I called the venture capital firm too—Investech. They wouldn't tell me much but I got them to admit they were having second thoughts about funding Success Videos."

"So Peter Brockway is up to no good."

"Apparently. The question is, did Deborah know that and would her knowing be sufficient reason to kill her? Hoffmeyer figured it out and no one's murdered him."

"Not yet anyway," Lauren pointed out. "Brockway wasn't with Deborah at the Arts and Flowers Ball. Does he have an alibi?"

"He says he had a woman with him at his apartment that night. He wouldn't tell me who."

"That sounds nebulous. It's possible he met up with Deborah after the ball and—" She finished the sentence by slicing a finger across her throat.

"Deborah was strangled, not slashed." Suddenly I felt depressed. Despite the glamorous TV image, detective work usually consists of mundane things: searching property records for hours in City Hall, combing through figures in financial statements, talking to people and winnowing what they said to find the one significant fact. Rarely did I have this close a connection to violence and unnatural death, and I wasn't finding it one bit comfortable.

"Still, Brockway could have done it," Lauren persisted. "Maybe you should warn this bookkeeper fellow to be careful."

"Perhaps you're right. Speaking of warnings, I've had a couple of my own." I told her about the threatening phone calls, making light of them. Nothing to worry about, just someone's idea of a joke. With luck I could convince myself and make the edgy feeling go away.

She frowned. "Who could it have been? Brockway? Or maybe the Mystery Stranger? Are you any closer to tracking him down?"

"Oh yes, the Stranger." I shoved the rest of my sandwich away. I don't have to track him down, I wanted to say. I know exactly who he is—my father. My other father, my biological father, my . . . no, not my real father. But the words caught like barbs in my throat. Tyler and Claudia knew. Even the police had figured it out. Lauren was a good friend; I confided in her about so many things. Why was it so damn hard to talk about Allen Fraser?

Lauren set down her coffee cup. "Jess, are you okay?"

I forced a smile. "Of course I am. Why?"

"I don't know. For a moment there, you looked . . . upset. Like you were thinking about crying."

"I'm fine." I glanced at my watch. "I'd better check in with the office. Be right back."

A heavyset woman with two fat shopping bags was jabbering into the pay phone at the back of the coffee shop, so I detoured into the ladies' room. I splashed cold water on my face, dried off with a scratchy paper towel, then did the whole routine again. When I came out, feeling a little more together, the heavy woman was gathering her bundles. As she lumbered away from the phone I grabbed it, beating out a black man in a Stanford sweater.

"Oh, Jess, I'm glad it's you," said Claudia when she answered. "Tyler wanted to be sure to talk to you if you called in."

She put him on the line. "Bad news," Tyler said. "Stuart phoned about an hour ago. The police have arrested your father for Deborah Collington's murder."

EIGHTEEN

"But, Stuart," I protested when I got the lawyer on the phone, "Gardino can't possibly have enough evidence to hold him."

"I pointed that out," Stuart Weingarten said. "But he seems to think he does. He's a careful man, Jess, and he takes the law seriously. He isn't known for arresting people on a whim."

"I realize that." I sagged against the wall. The black fellow in the Stanford sweater stood a few feet away, frowning at me and tapping his foot. "But I can't let myself believe Allen did it. He's not the type."

"Jess," Stuart said gently, "how long have you known this guy? Two or three days?"

"You don't understand."

"He told me, Jess. About being your father, I mean."

Damn Allen Fraser, I thought.

"He said it with great pride, too," Stuart continued. "Just be careful, okay? Don't shift your loyalties around too fast. Though if it helps, I don't think he killed anyone either. Which is helpful, since I've agreed to be his counsel."

"I'm glad. Thanks, Stuart." I surrendered the phone to the Stanford man and made my way back through the maze of tables. Lauren was putting on her fringed jacket, ready to leave.

"Good Lord," she said, "you look like a truck hit you. Are you sure you're all right?"

"The police have arrested someone in the Collington case. A . . . a friend of her family, the people I'm working for. It brings it all closer to home."

"Someone you know?"

I counted out change for a tip, slowly, precisely. "Someone I've met," I said finally. "I don't know how well I know him."

"Look, Jess . . ."

"Hey, I'm okay. Really." I picked up my own jacket, draped on the back of my chair. "Go on, I know you have to get back. I'll wait for the check."

Lauren watched me for a moment, then gave a quick nod. "Okay. Thanks again for that great poster. And let me know if I can help with . . . well, anything. I'm always happy to play Dr. Watson." She started moving through the chattering, munching crowd toward the door. "Don't forget to tell me about the necklace," she called back over her shoulder.

One-thirty. Half an hour to go before I could retrieve Deborah's necklace from the Friedberg store. Jack Emerich's office was just a few blocks away, so I headed there.

The receptionist said Jack would be right out. As I waited I studied the painting from my Art Institute days that hung on the far wall. It was a big square canvas covered with jagged geometric shapes and slashing diagonal lines. Indigo, cordovan, olive green. Rust and slate gray. When I painted it I had just had a huge blow-up with Dan—one of many as it turned out.

What had that fight been about? Closing my eyes to remember, all I could see was the red shimmer of the anger. I heard yelling without being able to discern the words. I felt Dan gather me into his warm, strong arms and sweetly kiss away my tears as if he hadn't caused them.

Perhaps this was the time I'd had two paintings in a juried student show—my first real exhibition. Dan was supposed to meet me at the artists' reception. All evening I scanned the doorway, watching for him, fending off queries of "Hey, where's Dan?" At last I went home alone. Hours later he woke me as he stumbled in, singing loud and off-key. He'd run into some buddies, they'd hit a few bars, he'd forgotten the reception. But no matter—the show would be up for three weeks, right? He'd see it at some point. And hey, I was good—they're be lots more shows and receptions. Why was I so mad about this one? It truly bewildered him.

I cocked my head to change my viewing angle. The painting might look interesting hanging from its top left corner, in a diamond shape. It was very different from the work I was doing now, which was softer, brighter, more luminous. Yet for all the anger it contained, this one had held up well. I wasn't one bit embarrassed to have it wear the little blue J. RANDOLPH at its lower right edge.

"Jess!" boomed Jack's voice behind me. "This is twice in three days. Must be my lucky week." I turned to meet his warm smile with one of my own. Big, bald, kindly, he'd always been one of my favorite people. I still wasn't sure why things hadn't worked out between him and my mother.

Once in his office, however, I let my smile slide. Jack gestured me into an armchair and leaned against his wide walnut desk. Behind him, through the window, sunshine poured onto a narrow green swatch of Telegraph Hill.

"What's the matter, honey?" he asked. "Don't deny it—I can see it in your face."

"I've got bad news. The police have decided Allen Fraser killed Deborah Collington."

I was glad to see that his reaction was shock, apparently genuine. "They've arrested him?"

"I'm afraid so."

"But that's absurd. Allen's no killer."

"I hope you're right."

"I'm sorry, Jess. This isn't how you and your father should have become acquainted. Lord, arrested for murder."

For some reason my mind flashed back to a Girl Scout father-daughter dinner. Mom came with me so I wouldn't have to miss it. After all, she had said, I'm your mother and father both. At first she joked that she was going to wear a man's suit and pin her hair up under a hat and pretend to really be my father, but I shrieked in protest—I could imagine nothing more mortifying. I was giddy with relief when she emerged from her bedroom on the big night in a neat dress of robin's egg blue. The next year there was Roger to take me, and I clutched his arm possessively the whole evening.

"No," I agreed. "It's not the way I wanted it. In fact I didn't want it at all. But we have to deal with things as they are. If I keep digging, maybe I'll find something to establish his innocence."

He sank into his desk chair and rubbed his smooth head. "What have you come up with so far?"

"Not much really. Not enough."

"You sound discouraged."

"I guess I am. I didn't think they'd arrest him. But Gardino wouldn't do it without a reason." There was a worn spot in the tweed upholstery on the chair arm. I caught myself digging at it with my fingers. "Damn it, Jack. I want to believe in him, yet I can't help wondering."

"I've known him for years, honey, and I can't imagine him doing such a horrible thing. Not murder. Sure, he's had his problems, but that was a long time ago."

"What problems?" I demanded. "You keep holding out on me, Jack. I have to know what happened."

"Please, Jess, I—"

"Is protecting your friend more important than helping me? Than being truthful? Damn it, you're family. My Uncle Jack. Doesn't that count for something?"

"Oh, Jess, sweetheart, of course it counts. But I promised Allen. I talked to him yesterday; he assured me he'd tell you himself, his own way. I guess . . . I guess this changes things, his being arrested."

Jack fell silent. I waited while he swept his hand again over his slick scalp. He'd started losing his hair quite young. I couldn't remember when he didn't have at least a bare tonsure and a high brow. In one of my bratty phases, around age twelve or thirteen, I took to calling him Uncle Chrome-Dome, which he endured with remarkable grace.

"We were all just kids," he began, "fresh into college. Allen, Mary, me—a whole crowd of us, lots of good times and parties. Then Mary became pregnant and they got married. Their families were against it, so they were on their own. They both dropped out of school; the rest of us didn't see much of them, though I tried to visit from time to time. They were under so much pressure. No money, Allen working this awful factory job, Mary with a new baby to care for."

"Me," I said.

"Yes, honey, you."

"But that happens to lots of people. They rise to the challenge and make it work. They grow up, for God's sake."

"I'm not excusing him, Jess. It's not excusable. I'm just telling you what happened."

"All right. Go on."

"Allen . . . well, he let the pressure get to him. One night he cracked up, I guess. Took it out on Mary." Jack's eyes were dark with remembered anguish. "I showed up at their place right afterward, thank God, and got her to the hospital."

"He battered her."

"I'm afraid so, honey. If it helps, so far as I know it only happened once."

"He beat up my mother!" I felt a white-hot fire surging through me.

"Afterward it was as if Mary had built a cold rock wall between them. They were both terrified it would happen again. Soon Arlette came along and Allen took off."

"What did he do to Mom? How did he hurt her?"

"Ah, Jess. It was a destructive situation. It was for the best, really, that they broke up. Like you and Dan, remember? Not all relationships work out the way we'd like."

"At least Dan never hit me. If he had, I'd have walked out." Or would I? It had been so hard to extricate myself, even once it became clear that there was nothing in it for me but pain. My mother hadn't walked out. Why not? And I realized—because of me. She'd stayed as long as she could because she kept hoping things would get better, for me.

"It's not that easy, Jess. When Arlette left him, Allen realized he had a problem. He went to a psychiatrist for a long time to straighten it out. Then he came back here and begged Mary for a second chance. But she had such dreadful memories. She could never believe he'd changed. She was terrified he'd hurt you—that's why she kept you apart."

She was worried I'd be hurt in his presence—that he might abuse me as he had her. As it was, I'd been hurt by his absence. Either way, I thought, the child loses. My mind raged in a tumult. The white fire leaped and danced.

"Jess?" Jack said anxiously when I hadn't spoken for a long time.

"I'd better be going." I pushed myself out of the armchair. "Thanks for . . . for letting me barge in on you."

"Remember, sugar, it was a long time ago. People change. He's not the same man now."

"I know." Although I didn't know really. That was the problem. At the door I turned. "I'm glad you told me."

"If there's any way I can help? If Allen needs someone to vouch for him or assist with bail—or if you—"

"Need a shoulder to cry on." I put my smile back on, very carefully. "Thanks, Uncle Jack."

"There are four things that determine the value of a diamond," old Mr. Friedberg explained. "Color, clarity, carat weight and cut. In jeweler's talk, the four C's."

We stood in a little laboratory behind the store. The bright lights and modern equipment in here contrasted sharply with the hushed, dim, old-fashioned interior the public encountered. He had proudly described all the instruments to me: binocular microscope, refractometer, polariscope, spectroscope, ultraviolet lamp, and a scale, the only thing I had recognized on sight.

When Joseph showed me to the lab, his grandfather had greeted me in rolled-up shirt sleeves. But right away the old man fastened his cuffs at his wrists, straightened his string tie, smoothed the white wisps over his rosy scalp. Customers were entitled to a certain propriety.

Deborah's necklace was spread out on a tabletop of translucent glass. A light source under the glass filled the stones and made them radiant.

Mr. Friedberg laid a gnarled finger on the pendeloque diamond. "Now, this one," he said fervently, "this stone is a treasure. It is rare for one so large to be so fine. It is nearly four carats—that is formidable for a diamond. The color is excellent, very white. And it surprised me how clear it is. There are a few small inclusions, little black specks of carbon. But if there were none, I would know it to be a fake. Look here, you can see for yourself what I am talking about."

He handed me a jeweler's loupe. I held it to my eye and trained it on the diamond. If there were little black spots, they eluded me.

"There, you see?" He beamed at me, like a father showing off the virtues of his children.

I shook my head. "I'm afraid I can't see a thing."

"Ah, well, you have not been trained for it. My papa began teaching me when I was only this big." He held his hand at hip level, his black eyes dancing with the memory. "And I have certificates from the best gemological institutes." That much I could see. They were all framed and hanging on the walls.

"This diamond is beautifully cut," the old man continued. "These days, often the cutter does not take care, so the stone is too shallow or has too broad a top. That is sad, for then it is less brilliant. It is robbed of its right to enchant, to dazzle. But the one who cut this—ah, he was an artist."

"What about the others?"

"Ah, yes. I looked also at several of the emeralds. This one here, and this one." He pointed with a pencil; his fingertip would have covered two of them. "They are fine stones, young lady—very lively, with good rich color."

"So the gems are genuine. This is a valuable piece."

He lifted a cautionary finger. "I cannot promise a price. My examination was too superficial."

"Of course not. But as far as you can tell . . ."

"The stones I looked at are of excellent quality, I am certain of that. A high price for this beauty would not surprise me, should you desire to sell."

"If only it were mine to do something with."

He scowled as he composed the necklace in its green velvet box. "Ah, yes. Evidence in a murder case. That is most unfortunate. There are stones that are jinxed, you know. They carry bad luck, which infects everyone who owns them. These may be some such. Perhaps it is just as well they do not belong to you."

He was probably right. These jewels had certainly brought bad luck to Deborah Collington. Or their twins had, the ones in the mysterious matching necklace that her father had turned over to the police.

"You know, young lady, there are many legends about the magic of jewels. The diamond is very hard, so that wearing one was once thought to make a warrior invincible in battle."

"That would be useful," I agreed as I put the velvet case in my satchel.

"The emerald is said to have power over the eyes," he went on. "Looking through emeralds improves the vision. And they can be used to make serpents blind. This is a great thing, because serpents represent evil. Ask Adam and Eve if you do not believe me."

Mr. Friedberg guided me out through the shop, stopping by the display case closest to the door. Inside it garnets gleamed, stones the color of cabernet sauvignon.

"By the way," I asked, "Has anyone come in today with jewelry to sell? A strand of pearls, gold earrings, a diamond-and-emerald ring?"

"What? More evidence for your murder?" His shaggy brows pulled into a look of disapproval.

"A robbery."

The old man drew himself up straight and proud. "At Friedberg's we do not deal in stolen goods."

I assured him I wasn't accusing him of dishonesty, as I thanked him, paid him and said good-bye.

"Come back any time, young lady. Whenever you want jewels to do justice to your beauty, come to me. I will give you the best. And bring your Dr. Watson, too." He gave a courtly little bow.

I smiled to acknowledge his compliment, as old-fashioned as the interior of his store. Then I went out onto the street, my satchel tucked tight under my arm. I was considerably more nervous now about carrying the necklace around. Next stop, the P&O office, where there was a nice safe safe.

To avoid provoking questions I waited until Claudia went to the john before stashing the necklace away. We rarely got into the office safe, so I wasn't too worried that she or Tyler would find it accidentally. It would be secure there until I could plan how to sneak it back to Bumblebee. I sat at my desk, twirling a pencil, my stomach twisting into kinks as I thought about Allen Fraser and my mother.

There was one message slip: Brad Collington had phoned. I punched out the number of Deborah's flat.

"You've heard the news?" he said glumly. "That lawyer called me, what's his name, Weinstein."

"Weingarten. I talked to him."

"I can't believe it. How could Allen do such a thing?"

"You think he's guilty?" Shock hiked my voice a full octave.

"I don't know what to think. That was my Debbie who got killed. My daughter!"

"But how can you—"

"Allen was my friend, Jessica. I trusted him. Have you ever been betrayed by a friend?"

"Please, Brad—"

"He knew how much I loved her. I know we didn't have the best relationship, but I was trying to fix that. And Allen comes along and . . . and—"

"Brad, no one knows who killed her." My hand had picked up the pencil, started drawing on a yellow legal pad.

"I believed his tale at first—being given the necklace, dropping her off at home. I thought she'd gone out again, some bum on the street, some drugged-up punk—"

"That could be exactly what happened." A man emerged on the yellow page, legs bent as though leaping, arms upraised, fists clenched.

"Then why arrest him? The police must have proof."

"Proof doesn't come until the trial." I faked a confident tone. "If it even gets that far—the police have been wrong before. Allen could be off the hook in no time."

"I don't want him off the hook. If he killed my little girl—"

"Damn it, why are you turning on him? Yesterday you were doing every fool thing you could think of to protect him. If he was innocent yesterday, he's just as innocent today." A mouth appeared—a round penciled O as if the man was screaming.

"You don't understand, Jessica. He—I'm afraid he has a history of violence. He beat up his wife—your mother. I'm sure you didn't know."

"One time. That's all. Jack said so."

"I thought he was over it. But now—"

"That was a long time ago, Brad," I said sharply. "It doesn't mean he killed Deborah. It just can't mean that."

The sound on the other end of the line was something like a sob. Or a crazy bark of laughter; it was hard to tell. "Oh, hell. I just don't know anymore. Thank you for your time and effort. I'm sorry it ended badly. I know Allen retained you on a professional basis. Send your bill to my office and I'll see you get paid."

"Wait a minute. Are you telling me to quit?"

"What's the point in continuing? Allen's in jail."

"He's my client, Mr. Collington. I'm on my way to the Hall of

Justice now. If Allen asks me to stop, that's one thing. But I'm not going to give up on him just because a disloyal, kick-him-when-he's-down, fair-weather, so-called friend tells me to." I jabbed the pencil at the heart of the sketched man. The point snapped off.

"Christ, Jessica, what do you want from me? My poor little Debbie is murdered, my partner is arrested—I only called to say thank you and good-bye."

"Good-bye?"

"I'm flying home tomorrow. Debbie's lawyer can handle the estate for now. I have to get back and tend to business matters. Especially now that Allen is . . . out of commission."

Protest seemed futile. "Isabel and Hud will be glad to have you home."

"Who? Oh, yes. This has been very hard on them too."

Poor little Debbie, I thought as I banged down the phone. Poor Mary. Poor Allen. Poor all of us.

NINETEEN Tieless, beltless, with even his shoelaces missing, Allen Fraser had aged noticeably since morning. He had not yet been issued the baggy orange jumpsuit that was standard garb in the jail, but he had taken on the anonymous quality, the diminished sense of self, that the uniform was meant to impart.

We stared at each other through the glass shield that separated inmates from their visitors and the rest of the outside world. Allen rubbed his chin as if he wished he could shave. The red hair was disheveled. His face was pallid; blue circles shadowed his eyes. But the change in him was more than just altered appearance. It was as though events had wrung some of the life force out of him.

"So, Jessica." Allen spoke into the mouthpiece of the phone hookup that allowed us to communicate. His voice sounded distant, distorted. It would have been hard to hear him anyway. Every station in the narrow visiting area was occupied, and the chatter, laughter, wails and sighs bounced and echoed off the hard surfaces. Next to me stood a young mother, hardly older than a child herself, with glossy black hair that spilled to her waist. She balanced a curly-headed toddler on the shelf to be admired through the window by a skinny youth with a pencil-stroke mustache.

Allen was holding himself together with visible effort. He made a valiant try at smiling, but his grimace fell far short of the charming, almost bashful grin that—I realized with a pang—I had come to like.

"Great father I'm turning out to be. What I should have done, I see it now, is hopped on that plane Monday night and headed straight back to New York."

But then you wouldn't have called me. I was startled by the thought and by the jab of disappointment that accompanied it. Then I thought of my mother. Bruised? Bloodied? Bones broken? How could I let myself begin to like this man? How could I betray her like that?

Yet when Brad Collington, Allen's partner and supposed friend, attacked him, I had jumped to his defense.

I closed my eyes; maybe that would help dissipate my confusion. When I opened them, I promised myself, I would see Allen Fraser coldly and dispassionately. Just another client. Nothing more.

"Running away wouldn't have helped," I said, looking at him again. "What you should have done is gone to the police right away."

"Oh, hell. That would have just landed me here three days sooner."

"Why does Gardino think you did it?" I didn't add, is he right?

Allen shrugged. "Hell, I don't know. I've got no alibi. People saw me leave that dance with Debbie. The next time anyone saw her, she was dead."

"That's not enough to hold you on."

"Then there's that blasted trade we made—my tie for her necklace."

"You told him about that finally? Even after Brad's elaborate ruse?"

"What could I do? The whole point of Brad's scheme was to keep me out of the hands of the cops." He spread his arms to indicate our grim surroundings—now look where I am. "I explained why Debbie gave me the necklace. I could tell Gardino didn't believe a word."

"If it's true, he'll come around to believing it."

"Swell. Twenty years from now someone will confess on his

deathbed and Gardino will show up at the pen. 'Sorry, Mr. Fraser, it was all a mistake, you can go now.' "

"You shouldn't be so hopeless."

"Why not? Has anyone come up with a better suspect?" He looked at me reproachfully.

"Damn it!" I snapped. "Give me time."

To my surprise and delight he almost chuckled. That was a good sign. "The traditional redhead's temper. Brad and I always joke that we make perfect partners. I have the red hair and he has the temper. Two halves of a whole."

"I hear you used to have a temper problem," I said quietly.

"You know about that?" Allen studied the drab wall behind me, avoiding my gaze. "Shit, of course you do. You probably grew up hearing all about what a monster I am."

"No. I just found out today."

"I won't defend myself, Jessica. I regret that it happened, that I was ever . . . the kind of young man I was. But I worked hard to overcome that problem, and I've put it behind me. I hope . . . I hope Mary was able to put it behind her also." He turned back, giving me a questioning look.

"I hope so too."

The silence that fell was heavy and thick. Allen leaned dejectedly against the window. Next to him the youth with the skimpy mustache made faces at the baby, who squealed with delight. A raspy voice from somewhere announced a five-minute warning, which raised the volume level in the room. Get it said now; visiting hours are almost over.

A client, I reminded myself. Forget family, forget all the rest of it. I wondered what I could tell him about my investigation so far. Was there anything conclusive, anything that would cheer him? No. Even the discovery of the new, identical necklace offered no solutions, only more problems. Maybe Tyler was right, maybe I should turn this one over to him.

"I talked to Brad——" I began.

"You did?" Hope flickered in his eyes. "What did he say? Has he talked to Gardino?"

"Not yet. He . . . he feels a little like you betrayed him. He'll come around."

Dejection swamped him again. "Maybe. That's one of his issues, betrayal. His best friend at prep school stole some things and got Brad blamed for it. Brad was expelled. Ever since, he's been a little leery of trusting people. He demands your loyalty, but he's slow to give you his."

"Odd sort to choose for a partner."

"It bothered me at first. But he learned he could count on me."

"Was that his problem with Deborah?"

"Part of it. He kept a tight rein on his kids. I guess she resented it."

"Look," I said. "Brad suggested I drop the case. I said it's up to you. But I haven't done you much good so far. If you'd rather get someone else . . ."

"No, no, Jessica, please," he protested. He reached out, pushing his free hand against the glass. "Brad has no right—I want you." This time he managed a good approximation of his charming smile. "I have great faith—I know you'll come through for me."

"Okay." I sighed. "Okay then. A couple of questions. Did Deborah say anything to you about cocaine? Using it, selling it?"

"No, nothing." He looked puzzled.

"What kind of car were you driving Saturday night?"

"Car? Oh hell, I don't remember. It was a rental. From AmeriCar."

"Can you describe it? Think."

His eyes drifted to a far corner. "A Ford Taurus. Smallish. Tan. Why, did someone see us together in it? That's no secret anymore."

"A neighbor saw a car . . . it probably doesn't mean anything." A large blue car, not a small tan one. Not Allen. If Allen was telling the truth.

A burly guard appeared, nudging Allen's shoulder. "Time's up."

Allen shot me a look full of pain.

"Come on." The guard gave him another poke.

"Jessica, help me," he whispered.

"Allen—" I wanted to touch him, to say whatever would make things right. But there was that damn glass between us, and the guard was already hanging up Allen's phone.

I watched helplessly as Allen shuffled off. Then I felt a tug on my hair. The baby, riding in his mother's arms, had grabbed a lock and was cooing with pleasure.

"Hey there, stop it. That's not nice," his mother said as she disentangled his fingers. I thought she was going to apologize for her son and I started to tell her she didn't need to. But instead, her eyes full of sympathy, she said, "Gee, lady, sorry about your father."

I stared after her, amazed. I tried to think—had Allen and I said one word about fathers or daughters? I couldn't recall the least little comment. And she'd been wrapped in her own visit anyway. Was our relationship that obvious on sight?

Inspector Nicholas J. Gardino of the Homicide Division was not pleased to see me.

"Goddamn it, Jess! I ought to have your license lifted. I ought to arrest you as an accessory. I ought to box your frigging ears."

"I'm sorry, Nick." I stood in the doorway of the homicide squad room. It was a tight space for fourteen detectives to work in. Jammed with wooden desks shoved together in pairs. Ringed with gray metal lockers and file cabinets. The walls were painted a nerve-deadening shade of ecru. There was a mammoth bulletin board on one wall, bearing various notices, a funny but unflattering sketch of the mayor and, incongruously, a poster of a child in a field of flowers. Its legend read: EVERY DAY IS A NEW AND BEAUTIFUL EXPERIENCE.

Several of Nick's colleagues were present, looking from him to me with interest and amusement. I was lucky to have caught Gardino in. Or then again, maybe not so lucky. "I may not have used the best judgment. It's an awkward situation."

"And it's considerably more awkward now, thanks to you. I can't believe you hid this guy from me all this time." Gardino gave me a disgusted look. He picked up a Styrofoam coffee cup, took a big swig of the contents, made a face, set the cup down again. His expression said he wished the cup were made of pottery so he could slam it down on the desk. Maybe it was the bad taste of the brew that made him feel that way instead of me.

I walked over to his desk. Like all the others, it was overburdened with papers, files, and stacks and rows of thick black binders. Each binder represented a case—one more violent death.

Almost lost among the official debris on his desk was a single personal touch: a photo in a plastic frame of a little girl, about six years old. She had a big gap-toothed grin and Gardino's bronze-colored eyes.

"May I come in?" I asked, although clearly I was already there.

"What for?"

"I'd like to talk to you."

"About this case? Jess, if you know what's good for you, you will leave this building right now and forget you ever heard the name Collington. Go back to helping shoe stores figure out which clerk's got his fingers in the cash drawer. Homicide's out of your league. Especially this homicide." He picked up a fistful of papers, riffled through them, whomped them down on the other side of the desk. When he looked up again I was still there. "Christ, Jess. Go. Beat it. Scram."

"I have a vested interest in this case, Nick."

"I know that. Shit. Okay, sit down. You get five minutes, that's it."

He pointed to a wooden chair, hard, unpadded. I'd bet none of his visitors stayed more than five minutes.

"Why did you arrest Allen Fraser, Nick? What evidence do you have?"

He lifted his fist, index finger upraised. "First, he had opportunity. He was seen leaving the Arts and Flowers Ball with the victim, which is the last time anyone saw her alive. Hell, he admits leaving with her. There's no one who can verify his movements from that moment until he showed up in his client's office in Palo Alto Monday morning. Second, means." Another finger shot up. "Deborah Collington was strangled. Fraser is a big man, strong enough to do that."

"So are lots of other men," I pointed out. "A woman could do it if she was enraged enough and managed to grab the right spot. Lucia Sanmarco, for instance."

"Who?"

"You know. Deborah's ex-husband's wife. She had plenty of reason to want Deborah dead. There was a woman at Deborah's flat late that night. A neighbor saw her."

"Jess—"

"Or Peter Brockway. Deborah's fiancé. They had a big fight the day before she was killed; I have a witness."

"Your efforts are noble, Jess. As far as I know neither of those people was seen with Deborah right before she was killed. Fraser had means, he had opportunity—"

"But no motive."

"How about money? Oldest motive in the book. That necklace is big bucks. People have been killed for much less. Believe me," he said wearily, "I know."

"What makes you think Allen Fraser needs money?"

"Come on, Jess, you know better than that. Need has nothing to do with it. Remember those guys on Wall Street a while back, got sent up for fraud and insider trading? They were pulling down a couple million a year, legit, in commissions and perks. You're telling me they needed money? All money has to do to be a motive is exist. And Fraser did end up with the necklace."

"He says Deborah gave it to him."

"He says. Why would she just hand someone a necklace worth a jillion bucks? Because she thought he had pretty eyes? Christ, even if he was the world's greatest lay, it couldn't have been worth that much to her. From what I hear she got laid all the time."

"She wanted Allen to give the necklace to her father."

"Who she hadn't spoken to in years. Does that make sense? No," he answered without giving me a chance to reply. "Look, Jess, I know Fraser is your father and that's why you're interested in this case. No, don't interrupt. I figured it out the instant I saw you together. You don't take after your mother's side, you know.

"So there you are—motive, means, opportunity." He counted them off on three upraised fingers.

"It's all circumstantial, Nick. You can't—"

"There's also his previous record."

"His *what?*"

"You know. The assault charge. Right here in San Francisco—I didn't even have to look hard for it. Battery involving his wife. For some reason she pressed charges; usually they won't. Of course it was years ago, but—" He stopped, giving me an odd look. Something must have shown in my face. "Christ. You didn't know."

"It's still not enough, Nick." I was fighting to maintain my composure. Remember, Jess, Allen's a client. Nothing more.

"Plus he lives in New York. I can't take a chance he'll run off home, or to Timbuktu, or someplace else I can't find him."

"Not to mention the fact that the media's breathing down your neck on this one," I shot at him.

"Media, hell. Try the mayor's office. Not to mention Her Highness, Lois Whittlesey Putnam herself."

Gardino leaned back in his chair, regarding me with sympathy. I was getting altogether too many sympathetic looks this afternoon. "But that's not why I arrested Fraser, Jess," he said gently. "The man did it—I'll swear to it."

"You're wrong, Nick. I know it. He's telling the truth. Deborah went back to her flat after the ball and then went out again." I explained about the ring on her bureau and the change of shoes and my theory that she'd left because of a phone call. Gardino listened attentively—I'll give him credit. He even took notes.

But when I was done he shook his head. "You may be right, Jess. It might have happened exactly like that. But that doesn't mean Fraser wasn't in the flat with her the whole time. Or waiting when she came out again."

He was right, damn him.

"Since I've told you what I know, maybe you can return the favor." Of course I hadn't told him everything—no mention of the second necklace, for instance, or the packet of white powder in Deborah's safe. But I didn't know yet how they fit into the picture, or whether I'd be doing Allen harm or good by bringing them up.

Gardino glanced at his watch. Five minutes was long since up.

"Please," I said.

He crushed the Styrofoam cup and flipped it toward a trashcan. "You already know what we've got," he said. "Motive, means and opportunity."

I waited.

He sighed. "All right. The way I figure it is this. Fraser and Collington leave the ball. Maybe they go back to her place, maybe not. Somewhere along the way something happens. Could be they get into an argument. Could be he puts the make on her and she knees him in the groin. Could be he just can't resist all those sparkly jewels dangling around her tender little throat. So he strangles her. He drives around, finds a likely spot to dump the body. Then he heads back to the clean white sheets at his hotel. Sometime around dawn old Sparky rolls out of his rat-eaten blanket and finds he's lying next to a corpse. Sparky's sensitive about that sort of thing so he bums a quarter from somebody and calls the cops."

"Who's Sparky?"

"A wino, hangs out down there in the Tenderloin. He does us favors sometimes, we do him one once in a while. He sort of keeps an eye on the neighborhood for us."

"Did he see anything that night, when the body was dumped?"

"He claims not, he was sound asleep. Coroner says she was killed around four o'clock, give or take a couple of hours. Sparky called us close to eight."

I had taken out my sketchbook. *Sparky*, I wrote. "What else, Nick?"

"There is no else. We did the obvious, you know. We talked to Brockway and the Sanmarcos and Deborah's neighbors and lots of other people. The finger doesn't point at any of them. It points, I'm sorry, Jess, at your Mr. Fraser."

"It's not enough. You know it's not. You need hard physical evidence before you can arrest him."

"Chrissake, Jess, calm down. You know I'm—okay, okay. I shouldn't be telling you this, but what the hell, the guy's behind bars. Jess, we got the murder weapon."

"Weapon? She was strangled."

"But not by hand. I know, the media implied it was manual, because we let them think so. You know us cops, we're notorious for holding something back, something only we and the killer know about."

My throat was so tight I could barely push words out. "Nick, what are you saying?"

"Deborah Collington was strangled with a necktie. The bruises on her neck fit with—"

"Nick, no—"

"Very handsome silk tie. Same color as her emeralds, how's that for ironic. With little gold stripes. It has a label from some swank New York men's shop. Mr. Fraser agrees that it belongs to him."

"But . . . but that's still circumstantial. It doesn't prove he strangled her with it. They traded—the tie for the necklace."

"Sure they did. Like I'm going to trade my house for a cardboard box. Jess, for your sake I wish it was someone else. Anyone else. But it's not. It's Fraser."

He glanced at his watch again. I stood up; I could take a hint.

"Now look," he warned, "just because I told you a few things, that doesn't mean I want you anywhere near this case. You get in the way again and I'll have your hide. Got it?"

"Yes, sir," I gave him a snappy salute, trying not to show how hard I'd been hit by what he told me. "By the way, who's your sweetheart?" I indicated the photo of the little girl.

Gardino's expression turned soft for the first time since I got here. "That's my kid, Amy. She lives with her mother up in Chico."

"Do you get to see her often?"

"Every couple of months. She was here over the Christmas holidays." He thought about that, frowned. "Guess I ought to give her a call."

"Good idea. Thanks for the talk, Nick." Before scooting out the door I added, "Incidentally, you may want to have that necklace appraised. It might not be what you think it is. And let me know when you find out, okay?"

TWENTY

The freeway's not normally my favorite place to be late on a Friday afternoon. But today I didn't mind inching down the Peninsula along 101, even though I was sandwiched between a smoky airport bus and a battered green pickup whose driver thought the traffic should open up at the sound of his horn like the Red Sea did for Moses. The drive would give me time to think, to sort out my crazy mixed-up feelings before I had to show up in a festive mood at my brother Keith's birthday dinner.

Arriving home from the homicide squad room, I had checked on Scruff at Mrs. Fiorelli's, taking him a chunk of Swiss cheese. "Enjoy, kiddo," I said as he chomped it down whole. "Rotten for your cholesterol but good for your soul." Mrs. F assured me that the kids adored him, and he seemed delighted at having playmates. Yet I felt guilty, uneasy. I kept telling myself the calls were a bluff, but what if there was real danger? Was I putting us all at risk? I wished I could take the dog with me to Roger's, where he'd be farther away, but Roger's allergy made that impossible.

Upstairs in my own flat I changed from my skirt and pumps to comfy brown cords and running shoes. I had to fix up Keith's birthday surprise. The illustration of King Arthur's Court stared up from my drawing board, still not quite done. Hastily I inked in the remaining section and blew on it to speed its drying; thank God I'd used a good porous paper. Of course I had intended to frame it, but—ah! I knew what I'd do.

I rummaged through the stuff piled on a table in the corner of my studio and came up with a sheet of the handmade paper I'd bought at a crafts fair last fall. Thick, heavily textured, a rich ivory color shot through with threads of silver and blue. With a bright turquoise pen I lettered an IOU for one mat and frame. I rolled the two sheets together and tied them with purple yarn.

At least I had collected the specially requested double-fudge torte from Irma's. Along with a chocolate chip cookie—you never know when one might come in handy. It's a well-known fact that chocolate chip cookies heighten your powers of perception. I was munching it now.

Going to Roger's house in Berkeley by way of San Mateo was doing it the hard way, especially at this hour. But I was hoping to catch Peter Brockway before he left his office. Leonard Hoffmeyer's story bore checking out.

The jazz on the radio shifted from a mellow clarinet solo to nerve-shattering percussion. The bus belched out a black plume of exhaust and slowed from ten miles per hour to none. Behind me, the pickup jockey blasted his horn. The bus driver jabbed his arm out the window, with his middle finger sticking straight up.

I almost didn't make it in time. As I pulled into the parking lot, Brockway emerged from his office building and headed down the walk past the freshly installed junipers. With him, leaning against him and gazing up adoringly, was his receptionist, Tina Margolis. She giggled at something he said, and he brushed his lips against her black hair.

I caught up with them as they reached a sporty maroon Mercedes, probably selected by his designer to match his office decor. Too bad it wasn't a blue Ford. On the other hand, would you take your own car if you were off to commit a murder? Brockway frowned as I approached. Tina looked confused.

"What do you want?" Brockway demanded.

"I heard an interesting story today," I said. "I thought I'd tell it to you and get your reaction."

"Story?" he said. "I don't get it."

"Leonard Hoffmeyer told it to me."

"Oh shit. That little bastard. Wait here, Tina. I'd better go clear this up." He unlocked the passenger door and let her in.

"Will you be long, Pete?" she asked anxiously.

He squeezed her shoulder as he glared at me. "Not a minute more than absolutely necessary." His face was even grayer and more haggard than it had been yesterday.

"Her car broke down," he explained as we walked toward the building, even though I hadn't asked. "I offered her a ride home."

He nodded to the security guard posted in the teak-lined lobby. I suggested we talk there, but he insisted on taking me all the way up to his office, so he could sit behind his imposing desk and use it as a barrier. I made my move in the game by not sitting demurely in the little chair he offered, perching instead on the corner of the desk. I picked up a rubber band, stretched it around my fingers, and aimed it like a gun at one of the production stills on the wall. Brockway grimaced but said nothing. I didn't fire.

It was his move. "What lies has Hoffmeyer been feeding you, anyway?"

"He claims you fired him. Is that a lie?" I found five stray paper clips and linked them into a chain.

"Of course I fired him. He was overstepping his authority, sneaking behind my back, interfering where it wasn't his job. I warned him—he didn't listen."

"According to him, you were the one interfering." I recounted Hoffmeyer's tale about the missing invoices.

Brockway's expression grew grimmer. "Len doesn't know what he's talking about."

"Perhaps not," I conceded, dropping the paper clips. There was a calendar on the desk, the kind with a plastic base and pages hooked onto metal loops. I picked it up and flipped idly through it, just to give my fingers something to do. "That's why I came to ask you about it. However, I did call Investech and the companies shown on the invoices. They back up his story."

"For God's sake, stay the hell away from Investech. You're really going to screw things up for me, messing around in something you don't understand."

"Why don't you explain it to me, then?"

"Listen," he said, leaning forward. "Even if Hoffmeyer was on to something, which he isn't, it's no damn concern of yours. You came here yesterday to ask about Deborah. How I run my company has nothing to do with her or you."

"Deborah was murdered," I reminded him. Ah, good, the page for last Friday. A notation about the board meeting at Pacific Playhouse. A red scrawl saying *C-Day, 11 A.M.* Just like the entry on Deborah's appointment calendar.

"You admit fighting with her on Friday, the day before she died," I went on. "A witness says your fight was about money. Another witness says something fishy is going on with your company's finances and the same Friday is involved. You can see how I might wonder if there's a connection."

"There's no connection," Brockway said emphatically. "Look, I'm sure Deborah's father means well, asking you to look into her life, but this nosing around doesn't help. It just adds to the pain. Drop it, okay? It would be kinder to everyone, even her family. Let them maintain their illusions—Deborah can be anything they want her to be."

Nothing on the page for Saturday, the day of the Arts and Flowers Ball. I dangled the calendar from my finger by one of its metal loops.

"Did you know that the police have arrested someone?" I asked casually.

"They have? Thank God. Who is the bastard?" His expression was a mixture of anger and relief.

"A friend of the family," I told him. "Her father's business partner."

"So why are you here? Your job is done."

"I don't happen to think he's guilty."

"The cops wouldn't arrest him without good cause. So you can damn well stop harassing me right now." Brockway stood. Interview over.

I set the calendar back on his desk. "Was Deborah seeing someone else besides you?"

"Of course not. Jesus, how nosy can you get?"

"You're sure? Hoffmeyer mentioned a name—Guillermo. I wondered if that could be Guillermo Reyes."

Brockway paled, then reddened. He knew the name. "Len's full of shit. If he thinks he can get some kind of cheap revenge by—" The phone rang; Brockway lunged for it. Saved by the bell.

He pointed to the door as he announced, "Good evening, Success Videos," to the after-hours caller. I jumped off the desk; this was the instant replay of the end of our conversation yesterday. Don't bother to show me out, Mr. Brockway. I know the way.

Despite the lights Brockway had flipped on when we came in, the office suite was thick with quiet, the sort of stillness that settles like dust on a place when no one's there to breathe the air or disturb it with motion. Apparently none of his staff had decided to impress the boss by working late on a Friday evening. Tina's desk was tidy— pens and pencils in their gray leather cup, typewriter covered, *Cosmopolitan* magazine in the in-basket. On her phone, the button for one line was lit. I eased the receiver out of its cradle.

"Please give it to me." Brockway was begging. "I'll pay you as soon as it's sold."

The voice on the other end was deep, with a strong accent: "I explained to you before, señor. I cannot provide credit. Not even as a tribute to the memory of our sweet Deborah."

"She stole that money, damn it. Both of you—don't tell me you didn't scheme it together. And now that the damn necklace is gone—"

"Yes, to police headquarters. I can see how that makes things difficult for you."

"I've got some other items to sell. But it will take me a while. If

I haven't got things in order by next week, Investech says no deal."

"Cash in full. Then I will let you have what you want."

"Be reasonable, Reyes. There's no way—"

There was a click as the connection broke. The caller had hung up. I gently replaced the phone and summoned the elevator before Brockway could come out and wonder why I was still here.

Tina Margolis was slumped in the passenger seat of the Mercedes, looking put-upon and phenomenally bored. No doubt she was wishing that she'd brought the *Cosmopolitan* with her. I tapped on the window. She looked up blankly, then rolled the window down. She was wearing a chunky black-stoned silver bracelet and a magenta sweater dress. The vivid color matched her lacquered nails, but it must have clashed badly with the burgundy tone of the office upholstery. I was surprised Brockway didn't have a dress code to prevent that sort of thing.

"What do you want?" she asked sullenly. "Where's Pete?"

"He'll be down in a minute. Sorry to hold you up, but it was important that I talk to him."

"Wish he'd hurry." She opened the car door, climbed out and stretched. "I'm all stiff, cooped up in there. You were asking him about Deborah again?"

"That's right."

"You know, it's creepy," she said.

"What is?"

"Well, you see someone, and she's alive, you know? She's laughing, she's talking about things. Just like me or you. Then boom—a few minutes later she's dead. Just . . . gone. And you think, she can't be dead, I just saw her and she was fine. I mean, my God, if it happened to her, maybe it could happen to me, you know?" She shuddered to illustrate the point.

"Wait a minute, Tina. Are you saying you saw Deborah a few minutes before she was murdered?"

"Well, not a few minutes, maybe. But the same night—that's what makes it creepy."

"But you saw her. Where? At the Arts and Flowers Ball?"

"No, at—" She shot a glance toward the building. "Pete said not to tell."

"Tell what? You can't hide information that would lead to a killer. You could be arrested as an accessory." I looked back too. No sign of Brockway.

"I don't know who killed her." She set her pretty mouth in a stubborn line.

"But anything you know about that night might help. Who she saw, what she did. It narrows down the possibilities, keeps the police from arresting the wrong people. Please—where did you see Deborah?"

Tina squirmed, looking uncomfortable. "At Pete's. We were watching, uh, movies on the VCR."

"And Deborah was there? When?" I concentrated hard, willing Brockway to stay inside.

"Gee, I don't know. Pretty late. The phone rang and I heard Pete argue with her. Then she came over. I was upset, I mean having his girlfriend barge in like that."

The phone call! It was real—Deborah *had* made a call after the dance, she *had* gone home. "Why did she come over?" I asked eagerly. "Was she angry about his date with you?"

"No, she didn't even seem to notice me. It was more like she was excited. Sort of . . . gloating, you know? Like she'd done something on purpose to make him mad and she thought it was funny."

"What had she done?"

Tina fidgeted, twisting her silver bracelet. "Where's Pete? I don't like all these questions."

"What if it had been you that was murdered? Wouldn't you want people to tell any remote thing they knew so your killer could be caught?"

"I guess so." She looked desperately at the building. Brockway still wasn't coming to rescue her. "I mean, Deborah was a real bitch, but I didn't want her to die."

"So you can tell me. What had she done that she thought was so funny?"

"I don't know. She said . . . you know, something like the necklace was gone and it was just too bad for him." She screwed up her porcelain face with the effort of thinking. "She said she had an emerald necktie he could make do with instead. Then she called up someone named George and said the same thing. That's all I heard. Pete made me go in the bedroom so they could talk in private. I could tell he was real mad."

"How long did she stay?"

"A while. I don't know. I got bored. I think maybe I dozed off."

"You saw her leave?"

"No, I—" Suddenly her eyes widened. "Hey, wait a minute, you're not thinking—Pete was there the whole time, I swear."

"But if you were asleep—"

"Not asleep, just dozing. I would have heard if he went out."

"What time did you go home?" I asked. Perhaps Brockway had killed Deborah, hidden the body and taken it out after Tina left.

"Go home? I didn't. Not until lunchtime. He never left for a minute, honest."

"Did you tell the police about seeing Deborah that night?"

"Nobody ever asked me. Pete said he'd take care of it." She grabbed my arm. "Come on, you can't really think Pete—the TV said it was that Mystery Stranger."

I smiled in a way that I hoped was both reassuring and noncommittal. "Last Friday," I said, "the day before your big date, was Peter in the office? I know he had a board meeting at Pacific Playhouse that afternoon. I mean earlier."

Tina looked perplexed at the shift of topic. She put a purple talon to her lips as she considered her reply. "Gee, I can't remember. You mean when he went to the marina?"

"The marina," I said carefully.

"Yeah, I think that was Friday morning." She seemed eager now, as if she'd decided that this answer would prove Brockway innocent. "Some friend of Deborah's was coming in from, uh, I don't know. Venezuela or someplace?"

"Colombia? Was it Guillermo Reyes?"

"Gosh, maybe. I'm not sure."

A man emerged from the office building. Tina brightened, but darkened again when she realized it wasn't Peter Brockway. The man got into a beige Buick and tried to start it. Its engine sputtered and died.

"Where is he, anyway?" Tina sulked, looking at her watch.

"I'm going to find him. I have a couple more questions to ask. Thanks, you've been a big help."

She clutched at me, looking scared. "Don't tell him I told you. About Deborah coming over, I mean."

"I won't say anything I don't have to."

"Wait, I'll come too."

That I didn't need. "No, please stay here. In case I miss him."

The security guard looked up as I strode into the lobby. "Hey, you gotta sign the log."

"I'll just be a second. I left a book in Mr. Brockway's office." I punched the elevator button. "It's okay, he's still up there."

The guard looked dubious. "You saw us go in together," I reminded him. "And he hasn't come out, has he?"

"No, but—" But I was in the elevator and on my way.

The reception area was dark, the feeling of emptiness heavier, more palpable. I reached for the light switch, then thought better of it and fished my pen-sized flashlight out of my satchel. Brockway's office was dim and shadowy; all I could make out were the pale rectangles of windows with the waning day behind them. I followed the flashlight's baby beam down the corridor until I found the men's room. I pushed open the door—nothing but blackness inside.

Where had Brockway gone? I went back to his office, looking for movement, listening for a soft flutter of breathing. Outside a car engine roared into life.

I got to the window in time to see the beige Buick kick up a spray of gravel as it finally left the parking lot. Tina Margolis was still pouting by the open door of Brockway's car. And Brockway himself was stumbling along the sidewalk carrying a large cardboard box.

Of course. There would be fire stairs, a delivery entrance.

I picked up the calendar on his desk. As long as I was here, I might as well doublecheck that interesting notation on last Friday's page. But that page was no longer there.

TWENTY ONE

The house stood dark and silent in the gathering dusk. It was smaller than I remembered, the yard weedier, the neighborhood more run-down.

The stucco walls had been tan when I lived there. Sometime in the intervening years—not recently—they'd been painted green, an unappetizing shade between lime and olive.

But someone still tended the rosebushes my mother had planted lovingly beneath the living room windows. They were covered now with pink and white blooms.

The front porch was deep in shadow. If I closed my eyes halfway, I could see little Jessie Fraser sitting on the top step, red pigtails dangling, a glass of lemonade and a box of crayons beside her, a coloring book in her lap. And lolling on the step below, her favorite doll, that silly, grinning Crazy the Clown. Whatever had happened to Crazy, anyway?

I hadn't planned to stop here. I'd only been back once or twice since Mom had married Roger and we'd moved up to his home in the hills. I was overdue there for dinner right now. But coming through Oakland I'd been pulled off the freeway as if by a magnet and drawn to this little house.

I stood outside a chain-link fence that hadn't been there before and surveyed the cottage and yard, looking for . . . what? Ghosts, perhaps. Some knowledge about myself that this house might contain, some imprint that the first thirteen years of my life could have pressed on its walls.

The windows, dark and blank, stared back. I wished there were signs of life about the place, something to keep it from looking abandoned and forlorn, to make it look like home—if not mine, then someone's. The rusty bike lying on the lawn, even the roses, were not enough.

I'd been there for maybe fifteen minutes, gazing, remembering, when an ancient station wagon pulled into the driveway. All the doors popped open and three little girls with dark, ribboned hair bounded out. Their mother appeared to be about my age. She handed the oldest child a grocery bag and unloaded a baby from its seat in the back.

Apprehension crossed her face as she saw me watching. She gave a nudge to one of her daughters, who had stopped to play with the bike—"¡No, Elena! Mete en la casa, punto!"—and herded them all inside. The door slammed. A glaring overhead bulb flooded the porch with light.

Little Jessie Fraser vanished. Maybe she had never been there at all.

I'm glad you came home, I told the woman silently. Thank God you came home.

Time to get to Roger's. I got in my car, switched on the ignition, shifted into gear. Suddenly, though, I couldn't see to drive.

Damn tears. They never come at a convenient moment.

". . . Happy birthday, dear Kee-eeth, happy birthday to you!" Fourteen yellow candles twinkled merrily on top of the double-fudge torte.

"Make a wish and blow!" yelled Teddy. Keith inflated his cheeks and gave a mighty puff; all the flames snuffed out.

"Hurray!" Teddy cried. "You get your wish. Tell us what you wished."

"Uh-uh, creep. No way I'm telling." Keith flashed Teddy a grin full of smugness and mystery. He pulled the spent candles one by one from the frosting and licked the ends.

"You're crazy, Ted," said Keith's best friend, Benjamin. "You tell a wish, it won't come true."

Teddy was undaunted. "I know what I wish. I wish there was no school, and I had a million dollars, and I'd pitch a no-hitter every time. Hey, let *me* have some candles."

Keith pointed the cake knife at Teddy's chest. "What I wish is, I wish I didn't have a pesty brat brother like you."

"Cut the cake, Keith," Roger said calmly before Teddy could react. "You know we can't eat until you've had the first bite. Some of us are getting impatient for our chocolate."

It was a familiar family gathering around the Randolph dining table. I was sitting in the chair that had always been mine, facing Mom's African violets on the sideboard and her prized Chagall print on the wall. Keith and Teddy and Roger were all in their accustomed places. Muggins, the fat and elderly brindled cat, was sprawled as usual behind Teddy's chair, disdaining to pay attention yet ready to pounce if an interesting tidbit should tumble to the floor.

But Mom wasn't there. I felt her absence keenly. We'd only had about half a dozen birthdays among us since she had died, and we hadn't found the knack of celebrating without her. At one point during dinner, as I was saying something to Roger, a movement at the other end of the table caught my eye and I turned, expecting to see her. But it was only Benjamin, sitting in her spot.

Suddenly I felt like a guest in this house.

I hadn't really lived here for ten years. Keith had been in nursery school when I moved into my first little studio apartment near the Art Institute. Teddy had been just learning to walk.

The two boys across from me were scarcely more than casual acquaintances. Keith, always tall and gangly, seemed to have shot up another two inches since I'd last seen him, yet that hadn't been so long ago—had it? Our mother's silky dark hair tumbled across his forehead; behind his glasses he had her brooding brown eyes. He read science fiction and fantasy, he tinkered with electronics, he played the piano. What else did he enjoy? Was he interested in girls yet? I didn't know.

Teddy, at eleven, was the exuberant one. He looked like his dad—stocky build, a freckled face that was wide and open, warm gold-flecked eyes, caramel-colored hair like Roger's had been before it softened into gray. Teddy was the athlete, the joke teller, the collector of lizards and rescuer of broken-winged birds. Once he had dreamed of being a cowboy—what were his ambitions now?

They had grown up together, grown up with Roger, all of them intertwined, a family. As for me—to my brothers I had been another adult, something of a stranger who tagged along for birthdays and Christmases and Sunday outings, but who was never really a part of things, who didn't totally belong. And now that Mom was gone . . .

It took the boys about two swallows apiece to consume half the cake and most of a gallon of mocha chip ice cream. Then Keith and Benjamin departed for the movies. Teddy gathered up Muggins and disappeared into the den to watch TV. I toted dishes into the kitchen while Roger put the kettle on to boil and measured Earl Grey into the teapot. When I went to fetch the cups from their usual cabinet, I found peanut butter and Tabasco sauce there instead.

"I rearranged the kitchen a bit," Roger explained, glancing away from me—furtively?—as he retrieved the cups from the shelf where the mixing bowls used to be. "Handier for my way of doing things."

We carried a tray full of tea things into the living room. Roger laid and lit a fire while I poured tea for both of us. I added cream to his cup, and started to spoon in sugar, the way I knew he liked it.

"Wait, skip the sugar, Jess." He patted his waist. "I'm trying to cut down a bit and after all that great cake . . ."

I dumped the sugar back into the bowl, feeling slightly and unreasonably hurt.

Roger settled into his customary chair, a leather-covered recliner that he had bought just before he married Mom. She had never liked it, but he insisted that it was the most comfortable chair he'd ever owned and had to stay. Gradually she had made the room her own—new drapes, fresh paint, her prints on the wall—but the old chair had remained. Now, though its leather was cracked and its cushions misshapen, it continued to hold the place of honor in the room.

I curled up on the sofa. When Teddy had made it past the toddler stage of spills and sticky fingers, Mom had had it reupholstered in light creamy wool. Her needlepoint pillows still adorned it, brightening the room with peach and pale yellow, spring green and sky blue. The bookcases flanking the fireplace were full of Roger's books, as they'd always been, and his piano stood in the corner. My lessons had only lasted a year before he and Mom got sick of hearing me bang my fists on the keys in frustration. Keith had taken to it well, though; he was becoming quite an accomplished musician.

On top of the piano was a row of photos in leather frames. Only one showed all of us. Mom was holding Teddy, a brand-new baby. Roger, beaming proudly, balanced three-year-old Keith on his shoulder. I stood to one side, the odd one. Black turtleneck, gypsy shawl, huge dangling earrings of ebony and brass. Eyes rimmed with heavy makeup, waist-length hair flying wild. That was before I learned that it's the work you do that makes you an artist, not the way you look.

The kindling crackled and sputtered. Then the first of the big logs caught and the flames danced high, orange and golden.

Roger and I sat in awkward silence. I couldn't remember the last time I'd felt uncomfortable with him. I watched his face. All evening I'd been trying to read the signs, to figure out what he thought about all this. When I'd arrived his embrace had seemed tentative. During dinner he had laughed less than usual, had given me strange glances, had avoided asking how things were going. Or maybe I was imagining it all.

We sipped our tea.

"Tell me about Allen Fraser," Roger said at last, in a carefully neutral tone. I was relieved. Perhaps naming it would put the specter between us to rest.

"I think . . . well, he seems pleasant. Attractive, charming, that sort of thing. He's a financial planner—you know, he counsels people on their investments." Steam rose from my cup and dissipated in the air. "The police . . . he was arrested today. For Deborah Collington's murder."

"Oh, Jess." His warm, deep voice held an undertone of pain. "How awful for you."

"He didn't do it. I've thought a lot about it—you know, am I being prejudiced? Is the fact that he's my . . . my father keeping me from seeing things clearly? But I really don't believe he's guilty."

Had there been a slight flicker in Roger's eyes at the word *father?* I couldn't be sure.

"You're a pretty good judge of character, Jess. The police could be wrong." He drank some tea. His cup, with its delicate border of pink flowers, was one I'd given my mother for Christmas when I was fifteen. "I know this is difficult for you—having him show up out of the blue, and under such terrible circumstances. It would be hard even if he were a paragon." He sighed; he frowned. "And from what I've heard, he never was that. Jess . . . be careful. There's just so much . . . potential for disillusionment."

"I heard about it. Jack told me. What he did to my mother."

"Ah. Well, it's just as well you know. I never understood why Mary wouldn't tell you. Didn't want to scare you off men forever, I guess. She worried the whole time you were involved with Dan, afraid you were repeating her mistakes."

"That was different," I said emphatically. "Besides, I had you as a positive model."

"You know, if Mary and your father had lived happily ever after, my life would be empty. No Mary in it, no Keith or Teddy. Or you."

I tried to imagine it. Little Jessie Fraser, growing up in a house with Mary and Allen, happily ever after. The three of us sitting at a table in some sunny, spice-scented kitchen. No more letting myself into an empty house after school, no more fixing lonely sandwich suppers because Mom was working late again. There would be little brothers perhaps—a happy, noisy, laughing family.

Only they'd be different brothers. Not Keith. Not Teddy. And I couldn't fix Allen Fraser's face on the man at the kitchen table. Nor, try as I might, could I make him look like Roger. The man faded out and so did the sunshine, until Mom and I were alone again in the little Oakland house.

What would have happened if my mother had given Allen Fraser that second chance?

I gave myself a mental shake. The past was done with. I needed to focus on my life now.

"Roger, tell me what you think. I'd appreciate your insight." I explained the Collington case to him as clearly as I understood it—which was probably not too clearly at that.

Roger was silent when I finished. He set down the flower-rimmed cup and got up to poke the fire. He fiddled with the red-glowing logs for an awfully long time.

"I'm not sure what to tell you," he said at last.

"I don't understand this. Why does having Allen Fraser come into my life make me feel like I've lost something rather than gained something? It's as if I'm in mourning."

"For the woman who was murdered," Roger said, but I could tell he knew that wasn't what I meant.

"No. What happened is dreadful. But I never actually knew her. Her death is a great loss to lots of people, but not really to me. She wasn't part of my life."

"Until now."

"Yes, until now." I poured us each another cup of tea. "No sugar," I said.

"Right." He had moved over to the window, and I joined him, bringing his cup. The curtains were open. The blackness outside was punctuated with millions of tiny lights. The window looked out across the Berkeley flats to the bay, the Marin hills and the Golden Gate. Through the branches of a eucalyptus I could see a single tower of the bridge, half swallowed in fog.

"Maybe I'm losing something too," Roger murmured. He turned to face me; his face glistened as the firelight struck remnants of tears. "I have a daughter and I'm afraid she's slipping away. After all, I'm not her real father—just an interloper who came into her life rather late."

I had a sudden, unbidden flash—myself at thirteen, a gawky, pimpled kid, running from the room in dismay when Mom told me she was going to marry Roger. She was all I had. If she and Roger had each other, who would there be for me? The night before the wedding I cried all through the black hours until sunrise, but then I got control of myself and hid my tears from my mother—hid them, I realized now, the way she had taught me by example to hide feelings, the way she had always hidden so much of herself from me.

"Roger, you *are* my real father. As real as I've got. Allen's coming back doesn't change things." I struggled to keep my voice steady.

"Yes it does. You may not want it to, and it may not change them very much. But it can't help changing things."

"But Roger—"

"Change is what life's all about, Jess. Mary's gone—God, how I miss her. You were out of the house before we'd hardly had time to get to know each other. The boys are growing faster than I can keep track of. Who'd ever have thought a little tyke like Keith would reach fourteen?" His half-smile didn't contradict the sadness.

I slipped my arm around his waist and studied our reflections in the window. We were nearly the same height, but other than that there was little resemblance. Allen Fraser was taller than Roger. Allen's hair was thicker, his face longer, his body leaner. Allen looked like me.

"I might be friends with him someday," I said, testing out the thought on both of us. "But not family. You're family, Roger. You and Teddy and Keith."

"Good." He gave me a quick squeeze. "Just remember that. And don't forget, family can be friends, too."

The telephone rang. "I'll get it!" Teddy yelled as he came careening through the living room. A moment later he appeared again, dragging his feet and looking disappointed. "Aw, it's for you, Jess. Some guy."

The guy was Tyler Parks. "Sorry to disturb your party, Jess. I knew where you were because you talked about picking up that cake at Irma's. I was sort of wishing I had some. I'm back on austerity rations."

"That'll be the day," I said, remembering yesterday's three-and-a-half-cookie lunch. "Why did you call? I can't ship you cake over the phone wires."

"If only you could. But no, that's not it. O'Meara and I are here at the office; I wanted to play with some numbers on the Meridian Insurance thing. And this call just came in. Jess, I meant it this morning when I said I should take over the case. This only confirms it."

"Tyler, what are you talking about?"

"Lady sounded really wacko. Yelling and screaming, calling you names, making threats. At first I thought she was a crank but—"

"Threats? What lady?"

"Oh, sorry. Thought I said her name. Lucia Sanmarco."

George's wife. Deborah's rival. I saw her standing in her living room, wild-eyed, ready to fling a handful of emeralds.

"Look, Tyler, I'll handle it. It's my case and it's going to stay my case, damn it."

I made him give the phone number he had finagled out of her. I thanked him, hung up and dialed.

"Mrs. Sanmarco? This is Jess Randolph. You were trying to reach me?"

"Randolph?" The woman's voice was high-pitched, shrill. "This is the whore? You send George home right now. He's mine, do you understand? He promised. I don't care what he gave you, he's mine!"

"Wait a minute. George isn't with me. There's some misunderstanding—"

"I understand everything, you filthy slut. I'll get you, I swear I'll—"

"Mrs. Sanmarco, listen—"

"That other one got killed. Remember that. It's me he loves—he promised." Suddenly the voice crumpled into sobs. "Why, George, why? How could you do such a thing?"

"What did he do, Mrs. Sanmarco?" I said softly.

"Please, George, come home now. I'm sorry I did it."

"Mrs. Sanmarco—"

"Help me. Please come and help me. I'm all alone. I'm scared."

The sobbing took over. Nothing I tried to say from that point on got through. I hung up the phone. Roger was standing in the doorway.

"What was that about?" he asked.

"I'm not sure," I told him. "But I think I'd better go find out."

TWENTY TWO

Everything about Lucia Sanmarco was thin and sharp, from her angular body to her long nose to her voice as she greeted me.

"You got nerve, coming here," she said.

She stood in the archway, swaying slightly, wearing a garnet-colored robe, ankle-length, tightly sashed. Her hands were thrust deep into huge patch pockets; her feet were bare on the marble floor. Tendrils of black hair had escaped from the knot at the back of her neck.

She was covered with jewels: ropes of pearls that wound round her neck, gold chains with ruby and sapphire pendants, the diamond choker from the portrait over the fireplace. Bracelets paraded up both arms; rings adorned every finger. On her head was a tiara, sloping precariously toward her left ear.

The elevator door hissed shut behind me. "You asked me to come, remember? You said you needed help."

"Where's George?"

"I don't know. Why did you think he was with me?"

Lucia shook her head as if to clear it. She pulled her right fist from her pocket and pointed it toward me; she was holding a snub-nosed revolver. But it wasn't aimed—she was merely displaying it as an object of curiosity, a toy.

"Look. I found it in George's study," she said. Her eyes glittered like her jewels. "I wish I'd found it long ago."

"May I see it?" I reached out to take it. She snatched back her hand.

"No! I need it." She cradled the gun to her breastbone as she rocked back and forth under the arch. For the space of a heartbeat I thought she was going to pull the trigger.

But she dropped her arms to her sides. I felt my caught breath slide out.

"Jess Randolph," she slurred, slipping the gun into her pocket. "George always did like them tall and pretty." She spun unsteadily into the living room, the silk robe rustling as it swirled about her legs. "Siddown. We better have things out."

On the coffee table was a nearly empty bottle of vodka and a cut crystal glass half full of melting ice. Lucia splashed the last drops of liquor over the cubes. I wondered if the bottle had been full at the start of the night.

She gulped from the glass and gave a small nod of satisfaction. Her face was in chiaroscuro, half shadowed, half etched in light from the room's single burning lamp.

Lucia looked like a lost child in this place. George had his pipe-stand and easy chair, but there was little clue to a real Lucia in the designer's impeccable, impersonal decor. Even her portrait over the fireplace was an outsider's interpretation. The artist had seen a younger woman, tentative and slightly bewildered, with only an edge of resemblance to the gawky, sad-eyed woman in front of me.

She stood there for a long moment, her only motion a faint tremor, her eyes fixed on the blue drapes that were pulled tight against the darkness outside. I thought she had forgotten me until she turned, gestured with her glass and asked, "What'll you have?"

"Nothing, thanks." I'll take the gun, I thought, but of course that was not what was being offered.

"I told you to sit." Lucia sank onto the sofa. I looked around. The antique chairs appeared too delicate to be inviting, but to sit in

George's armchair would be a blatant invasion. I sat at the sofa's opposite end.

"George thought he kept you a secret," Lucia said. "But I found your card, right there in his pocket. See, I'm a detective too." I could pick out her overprecise enunciation as she struggled to keep the liquor out of her voice. Yet in a way she seemed disconnected from the sounds she made. It was as if her voice emanated from some point two feet to her left.

She banged the empty glass on the coffee table. "You're gonna leave him alone, Jess Randolph. My husband. I'll see to that."

"I'm not after your husband," I tried to assure her. "I was here yesterday on business. I'm investigating the murder of Deborah Collington."

"You're on her side?" she shrilled. "That horrible creature? Someone did the world a favor, killing her."

"I'm not on anyone's side. I'm trying to help her family understand what happened. Her death has affected a lot of innocent people."

"George was showing you jewels." Her voice was anguished. "Bright green emeralds all over the table. Take your pick, I bet he said. Well, you won't get any of *my* pretty things, not like her. Today I took them all out of the safe deposit box. See?"

Lucia stood and wobbled in a circle, arms wide so I could admire her finery. In the dim room, the stones had little flash or fire. "I'm gonna keep them with me always."

"Why weren't those emeralds in the safe deposit box?" I asked her.

"They jus' came." Lucia dropped down into the sofa again and picked up her glass. She looked disappointed to find it empty. "From Reyes."

"Guillermo Reyes?"

Her answer was a shudder, a look of disgust. "I hate him. Don't you hate him? Such an awful, awful man. Always luring George off to do . . . wild things." She ran two fingertips around the rim of her glass. One ruby-painted nail was a perfect oval. The other had been bitten to the quick.

"He introduced George to that horrible creature. Those emeralds, I bet they were for her. But now she's dead, she's dead, so George was going to give them to you."

"They were for Deborah Collington?"

"He never gave her up, you know. She humiliated him, she ran around with every man she could lay her filthy hands on. And that bastard . . . he never, ever gave her up."

"But he divorced her. He came back to you."

She was rolling the glass in her hands like a child forming long strings out of modeling clay. "I was the only one who would ever understand. Good, I told him. Now you know what it feels like when someone destroys you. When you can't go anywhere because everyone's pointing and laughing. When the hurt goes so deep it's like marrow in your bones."

She was squeezing the glass so hard I was afraid she'd crush it. "I don't get it," I said. "You married him again even though he hurt you so badly?"

"Of course. It meant I won."

She upended the empty bottle. Nothing came out. With a heart-deep sigh she carried the glass to an ornate cabinet in the corner. When she opened it I could see bottles of liquor inside, mates of the dead soldier on the coffee table.

"Except I didn't win at all," Lucia said into the depths of the cabinet. She took out a fresh bottle and a clean glass, loaded both glasses with ice from a silver bucket and filled them with vodka.

She brought me one. "You have to," she pleaded. "Don't make me drink alone. It's been so long . . . so goddamn long."

I took the glass but set it on the coffee table. I wasn't sure what I was contending with here in Lucia Sanmarco. Dulling myself with a drink was not a good idea.

Lucia pulled herself into a ball at the far end of the sofa, tucking her feet up under her. "George promised it was all over. So lonely, I believed him. Such a fool." She shook her head, as if she couldn't believe her own naivete. "He kept giving her things . . . that apartment . . . that awful store. He . . . he gave her my necklace."

"The one she was wearing the night she was killed," I said.

"It's mine! George gave it to me when . . . when . . . our baby . . ." Her words strangled, then gushed forth. "She was born too early, only seven months, we were going to name her Angelina. My little angel. I never even got to hold her."

"I'm so sorry," I whispered. It sounded clumsy and inadequate.

Lucia's long red-tipped fingers tangled the chains around her throat. She rocked back and forth, looking somewhere far beyond me as she talked. "I was still in the hospital. George brought it to me. Not to make it up to me, nothing could do that, but to show . . . he still loved me. Even without the baby, even though the doctors said I could . . . never have another. I hardly ever wore it. It reminded me too much of . . . of . . . but don't you see? It was the most precious thing I owned.

"Angelina's necklace. I used to dream . . . on her wedding day . . . I would clasp it around her neck, she'd look so beautiful. So beautiful." Lucia's face was rapt, her eyes brimming. Somewhere in shadowed corners her lost child hovered. "I couldn't believe it . . . George said he was giving away Angelina's necklace . . . to that slut."

"Why did you let him?" I asked gently. "Didn't he know how much it meant to you?"

"I told him no, no," she wailed. "He promised he wouldn't, he promised, he promised. Then one day . . . I saw something on TV, it was all about how they save babies now, they work miracles, only . . . only it's too late. I felt so awful. I went to get Angelina's necklace, just to hold it, be close to my baby. But it was gone."

"You mean Deborah had stolen it?"

Tears were spilling down her cheeks, leaving dark trails of mascara. "No, no. George . . . he said he had to . . . he said . . . so that creature would leave us alone. I thought maybe it's worth it . . . just to be rid of her. I'm such a fool." She stoppered her eyes with the heels of her hands, but the tears kept coming. "I'd give anything to have it again. Oh Angelina!"

Her tiara fell into her lap as sobs wrenched her thin body. I felt truly sympathetic, but awkward and embarrassed too. I touched her arm, hoping to offer comfort, but she went tight as a wire. So I watched helplessly until the sobs subsided into whimpers and the whimpers finally ceased.

"I'm sorry," I said. "I understand better now. It's a lot to endure."

"George promised he'd get it back. This week I'd have it, he said so on Saturday. But now it's stolen, gone, all gone." Lucia looked up, blotchy-cheeked and red-eyed.

She picked up the tiara and twirled it round and round in her hands. The storm seemed to have cleared something within her. Her body was less taut, her voice steadier, her manner more calm.

"Please—go away."

I was tempted. It was nearly midnight. Three hours' sleep last night, a wracking day, now dealing with someone in worse turmoil than my own—I was not at my sharpest. I stood up, almost relieved that she was kicking me out.

Except—*Jessica, help me*, Allen Fraser had said.

How would I get this opportunity with Lucia again? "Please give me another few minutes. I'd be really grateful if you'd answer some questions. . . ."

Lucia stared at me, not quite vacantly. Her eyes were brown. Or perhaps smoky gray—in the low light it was hard to tell.

"What happens if you find out who killed her?" She had yet to refer to Deborah by name.

"With luck, the murderer will be brought to justice and the healing process can begin."

"The pain never heals." Her drink had been sitting neglected, but now she picked it up and polished it off.

"I'm trying to learn everything I can about Deborah. Then maybe I can reconstruct where she went late Saturday night and why. Something you think is insignificant could help." I sat, hoping she'd forgotten she'd asked me to leave. "You didn't go to the Arts and Flowers Ball?"

"No," she moaned. "I was here . . . watching TV. I used to be on their committee. I loved parties like that, before . . . before . . ."

"And George was with you?"

Lucia shook her head. "He was out."

"Out where?"

"I don't know." She nibbled a red fingernail. "With someone. Business. It was a man. He promised."

"Why didn't you go along?"

"I . . . I wasn't invited. George keeps me away . . . from his business. Don't worry your pretty head, he says. Of course, *she* was different, *she* was fascinated by every detail. And the damn bastard ate it up."

"Then why doesn't he encourage your interest now?"

"No, no, it was a mistake. He said so." She made her voice deep, mimicking George. "She knows too much for her own damn good or mine either." Then in her own whiny treble: "That's why . . . that horrid shop . . . to keep her nose out of his business."

She was drifting in and out of focus. I felt helpless, trying to direct her line of thought. "But you don't know who he went out with Saturday night?"

"They met at the restaurant. It was a man. George promised."

"What time did he get home?"

"I was sleeping. Sleeping. I heard voices—loud ones, yelling. The man brought George home. I came out to see, why are you yelling? But the man was in the elevator. Going away, away."

"They were arguing? What about?"

"I . . . I don't know." But she did. I could tell by her sudden wariness, the stab of fear in her eyes.

"Please tell me—it could be important."

"It wasn't about that awful—" Lucia stopped abruptly.

"What is it?" I probed gently.

"He said it was her fault. Someone's . . . suing George? A lawsuit, I don't know why. Something about . . . the gemstones aren't real?"

She gave her head a puzzled little shake. "But the man Saturday, I think he's in trouble too. He kept saying, it's all your fault, George. And that horrid slut. It's her fault too."

"Did you see what the man looked like?"

"Tall . . . he was tall."

"Red hair?" I didn't want to hear the answer. Could Allen have had some reason to be in touch with Sanmarco? He said he'd arrived late at the Arts and Flowers Ball.

"I don't know, I don't know."

"Is that why you think George was still involved with Deborah? Because of this lawsuit?"

"No, no, the money. All my Papa's money. Every month he pays her. Three thousand dollars, four thousand, more sometimes. He thinks I don't know. A special account, everything goes to his office, but once . . . a check . . . he didn't sign it. The bank called here by mistake.

"We can't afford all that. We're not rich. People think . . . oh, lots of money. But no, it's Papa's, he left it to me. Almost gone now." Lucia's voice rose to a wail. "Gone, gone. Oh, George, what have you done . . . all Papa's money!"

"But what about the gem investment firm? Surely he makes money there."

"Papa's money. Papa gave him some . . . for starting his business. Long ago, long ago. The rest he left to me. I'm sorry, Papa. So much money . . . all gone . . . to that whore." She looked at me bleakly. "When the bank called I told him . . . told George . . . give me Papa's money back. And George . . . he promised . . . it was the last time. He told her so. No more money. And I'd get my necklace back."

"He cut her off," I mused. "I wonder why." I wondered also how much Lucia's tale could be trusted.

"Where's my necklace? Do you have my necklace?"

"No, of course not." Except I did have it, hidden away in the P&O safe. Or one just like it. "Were George and Deborah seeing each other socially, too?"

Lucia reared up, eyes flaming. "You have no right to be jealous. He's mine, damn it." She slapped me hard.

"Of course he is," I said soothingly as I rubbed my stinging cheek. Better not start up that line of thinking again.

"She got engaged . . . I thought, finally it's over. To that man— what's his name?"

"Peter Brockway."

"Mr. Parkway. Peace at last. But no, no."

"What do you mean?"

"The loan . . . George gave it to Parkway. She made him."

"A loan? For what?"

"I can't stand it. George has no right, no right at all—"

Lucia pushed up out of the sofa, took a couple of faltering steps, then turned back to pick up the tiara. She set it squarely on her head, as if it would help her walk more steadily. She disappeared through archways to some place deep in the penthouse. I debated following her, but with the gun in her pocket and her unstable condition, that didn't seem wise.

She returned with a manila envelope and pulled out a sheet of paper. "What does this mean? Her name is on it, it can't be good."

But when I reached for the paper she jammed it into the bosom of her robe. "No!" she cried, waving the envelope at me. "You'll give it to George. I need all this, it's ammunition."

"Ammunition?"

"In case . . . another divorce. I can't stand it much longer."

Her eyes glittered; she had spotted my untouched drink. Dropping the envelope, she picked up the glass.

"Lucia? You've had enough."

"Yes. But not of this." Lucia's voice had gone dull and flat and distant. She leaned against the fireplace mantel, sucking at my drink. Above her head, the younger, fresher Lucia Sanmarco of the portrait looked out over the room. To be true to its subject now, the picture would require more blues and greens in the skin tones, purple at the rims of the eyes, umber to sharpen the planes and hollows of the cheeks. The white catchlights that gave life to the eyes would have to be painted out.

"I hate it here," Lucia said. "Before *her* we had a wonderful house. Angelina's room was all fixed up. Then George . . . left. I was all by myself. A horrid little place, cramped, dark. So dark. I . . . I got sick. Finally he came back, we moved here, a brand-new start, he said. I thought it would be . . . just like before. But no one I know lives here at all. George is someone else now. And Lucia . . . where is she?"

Neither of us had a good answer to that. She swallowed the last of the vodka and set the glass on the mantel.

"If George was still involved with Deborah—" I began.

"You think . . . he killed her? Just because it's better she's dead . . . but he was already home when she called."

I jumped up abruptly, without thinking. "Deborah phoned here that night? Are you sure? What did she want?"

Lucia shrank away, grabbing at the mantel for support. "She said, 'I gave it away, you and Peter can fight it out.' I . . . I listened . . . on the extension. She was laughing. Someone was yelling, a man. In the background, yelling. It was late. I was scared, out alone in the dark so late."

"You went out? Where did you go?"

Lucia's eyes widened, round circles of fear. "No, no, I mean *she* was scared, she must have been scared, someone grabbing her so late at night!"

"You said *you* went out, Lucia. Where did you go? I'm not going to hurt you. Please don't be afraid to tell me."

She fluttered her hands in front of her face, as if to brush something away—my question, a memory, an imaginary spiderweb. "No, I didn't. Where's George? He should be home by now." Her voice peaked, high and shrill. "I thought he was with you. Could he have another whore already? We just got rid of that other one."

I held her bony shoulders, trying to steady her. "Where did George tell you he was going tonight?"

"Sailing." She trembled under my hands. "A sunset sail, the man from last Saturday. He promised."

"It's past midnight. Late to be sailing."

"I didn't believe him. I thought he was with you." Tears were welling up again. "Goddamn bastard." She fumbled for the glass on the mantel. It was slippery with condensation and crashed to the hearth, slopping ice onto the expensive Chinese rug.

I bent to pick things up, clunking cubes and shards into the other glass, blotting at the wet spot with my sleeve. When I glanced up I froze. Lucia was caressing the gun.

"How does it work?" she asked. "Do I just pull the trigger?"

"Give it to me." I raised myself slowly, hoping not to alarm her. "I'll take care of it for you."

"I should have used it on that horrid creature," she murmured. "I should have done it long ago."

But instead you went out that night and strangled her—the thought leaped into my mind; it had been lurking at the edges all along.

"Deborah's gone now," I reminded her. I inched carefully to her side.

"Too late," she moaned. "Too late."

"Don't think like that. George will be home soon to take care of you." I took her hand gently and tried to ease the revolver out of it.

"No!" Lucia whirled from my grasp, gun flailing. She staggered against the fireplace, then faced me, trembling, with a look of terror. She pointed the gun at my stomach, my throat, my chest. Everything inside me was in knots.

"Give it to me, Lucia."

The gun wavered, steadied, wavered again. She gave that perplexed little shake of her head.

"Give it to me or put it away."

She was shaking as though an icy wind were sweeping through the room. I felt the chill too.

"Lucia—"

"I want . . . I want . . . oh, damn that bastard! Goddamn it all!"

The thudding of my heart seemed to echo through the room. I reached out. "Everything will be all right. Let me have the gun."

She twisted away. With the sudden motion her face turned green, and she lurched from the room. A moment later I heard a shot and a clatter, followed by the sound of retching.

I found Lucia Sanmarco heaped on a cool hard bathroom floor, next to the toilet into which she'd thrown up. Garnet-colored silk, black hair, tangled jewelry, all limp and lifeless. The gun was in the tub. Head-high on the wall, cracks webbed out from the bullet hole.

But there was no blood. Thank God there was no blood.

The tiara had tumbled into the toilet bowl. Fighting back a wave of nausea of my own, I fished it out with a wad of toilet paper and tossed it into the sink. I pushed the flush handle down and bent to help Lucia Sanmarco.

"Lucia?" I whispered. She moaned softly.

I ran cold water into a washcloth, wrung it out, and let the water swirl over the tiara while I sponged her face.

"Can you get up?"

She moaned again. Her eyelids quivered, opened, shut once more. I slipped a hand beneath her head.

"Come on now, you can do it." Slowly, cautiously, I maneuvered the dead weight of Lucia to her feet. She leaned heavily against me as I turned off the tap.

"Which way is your bedroom?"

She flopped a hand in reply. I peeked into doorways as we shuffled down the hall—George's study, an exercise room, a linen closet piled with ill-folded towels. Finally we came to a rose-and-silver room containing a king-sized bed. I pulled down the heavy damask spread and lowered Lucia onto the mattress, tucking her robe around her legs.

Lucia made no movement, no sound but the slightest whistling of breath. I started to remove her jewelry and put it on the nightstand. She'd be more comfortable without it.

But I changed my mind. She wouldn't be more comfortable at all. She wanted to keep her pretty things with her always.

TWENTY THREE I fished the gun out of the bathtub. A small-model Colt revolver, not dissimilar from my own .38. I unloaded it, putting it and its bullets into my satchel. Given Lucia's frame of mind, it wasn't safe to leave them in the apartment. I would have to return them to her husband.

The revolver felt heavy, more of a burden than its physical weight would account for. I trained in the use of firearms when I started working for P&O, and I go to the range to keep in practice. But I've never felt comfortable with the idea of guns. Mine stays in the safe at the office; I almost never carry it.

Lucia's envelope of divorce ammunition was on the living room floor. I pushed that into my satchel too. So someone was suing George Sanmarco for misrepresenting the gems he sold. I thought of the emeralds George had shown me. What would my new friend Mr. Friedberg say about those stones?

George's study was the best bet. He'd probably stashed them in a wall safe, which would do me no good. But perhaps there was a false-bottomed drawer or a hollowed-out book. . . .

And perhaps Sanmarco would walk in and catch me looking. I almost chickened out. But surely, I convinced myself, some sound would warn me he was approaching. I could slip out of the room unnoticed and explain, as I emerged from the hall, that I'd merely been putting his passed-out wife to bed.

The walls were lined with antique nautical prints; there was no safe concealed behind any of them. The desk drawers held nothing of interest. An old typewriter on a stand was pushed into a corner, displaced by a personal computer. But it was a real typewriter, not a disguised miniature vault. I began to worry that I'd strike out—no incriminating papers, no information on Guillermo Reyes, no emeralds.

It took me twenty heart-pounding minutes, with a third of my attention devoted to the search and two thirds to listening for the clunk of the elevator mechanism or the tap of shoes on the foyer tiles. But at last, paydirt—a model clipper ship sailed on a table in front of the window; cached in its hold was the little pouch of emeralds. I helped myself to two, hoping they were a representative sample. As long as the pouch felt full, George might not notice a couple were gone.

Before leaving I checked on Lucia. She was curled on her side with one arm flung over her face, and her breathing was shallow but peaceful. As I pulled up the spread, which had started to slide, her thin little voice whimpered, "George?"

"He'll be here soon," I whispered.

But it was now close to one o'clock. I was wondering myself about the question Lucia had been asking all night.

Where was George Sanmarco?

Boats glistened like chunks of ice in the green-white glare of the security lights. Out in the black bay, a beacon pulsed, pulsed, pulsed at intervals, warning vessels away from the rocks of Alcatraz.

The night had turned misty and cold. Fog blotted out most of the nearby Golden Gate Bridge. I got out of my car and pulled on the old brown sweater I keep in the trunk for such occasions. Salt was tangy in the air.

The marina was full of eerie noise at one A.M. The security lights crackled and buzzed; the docks creaked and moaned as currents shifted them. Out on the boulevard traffic still thrummed steadily.

Music and faint laughter drifted across the dark water from a party on a distant yacht.

A dozen or so cars were parked in the marina lot but hardly anyone was about. A man in stained, shabby jeans and cracked shoes was sprawled on a bench, a tent of newspaper sheltering his face. There was a broken bottle under the bench; I caught a sour whiff of cheap wine.

Far down the walkway a pair of silhouettes merged into one as a couple stopped strolling to embrace. What a lovely idea—I wished I had someone to hug at that moment, someone who would let me trade a little of my confusion and weariness for a morsel of calm and strength. I found myself thinking of Kit Cormier. His steady manner, his solid shoulders, his blue, blue eyes. Perhaps even at this moment his call was waiting on my answering machine. But no—I remembered the photo of pretty Sara.

The shadow couple kissed ardently. I looked away. Watching hurt too much.

I had come here hoping to catch George Sanmarco as he returned from his midnight sail. I wanted to be rid of the gun, to return it quickly to its owner. And to ask him a few questions while I was at it.

But I had missed him. *Sweet Lucy* was already home, bobbing gently in her slip. No lights on her, no sound. Tied up for the night, shipshape and secure.

Except . . . as I got closer to the pier the boat looked odd. A wide, dark splotch marred the ice-white surface of her deck. Something heavy was dragging from the line that held her to the pier. A large, bulky object floated beside her in the inky water.

Oh God. I did not want to know what it was. Yet I had to know—I was afraid I knew already.

The metal-mesh gate to the dock was locked. I climbed onto the railing, grabbed the top of the gate, and gained a foothold on the pneumatic closing device. At the top I teetered. What if someone was still there, waiting, hiding? Then I dropped, *thud*, to the wooden dock.

I paused, expecting to hear an alarm shriek. But no—just the creaking and moaning, just the spitting sound of the lights. I made my way to *Sweet Lucy*.

George Sanmarco's face floated below the surface of the water like a pale round fish. Eyes wide open, gaping, blank. Shirtfront spattered, stained with blood. His jacket billowed, trying to drag him deep, but his feet were tangled in the lines that held the boat fast.

The sight was like a jab to my stomach, knocking out air, replacing it with nausea and the taste of bile.

The black puddle on the deck was blood, its smell sharp and metallic. It was smeared, as if someone had hauled the body from where it fell to dump it in the water.

Oh Lord, oh God, oh sweet Jesus Christ. Don't touch anything, I said to no one. Take ten deep breaths. Call the cops. Call homicide.

The gate opened with a latch from this side. The drunk on the bench twitched and groaned when it clanged shut, but he didn't waken.

Poor Lucia. Lost and alone in her penthouse. Truly alone now. I'm sorry, Lucia. I'm so sorry.

Across the boulevard was a twenty-four-hour Safeway, busy even now, with a phone booth in the gloom by its side wall. The security lights in front were orange, casting garish mock daylight over the parking lot. A guy came out of the store with two six-packs of beer, another lugged a sack of kitty litter, a woman trundled a cart loaded with groceries. So normal, so normal. How could people carry on ordinary activities with death so close, with George Sanmarco's body trapped in the frigid water just a couple of hundred yards away?

I punched nine-one-one. The voice that gave the report to the dispatcher must have belonged to someone other than me, because it managed to sound calm and rational.

I hung up and leaned my forehead against the phone while spasms racked my body. When I could walk again I crossed the road to my car. Nothing I could do now but collect myself and wait for the cops.

"Christ, Jess, what am I supposed to think?" Nick Gardino stopped his pacing in front of me. He looked fatigued, disheveled. Further down the dock cops were swarming over *Sweet Lucy*, popping flashbulbs, dusting for fingerprints, swabbing up samples of blood.

I didn't answer. I was slumped against the metal gate, staying out of the way while the police did their thing. I had pulled up the cowl neck of my sweater and drawn my hands inside the sleeves. The fog had thickened; I'd stood for two hours in the cold. I was sure that was why I was shivering.

Beyond the gate a cluster of people had gathered, from the Safeway, from nearby apartments, from out of the air. The drunk who'd been napping on the bench wasn't among them; he'd slithered away at the first sign of the police.

"You show up at the Collington woman's funeral," Gardino railed on. "You show up again at her flat the night it's broken into. You turn out to be related to the guy who killed her. Now you're on the scene of a new homicide."

"Doesn't this prove Allen Fraser is innocent?" I asked. "He couldn't have killed Sanmarco. He's locked up in your jail. What could be a better alibi?"

"It's a super alibi for tonight. It means zip where the Collington killing's concerned. That happened last weekend, remember?"

"Come on, Nick. The two murders have to be connected."

"The only connection I see is that in both cases I find you poking around. She was strangled, he was shot. Different m.o.'s, or hadn't you noticed? Different m.o.'s mean different perpetrators."

"Not always." The police had hauled Sanmarco out of the water and stretched him out on the deck. The medical examiner poked and prodded at the sodden remains.

"No, not always." Gardino rubbed a hand across his eyes. "Christ, I gotta find a different line of work. Bricklayer. Shoeshine boy. They don't have to deal with this kind of shit. Once they go to bed they can figure on staying there. Till the rosy-fingered frigging dawn, or however the hell the line goes."

"A woman and her ex-husband both murdered in less than a week—that's too much for coincidence, Nick. Deborah and Sanmarco were still involved with each other. I know it for a fact."

"For my money the wife put him down. Most homicides are family matters, Jess, you know that."

"Except I was with her tonight. I told you."

"Yeah. From maybe ten-thirty on. For all we know he was killed at suppertime. You said she was acting loony."

Drunk and agitated is what I had said. I had told Gardino about my visit to Lucia, about her vodka and her loneliness and her worry about her husband's whereabouts. I told him she'd said George was sailing and that's how I'd happened to come down to the marina. I hadn't told him about the gun in my satchel. All I needed was to have it turn out to be the murder weapon. Gardino had not been thrilled to find me here. It would be just my luck to have him start thinking of me as a suspect.

Suddenly it hit me—this rationalization was just like Allen Fraser's refusal to go to the police. Like father, like daughter, a little voice snickered. Damn, damn, damn.

But I still didn't mention the gun.

"Done 'bout everything here we can, Inspector." It was Humphreys, the black detective who'd investigated the break-in at Deborah's flat. The others were loading what was left of George Sanmarco into a body bag. After a few moments they came trooping down the dock with it and passed us, through the gate. Two men stayed behind to guard *Sweet Lucy* until morning, when daylight might reveal something that had been missed; it's hard to put a police seal on a boat.

"I better go break the news to the widow," Gardino muttered. He looked like he did not relish the task. "It's got to be done, and her reaction might tell me something."

"Let me come with you." The prospect didn't entice me either, but somehow I felt I should be there.

"Jess, listen—"

"She's in a bad state already, but there were a couple of moments when we had a sort of rapport going. My presence might help."

I could see in his face the little battle he waged with himself. "Okay," he said finally. "Come on."

Gardino leaned on the buzzer at the entrance to the Sanmarcos' building. And leaned. And pounded on the door in frustration.

"She was pretty well out of it when I left," I told him. "I don't know if the buzzer would be loud enough to wake her."

"Damn. Guess I'll have to find a phone."

I tried to remember if there had been a phone on the nightstand by the bed. "I think you'd have the same problem."

"Damn building's got to have a manager." He began punching buzzers at random.

"That won't do any good," I told him. "Even if you get in, you need a key to get the elevator up to that floor."

"Shit." He peered through the glass panel into the lobby, then turned to me. "I don't suppose you know who to call to come stay with her. Friend, relative, anybody whose presence would be a comfort? Help her through the hard part?"

"No. She didn't say . . . I don't think she has anyone like that." The realization filled me with sadness, chilling and intense. I pulled the old brown sweater tight around me.

"Come on," Nick said, with a hand at my elbow. "I'll give you a ride home."

"That's okay. My car's down at the marina lot."

"I'll drop you off there then." He gave me a long look. "You *are* telling the truth, Jess."

"Lord, Nick—" I started to protest.

"Okay, okay. You'll come in tomorrow of course and give us a statement."

"Of course."

It was three-thirty when I finally, gratefully, stretched out in bed. The blinking light on my answering machine could wait. Lucia

Sanmarco's manila envelope could wait. I couldn't deal with one more thing tonight. Except sleep.

But sleep kept out of reach for a long time. There were haunts in my bedroom; I saw them every time I tried to shut my eyes. A woman lying broken on a hospital gurney. An ashen phantom behind a glass wall. A sobbing garnet-colored specter with a tiara and gun. And a face, a face that floated beneath the water like a pale round fish.

TWENTY FOUR

Rat-tat-tat.

At first the sound seemed faint and distant. Gradually it grew louder and closer.

Rat-tat-tat.

The wind banging loose lines on a boat. Heavy footfalls on a wooden pier. An explosion of gunfire knocking a body off a deck. I burrowed deeper into pillow and blankets, trying to muffle the noise.

Rat-tat-tat.

I peeked out of the covers and groaned. The slant of light in the room told me it was well into morning—long past the hour I'd intended to get up.

Rat-tat-tat.

Someone was pounding on my front door. The buzzer was broken. I'd mentioned it twice to Mrs. Fiorelli, but it still hadn't been fixed.

I didn't want to see anyone. No one at all. I wanted to lie in the dark and shake. I wanted to play loud, crashing music that would fill up my head and drive out everything else, leaving no room for memories of last night.

But the knocking continued. I dragged on my robe, pushed my fingers through my tangled hair and headed down the stairs. Through the peephole I saw Mrs. F, her fist poised to attack the door again. I unlatched it and tried to wish her good morning, but my words were only half out when a gleeful Scruff bounced against my stomach.

"Hey, get down, kiddo," I told him, grinning. "I'm happy to see you too, but I'll be even happier if I stay upright." Scruff danced about on the porch, his tail pumping wildly.

"Oh, dear, I warned those kids," fretted Mrs. Fiorelli. "Davy! Come out here and get the dog." My landlady is in her seventies, a short, square, sturdy woman with amazingly little gray in her thick coil of hair. At the moment she was covered bosom to knee in a vast flowered apron.

Davy, a boy of about ten, shaggy-haired and toothpick-thin, emerged from the open door of her flat. A couple of the smaller children trailed behind, wide-eyed. Davy reached for the dog's collar.

"That's okay." I rubbed Scruff's muzzle, scratched his silky ears. "I'll take him for a while."

"You sure?" asked Mrs. F. "I don't want anything to happen."

"I'll bring him back when I go out."

"If the dog's in danger, what about you, up there all alone? You want, I'll call the fellas, get them to come down and keep an eye on you." The fellas were Frank and Nelson, the top-floor tenants. I assured her I could take care of myself. Mrs. F is slightly old-fashioned. She assumes other women need men to take care of them, even though she herself had fared just fine without one for nearly four decades. Her delight was tempered with dismay on my behalf when Dan moved out of the flat for good.

She started to herd the kids back inside but stopped abruptly, pulling an envelope from her apron pocket. "Oh my, what am I thinking? Here's why I was knocking. Davy was playing out here this morning and found this. I don't know why these kids gotta play on the stoop when there's that lovely garden out back." She shook her head, puzzling over the mysterious ways of children. "But anyway, it says urgent, so I thought I better get it to you quick."

The envelope was plain white, business size. My name was typed on the front, slightly off-center. Underneath it indeed said URGENT. Had it been there when I arrived home last night? As tired and upset as I'd been, I could have missed a steamer trunk, never mind an envelope.

Davy was hovering half in, half out of the doorway. "Any idea who delivered this?" I asked him. "Or when?" He shook his head energetically, making his hair flap to and fro.

"He said it was just lying there on the mat," Mrs. F explained. "I've been in the kitchen all morning, so I didn't see."

I turned the envelope over. Sealed tight. No marks on the back.

"I tried your doorbell but it didn't ring. Now, sweetie, you gotta tell me when something goes wrong. How can I fix things I don't know are broken, tell me that." She stood there expectantly, waiting for me to open it. I didn't. "Look here," she said, changing tactics, "I'm baking pizza for the kids. Come by in an hour, I'll give you a nice fresh slice."

That way, she could pump me about the strange missive while I ate. "Sounds great. I have to work, though. I'll bring Scruff back when I leave—thanks for keeping him."

But the instant I was back upstairs, I ripped the envelope open. The message inside consisted of three crude sketches. The first showed a stick-figure woman hanging from a noose; the initials *D.C.* were written on her triangle skirt. The second depicted a dog impaled by a knife. The last had another stick figure with a gun aimed at her little valentine heart. This one was labeled *J.R.*

Underneath the drawings someone had typed: *One down. Two to go if you don't lay off.*

It was supposed to scare me. But what jolted through me was anger, the white hot flash I was beginning to know too well. I balled up the paper and flung it across the room.

I stomped into the kitchen to put on the teakettle. The clock on the stove said nine-thirty. I had set my alarm for seven; it must not have gone off. Or maybe it had buzzed and I'd shut it off in my sleep—one more noise in a dream filled with the shriek of sirens.

Scruff was eager, so I threw on some jeans and we made a

round-the-block dash. The fog was receding, the spring sun growing strong. I was too edgy, though, to take pleasure in it. I kept looking around for sources of menace. The elderly man sweeping the sidewalk in front of the cafe, the two shabby guys playing cards at the curb, the fellow dog walkers, the black kid at the bus stop—they all seemed to be eyeing Scruff and me, weighing the right moment to strike. When we reached home Scruff whined, straining against his leash to persuade me to stay out longer. But I held firm.

The kettle was shrilling as we climbed the stairs. The world was too damn noisy this morning. I appeased Scruff with Swiss cheese and carried my tea to the living room table.

One down. I shivered. Two down really, now that George Sanmarco was dead. The missive must be from the loonie who'd been calling. Was I getting closer than I realized? Closer to what? Or to whom? Anyone could have found my flat and left the note. Even Sanmarco could have sketched the cheery greeting yesterday and paid someone to deliver it.

Anyone except Allen Fraser—this would have been hard to arrange from jail.

I didn't dare let myself think about violence happening to me. I couldn't tell Tyler about the threats—he already was looking for an excuse to pull me off this case. So, I'm sure, was Gardino—he'd love it if I came sniveling to him about some vague menace.

If anything happened to Scruff, I'd . . . I'd . . .

I dropped my head onto my hands. I shouldn't let this bother me. If only I didn't feel so exhausted. Last night's few moments of haunted sleep had done me no good at all.

Jess, oh Jess, go back to bed, help your father and wind up—

Something damp landed on my toes. Scruff, sensing that I was feeling low, had brought a gift to cheer me—an old knee sock, once blue, now dingy gray, which we used for playing tug-of-war. He waited, tail waving, for me to start the game. I wanted to hold him tight, protect him, keep him safe. To gather him up and bury my face in that soft amber fur. But he wouldn't tolerate that for a minute. Scruff was a dog of action—none of that mushy stuff for him.

And none for me either. We played one game, which I let him win. Then it was time to get to work.

The little red eye on my message machine was still winking from last night. Kit Cormier at last, I prayed to the love god. Please let it be Kit.

But no, neither of the messages was from the gorgeous blue-eyed photographer. Far from it—the first caller was Evan Krausgill. "Hey, doll, give me a jingle. We've got something stra-ange going on at the theater I want to talk to you about." I didn't bother to write the phone number down.

The other message was from my friend with the muffled voice, warning me yet again to stay away from the Collington case. Damn it, I was going to solve this thing just to spite whatever jerk thought I could be so easily scared off. I punched the erase button, sending both messages into oblivion.

Perhaps if I looked at all my case notes and documents together, they would tell me something new. I organized it all on the living room table—my sketchbook, the newspaper clippings, the Success Videos invoices that Leonard Hoffmeyer gave me. Grabbing my satchel to take out Lucia's envelope, I was surprised by its weight.

Of course—George Sanmarco's gun.

I ripped a page from the sketchbook so I could organize my thoughts in writing. Assuming I had any thoughts, as fatigued as I felt.

The contents of Lucia's envelope were disappointingly meager. All it contained was a few papers, dated two weeks ago, pertaining to the lawsuit she had talked about.

Translated from legalese, they seemed to say that Sanmarco was being sued by one Bernard K. Tauber of Lincoln, Massachusetts, for misrepresenting gems he had sold to Tauber. The top-quality emeralds in question had turned out to be cheap synthetic stones. A placating letter from Sanmarco said the wrong stones had been shipped in error and offered to refund Tauber's money. Tauber's heated reply announced that he intended to keep Sanmarco and his cohorts from ever preying on innocent people again.

What had Lucia said? Something about the lawsuit being Deborah's fault. But Deborah's name was not mentioned.

There was something else Lucia had mentioned—a loan, engineered by Deborah, that Sanmarco had made to Peter Brockway. In my mind I saw Lucia stuffing a paper down the front of her robe. Damn it, if only I had remembered it when I was putting her to bed and could have retrieved it.

Why would Sanmarco agree to give his ex-wife's fiancé a large loan? Brockway hardly seemed the best credit risk.

It all centered around last Friday. The Success Videos invoices were supposed to be paid last Friday. Deborah and Brockway had battled noisily about money last Friday. Both of their calendars had mentioned a mysterious C-Day, which somehow involved the emerald king, Guillermo Reyes. C-Day was last Friday.

And the next night Deborah Collington was killed. Killed *after* Allen Fraser had delivered her safe at home. *After* she had gone over to Brockway's apartment, after she had talked to Sanmarco on the phone, after Lucia Sanmarco had gone out into the dark night to look for her.

Perhaps it all meant nothing. Perhaps Deborah encountered some crazy on the street, some guy hopped up on crack or smack who needed a fast few bucks and wasn't fussy about what he had to do to acquire them.

Except George Sanmarco was also dead. The two murders had to fit together. But how?

Nothing helpful had emerged on my sketchbook page. All I'd accomplished was a doodle of *Sweet Lucy*, a skull-and-crossbones flag fluttering from her mast.

Or maybe not *Sweet Lucy*. My mind flashed on a photo—Deborah and Sanmarco drinking champagne with Reyes on the deck of the *Esmeralda*. I got up to call Kit Cormier, not one bit sorry to have come up with an excuse.

Kit's voice was just as I recalled it: a warm, husky baritone—true music. "I'm glad you called," he said. "You must have gotten my message."

"Message? No." Did this mean he'd tried to get in touch? Hooray!

"I phoned your office yesterday afternoon. Just an impulse. I had an appointment near there and thought maybe I could meet you after work for a glass of wine of something. But your secretary said you were gone for the day. Out tracking down clues?"

"Something like that. Now I wish I'd stayed at the office." I forced myself not to think of the leather-framed photo on his shelf. *Love, Sara.*

"How's your investigation going?" Kit asked.

"I've hit a snag," I admitted. "Could I come by and look at that magazine again? The one showing the party on the South American yacht? I was an idiot not to have borrowed it to make a photocopy."

"I'm glad you didn't. This way I get to see you again." He was on his way out but would be working in his darkroom in the afternoon. "Press the doorbell hard so I'll hear you."

The prospect of seeing him gave me a pleasurable tingle. But I didn't get a chance to savor it. The phone rang the instant I replaced the receiver. It was Nick Gardino.

"We finally roused the Sanmarco woman," he said, sounding weary. "Christ, the hysterics she threw."

"Her husband was murdered, Nick. Give her a break."

"I know, I know. I wasn't expecting her to dance a jig, but some people take bad news with fortitude. This one just came unglued. I haven't even been able to question her yet. Which brings me to why I called. What time did you get to her home last night?"

"Quarter past ten. I left just before one o'clock. I told you that." I'd arrived at the Sanmarco apartment barely twelve hours ago. Amazing—it felt like days had passed.

"Bear with me, Jess. Last night's a bit of a blur. I haven't had any sleep yet. Anyone see you? Coming or going?"

"I don't think so, but people knew I was there. Mrs. Sanmarco talked to Tyler when she was trying to reach me and he called me at my father's place. So—"

"Your father's place." Nick's voice was cold and flat.

My own voice came out louder and sharper than I intended. "My stepfather's. Roger Randolph's. Damn it, Nick, you know what I meant. Why does it matter what—"

"Calm down, Jess. Two hysterical women in one morning is more than I can take. It matters because the preliminary guess is that Sanmarco could have been shot as early as eight P.M. If you weren't there until after ten, the wife's not off the hook."

"But she couldn't have done it. In her state of mind she would have confessed the minute I walked in. What about the man Sanmarco was sailing with?"

"The phantom business associate. There was no appointment on his calendar. Mrs. Sanmarco couldn't come up with a name."

"Have you arrested her?"

"I don't make arrests unless I'm sure, Jess." He paused to let that sink in. "Oh, by the way, I checked out that necklace like you suggested. The appraiser says it's very pretty glass."

Gardino signed off by reminding me to come in and give my statement. I slammed the receiver down, inspiring a startled yip from Scruff.

"Tomorrow," I promised the pup, "we'll go to the beach and you can have a grand romp. But today you go back to Mrs. Fiorelli's where it's safe, because I have too much to do. First I'm going to finish that damn Videau report and get it out of my hair. Next I have to deliver my paintings to the Hammerwood Gallery. Then I have to check out some emeralds and find a man who discovered a body. I need to call Tyler and ask him to please follow up on Bernard Tauber while I'm out running around. I've got to give the cops their damn statement.

"And Kit"—I gave Scruff a quick hug—"yes, I get to see Kit. Maybe today won't be so bad after all."

I tossed my jeans onto the rubble of blankets on my bed and was halfway into a pair of gray wool slacks when the phone rang again.

"Hey, babe, it's me. I was getting worried I'd somehow missed your call."

"Hello, Evan." The elation I felt about visiting Kit whooshed out of me like air from a leaky balloon. "I got in late last night. Just listened to my phone tape a moment ago." That was true enough. He didn't need to know that I'd planned to ignore his message.

"Look, doll, I know you said you don't go out socially with guys connected to your cases. But there's no reason we can't get together for a little sleuthing, right? There's something weird going on we need to look into."

"Evan, I'm really busy right now."

"No, I mean it. I'm talking about hiring you, a purely professional relationship. Someone broke into the theater Thursday night; that's why I called. Then I got here this morning and damn if it hadn't happened again."

In spite of myself, I felt curiosity click in. An occupational hazard. "Was anything taken?"

"Not that I could tell. That's the weird part. But I got to thinking, hey, good old Deb was one of our stars, right? Maybe this is connected to her murder. Come on over and I'll show you what I've found."

Reluctantly, I agreed to meet him later. The chance seemed slim that the shenanigans at Pacific Playhouse had anything to do with Deborah Collington. Evan was probably staging a little show of his own as a ruse to get us together.

But I didn't dare not check it out.

TWENTY FIVE

Huge, flat faces stared from the walls. Skin tones of pale grayed blue, hard-edged hair in midnight colors, blank eyes the size of dinner plates. Very cool, very unemotional.

"What a jolly crowd," I said. I stood in the middle of Hammerwood Gallery and gazed back at them, a painting of my own sheltered in my arms.

"A laugh a minute," Darlene Chong agreed. "With all this raucous partying going on, it's amazing I get any work done."

Darlene, Muriel Gittelsohn's assistant, was seated behind a white laminate desk at the rear of the room, with a bookkeeping ledger spread open in front of her. A crystal vase on the desk held long stems of gladioli in colors that harmonized with the art: lavender, purple, indigo.

She rose and came toward me. She was about my age, small and elegant, with a thick black curtain of hair. Her suit was bright pink, adding an upbeat note to the gloomy tones that dominated the room.

"Muriel thinks this artist is enormously talented," Darlene said, with a disbelieving shake of her head. "Frankly, though, I'll be delighted to see these things go. It gives me the creeps to have them looking over my shoulder all the time. The Ars Nova exhibit will be lots more fun. This is your contribution?"

She took *Seascape III* away from me, leaned it against the desk, and stepped back to regard it from an appropriate distance.

"One of them. The rest are in the car." I pointed through the plate glass window to my Toyota, sitting in the middle of the Union Street traffic with its hazard lights blinking, daring the meter maid to come along. There hadn't been a parking place within blocks, and the paintings were too cumbersome to haul very far on foot.

Darlene eyed the picture appraisingly, tilting her head first one way, then the other. I looked at her, looked at the picture; to my surprise the volume of my heartbeats notched up louder as I awaited her verdict. I *knew* the painting was good. I liked the rhythm of the lines, the play of light across the surface, the tension among tan and yellow, cobalt and aquamarine. In fact, this was one of the samples that had convinced Muriel Gittelsohn to give me a slot in the Ars Nova show. And yet, and yet . . .

"Very nice," Darlene pronounced, and the warmth in her voice suggested she meant it. My reaction was relief rather than gratitude, followed by annoyance at myself for letting it matter. If I knew it was good, really knew that within myself, why wasn't that enough?

"Thank you," was all I said. She showed me where to put the painting in the storeroom and helped me carry in the others. There were six all together. Unfortunately, the one I'd hoped to complete in time wasn't among them; it still sat unfinished on my easel, to remind me how Allen Fraser's arrival had disrupted my life.

I had spent a long time this morning in my studio thinking about my options. I could deliver the others to Hammerwood and then spend the rest of today slapping paint on this last one, rushing it still wet to the gallery in time to hang it in the show. But it wouldn't be the painting I had intended it to be, the one I could see it had the potential to become. And no matter how well it seemed to turn out, I would never really like it.

Besides, I had other things to accomplish today. Freedom was a relative thing: for me, it meant having time to paint. But for Allen the stakes were so much higher. If I compromised my effort on the

Collington case, I wouldn't like *myself* very much, and that was far more crucial than liking a painting.

Yet I had committed to six paintings for the show, so I took an early picture down from my bedroom wall. My work had grown since it was done, so I hadn't planned to show it. But I'd been pleased with it then; it wouldn't embarrass me.

As we tucked the last painting into the storeroom, Darlene asked, "You're coming in the morning to help us hang the show, aren't you? I think all the other artists will be here. Around seven—we'll have coffee and pastries to wake everyone up."

"Of course. I wouldn't miss it for anything." I offered a quick prayer to the art god that the Collington investigation wouldn't interfere.

"The reception will be fun, too. We always get a great turnout for the Ars Nova party."

"I can't wait. See you tomorrow."

I was almost out the door when Darlene called after me. "Wait, Jess, I almost forgot. That Duplisea canvas you were asking about? I called a couple of people for you. One was Lou Sutton; it's the type of thing he handles. Well, he said a man had been in yesterday trying to sell him a painting like the one you described."

"Sutton Galleries? Darlene, may I use your phone?"

She let me call from the white desk. The painting Lou Sutton had seen was almost certainly the one from Deborah's flat; his description tallied with my memory of it.

"Actually, the fellow showed me a Polaroid of it," Sutton told me. "Inheritance from an uncle, so he said."

"You didn't offer to buy it?"

"No. It's not Duplisea's best, you want the truth. I might have taken it on consignment, but the man wanted cash on the barrelhead, this instant. Wouldn't leave an address or phone number in case I changed my mind, not even a name. I kind of suspected the painting might be hot."

"What did this man look like?"

"He was rather a pretty fellow. Tall, fair-haired, a little gray around the edges. Looked a bit haggard for my taste, though—like he'd been under a lot of stress and strain lately. That'd figure, wouldn't it, if he's pushing stolen goodies."

I thanked Sutton, hung up and said good-bye again to Darlene.

The meter maid hadn't resisted the challenge. I walked out of Hammerwood just in time to see her shove a forty-dollar greeting under my windshield wiper. I ripped it out, balled it up and tossed it under the passenger seat.

I drove down Union Street, heading toward Van Ness where I would cut across town to the Tenderloin. The fog had totally dissipated, and shoppers were out in force to enjoy the Saturday sunshine. No doubt it would be a great business day for the neighborhood stores.

Which was why it seemed strange and sad, as I passed Deborah's boutique, to see that the neon butterfly was dark and a sign on the door said CLOSED.

"Right here's where I found her." Sparky stopped halfway down the alley and aimed a stubby finger at a spot beside an overflowing dumpster. "Looked like one of them fairy-tale princesses, that pretty dress, all them golden curls."

"Only ain't no handsome prince ever gonna wake her up," the woman with him said. She hugged herself with her skinny arms. "Take more'n a kiss to help that lady."

I stared at the place where Deborah Collington's body had lain. Scraps of old newspaper, crumbs of plastic fast-food cartons, dog droppings, a litter of broken glass. Someone had smeared obscenities along the wall bounding the alley; underneath, someone else had abandoned a hypodermic needle, a plastic spoon. Weeds struggled to survive in the cracks of the pavement. There was a stench of urine and rotting garbage, intensified by the warm springtime sun.

There was no sign of Deborah here now. She'd been strangled so there were no bloodstains, and the chalk outline the cops had drawn around her body had worn away. A week ago today she'd been getting ready for the Arts and Flowers Ball. What had her mood been on her last day alive? Excited and happy at the prospect of a party? Angry and frustrated because of her fight with Peter Brockway? Late that night she'd been laughing—both Tina Margolis and Lucia Sanmarco had said so. And a few hours later she'd been dumped here, lifeless, like so much rubbish.

"Thank you for showing me," I whispered, turning, eager to be away from here. We walked back out to Turk Street. A flap of yellow police-line tape still fluttered from the edge of the corner building, along with remnants of flyers touting rock concerts, palm readers, drug rehab clinics.

The Tenderloin was changing, becoming a family neighborhood as Asian refugees moved into the residential hotels that had been the exclusive province of winos, drug addicts, elderly people down on their luck. But there was still a bar or a liquor store at just about every corner, and that's how I had searched for Sparky.

I'd left my blazer in my trunk, putting on the old brown sweater I'd worn last night as a sort of camouflage. Then I started at the liquor store closest to the alley and fanned out until I found one where the clerk was able to tell me about him: Sparky bought vodka by the pint and beef jerky by the stick, he fancied himself a natty dresser, and he hung out during the day at an Ellis Street bar called the Gold Top, hoping someone would spot him for a game of pool.

Sparky turned out to be a small man of some indeterminate age between perhaps fifty and eighty. His jeans were clean but faded, frayed at the cuffs and holey at the knees. He wore a yellowed dress shirt and a shiny blue polyester suitcoat that was two sizes too large. There was a greasy red polka-dot tie knotted at his neck and a matching handkerchief poking out of his breast pocket. He had little hair, but a matted gray beard brushed the top of his tie and his eyebrows were thick and bristly.

Nick Gardino had told me Sparky kept an eye on things in the neighborhood for the police, so I used Nick's name and a twenty-dollar bill to get his attention. Sparky snapped the bill out of my hand and agreed to show me where he'd found Deborah's body. He hoisted a battered bedroll as we started to leave the Gold Top; I suspected it went everywhere with him.

The woman probably went everywhere with him too. Sister, daughter, lover, friend—it was hard to tell their connection. She emerged from a murky corner and grabbed his arm as we headed for the door; whatever the relationship was, she didn't want me horning in on it.

Sparky introduced her as Star Sister. She was a relic from the past: dressed in layer upon layer of tattered and grubby flower-child clothing, with strings of seeds and feathers around her neck. Her feet were bare, grayed from street grime. Her hair hung loose to her waist, and in the dusky light of the bar I thought she was a kid. But out in the sunshine I could see the gray threaded through her hair and the lines etched around her glittery green eyes.

"Can't tell you much," Sparky said now. We stood at the mouth of the alley. Across Turk Street a handful of small black-haired boys, Vietnamese perhaps, or Cambodian, were playing some sort of game with a ball. "I told that cop, I didn't see nothin'. I had my gear up there at the end of the alley. The way them three buildings come together, it makes kind of like a shelter. The wind don't get up there, see. I sleep here a lot on account of that."

"Yes, I can see it would be a good place." I shuddered. What an awful place to have to call home.

"All I know is, she weren't there when I got here. Woke up in the morning and there she was, just layin' there, all cold and blue."

"What time did you . . . go to bed?"

"Gold Top closes at two. They all do. I come here right after that."

"And you didn't see or hear anything?"

He shrugged. "I was sleepin' pretty sound."

Star Sister snorted. "Huh. Passed out, more like."

He gave her a sudden, fierce look. It surprised me; his attitude toward her had been affectionate and protective, his manner in general mild. "Hush up," he commanded sharply. "You wasn't here. You don't know nothin' about it."

Her eyes darted up the alley, back to Sparky, then to the ground. She took a furtive little step backward. Sparky was lying, I realized: Star Sister had been here that night.

I turned to her, hoping to make my questions sound gentle and unthreatening. "Do you sleep here in this alley too?"

She glanced at him. "Sometimes. So what?"

"But you weren't here that night?"

She shook her head in vigorous denial.

"Then what makes you think he might have been passed out?"

"Shit, he's passed out more nights'n not." She was looking down at her feet. Her toes had found a bottle cap to play with; they were rolling it round and round. "I don't know about that night for sure."

"Where were you, if you weren't here?"

She shot another look up the alley, her eyes glistening with sudden tears. "I don't gotta tell you. You ain't no cop."

"No, I'm not. I'm just trying to find out what happened, so whoever killed that poor woman won't get away with it."

"What's it to me?" Her voice was trembling. "Why should I care, some rich bitch gets killed?"

"She ain't gettin' mixed up in this," Sparky interjected. He put his arm around her, shielding her against his body. She burrowed her face against his shoulder for an instant, then peered at me through a cascade of dull hair. Tears had made dirt-edged furrows down her face.

"You do know something, don't you," I said softly to Star Sister. "You'll feel better if you tell it." Sparky started to protest, but I stopped him. "It's her decision to make. Not yours."

Sparky spat onto the sidewalk. "Cops come down on her too much already. They bust her for sellin' junk, they haul her in for solicitin' when she ain't never done nothin' like that. I talk to cops some, they make it worth my while. But I ain't gonna let 'em come down on Star."

"They won't come down on her for helping them. You know that."

"What if the guy what did it finds out she told? He'll come back and waste her too."

"There's no way he could learn about it, not until the police have him in custody. And then he couldn't do anything to her."

"Maybe you'll tell him," he persisted. "How do we know you ain't mixed up in it?"

"No, Sparky," Star Sister said, pulling away from him. "I saw her face up there in the alley. She wasn't in on no killing."

"Don't you tell her nothin'."

She pushed her hair out of her face, giving me a sly look. "Can I get twenty bucks too?"

"Star! We showed her where. That's all we gotta do."

"You heard her. She said I could decide myself." Star Sister reached out a chapped and grubby hand. "Can I? Twenty dollars?"

I took out another twenty-dollar bill. Sparky folded his arms across his chest, looking disgusted.

Star Sister took the money and gazed at it. Gently, respectfully, she touched Andrew Jackson's cheek. Then she folded the bill four times, making precise, careful creases. It disappeared into the layers of her clothing.

"He had a hat," she said.

"What?"

"The man who left her. He wore a hat—you know, one of them businessman hats." She pantomimed a round brim, a creased crown.

A vision came before me—Allen Fraser at the funeral, his foolish fedora pulled low in his attempt at disguise. Oh, please, God, it couldn't be.

"What else did you notice about him?"

Sparky put an arm around her again. "Star—"

She shrank back against his side. "Mostly just the hat. It was real dark, you know? All I could see was like a shadow outline."

"Just the hat. Nothing more?" I felt exhausted, defeated. Don't be silly, Jess, I told myself. There are lots of hats in the world. But I couldn't shake the sudden feeling of panic. What did I really know about Allen Fraser? How much of my judgment was based on wishful thinking, on silly assumptions about what any father of mine must be like?

"Well, I followed him out of the alley, you know? I didn't know he—what he had dumped there. I was gonna—I mean, I thought maybe he had money, see. But when I got to the street, he was back in his car already."

"And you saw the car?" I asked.

"Yeah, a big car. Blue."

"Was there anything unusual about it?"

She twisted her fingers in the seeds and feathers of her necklace. "It had like this little sticker on the bumper. From AmeriCar Rentals? They got an office with a big sign, near this soup kitchen I go to sometimes. So I recognized the design."

There was a screech of brakes and the blare of a horn; I whirled. The Asian kids' ball had escaped into the street, and one of the boys had dashed into the traffic to retrieve it. When he was safely back on the sidewalk I turned around again. Sparky had hoisted his bedroll to his shoulder, and he and Star Sister were shuffling off.

I stood there trembling. A big blue car, Star Sister had said. Deborah's neighbor Jerome Argyle had seen a big blue car staked out in front of her flat on the fatal night. And the man driving it had been wearing a hat like Allen's.

In a nearby bar I found a pay phone. I called Tyler and asked him to check AmeriCar's records. Allen claimed he had rented a small tan Ford. I had to know if he was lying.

The places were only a mile apart, yet there were worlds of difference between them. I was wearing my blazer again, yet entering Friedberg's Fine Jewelry I felt as though I was dragging the dirt and stench of the Tenderloin alley behind me. I tried to picture Star Sister in here—her gray feet padding across the thick beige carpet, her fingers clutching at her seeds and feathers, her eyes gaping in bewilderment at sapphires and rubies and jade.

The Friedbergs, grandfather and grandson, were at the counter showing a tray of diamond rings to a handsome young couple. The old man looked up as the door chime announced my arrival. Twinkling with recognition, he excused himself from the group to come and greet me.

"Ah, Miss Sherlock Holmes. Such a pleasure," he said. He was dressed as he had been yesterday, in what was no doubt his uniform: the black suit, the white shirt, the black string tie.

"Today perhaps I can sell you a trinket or two?" he asked. "Or is this once again"—his voice dropped to a conspiratorial whisper—"an official detective mission?"

"I'm afraid so. I was hoping you could tell me about these stones." I showed him the two emeralds I had taken from the hold of George Sanmarco's model ship.

"Ah, yes." He held up one of the tiny beveled rectangles to let the light flow through. "You are sure this is for a murder investigation?" he asked, smiling. "You have not concocted some fanciful tale to amuse an old man? I would prefer to think that you have a gentleman friend who treats you to such elegant things. You are perhaps a little suspicious of his generosity, so you are checking up."

I laughed. "If only that were true."

"Ah, a great pity. Come with me." He led me back to his brightly lit lab, where I sat on a tall stool while he made his inspection. He was humming—a cheery, flat little tune. But as he worked the song slowed, faltered, finally died. When he looked up his shaggy white brows were pulled together in a deep frown.

"Where did you get these, Miss Sherlock Holmes?"

"They're not real," I said.

He shook his head regretfully. "It is just as well that they were not given to you by a gentleman friend. For then I would have the sad duty of informing you that your lover was not to be trusted."

"They came from a man named Guillermo Reyes."

"Pah! Him!" The black eyes blazed. "The Buenaventura Bandit, my grandson calls him. The Colombia Crook."

"You've dealt with him?"

"In the past, but no longer. He is a wholesaler of emeralds, but also he owns a factory for making synthetic gems. That is fine, but with him the two businesses are too closely connected. One can never be sure what one is getting from Mr. Reyes."

"Do you know where I can reach him?"

"In Colombia I presume. We keep no files on bandits. Please, permit an old man to give you some advice. Yesterday you ask about George Sanmarco; today, Guillermo Reyes. These are not suitable men for a charming young lady like you. Now Joseph—my grandson, you have met him here—he is a fine young man, a good family, a prosperous career awaits him in this firm."

I decided I'd better head off the doting grandpa before he turned matchmaker. "I don't want to keep you. You've been very generous with your time. Thank you."

Mr. Friedberg stared down at the two green stones in his palm. "Yesterday, the magnificent necklace, ah yes, that was a treasure. But these—pah, they are trash. Skillfully cut, I will grant you, and well colored. For those who are satisfied with costume jewelry, they would do." His face showed what he thought of those people. "But for someone who understands true beauty—nothing but trash."

He handed the bits of glass back to me. "You will not blind any serpents with these, Miss Sherlock Holmes."

TWENTY SIX

"Jess! Baby! Glad you could take time out of your busy schedule!" Evan Krausgill flashed his impossibly white teeth at me, tossed his arm around my shoulder and swept me into the hallway of the former Sunday school wing. The diamond stud in his ear had been exchanged for a little gold hoop, like a pirate's. He was wearing tight jeans and an equally tight vermilion polo shirt, the better to show off his firmly muscled physique.

"Are these break-ins a stroke of luck or what?" he said. "I know that sounds crass, but hey, they gave us an excuse to get together, right? Let's celebrate. There's a very pleasant white wine in the fridge."

"No, thanks." I wanted to keep this as businesslike as possible. "Tell me what happened."

He pushed open a door. Tacked to it was one of the promotional posters: the galloping umber shadow of the horse, the blood-red letters.

"In here. I'll show you."

The first thing I noticed was the sound: *thdr-thdr-thdr-thdr-THWAP-thdr-THWAP.* Next I became aware of pungent smells of sawdust and turpentine.

The room was a large carpentry shop. Big double-hung windows, gridded with small panes, let in lots of light. There was a table saw, a crosscut saw, a radial arm saw. A workbench stretched along one wall, with hand tools hanging from pegs above it. In one corner was a bin of lumber scraps, in another a rack that held huge cloth-covered flats like overgrown artists' canvases. Linoleum tiles, once gray, were now speckled with color—brown, green, blue, here and there some orange and purple. That made me comfortable; I always feel at home in places with paint spattered on the floor.

In the middle of the space stood a bulky table and three clumsy, overscaled wooden chairs—furnishings for *Blood Wedding*, no doubt. On stage, with the right lighting, they would probably look like ornately carved Spanish antiques. But here in the harsh fluorescent glare, you could see how stock moldings and paint had been used to create the illusion.

"This is our scene shop," Evan announced unnecessarily. "Used to be three classrooms. We knocked out the walls to make one big space."

A contraption that looked like a beer keg was the source of the odd *thdr-thdr* noise. A rubber hose snaked out from it; the end was held by a ponytailed fellow in grubby workclothes who was repairing a flat. The *THWAP* came as he pushed the gizmo at the end of the hose against the flat's frame.

"A compressor," Evan explained. "It drives the power stapler."

"I thought you weren't using scenery for this show."

"Just a few flats to screen the stage entrances. Mike here is making sure they're in good shape before we start painting them."

"Is this the room that was broken into?" The shop looked disordered, but no more than you might expect a week before opening night. Nothing to resemble, say, the derangement of Deborah Collington's apartment.

"Yeah." Evan stood back, arms crossed over his chest, a slight smile twitching beneath his black mustache as he watched me.

The only thing that appeared odd was one of the windows. Cardboard had been taped over the pane right under the latch.

"That's where your thief got in."

"Very good." Evan clapped his hands as if in delight. "You *are* a real detective."

"I wasn't aware this was a test." I walked over to the window and looked out. About ten feet back a high wooden fence separated the theater property from the backyards of the houses on the next street. Scraggly bushes grew in the strip in between; some of the twigs looked as if they might have been broken by something moving through them. The windowsill was only about four feet above the ground.

Evan moved up beside me. I felt his hand come to rest between my shoulder blades. I shifted, subtly I hoped, to get out of reach.

"I was the first one here yesterday morning," he said. "I came into the shop to get something and right away I see, hey, the window's been smashed. Glass all over the floor. I called Mike"—he jerked his head toward the young man working on the flat—"and he brought in some glass to fix it. Nothing else was disturbed so we didn't worry about it much. Figured it was the neighborhood kids, you know, high spirits getting out of hand. But this morning, damn if the same pane isn't smashed again. It would be simple to reach in and unlock the window. Then someone could just raise it and climb in." He flipped the latch and shoved up the window to show me how easy it was.

"But why, if nothing was taken?"

"That's what you're here to figure out. Think about it: a glamorous private eye shows up asking about a star actress who's just been murdered. Then that very night we get broken into. Damn funny coincidence, right?"

He slammed the window shut and turned to me, eyes gleaming. "Wouldn't it be great if we solved Deb's murder right here? The media would go wild! Already our advance sales for *Blood Wedding* are way up because of all the press attention. I was thinking, it's too bad that if she had to die, she couldn't have been killed here so we could really capitalize on this. We need the publicity lots more than Lois Whittlesey Putnam and the Arts Council."

I stared at him. The idiot was serious. I could just imagine it—the

PR director murders the star in order to generate publicity and funds for the financially strapped theater. A preposterous thought—or was it? I made a sound somewhere between a laugh and an angry sputter.

Evan looked hurt. "Hey, I loved Deb as much as the next guy. More even. But I can't change the fact she got killed. We've been handed a situation, it's up to us to make the most of it."

It wasn't worth a reply. I sat on one of the immense Spanish chairs and changed the subject before I could get really, fruitlessly mad. "Might Deborah have come by here for some reason after the Arts and Flowers Ball? She seems to have been doing some running around between the time she left the dance and the time she was killed."

He perched on the workbench, which made him higher than me. "She couldn't have gotten in. No key. Only a few of us have keys."

"How about a locker or something? Did she keep anything here, something someone might have wanted?"

"Nah, we don't have any—wait a minute." He snapped his fingers. "Brockway's closet."

"What?"

"Jeez, how could I have forgotten? Peter Brockway rents this little storage room from us. He says he'd rather pay the money to the theater than some self-store operation. He probably does it because he feels guilty about being too broke to fork over any really big bucks after we made him a board member and all."

"May I see it?"

"Sure, let's go." Evan hopped down from the workbench. He led me down the corridor to a door close to the stage entrance. It was secured by a combination padlock on a hasp. "This is it." He rapped on the door. "Nobody home."

I didn't laugh. A little thrill of excitement shot through me. There were answers behind this door; I could feel it. I twirled the padlock dial, listened hard to the clicks, wishing I knew more about locksmithing.

"What does Brockway keep in here?" I asked.

"Haven't the foggiest." The glint in his eye reflected the larceny that no doubt dwelled in his heart. "We can find out, though. Wait here."

He disappeared into the scene shop, coming back with a hammer and a stout screwdriver. "There are advantages to having a well-equipped workshop just down the hall," he said. Fitting the screwdriver blade against the top edge of the hasp, he began to pound.

"Look, Evan—" I started to protest. I wanted badly to see what was behind this door, but if I was going to indulge in breaking and entering I would rather do it without causing such obvious damage.

"We could take the door off the hinges but this'll be faster. Screws on this thing are probably pretty short." He had wedged the screwdriver behind the hasp and was wiggling, pushing, prying it. With a ripping sound, the screws tore out of the wood.

Evan stood back and grinned. "After you."

The hallway light revealed a small, shadowed, windowless room filled with dim, boxy shapes. In the old church days this space had likely stored candles, choir robes, offertory plates.

Evan nudged me inside ahead of him and slammed the door, plunging us into darkness. "Aha, me pretty," he intoned in a dreadful matinee-villain accent, "at last I haff you vhere I vant you." I felt a groping hand on my arm; another poked at my ribcage.

Wonderful—trapped in the blackness with someone who assumes his amorous attentions are as welcome as a lottery win. With someone who thinks murder is a clever publicity stunt.

"Evan! Cut it out! Right now. Open the door. Is there a light in here?"

"Jeez, lady, just a little joke—"

"Now," I commanded. A light flashed on, a bare bulb in an overhead socket. "The door," I said.

"I can't open the door. What if Mike comes out and sees us sleuthing around in here?"

It would hardly be a secret with the padlock dangling uselessly from the doorframe. I shoved Evan aside and opened the door myself.

The boxy shapes proved to be cartons. Dozens of them, stacked to the ceiling, all imprinted with the Success Videos logo. I hauled one off the top of a stack and nearly tumbled backward; it was heavier than I expected. It was sealed as if ready for shipping. An address label directed it to Peregrine Video Stores.

I used my Swiss army knife to slice the carton open. Videotapes. *Time Management for the Busy Executive. The Power System for Stress Control. Negotiating a Better Compensation Package*—maybe I should watch that one and have a little chat with Tyler.

"Aw, shit." Evan looked disgusted. "All that work, and there's nothing here but overflow from Brockway's warehouse."

"I'm not so sure that's what it is." I examined more of the cartons. Shipping labels on every one: Peregrine Video Stores, Raleigh Enterprises, Executive Development Systems—all of them names from the past-due invoices that had so upset Brockway's bookkeeper, poor moon-faced Leonard Hoffmeyer. No wonder the customers had refused to pay.

I worked my way around the room. Tucked behind a low stack of cartons I came upon a large, flat, rectangular something, wrapped in brown kraft paper. I ran my fingers along the top edge.

"What's that?" Evan asked.

"I don't know."

"Let's find out." Grinning again, he started to rip off the paper cover. "Could be a clue."

"Wait! Don't damage it."

Evan grabbed a corner and tugged. "Let's take it to the greenroom. Right across from the shop. We can unwrap it and get a good look."

There seemed to be no choice. Besides, I was as curious as he was. Together we wrestled the awkward thing from its hiding place.

The greenroom turned out to be a lounge. Overstuffed chairs, game tables, a kitchenette unit, an array of photographs from past productions. The walls were beige, the curtains blue, the upholstery maroon vinyl.

"Greenroom?" I laughed.

"Theater talk. It's the traditional name for the place where the actors relax when they're offstage. Green paint was probably cheap in Shakespeare's day."

We leaned the big flat shape against the ungreen wall. Evan was ready to tear into the wrapping, but I stopped him. Better that the package should still look more or less intact when we put it back. I slit the tape at the corners with my knife and carefully peeled the paper back.

It was upside down but there was still no mistaking it. Even if the spiky signature hadn't given it away I would have recognized Gerard Duplisea's work: that exploding double helix of chartreuse, orange, magenta, saffron. The one other time I had seen this painting, it had been hanging above the black lacquered credenza in Deborah Collington's dining room.

Evan wrinkled his pretty face at it. "I can see why Brockway hid this thing away. Ug-lee!"

"You may think so. It happens that this fellow is hot stuff in the art market right now." And the prices he gets stretch well into five figures, I added, but silently—no point in putting ideas of thievery in Evan's head.

In fact, I realized, Evan might have stolen this painting already, from Deborah's home. He could have hidden it in Brockway's storeroom and led me to it because—why? Well, because he wanted to plant suspicion on someone else and Brockway was handy. Because they were conniving on some scheme and had had a falling out. There were lots of possible becauses. Evan might have staged this whole little drama—broken window, padlock, screwdriver, and all—to throw me off track.

But that didn't really make sense. What made sense was—a scenario popped into my head, one possible solution to the Pacific Playhouse break-in.

Suppose it was Brockway who ransacked Deborah's flat, hunting for something that would tie him to her murder. Or searching for the necklace, thinking it would solve his financial problems—he wouldn't have known that the one supposedly found on the doorstep was just a cheap copy. Perhaps the ripping apart of everything had been a ruse.

Of course he can't find the necklace because the police have it. But this painting is there, and however dreadful it looks, it's valuable. He grabs it, planning to stash it in his storeroom until he can sell it. He has no keys to the theater, yet he doesn't want to risk carting in stolen goods during the day when someone might see him. So he breaks the window and—

But what about last night? It was the same mode of entry, it had to be the same person. Why would Brockway come back?

"Come on, Evan, let's put this away. Got any tape?"

Together we rewrapped the painting. As we maneuvered it back into its hiding place, Evan dislodged a carton, which landed on my toes.

"Whoops, sorry. Bet that smarts."

But this one wasn't heavy—it weighed hardly anything. Nor was it sealed like the others; someone had closed it by weaving the flaps together. I shook it; something shifted inside. I had a fleeting picture of Peter Brockway outside his office building, clutching a carton to his chest as he jogged through the dusk toward his car. If this was the same box, his bringing it here could explain the second break-in.

"Hey, what's in there?" Evan demanded, eager as an eight-year-old on Christmas morning.

I picked up the carton. Whatever it held, this time I didn't want him panting over my shoulder while I found out. It was bad enough that he'd seen the painting.

"Thanks, Evan. You've been a big help."

"Wait a minute. Aren't we going to open that?"

"Not here. I, uh . . ." Think fast, Jess. "Look, Evan, you may put yourself in danger if you know too much. I shouldn't have let you get this far involved."

He looked thrilled by the prospect. "A little danger doesn't bother me. Besides, wouldn't you be in danger too?"

"It's part of my job. It's not part of yours."

"Does this mean it's Peter who did Deb in?" Evan braced himself in the doorframe, blocking my way.

"I don't know what it means. Let me by."

"What about our break-ins? We're going to solve them, right? What's our next step?"

"*My* next step is to do some investigating. *Your* next step is to stay out of the way." I could see it now—if he tried to help, he'd do it with the whole Channel Five News team in tow.

"Come on, you can't take that." He snatched at the box. I yanked it away. Thrown off balance, he toppled into a stack of cartons. I dodged around him and pushed my way out.

"What if Brockway finds it missing?" he wailed. "What if he thinks I—"

"Too late to worry about that," I called back. "He'll know something's up when he sees the lock ripped off the door."

I stepped outside. Evan came loping after me.

"But what are you going to do?"

"I can't tell you, Evan," I said with exasperation. "Don't you watch TV? No detective ever solved a case by telegraphing every move in advance." I didn't bother to mention that I had only the remotest idea what my moves would be.

Ocean Beach was four blocks away, beyond Evan Krausgill's prying range. I parked downhill from the Cliff House, overlooking the long expanse of sand, and opened my window. Fresh air might clear my muddled head.

It wasn't spring out here. A thick bank of pewter-gray fog hung heavily on the water, obscuring the horizon. Ragged clouds scuttled eastward over Golden Gate Park. Sand and trash blew across the road. The wind, strong and cold, carried the briny smell of seaweed. The occasional people strolling on the beach were wearing jeans and parkas with the hoods pulled up.

Below me, a few intrepid surfers bobbed on the tide, as sleek as seals in their wetsuits, patiently enduring the freezing of buns and toes as they waited for the payoff—that one grand ninety-second joyride that would make it all worthwhile. It suddenly occurred to me that detective work followed much the same pattern.

The carton waited on the seat beside me. Was this where the payoff would be? I almost didn't want to open it—Pandora had gotten into a lot of trouble that way. I closed my eyes, thinking longingly of my bed. My head filled with the hum of traffic, the squeal of gulls, the soughing of surf. For a moment at the theater I'd had a wisp of an idea, a solution. But now I couldn't think what it was.

What if the box held the wrong answers, answers I didn't want to know? What if Allen Fraser was somehow implicated after all?

No, he had to be innocent—for my sake. My father had always been a dark void in my life, one that Roger, as dearly as I loved him, could never really change. Now I had someone to fill that emptiness. I couldn't bear to have him be a villain.

He's not the same man now, Uncle Jack had said. But how could I know? I had no memory of his hitting my mother, no memory of him at all. Except for the fleeting recollection of a stranger, the man who gave me Crazy the Clown on the night he came to beg my mother for a second chance.

Mom had never let me know about my father. She had refused to tell me the truth, to allow me to make my own judgments. She thought she was protecting me by burying him deep in the shadows, but that protection had brought its own burden of hurt.

I sat for a long while, staring through the windshield as the breakers smashed against rocks and sand.

Okay Jess, I sighed, get hold of yourself. Act professional. I tugged at the carton flaps.

Brockway must have grabbed whatever box had been handiest. He didn't need such a large one for the little heap of papers inside. Last Friday's page from his desk calendar—the one with *C-Day* scrawled in large letters—floated on top of the rest.

Beneath the documents I uncovered a litter of jewelry. A string of pearls, a pair of hammered-gold earrings and, wedged in a corner, the beautiful ring with the off-center emerald and the three small diamonds. But something seemed to be missing.

I closed my eyes, trying to summon a picture of Deborah's dresser with the jewelry strewn on top. A bracelet, that was it—a chunky silver-and-onyx bracelet. My mind's-eye picture shifted, showing me a nervous Tina Margolis fidgeting with a bracelet on her wrist. Did she know it was Deborah's? Had Brockway shown her the jewelry and let her choose? Surely anyone with sense would have picked the ring.

I lifted out the papers and flipped through them. Correspondence with Investech, the venture capital firm. Copies of financial statements. Invoices addressed to Peregrine Video Stores and other customers—the same invoices that Leonard Hoffmeyer had copied and brought to me. Wait—did that paper say Sanmarco?

Yes—it was a sheet of George's personal stationery. This was the document that had so upset Lucia: a letter of agreement spelling out the terms of a loan made by George Victor Sanmarco to Peter S. Brockway in the amount of fifty thousand dollars, purpose unspecified, collateral as provided for in a separate agreement. The letter, signed by both men, was dated about a month ago, prior to the filing of Bernard Tauber's lawsuit. Repayment in full was due last Friday, the day before Deborah Collington's death.

There was a second page, handwritten in purple ink:

As collateral for this loan, I pledge the diamond and emerald necklace given to me by George V. Sanmarco. Should repayment not be made in accordance with the agreement, I will return said necklace to Mr. Sanmarco. This necklace is known to all parties and it is agreed that its value is more than sufficient to discharge this debt.

There were three signatures on this sheet—Sanmarco's, Brockway's and a snaky squiggle in the same purple. It was illegible but it was clear to me whose it was.

So that's what had happened. The loan had not been paid back. But rather than turn the necklace over to Sanmarco as promised, Deborah gave it to Allen Fraser, apparently on a whim. Later that night she got in touch with both her fiancé and her ex-husband, laughing—gloating, Tina Margolis had said—about something she had done. The impulsive gift was a doublecross of Brockway and Sanmarco.

But she was going to doublecross them anyway. I couldn't believe she'd gone to the trouble of having a duplicate made with fake stones just to have a souvenir. No doubt George had had the original appraised when he bought it; if the necklace he got back from Deborah was identical, why would he suspect that it was not the same one?

That left one big question: What happened to the loan money? Brockway had expected to have cash enough by last Friday—C-Day—to pay off the phony invoices, make his company look good to Investech and repay Sanmarco, all at the same time.

What was the fastest way to turn over that large a sum and make enough profit to do Brockway some good? A drug deal. I remembered the bag of white powder I'd found with the necklace in Deborah's safe, and the ambiguous note that had accompanied them, signed by Guillermo Reyes.

C-Day—Cocaine Day?

One of the surfers caught a wave. I watched him ride, tipping his body this way and that to maintain his precarious balance, until he vanished in a burst of white foam. After several long seconds, I saw him pop up near the rocks and start paddling out for another try.

My elusive thoughts about a solution to this case were starting to drift back.

I wasn't sure of the details, but it was obvious who had reason to want both Deborah and Sanmarco dead. I turned the key in the ignition. When I was through with giving my statement at the Hall of Justice, I would go up to the jail to visit Allen. Finally I had something to tell him that might give him hope.

TWENTY SEVEN

"Good news," I said as cheerily as I could into the mouthpiece. I had to speak up in order to hear myself over the clamor of the Saturday visiting crowd.

Allen stared blankly through the glass. He didn't say a word. His gray eyes held no light at all.

I tried again. "I found out who broke into Deborah's flat."

Today he was wearing one of the jail-issue jumpsuits—orange, shapeless, so much too large that I could barely detect the shrug of his shoulders. Damn it, how about a little response here, a little enthusiasm?

I explained what I had discovered at the theater. "Of course it doesn't prove he killed her. But it means he had a motive. And his alibi is shaky, so—"

Allen shook his head as if he couldn't take it in. "But why kill her now? What would he gain? Later maybe, after they were married and he would inherit . . ."

"She betrayed him," I said. "I'm not sure how, but she took all that money and left him holding the bag. It was a desperate situation for him, and she not only betrayed him but gloated about it."

"Betrayed," he murmured. "Poor Brad. If that's how she died . . . it will be so hard on him. I told you about him, that time in school . . . Brad always says it wasn't getting punished—expelled—that made

246

him so furious. It was being betrayed. That breaking of trust. To have his daughter do that to someone . . ." He finished the thought with a sigh, shuffled his feet, dropped his glance to the floor.

"It's an awful feeling," I agreed. I knew it well—the rage, the helplessness, the shame, the disgust with yourself for having been willing to trust. I had felt it one day when I left P&O early because I was coming down with the flu. Aching and exhausted, I walked into my apartment, mine and Dan's, and discovered him in bed with an Art Institute sophomore, a curvy little sculpture major with jagged blond hair. He was astounded that I got upset, that I threw things. When he moved out the next day, for the final time, it was her place he went to. I didn't know where he was now.

"Are you going to tell Gardino about this?" At last Allen was looking at me.

"Not yet. All I've got is speculation. He just warned me again to stay far away from this case. I was downstairs giving my statement about finding Sanmarco's body and—"

"Body?" Allen looked shocked. I told him about my grisly discovery.

Pain fought with hope on his face. "But . . . doesn't that mean . . . it proves I didn't kill anyone."

"You didn't kill Sanmarco. Gardino doesn't see that the same person must have done both murders. George found out a week or two ago that he was being sued—someone named Bernard Tauber. The motive might be there."

"Tauber?" The flicker of life had burned out again. "Means nothing to me. The painting you found—did you tell Gardino about that?"

"Confess to breaking and entering? No, I need more, some definitive proof about the murder. I'm going to see if I can arrange a little confrontation." I sketched out a plan I had worked up on my way to the Hall of Justice.

Allen frowned. "But—won't that be dangerous?"

"I can handle it."

"Maybe you should get someone to help you."

"Why? It will be easier to do it alone. I'll arouse less suspicion."

"I'll worry about you. Get Brad to back you up. Or those partners of yours, that man Parks. And O'Meara."

"O'Meara? Haven't you been paying attention these past few days? O'Meara's a *dog!* An Irish setter."

He tried to brush it off. "Oh. Of course . . ."

"Where do you get off, anyway, worrying about me?"

"You're my daughter, Jessica, naturally I—"

"I could have been in danger thousands of times over the last thirty years, and where were you? What did you care? Talk about *betrayed!*" I could hear my voice rising in volume, in pitch.

"Jessica, I never—"

My whole body was rising. I was on my toes, bracing myself against the glass.

"Betrayed! That's exactly the word. Betrayed. My mother—God, what you did to my mother!"

"One time, Jessica! One awful mistake. Must I pay forever for—"

"You have no concept what it was like. Everything in our lives was formed by what you did! And you—you were gone—three thousand goddamn miles away. And you have the nerve to say you're *worried?*"

The crowd had fallen silent; I could feel the heat of their eyes. I didn't care.

"Jessica, please!"

"Jessica! You don't even know my name. No one calls me Jessica. I'm Jess! Just Jess! Uncle Jack tells you everything about me—didn't he even tell you my name? It's Jess! Jess! Jess!" I pounded on the glass to punctuate it. *Bam! Bam! Bam!*

A guard grabbed my arm, hustled me off. I looked back at Allen. Behind the glass he was crying, sobbing openly, not trying to hide his anguish.

At last, I thought. Thank God, at last, at last. I realized I had been wanting to make him do that from the moment I met him. To make him share my pain. I had been wanting it for thirty years.

■   ■   ■

I felt awful. I hunched into a corner of the down elevator and berated myself for blowing my cool. I had always been so proud of my ability to hide my feelings, to control my emotions. It's what makes me good at detective work, that containment, that discipline.

Mom taught it to me. She was so incredibly self-contained. I never saw her angry, never saw her exhilarated, and I learned to respect her aversion to strong emotion by never showing any myself. Now, with a pang, I understood that beneath her calm surface, her experience with my father had always festered.

What if she hadn't been protecting me? What if her refusal to let me know him had been a way to control me, to enroll me in her own pain? Uncle Jack had described how she built a cold rock wall between herself and Allen, and I couldn't blame her for that. But for years after he left she continued to hide behind it, sealing herself from the world. Even—the thought was piercing—even from me.

She had never been able, or willing, to give up the pain. It was, I realized, her principal legacy to me.

That and her love for art.

A sudden, fierce longing burned through me. I was a kid again. She and I were making one of many Saturday-morning museum visits, and she was showing me magic—how Vermeer molded figures with nothing but light and shadow, how gardens and cathedrals emerged glowing from Monet's dashes of color. And there was that proud day when she had finally siphoned off enough money from our meager household budget to buy her Chagall print. We toasted our good fortune with cups of cocoa. The print was now hanging on Roger's dining room wall.

And always she had encouraged my scribbles, had stretched the budget even farther to send me to art classes. It was her way of showing love.

The elevator became loaded with bodies as it descended floor by floor. The cramped space filled with odors: sweat, last night's garlic, peppermint gum, drugstore perfumes. I felt dizzy. People glanced at me; I must have looked dreadful. They quickly looked away.

What I found wonderful about art was the chance it gave me to express things I never felt comfortable showing any other way. The hardest thing I had to learn at the Art Institute was how to allow myself that freedom, that letting go. In my second year I had a great professor, a huge white-haired bear of a man, who pulled it out of me, who taught me how to break through the restraints and blocks, how to unbox my feelings and put them on canvas. Until then my work was neat and tidy but lifeless, afraid of its own vision, void of the passion that makes something art.

But I could only make it happen in my paintings. That was my problem with Dan, the unbridgeable gap—I saw it now with shimmering clarity. He was full of emotion, of drama, of wild and abandoned self-expression. I was both attracted and repelled by his exuberance, as he was by my reserve. He always argued that I was holding out on him; maybe I really was. He kept trying to squeeze himself into every corner of my life, my thoughts, my emotions. I began to hate him because he made me feel things and then abused those feelings.

Forget Deborah Collington and George Sanmarco and whoever killed them. I needed to hide in my studio and paint. To hold that reassuring brush, to let the colors show me their homes on the canvas. To spread my feelings out on that huge flat rectangle where I could deal with them. The hell with this case anyway.

The elevator thumped to a halt at the first floor. When everyone else had exited I peeled myself away from the back wall. I walked through the marble lobby, past the security checkpoint, out the Hall of Justice doors. The abrupt shift into sunshine made me squint.

"Jessica?"

I looked up. Brad Collington greeted me by gallantly tipping an imaginary hat.

"Oh. Brad. I thought you'd gone back to New York."

"I changed my flight to tomorrow. I wanted to see your father before I left."

"Good. He'll appreciate having a friend."

Collington started to say something more but didn't. Perhaps something about my appearance discouraged conversation—although he looked at least as haggard as I must have.

"I went by Bumblebee," I said. "You closed it."

He shrugged. "It seemed best. I went over the books with the lawyer, and the place was hardly holding its own. In fact it looked like Debbie was planning to shut it down herself."

Neither of us could think of more to say. We watched each other warily for a moment, then he walked on inside. At least he was now on Allen's side.

In front of me Allen's image loomed, weeping in his glass cage. I was dismayed, yet thrilled, to feel another surge of satisfaction.

I had never even known that I was feeling such pain.

TWENTY EIGHT

I twisted down the rearview mirror so I could see my face instead of the rusty blue station wagon parked behind me. Not that my face was much more attractive than the beat-up old car. Wan skin, splotchy cheeks, red eyes sunk in dark hollows. I wiped it with one of those foil-wrapped towelettes, tugged a brush through my unruly hair, dabbed on fresh makeup. Which lipstick would enliven me more, the coral or the plum? Which color would Kit Cormier find more appealing?

The mirror, always merciless, told me that if irresistible was what I was after, I had a long way to go. I pushed at my hair some more, got out of the car and headed down the sidewalk toward Kit's studio. My heart was beating a tattoo against my ribs, loud enough to resound all over South Park. As I pushed the bell, a gust of goddamn wind tossed my hair in twelve different directions.

I thought my memory might have been exaggerating, but Kit Cormier's eyes really were a brilliant winter-sky blue. There he was, standing in the doorway, wearing jeans and a khaki shirt with epaulettes that emphasized his wide shoulders. I was peripherally aware of the tousled brown hair, the neat beard, the strong square hands. But I couldn't focus on anything but that incredible blue.

He greeted me warmly. Maybe—please!—he was genuinely glad to see me. But perhaps that was just his manner, an egalitarian friendliness available to anybody. Or just to women. Or . . . I gave myself a mental shake. Stop it, Jess. This is a business call. You have something to accomplish here.

He led me to the sitting area in the corner of his studio. A fuzzy green sofa with lumpy-looking cushions, three or four director's chairs, a low round table covered with proof sheets and glassine envelopes containing strips of negatives. He took some beer from a mini-refrigerator and poured it into a pair of wineglasses.

Our fingers touched as he handed me one. An electric current shot up my arm and through my whole body.

"It's not Dom Perignon, but it's the best I've got on hand. Wasn't there some brand that called itself the champagne of beers?" He lifted his glass in a salute. "Here's to a successful investigation."

His smile would have melted chocolate, I'm sure. It certainly melted me.

"I'll drink to that," I said.

Deborah Collington seemed to watch us from the wall. It was that wonderful photo—Deborah vibrant, laughing, haloed with sunshine. I scanned the desk for the other, possibly more important picture—Sara, the girl with coffee-colored hair. It was gone. My heart jumped. They'd had a quarrel? She was ancient history and Kit had finally tossed her photo out?

No, wait. There it was. It had merely been moved to the round table. Damn, damn, damn. Definitely just a business call.

"The reason I'm here—"

"I'm all ready for you," Kit said, tapping a magazine on his desk. It was the issue of *Bay Breeze.* "I dug this out this morning, when you said you were coming over. It's an extra copy. Here, give it to Deborah's parents."

"Her parents?"

"That's why you want it, isn't it? You said the other day you were investigating for her family, so they could find out what her life was like. I should have thought to give you the spare copy then."

"Oh, yes. Right." I flipped through the pages until I found the merry band of revelers aboard the *Esmeralda.* "They're having such a good time here. It's hard to believe that two of these people are dead now."

"Two of them?" Kit's eyebrows lifted in surprise.

I told him about George Sanmarco's homicide. "The thing is, Guillermo Reyes must be involved somehow. Everywhere I turn in this case, his name comes up."

"You think he killed them? But I thought they caught the guy who murdered Deborah. That Mystery Stranger."

"The police have made a mistake. He's not guilty."

"And Reyes is?"

"He's guilty of something. Maybe not murder—I have an idea who did that. But he sold Deborah a necklace with fake jewels. And I'm certain he was supplying her with cocaine."

"That's enough to hang him for." Kit scowled, a cloud darkening the sunny blue of his eyes. The other day, too, an expression of pain had flashed across his face when the subject of cocaine came up.

"I agree," I told him. "But if he's in Colombia—"

"He's not—he's here in the city."

"He's *what?*"

"Yep. I just saw him last night."

"Where?" I asked eagerly.

"Lois Whittlesey Putnam threw a reception for that Latin American dance troupe that's appearing at the Opera House. I was there to take pictures. Reyes was quite the center of attention, being a friend of Deborah's. You should have heard everyone buzzing away about her murder. Most of them had been to the Arts and Flowers Ball, so they felt a connection, like it was their own personal juicy little crime."

"I've got to talk to Reyes. Any idea where I can locate him?"

"I heard him tell someone he was staying on his yacht. He had it at the Heron Point Marina when I did the *Bay Breeze* shoot. You know, in Brisbane, down near the airport. Wait a minute, there's a column about the party in this morning's *Chronicle*. The grande Madame Putnam is a genius at getting her name in print. Maybe it says something about Reyes."

He found the newspaper on the table and held it out. I took it, trembling. All day I had avoided the paper, averting my eyes as I passed the vending boxes. The story I had been dodging was on page one above the fold, as I'd known it would be. MYSTERY STRANGER FOUND, screamed the headline. NEW YORKER ARRESTED FOR COLLINGTON MURDER.

"Oh shit," I said softly, sinking into one of Kit's director's chairs. Now that it was in my hands I couldn't let go. I read the sad tale from beginning to end.

"What's the matter?" Kit asked when I was done.

"Nothing. Why?" I laid the newspaper on the table.

"Your face looked, well, odd, while you were reading. Like you were—forgive me if I'm prying—like you wanted to cry."

I raised a hand to flick away any possible tattletale tear. "No, I didn't."

"You're not glad they caught the guy? It makes your job easier, doesn't it? Saves you a lot of work."

"I—oh damn." And like a silly, stupid, idiot fool, suddenly I *was* crying after all.

"You know him, is that it? Is he someone special?" Kit crouched beside the director's chair, bringing his face to my level. He handed me a handkerchief. I clutched it eagerly, blotting it at my face.

"Oh goddamn it to hell," I said, and before I knew what I was doing I had blurted out to this man, this almost total stranger, this person I had hoped to impress, the whole long sordid saga of Allen Fraser and my mother and their marriage and me. The story I hadn't even been able to tell Lauren, one of my best friends. That I hadn't really let myself share with my family or my P&O colleagues who were like family too. I told it between great gulping sobs as I twisted and wrung his handkerchief in my hands.

Kit sat quietly on the floor and listened. He didn't interrupt, didn't ask questions, just let me rattle on until I ran out of energy and words and tears. When I had finally been silent for a moment he said, "Your father must love you."

255

That made me ready to rave again. "How can you *say* that! When for all those years he didn't even—"

"I know, I know." He grasped both of my hands to calm me. "But your mother ordered him out of your lives, and he respected that. He didn't fight for custody, didn't kidnap you the way you hear so much about these days, he didn't disrupt your lives or—no, listen to me. He tried to send money, he kept up with you through this Uncle Jack you mentioned. He didn't contact you until after your mother died so she wouldn't get upset—"

"Two years! Two years he waited after she died. That's how eager he was to see me!"

"If he got in touch the minute her funeral was over you would have considered it ghoulish, right? Seems like a no-win situation to me."

"He beat her up! He battered my mother!"

"Yeah." He sighed. "That's the sticky part, all right. I can't condone that. But you did say he acknowledged the problem, spent a long time in therapy working it out."

"Damn it, Kit, I—"

"I might be all wrong, Jess—I don't know the man. But it's possible, isn't it? It could be the way I said—that in an odd way he loves you."

"Hell of a way to show love," I grumbled.

"Yes. I think . . . that's the hardest thing to do when you love someone. To leave them alone."

I looked up. Kit had let go of my hands and was gazing into a corner with that clouded look in his eyes.

"You're speaking from experience," I said. "A . . . a child of your own?"

"No." He shook his head. "My little sister. Sara. I watched out for her after our parents died. She was eighteen, on her own, but still a kid really. She was so sweet and . . . vulnerable. And she was all the family I had left." He picked up the small framed photo, stared at the girl for a moment and handed it to me.

A sister. Not a wife, not a girlfriend—thank God. I shoved the thought aside, ashamed to be letting my happy relief intrude on his pain.

"She started going with a guy who was dealing cocaine. He was at Stanford, headed for law school, charming and witty—I was really happy for her until I realized what was going on. Soon she was even more in love with the coke than she was with him. Hell, I tried the stuff myself a few times. At first I thought it gave me this incredible eye, this vision. But then I'd look at the photos when I came down from the high and they'd all be shit. So I gave it up. But Sara . . ."

How had I missed the family resemblance? As I looked at her picture, it was so clear—the arch of the brow, the blue of the eyes.

Kit went on. His voice was calm, matter-of-fact. Somehow that made his hurt seem deeper than if he'd been weeping. "It became her whole life. She turned into a different person. I couldn't bear to watch it. I tried to get her to enroll in treatment programs. She insisted she had no problem, it was her life, she was in control. We had incredible battles. Finally I dragged her forcibly to a clinic. She ran away. I never saw her again."

"And you don't know what happened to her?"

"Oh, I know." He fiddled with his shoelaces. "Couple of months later they found her in an abandoned house in Hunters Point. She'd been dead at least a week from an overdose."

"Oh Lord. How awful." I put a hand on his shoulder. He didn't pull away.

"It was a long time ago. Seven years now. Sometimes, though, I still can't help thinking—what if I'd let up on her? Not pushed so hard. Maybe she wouldn't have needed so much to prove me wrong. And then she'd be . . ." He let the thought dangle. Shaking his head he rose and walked over to the refrigerator.

"Your father—that's a different situation, I know. But the point is—it's so damn hard to know what's the right thing to do when you love someone. Maybe he did his best, like I did my best for Sara. Think about it."

I set down Sara's photo and the damp, wadded handkerchief. If only I knew the perfect, comforting thing to say. Kit had been using his pain to salve mine. I wanted to return the favor. But mine was so new, so fresh—or at least, so freshly acknowledged. Perhaps after seven years . . .

"I've done far more thinking than I care to lately," I said. "But I've got to do some more if I'm going to get him . . . my father . . . out of this mess. Whatever else, I promised him. I like to keep my promises."

I stood up, feeling thoroughly discouraged. What a jerk I was— coming here with my silly fantasies. And then instead of charming him, all I do is dump my problems on him and dredge up his sorrows.

Kit had refilled the wineglasses with beer, and he offered me one. I told him no. "I'd better get on with it. I want to see if I can track down Guillermo Reyes."

"Can I help? I'll come with you."

My spirits lifted a little. Maybe—maybe he liked me after all. Every part of me ached to say yes. But with him along, I'd be distracted by the desire to make a different sort of investigation. "I'd better go alone. You've helped a lot already."

He walked me to the door. "Kit?" I said. "You might be right about Allen—I'll have to think it through. Thank you for . . . listening. For being kind. I don't usually impose my troubles on strangers."

Kit wove his hands into my hair and smiled. The clouds vanished from his eyes; for a moment I lost myself in that clear winter blue.

"Tell you what then," he said. "Let's not be strangers."

His kiss set all my nerve ends zinging, clear to my toes.

TWENTY NINE

"*Esmeralda?* She's that big mother out at the end." The kid leaned against the fuel pump and pointed down the line of boats. Guillermo Reyes's yacht was longer and higher than any of the others. Its cabin was cream and teak, its hull a deep, rich emerald green. Sun spangled the water. Heron Point Marina was on the bay, well away from the ocean fog.

The boy was probably about fifteen, though he looked younger. He was shirtless, with jeans slung low on skimpy hips. His scrawny chest was all ridges and grooves; I had to resist an urge to count his ribs. He had a huge frizzy halo of hair that looked like it weighed more than all the rest of him.

"Man," he said fervidly, "how much bread you spose it takes, get you a boat like that?"

"Whole boatload of bread, man," answered his buddy, who was sitting on the dock, his feet hanging over the water. This boy was pudgy and soft. His fat back rested against a sour-smelling carton of empty beer bottles, detritus from someone's shipboard party.

The two of them nearly tumbled off the dock laughing. When they had recovered, I asked about the yacht's owner.

"Yeah, I know him," said the skinny one. Now he was frowning. "Evil-lookin' dude. He asks me to help him out sometimes, run errands and stuff. I don't like him much."

"But man, he do give real good tips." The pudgy kid poked his buddy's foot and smirked. "Better'n money."

The skinny boy jerked away. "You shut up, pig-belly."

"Shut up yourself, rat-face." The pudgy one lobbed a beer bottle into the bay.

"What's better than money?" I wondered aloud.

"I ain't tellin'." The skinny kid busied himself with putting some rags in a bucket. "I wanna keep this here marina gig."

"I bet I know what Reyes gave you." I whispered my guess into his ear.

"Hey, lady, I don't use that shit," he protested. "I didn't even keep his ol' tip."

"Nope," grinned his porky pal. "You gave it to your friends who ain't stupid like you. Your friends get to have fun and make real money. We don't gotta squirt gas in no dumb boats, make five bucks a fuckin' hour."

The scrawny kid flung himself at his buddy, catching him off guard and pitching him into the oily water. At the sound of the splash he rubbed his hands in pleasure. "Ol' pig-belly gonna get me in trouble," he muttered. "He ain't even spose to be hangin' round here while I'm at work."

I knelt down to haul his dripping, sputtering friend back onto the dock. The boys squared off, fists raised. I stepped between them, hoping they wouldn't throw their punches at me.

"Look," I told them, "I'm not here to cause anyone trouble. I just want to see Guillermo Reyes."

"What I tell you, man?" the pudgy boy pouted. "She don't care if the dude give you a tip. Why you think she be lookin' for him? Same as ol' blondie last week."

"A blond woman came to see Reyes?" I asked. "Was she a little younger than me? About this much shorter?"

"Yeah. She come here a couple times." Grabbing a fistful of rags from the bucket, he edged away from his friend and began mopping dry.

"When? What days?"

The scrawny kid folded his arms across his bony chest. "That's her business, ain't it? What are you, heat or somethin'?"

What story could I improvise that he would buy? "She's my sister. She's missing. She talked about Reyes a lot, so I thought he might know something that would help me find her."

"Then ask *him* what days he saw her."

"I don't know if I can trust him. It would help, hearing it from someone else. So I'll know if he's telling the truth."

He relaxed his rigid posture slightly. I tried a compliment. "You're a good judge of character. You said yourself he's an evil-looking dude. I just want to find her."

He chewed his lip, thinking it over. He glanced toward his plump buddy for guidance, but the other boy pretended to be preoccupied with wringing out his T-shirt.

"I'm scared for her," I persisted. "Do you have a sister?"

"Yeah. Two of 'em." He dropped his meager arms, sighing heavily. "Musta been Thursday when Reyes sailed in, cause it was payday."

"Five bucks an hour," snorted the pudgy kid. "Gives every penny to his mama, too."

The skinny boy glared him. "Blondie shows up maybe an hour later. That's the day he gimme the . . . that tip ol' pig-belly blabbed about. Next day she's back with some downtown-type dude. They're actin' all sweet and gooey together. They go down to Reyes's boat, and a few minutes later the dude comes steamin' back by hisself, lookin' like he wanna shoot somebody. That's all I ever saw her."

"Is Reyes on his yacht now?"

"Hey, you don't need him, lady," said the chubby one. He squeezed water out of a white tennis shoe. "Ol' rat-face here, he think he gonna get some kinda award for stayin' clean, but I be glad to help you out. I got great shit. Give you a swell deal." Never mind my story—he was sure he knew the real reason I had come looking for the *Esmeralda*.

"Thanks, but I really need to see Reyes."

The skinny kid pointed toward the marina parking lot. "See that big Cadillac? That's his, he rents it. I ain't seen him come by so I guess he must be on the boat."

A rental car? Could it have been Reyes that Star Sister saw? Or Jerome Argyle? The only Cadillac I could see was silver, not blue. But it had been night; surely they could have been mistaken in the darkness.

The skinny boy moved toward his friend. "Hey, man, sorry I blew."

"Yeah, well." The plump one shrugged, then grinned. "What the fuck, man."

A group of people, laden with beer coolers, life jackets and other gear, clambered off a sailboat near the *Esmeralda*. If I was quick, I could slip through the gate to the dock as they came out. If Guillermo Reyes was there . . .

A frisson shook me, as chilling as when the sun vanishes behind a thunderhead.

Reyes was the key to the whole case; I just knew it. But I couldn't shake the feeling of unease. I gave a P&O business card to the skinny kid along with a twenty-dollar bill and a quarter for the phone.

"Look, if I'm not back in half an hour, call this number, okay? Tell the person who answers to send help. There's a reward in it for you if you do."

Guillermo Reyes was up on his rear deck, polishing the already-gleaming brass trim, smoking a clove-scented cigarette as he worked. He was much larger than the magazine photo had suggested. With his black hair and mustache and strong-muscled arms, he looked a little like Evan Krausgill—but more massive, more powerful, more dangerous. He moved with the grace and economy of a cat.

I stood on the pier and waited for him to notice me. He didn't acknowledge my presence, but as he continued to work he began to play to the audience I provided. Finally he stood, tossed the cigarette butt overboard, and wiped his hands on his jeans.

"Tell me, señorita, is it the ship or the captain that fascinates you so?" His smile was warm, but his eyes were black ice.

"I'm Jess Randolph," I told him. "Deborah sent me."

Expressions flitted across his face—surprise, annoyance, apprehension. He settled on polite puzzlement. "Deborah? I am afraid I do not understand."

"Deborah Collington. I'm a friend of hers. She said you might help me."

"But Deborah—I am sorry if I bring you sad news—"

"She's dead. I know." Taking a deep breath I plunged into the story I'd concocted. "Last week I saw her and I told her about this problem I have. She gave me your name. Then she was murdered and I thought, well, maybe I can solve things somewhere else. But that didn't work out, and now I'm, uh, getting kind of desperate. So here I am." I tried to look helpless and appealing and addicted.

Reyes's eyes fixed on me, glacial, unblinking. I refused to squirm.

"Please come aboard, señorita. For Deborah's sake I will be glad to assist you if it is within my power. Kindly first remove your shoes." He indicated the ladder hanging over the side of the boat. I climbed up, shoes and satchel in hand.

"She is lovely, my *Esmeralda*, is she not?" Reyes said. "Never am I so happy as when I am on the ocean, sailing between Colombia, my home, and San Francisco, my favorite city."

The yacht was indeed beautiful. We sat on the molded bench that ringed the deck, watching other pleasure boats head in toward shore. A pair of gulls nearby squabbled over a scrap of fish. Across the bay, Oakland had taken on the rose-gold glow of late afternoon. To the west the gray fog was slithering over the Peninsula hills.

Guillermo Reyes struck a match to light another cigarette, scenting the air with clove and sulphur. The square-cut emerald in the ring he wore seemed as big as the front lawn of the Oakland house I grew up in. "How may I help you?" he asked.

"Deborah said you could, uh, sell me something."

"Of course. The emeralds." He smiled; again his eyes were not touched by it. "The proudest and most beautiful product of my country."

"Actually—"

"*Sí*, I understand," he said. "If you cannot afford the genuine stones, my company manufactures excellent synthetic gems. Emeralds, diamonds, whatever you wish. *Muy elegante*. Only the expert can distinguish them. But for you, señorita,"—he bowed gallantly—"to enhance your special beauty, that lovely flame-colored hair, for you the emeralds are best."

"Deborah bought some of your fake ones. She had you make a duplicate of a necklace."

"How do you know that?" His voice was sharp, staccato. "She said it was to be our secret."

"And George Sanmarco. You sold him fakes too."

"They are synthetic, señorita, not fake. Señor Sanmarco was a colleague. He bought many things from me. *Sí*, I say *was*. I have heard of his death on the radio." The black eyes seemed to bore through me. If I wasn't careful I'd blow this.

"Such as cocaine?" I attempted to sound eager and hopeful, not accusatory.

He turned away, as if in disgust. "Is this what you came for? Because I am from Colombia, you think I must deal in *la cocaína*? It is true we have many troubles from the drug trade. I weep for my country. But to assume that I am part of that evil just because Colombia is my home—that is an insult, señorita. An insult and an injustice."

"Deborah said—"

"No, I am sure she did not." Reyes was pacing, two steps and turn, in the constricted deck space. "If you were so desperate, señorita, Deborah could have found a way to help you herself. Or sent you to her friend at the theater. You are what? *La policía*? I did not kill her, señorita—not her, not Sanmarco.

"She came here to see you before she died. Twice. On Thursday and on Friday. Isn't that right?"

He was leaning over me, his huge bulk blocking out the sky. "So. It is information you are wanting. *Muy bien,* I will give you some. But I am a man of business, señorita. What do you offer me in exchange?"

I tried to stand. "What I—"

"Yourself perhaps?" His hands locked onto my shoulders; he yanked me to my feet.

Reyes's face loomed mere inches above mine. I could smell his damp breath: whiskey, tobacco, clove. Fear wrenched my stomach as I tried to pull free.

Quickly Reyes shifted his grip, twisting my arms behind my back, crushing me tight against his chest. "You are not so beautiful as Deborah, señorita, nor so willing. But one who is not willing can be amusing too."

His mouth came down hard on mine. I stamped on his foot, dragged my arm loose, clawed at his face. I jerked my body, trying to get into position to send a knee into his groin.

The smack of his fist against my temple caught me by surprise. My head rang. The world began to dance and reel.

"Come," commanded a rough voice from somewhere. "We will go below." I was prodded and shoved. Then I stumbled through a short, narrow doorway and down steep stairs.

THIRTY

Pain sang through my left knee where I had landed when I fell, veritable arias of agony. My temple throbbed. My jacket and shoes were gone. I was lying on a bunk, one of two wedged in a V into the bow of the *Esmeralda*. The low teak-lined ceiling seemed to be pressing down on me. A pair of salt-filmed portholes filtered twilight into the gloom.

My wrists and ankles were tied with rope to cleats at the corner of the bunk. The cords had several inches of play so I could move a bit, but that did me little good. Pulling only tightened the knots.

"You have spirit," Guillermo Reyes said with approval. He was standing between the bunks, rubbing his cheek where my fingernails had left a track of blood. "A private investigator. That is a very impressive job for a woman to do." He had searched my satchel, found my business cards and the photostat of my license.

"Let me go, Reyes."

"You have nothing to fear, señorita. This is a business arrangement, that is all. When we have completed our exchange, that will be the end of it."

In the dimness I could sense more than see his icy smile. "You will enjoy yourself, señorita. It is too bad that you can no longer ask your friend Deborah. She would assure you that I am very skilled in these matters. This with the ropes, it always gave her great pleasure."

I could hear the *putt-putt-putt* of a boat returning from an afternoon sail. I envisioned a happy family on board, reddened by wind, enjoyably tired. Other pictures flitted through my mind: My mother at her easel. Scruff running in the park. Deborah Collington sighing beneath the massive weight of Guillermo Reyes. George Sanmarco caught in ropes, floating dead in black water.

Concentrate, I told myself. How are you going to get out of this? If I hadn't jammed my knee I might have been able to fight him off. But now . . .

The pain reached for the high notes; I bit my lip to keep from crying out. Then it sank to tenor level.

Reyes went into the main cabin. A cupboard door clicked open and shut. He returned with a glass and a bottle of whiskey and sat on the opposite bunk.

"To show you that I am an honorable man, I will uphold my part of our bargain first."

"We have no bargain. Cut me loose, damn you."

"But we do. I drink a toast to it." Liquid sloshed into the glass. "You wish to know why Deborah came to see me before she died. It cannot hurt her now to tell you. First, she came because we are old friends. We loved each other in our way, she and I, but we held no illusions. We were, you might say, useful to each other."

"Useful how?" I forced my attention away from a new crescendo of pain. Keep him talking, Jess, give yourself time to think.

"That is the second reason she visited me. I had brought her some things from Colombia—the duplicate necklace and, as you have guessed, señorita, a little cocaine."

"Was she dealing? Did you supply her regularly?" There—if I twisted my wrist just right, I could get the fingers of my right hand, the one away from Reyes, onto the knot at the cleat.

"I do not traffic in such commodities. Sometimes I would bring her a little treat, that is all. But this was different. You may know she planned to remarry."

"To Peter Brockway."

"A foolish man, with no talent for money. Last month Deborah sent me funds to purchase a great deal of cocaine. Señor Brockway would sell it, she said; the profit would save his business. We arranged to meet, the three of us, last Friday. But Deborah decided she had a better use for the profit, so she came a day early, as soon as I arrived. She had found a buyer, a young man at the theater where she appeared in plays, who makes his money in this way. She said he was most thrilled to have such high quality as I brought."

"From the theater? Evan Krausgill—it must be." Was the knot really loosening? Keep him talking, keep him talking.

Even the shrug of his huge shoulders seemed threatening. "I do not know the name. The next day we told Señor Brockway the story we set up, how I am in danger of being caught by the customs officials and must dump the goods overboard. It is a fiction, of course. The *Esmeralda* is registered in San Francisco. No one pays attention when I come or go."

"What—" Never had my mouth felt so dry. I tried again. "What did Brockway do? When he found out?"

"He demanded the money back, but of course that is impossible. It has gone to pay my suppliers. Now he wishes me to provide cocaine on credit so he can pursue his scheme."

"You have more here to give him?" I picked at the knot with tiny, imperceptible movements. Please, let them be imperceptible.

Reyes chuckled. "You are very interested in *la cocaína*, señorita. *Sí*, I have more. I will make sure you have plenty before you leave."

"I don't want any."

"Oh, but you do." He squeezed my arm, stroked my cheek. I froze, praying he wouldn't notice the loosened cord.

"As to Señor Brockway, I have explained that it is bad business to extend credit. But he refuses to go back to where he got the first money."

"Sanmarco. He loaned it to Brockway." I slipped the end of the cord through a loop. Partway there. What would I do when I got it untied?

"*Sí*, a favor to Deborah. He had reason to make her favors. She knew, you see, how he sells the synthetic gems as real ones. People are such fools, they will buy a gem and believe anything you say about its value, because they want to believe. They will not even get it checked."

"But he gave certificates. Proving the stones are real. I saw some."

Reyes laughed. "It is easy to make a false certificate, I assure you."

"And you—you're part of this scheme? Selling fake gems?"

"Not fake, señorita, synthetic. I told you, I am an honorable man. I do not misrepresent what I sell. Sanmarco knew what he bought, which stones were genuine, which were synthetic. What he told his customer is not my responsibility."

"That's why it was so crazy. Their divorce settlement. Deborah was blackmailing him." Pain beat against my temple like a drum.

"Pobre Sanmarco. I warned him at the beginning not to be so trusting of her." Reyes poured himself more whiskey. "But the time for favors was over. Someone was suing George, it would all be revealed in the court, *el escándalo grande."*

"He'd quit paying for her silence?"

"Just last week he told her so. But Deborah was clever. She would sell her home and her shop, she would have money from selling this cocaine. She could live very comfortably in my country."

"In *your* country?"

"Why not? Señor Brockway is becoming a poor man, and Deborah would not love a poor man. Señor Sanmarco would no longer pay her. She had grown tired of playing shopkeeper. I am handsome, no? I am rich. She was beautiful and full of spirit. Why should we not sail away together? It is only sad that she died so soon, before we could carry out this lovely plan."

Reyes did not appear to be mourning, however. He put down his glass and slid over to my bunk. He felt heavy and oppressive next to me.

"It is true, señorita," he murmured. "I like a woman with spirit." The smoky smell of him was overwhelming. He ran his fingers down the length of my body.

Another boat putted by. It sounded like it was maneuvering into a nearby slip. When the engine cut off I could hear voices, people calling cheerily to each other as they tied down the vessel and packed up their gear.

Maybe if I screamed—

Reyes squelched my outcry, smothering my mouth with his in a mockery of kissing. I gagged, coughed, tried to bite.

He lifted his head; I was glad I couldn't see those icy eyes in the murky light.

"*Sí*, full of spirit. I have upheld my end of the bargain. Now it is your turn to give me what I want."

He kissed me again. He rubbed my hair, my cheek. His hands cupped my breasts. I fumbled frantically at the knot. Please, make him be too preoccupied to notice.

Nothing in our nonexistent bargain said Reyes wouldn't kill me when he was done with—whatever he intended to do. He had promised me plenty of cocaine before I left the *Esmeralda*. It would be easy to explain to the authorities—the señorita was strung out when she arrived, officer. She stumbled over the side. I could not reach her in time. *Qué lástima.* Such a pity.

He began to unfasten my shirt buttons.

At last—the rope fell free from the cleat. I twisted toward Reyes, aiming my thumb at the hollow of his throat.

A thud jarred the boat, as if a rock had struck it. Reyes snapped his head toward the sound, making me miss.

Another thud, and another, and the sound of shattering glass.

"*Mierda!*" Reyes threw me back onto the bunk and sprinted through the main cabin.

A shout from the neighboring boat: "Hey, you kids! What do you think you're doing!" Another thud.

Reyes's footfalls sounded on the steep stairs to the deck. I groped at the knot on my other wrist. Quickly—I might only have seconds.

Another yell from outside: "Hey, lady, you in there?"

The second wrist was free. One ankle was free. I could hear Reyes on the deck, bellowing a string of Spanish and English curses.

I grappled with the rope on the other ankle. My hands were sweaty; panic made my fingers slip. This was a different type of cord, nylon, slick. I looked around feverishly. My blazer and satchel had been tossed onto the other bunk. If I scrunched up at the foot of my bunk and stre-e-etched . . .

A dark shape shadowed the cabin door.

I snagged the satchel strap and pulled. The bag fell heavily off the bunk; I almost dropped it. Tightening my grip I hauled it up.

I sifted frenziedly through the contents. Pencil. Lipstick. Hairbrush. At last I felt what I was searching for—thank God Reyes hadn't taken it. My Swiss army knife.

Footsteps clattered down the stairway. I sawed at the final cord.

Reyes's face was as dark as a storm at sea. *"Idiotas!"* he raged. *"Zonzos!* They throw bottles at my boat! I have chased them away." He stood over the bunk, arms tight across his chest. "They say they are looking for the red-haired lady. Who knows you are here, señorita?"

Pain screamed through my knee as my feet hit the floor. I prayed he wasn't armed. My small blade wouldn't stop him unless I hit just the right place.

"Your price is too high, Reyes."

"Do not think that your toy knife frightens me, señorita." He lunged at me. I ducked under his arm, thrusting the knife upward. He howled as I struck soft flesh.

In the doorway appeared a small dark face, framed by a vast mane of frizzy hair. "Hey, lady, you okay?"

Reyes whirled. *"Chingao!"*

I dashed for the stairs. "Out of the way. Quick!"

Looking startled, the skinny kid bolted backward. I scrambled out into the waning daylight, into the sweet, fresh, salt-smelling air.

The boy leaped to the deck. His pudgy pal was waiting. They broke into grins as I jumped down from the *Esmeralda.*

"We do okay, lady? You gonna give us the reward?"

A few slips down, two men on a small boat were watching. "What's going on?" one of them called. "You need help?"

"No. Everything's fine." I was half-running, half-stumbling. The kids trotted beside me. My head pounded; my knee yelped with every step. The dock felt strangely cold underfoot.

The air was cold too. The skinny kid had put on a Forty-Niners sweatshirt. His buddy wore one that said BORN TO BE WILD. I realized my blazer and shoes were still on board the *Esmeralda*.

We opened the gate at the end of the dock and plunged through.

"What's that?" asked the pudgy kid, pointing to my wrist. A cord still dangled, the one I'd untied at the cleat. I removed it and gave it to him. "A souvenir," I said.

The scrawny boy bobbed up and down for attention. "I tried that phone number like you said, lady. But it was just a dumb ol' answering machine. So I said to ol' pig-belly here, maybe we better rescue you."

"It was my idea, throwin' the beer bottles," said the pudgy kid. "I get the reward too."

"Thanks. You both did good work." I got out my wallet and gave them each a fistful of bills. I didn't even care what denomination they might be.

"Get out of here," I warned them. "Stay away from Reyes."

When I reached my car I was trembling so much that I could barely fit the key to the lock. I sped out of the marina lot. At a convenience store I stopped and managed to cope with the pay phone. But before I dared to get on the freeway I had to pull over and let the shaking stop.

THIRTY ONE My apartment was too empty. My footsteps, even my heartbeats, seemed to echo.
Shadows in the corners made me jumpy. I needed company. I
wished for Kit, for Tyler, Lauren, Roger—anyone. I almost wished
for Dan.

Even Scruff wasn't there to bound at me in fervent greeting. But
I could fix that. I went downstairs and pushed Mrs. Fiorelli's bell.

Davy answered the door, his round brown eyes widening in
dismay at the sight of me. He ran down the hall. "Aunt Rosa! Aunt
Rosa!"

Mrs. F came bustling to the door, wiping her hands on her vast
apron. "Oh, sweetie, I'm so sorry. He was only out there a few
minutes. I don't know what happened."

Apprehension welled up in me. "What are you talking about? I
came to see Scruff."

"Davy let the dog out in the yard this afternoon." She glanced
back at the boy, who was lurking, looking terrified, at the back of
the hall. "When he went back to call him in—Scruff was gone."

Gone. The muffled-voiced caller had won. I felt sick to my stomach.

"I can't imagine how he got out," she said anxiously. "He didn't
dig, and the fence is high and sturdy. You know I just got it repaired
last year."

"He didn't get out. He was stolen. Did you see anything at all? Anyone strange hanging around?"

She lifted her arms helplessly. "In this neighborhood, who isn't strange? I heard him barking. I thought he was after a cat. I'm so sorry."

"It's not your fault. I should have taken him somewhere farther from home. Tell Davy I'm not angry."

I wasn't, not at the boy. But I was furious at whoever had abducted Scruff—and at myself for failing to protect him. I hoped that abducted was all they'd done to him. And that made me wonder—what did they have planned for me?

I combed the yard for clues but by now it was too dark to see much. Dispirited, I trudged back upstairs.

I needed to eat—I'd had nothing all day. I fixed a sandwich and a cup of tea, to which I added a generous shot of brandy. The first bite of the sandwich hit my stomach like a ball bearing. Automatically I put the rest of it in Scruff's dish, the way I often did with leftovers. But he didn't run up as usual to scarf it down. The shakes hit me again.

No one answered when I called P&O, but Tyler was at home.

"You okay?" he asked. "Your voice sounds weird."

"I'm all right. It's been a rough day." If I told him about Reyes, or Scruff, he'd try again to yank me off the case.

"Come over for dinner. I bought one of Irma's great blueberry pies." Tyler believed that the right dessert would cure anything. "I won't even bug you about the Videau report."

"I'll have you know I finished it this morning." Telling him so didn't give me the pleasure it should have. "Did you find out anything?"

"Sure did. I haven't gotten anywhere with AmeriCar Rentals. But I reached Bernard Tauber. He's a real estate man in Lincoln, Mass, outside Boston. Big booming voice—you know, hearty yet gravelly at the same time. My mental picture is a guy about two hundred fifty pounds, losing his hair, smoking a cigar."

"A man after your own heart."

"Aw, c'mon, Jess. I haven't smoked in weeks and you know it."

"I give you full marks."

"Okay, listen. Tauber's real estate business is doing better than okay, he's got spare cash, so he starts buying gems from Sanmarco as an investment. Emeralds, his favorite color's green, I guess because it's the same color as money. The first few he checks out with a Boston appraiser, everything's swell, and besides they've all come with their pedigree papers. So after a while he decides to skip the extra expense."

"Just what Sanmarco's counting on."

"Exactly. So not long ago he goes to sell them off, he wants the cash for something else. And surprise, the latest purchases turn out to be fake."

"Not fake," I said wearily. "Synthetic."

"At first Tauber thought it was an honest mistake. Besides, he was safe, because Sanmarco's sales contract had this clause where he guaranteed to buy back the stones. But Sanmarco said no deal. He accused Tauber of keeping the real stones and trying to scam him by screaming fraud. So Tauber got pissed and decided to sue."

"But he wasn't angry enough to fly out here and gun Sanmarco down."

"Highly unlikely. But brace yourself for this, Jess. He's also suing the financial advisory service that turned him on to Sanmarco. Fraser and Collington Associates."

It was like a physical blow. "Allen. Oh shit."

"I'm sorry, Jess."

"Damn it to hell, anyway." Suddenly everything was too much. The tears came in a torrent. I was infuriated with myself—I'd done enough crying for one day.

"Jess? You want me to come over?"

"He lied to me, the rotten bastard. He said he'd never heard of Tauber."

"Give me ten minutes. I'm on my way."

"No! Please don't." I willed myself to stop. "Enjoy your pie. I have things to do tonight. Parts of this case are beginning to come together."

"Better tell your big brother Ty about it."

If I did, he'd insist on coming along. I had to handle it alone. I couldn't let myself get spooked by what happened this afternoon.

"I'm just going out to catch a petty sneakthief. I won't need backup. I'm going to try out your new toy, that night-vision scope."

"No, you're not. I shipped it back today. One of the lenses was cracked."

"Damn. Okay, I'll go to plan B."

"Do the cops know what you're up to? You know our policy."

"I . . . don't worry. I'll make sure that base is covered."

I had to assure him twice more that I was fine. Finally I got him off the phone and let myself finish sobbing.

It took two phone calls to set things up.

Plan B involved talking Kit Cormier into lending me a camera. Mine was at Roger's. I had taken it to shoot pictures of the birthday boy and forgotten it in the confusion of Lucia Sanmarco's summons. There wasn't time to cross the bay to fetch it.

The other call reached an answering machine. I left an anonymous message; I hoped it would be intriguing enough to lure my quarry.

I dreaded phoning Gardino. I had only suspicions, no proof. If I turned out to be wrong, he might decide I'd do anything— even violate the law and the terms of my investigator's license— to save my father, a man he was sure was guilty. He would not be easy on me.

Someone else answered Gardino's line. "Homicide, McCabe."

I explained who I was and asked for Nick. He wasn't there.

"Can I reach him at home?"

"Nope. He's incommunicado for a couple of hours at least. Got off duty a while ago and had a sudden urge to drive up to Chico and see his kid."

"Good. I'm glad he's doing that."

"Probably passing Arbuckle right about now. If it's urgent, I can get the Highway Patrol to flag him down."

"No, I'll contact him later." Okay, Jess, I thought. Looks like it's up to you.

Using the camera instead of the night-vision scope, I'd have to reveal my presence. There was no way to avoid needing the flash. That meant a confrontation: it would be wise to have it on tape. I got my small voice-activated recorder from my studio, loaded in a fresh cassette and put it in my satchel.

I cleaned and loaded George Sanmarco's gun. His Colt was less powerful and accurate than my .38. I thought about going to the office to pick up my own weapon. But having laid my trap, I didn't know how quickly it would spring; I needed to get to my destination. I didn't like carrying a gun at all, but after today I felt in need of protection.

My head pounded. My wrenched knee throbbed. All my muscles and bones ached from tiredness. I craved another cup of strong tea with a healthy dose of medicinal brandy. Only this was the wrong time for such therapy. I settled for a shower, very long, very hot.

It failed to make me feel better. I scrubbed myself hard three times, but I couldn't slough off the day's events. Reyes leaning over me with his hot, whiskeyed breath, his hands slithering on my skin. Star Sister shuffling her gray feet in the squalid alley. My outburst at the jail. Allen's sunken, tear-filled eyes. Impressions jumped and tumbled in my brain.

And then a couple of pieces clicked into place. I shut the water off and toweled myself dry. I'd been close to right about the why of the slayings, but wrong about the who. Now I was sure I knew who the murderer was.

I needed hard evidence. A way to trap the killer. Until I could figure that out, I decided, I'd better proceed with my original plan. Though not guilty of homicide after all, my target had nevertheless committed several crimes. Not only that, if I was right, the person I was after would be the real slayer's next likely victim. With luck I might keep someone safe.

Fog had congealed into misty rain out near the ocean. The street-lights and neon signs wore ghostly halos.

But the Pacific Playhouse sign was dark. The whole building was dark. I huddled, damp and chilled, in the juncture of the two wings. After a while I gave up. Time for plan C. Shivering, I began to creep around to the rear of the theater.

A hand touched my shoulder. I nearly jumped out of my skin.

"Hey, calm down. It's me." Kit, with the camera.

"Oh! I'm glad it's you. Thanks for bringing me this."

He touched me again—another shock, this one more pleasant.

"Sure you don't want me to stay? I don't like your doing this alone."

"It's my job. It's easier alone." Part of me wanted to yell: yes, stay with me! But I didn't really know him—how he would react to what I hoped to do, whether I could trust him in a tight situation. "There shouldn't be any problem. It's only some prankster breaking windows for kicks. No one's been hurt, nothing taken. The staff is just getting tired of sweeping up broken glass."

"I'll help you catch him." Kit smiled. "Hog-tie him, give him the third degree—"

"I'll take good care of your camera, Kit. I promise. Now please go, before the culprit shows up."

"The camera's not what I'm worried about."

I was silent.

"Whatever you say, ma'am." He gave me a quick hug, a brief brush of his lips against my damp hair. Then he drew me close, enfolded me, gave me a real kiss.

My body remembered Guillermo Reyes and shuddered. Kit

pulled back with a hurt, questioning look. In the darkness his eyes weren't blue but slate gray.

I had to fix this. I clutched him, giving the kiss back doubled.

It was with great reluctance that we released each other. He smoothed some soggy hair off my forehead. "Take care," he whispered. It sounded like music.

I watched Kit walk back to his car and drive away. His headlights sent out twin cones of yellow to pierce the black rain.

It was easy to punch away the cardboard and unlatch the window. My knee protested fiercely as I heaved myself through. The cardboard had been attached with masking tape; I pressed it back in place.

Heavy, dark, strange shapes haunted the gloom: power drills, stacks of canvas flats, sharp-toothed saw blades, jagged ends protruding from the lumber bin. My flashlight beam darted across them as I got oriented.

Then I cut the beam. I settled down on the workbench to watch and wait.

THIRTY TWO

And wait. And wait. I was fighting to stay alert, to keep watching the huge dim rectangle of the window with the broken pane.

How good it would feel just to curl up on the workbench and sleep. A hard mattress, but right now anything would do. Besides, it was softer in its way than that frightful bunk on the *Esmeralda*. A phantasm of Guillermo Reyes loomed up—I forced it away. Think of pleasant things, Jess. Chocolate chip cookies. The exhibit opening tomorrow with six of your paintings. Kit Cormier—God, how I wish I could have let him stay. Let him help, let him hold me. Know that he was in the same room, breathing the same air. My bedroom, my own soft cozy bed—

A noise.

A tiny noise, yet loud enough in this silence to jolt me awake. Only it was coming from the wrong direction. A clicking like a key in a lock, a shuffle of steps in the hall. I sat up, tensed.

The door to the scene shop eased open. Too dark to tell who was there.

A flashlight switched on, its pool of white light bouncing off table saws and scrap wood, just as mine had. I scrunched myself as small as possible to stay out of the beam and tried to figure out where its source was, so I could aim the camera.

"Anybody home? Jess? You here?" It was a whisper. Had Kit come back? How had he gotten in?

The light caught my toe, dipped away, returned and lingered. "Hey, there you are, doll!" Evan Krausgill—just what I needed. He sidled up to the workbench, no longer bothering to whisper. "I guessed you might come here tonight. Couldn't bear the thought that you'd catch our master criminal by yourself, so I came to help. No action yet?"

"Douse that light, damn it. You want to screw everything up?"

"My, my. Such language." He plunged us back into blackness.

"Where's the TV crew?"

"What?"

Sarcasm was lost on him. I directed the camera toward the window again.

"Never mind. Did you really come to help? Or are you the reason I'm here?"

"What do you mean?"

I wished I could see him. It was a great disadvantage, not being able to observe his reactions. At least the tape recorder was whirring away in case he said something incriminating. Was he armed? I eased Sanmarco's gun out of my satchel to have it ready. Just in case.

"You're PR director for a nonprofit theater that's strapped for cash. They can't be paying you much. Yet you live in Pacific Heights, drive a classic Jag. 'Evan iz great,' says your license plate. You wear diamond ear studs."

He laughed. "Trust fund, babe. My old man was loaded."

"I heard about the coke you bought from Deborah. Just two days before she was murdered. That's where your money comes from, isn't it."

I could feel him step closer. He smelled of some musky aftershave. "Come off it, Jess. You can't be thinking—"

There was a clatter at the window and a *whoomph* as the cardboard broke away from the empty pane.

Evan jumped. "Hey!"

"Shut up!" I whispered. "Don't move."

Something reached through the space and undid the latch. The window lurched upward. A shape climbed into the room.

I triggered the camera. The room flared white in the burst of the flash, then blackened again, except for some dancing points of color.

"What the hell!" the intruder yelled. I shot off the camera again.

Suddenly the scene shop was flooded with light as Evan, damn him, hit the switch to the overhead fixtures. Peter Brockway stood near the middle of the room, rubbing his eyes to shut out the brightness.

"Hello, Peter," I said. I'd have to make the best of a bad situation. "Come to get Deborah's painting?"

"Jesus!" He waggled his head bewilderedly, trying to adjust his vision and his thinking to this turn of events. "What painting?"

Beside me, Evan was quivering with excitement. If only he wouldn't do something else stupid.

"The Gerard Duplisea oil you stole from her flat."

"Me? What is this?"

"I found it, Brockway. The videos too, the ones you swiped from your own company to make Investech think your sales were up."

"*You* left that message on my machine?" Brockway slunk backward. "What's your game? Blackmail? I haven't got money."

Evan slithered around the room to stand guard by the window. Maybe he had some sense after all.

"You were looking for the necklace," I said. "Only it wasn't there—the police had it. So you grabbed whatever was valuable and easy to carry. The painting. Her jewelry. I don't know how you missed her gun."

"You're insane. I had a key—why would I bust down the back door?"

"Is that what happened? How do you know? The news reports didn't say so."

"But—they must have." Brockway stared at me. His face had gone slack and gray. The rest of him was twitching.

"If you'd used a key, the police would have guessed who it was right away. Better to make it look like some punk who heard about the necklace on the six o'clock news."

"You can't—you're crazy!" Brockway whirled, flailing an arm toward Evan. "What about *him?* Deborah's murderer is right here and you can't even figure it out."

"Oh no, you don't." Evan edged away warily.

"What'd she do, Krausgill, screw you over on the dope like she did me?"

"Hey, man, I—"

Brockway sprang, catching Evan by the throat. Evan tugged at Peter's arms, his gym-trained muscles straining, but he couldn't break the frenzied hold. They hit the floor, thrashing and kicking. Evan gasped; he was turning purple. He brought his knee up hard into the other man's groin. Brockway shrieked and let go.

Evan rolled away. He scrabbled on his knees to the door, pushed to his feet and dashed out.

"Oh Jesus," moaned Peter, curled like a prawn on the floor. "You let the son of a bitch get away."

I stood over him with Sanmarco's gun. "He didn't kill Deborah."

"You can't think I did it!" Slowly and painfully he crept into a sitting position.

"The cops might think so. You have motives. You couldn't pay back the man who'd lent you money for your drug deal. Your fiancée had double-crossed you."

"No! I would never hurt her. Even though she betrayed me—I loved her! Don't you get it? I loved her."

"Tina Margolis told me how she showed up at your house right before she was killed. You're just lucky Tina fell asleep and didn't witness what happened."

"Deborah left again! She called Sanmarco from my place and went over there. I swear—I never killed anyone. Okay, you're right about the break-in, but—"

At last, I had it on tape. I could take him to the police. In jail he'd be safe.

"Come on, Brockway. You've got a lot of explaining to do to the cops. Believe me, you're better off in their hands. When Deborah's estate gets sorted out, the killer will realize that you and she and Sanmarco had your business interests all tangled up, thanks to that necklace. And he may decide you know more about their deaths than you really do."

"What—you know who killed her? Who? Tell me who!"

"No. I need to get proof first. Just be glad you'll be out of his reach."

But I had lost his attention; he was gawking at the door behind me. Was Evan back? I turned.

In the doorway stood the man whose name I'd just refused to say. He was wearing a hat. Allen's disguise fedora. He held Deborah's Beretta pistol in his hand.

"I prefer your previous speculation, Jessica," Brad Collington said. "It will explain things so well when the two of you are found here in the morning, shot to death."

THIRTY THREE

"Give me your gun, Jessica."

I clutched the Colt tighter. Collington had the Beretta leveled at me. Peter Brockway sprawled on the floor, ashen and open-mouthed, probably not even aware of the whimpering sounds he was making.

There was no way I'd be able to shoot first. Reluctantly I handed Collington the gun. Now he had one aimed at each of us.

But what was he doing here?

"I'll let you kill Jessica with this, Brockway," Collington said, indicating the Beretta. "It was Debbie's; it would be logical for you to have it. And it's the one that killed Sanmarco, so the cops will assume you did that, too.

"Then I'll shoot you with Jessica's gun and put it in her hand. She was on to you, you tried to kill her, she fired in self-defense—a plausible story, don't you think?"

He smiled, a patrician smile under the dapper hat. The successful businessman, the pillar of the community. Looking at him made me feel sick.

"I kept warning you away from this case, Jessica. But you're just like Debbie—won't listen to reason. You don't even love your dog enough to stop a course of action that could bring him to harm."

"Scruff! Where is he? How did you—"

"It was easy. You're right—he'll come to anyone for a few bites of Swiss cheese."

"Is he alive? Is he all right, damn you?" I wanted to leap at Collington, pound him to a pulp, tear out his eyes. But he had two guns. I'd never get near him.

"Don't worry, Jessica. In a few minutes you won't care. When Allen asked me about Bernard Tauber this afternoon, I knew I'd have to do more than scare you. You were getting too close."

"That's how you knew you'd find us here," I realized. "Allen told you."

"Yes, he was quite excited about your plan. Your father is very proud of you, Jessica. Of course he thought you were after Brockway here. But I knew it wouldn't take you much longer to figure out the truth."

"I did figure it out—once my head cleared enough to realize Tauber didn't have to be dealing with my father. There are two people at Fraser and Collington. Then I remembered—it was you who suggested that Allen wear that damn hat." Hot tears stung my eyes; I blinked them away. "You were hoping he'd be mistaken for you. You wanted him to take the rap."

"The hat was just a small precaution. I encouraged the police to think Deborah was killed by some random mugger." Collington smiled slightly. "But what I'm about to do will gain Allen his freedom. You said I should help him out."

We were in a workshop full of potential weapons—hammers and rasps, all kinds of saws, things to cut and gouge with, blunt instruments. What could I use, what could I reach in time? I glanced at Brockway. He was cringing on the tiles, gaping at Collington, his face bloodless under the gray. He wasn't going to be much help.

My flashlight and Evan's were on the end of the workbench. If I eased over there slowly . . .

"Stop right there, Jessica. Don't move again."

"I don't get it," Brockway whined. "Who's Tauber?"

"A client of Sanmarco's," I said. "Introduced by Mr. Collington here. George sold him fake gems, claiming they were real. Tauber was suing them both."

"Shut up," said Collington.

"You were in it together, weren't you? Sanmarco pushed emeralds—Guillermo Reyes sold him both genuine gems and artificial ones. George would start the clients with the real thing, then substitute the fakes on subsequent orders once trust got built up. And you got a cut of the take from clients you referred."

"Very clever." Collington looked amused. "You have a sharp mind."

"What did Allen get?"

"He knew nothing about it, Jessica. I hope that comforts you. Now then, Brockway, you get to shoot first."

"Wait," I said quickly. "Let me tell you what else I've come up with." I was beginning to feel wobbly; I needed to sit down. How long could I keep Collington talking? Would it do any good?

"You said the other night at dinner that you went to Boston last weekend to see a client. It was Tauber you saw—you wanted to talk him out of making a stink. But he was stubborn, and time was getting short. So you flew out here on Saturday, letting your wife think you were still in Boston. You rented a car, a blue Ford, right? And you took George to dinner—to what? Work out a strategy?"

"I had to convince Sanmarco to settle quietly. Tauber wouldn't negotiate with me alone—he insisted any deal had to be with both of us or neither. Going to court and having this become public would ruin me. Other clients would find out and sue. There might be a criminal prosecution. I'd end up losing everything."

"But Sanmarco refused to settle?"

"He couldn't—he didn't have the cash. And do you know why? Because my daughter was blackmailing him. My daughter!"

"So you went to confront Deborah. What happened?"

There was a low, squat metal tank close behind me. I sank down onto it.

"It won't matter if you know everything," Collington said, "since you'll be able to do nothing about it. Deborah wasn't home. I waited in my car until she got back—two, three in the morning. I was surprised when Sanmarco's wife showed up and rang Debbie's bell; thank God she didn't notice me. She went away when no one let her in."

Brockway was listening with his jaw dropped, his eyes huge with terror.

"Debbie was amazed to see me, especially right after talking with Allen. Everything I'd asked Allen to tell her was true, you know. About making up with her. Starting over. God, I had such dreams."

Collington quivered with nervous energy. But the guns didn't waver. "She wouldn't let me come upstairs, I don't know why, invasion of privacy she said."

I could understand that. An absent father turning up out of the blue . . .

"So we drove out to the beach and parked to talk. Debbie told me about the trade she'd made with Allen, giving him the necklace for me. She had his tie dangling around her neck. In the darkness I could just barely see her face. For a moment I deluded myself that she was my sweet little girl again."

"But she turned out not to be," I prompted.

"I explained why I was there—Tauber, the settlement I needed. You know what she did? She said it served me right. 'Well, well,' she said, 'I've got a crook for a father. I always knew it.' And she laughed at me. Christ, I've never been so *angry*."

The anger was still there. His handsome face was contorted with it. "Then she said, 'Maybe I should tell the world what a rotten criminal bastard I have for a father. I could tell mother, Bradford, Allen, all your clients. I could write a letter to the New York District Attorney, or maybe the newspapers.'

"She asked how much it was worth to me to have her keep quiet. Can you imagine—blackmailing me. Her own father. Just like she'd done to Sanmarco. A thousand a month, two thousand, there'd never be an end. She asked for the necklace back as a down payment. Offered to return Allen's tie in exchange."

"Then what happened?" I asked. But I already knew.

"I didn't mean to do it. Not to Debbie. I was so angry. The necktie—it was just hanging there. I yanked the ends, twisted, pulled. It happened so fast."

"You killed her! You killed her!" Brockway moaned, as if he had just caught on.

"And Sanmarco too," I said. "He figured it out, didn't he?" There was a rubber hose attached to the tank I was sitting on. All the fear I was struggling to keep out of my voice was working in my fingers, twisting and bending the hose. "He demanded the necklace back."

Collington's voice grew strident. "He wanted to sell it, use the money for Tauber. With Sanmarco dead, Tauber's just dealing with me. I'll buy him off with the necklace myself."

"No, you won't. It's a fake too. Worth a few hundred bucks, tops."

"You're lying!" Collington yelled.

All at once I realized what I was sitting on. Slowly, jerkily, I reeled in the hose, hoping he'd think it was activity born of fidgets and fear.

"The one Deborah gave Allen is a copy. I know where the real necklace is."

"Nice try, Jessica. But I'm still going to kill you. No, I forgot. Peter here is going to kill you. Now."

"Look, Collington," pleaded Brockway. "We can make a deal. We can—"

"Shut up. You've got nothing to offer me, nothing." Collington shoved the Beretta into Brockway's flailing hand.

Brockway was panicked. "Oh please, I can't, I can't, don't do it, oh God please—"

Collington's tongue flicked over his lips like a snake's.

"Shoot her." He pushed the Colt against Brockway's ear.

Brockway moaned. He raised the Beretta with both hands and pointed it shakily, his eyes screwed shut.

"Fire it. Now."

I grabbed a block of scrap wood. Flung it out. A better aim than I'd hoped for—it smacked Collington's shoulder. The Colt fired, but he'd been distracted almost enough.

A red stain spread on the arm of Brockway's shirt. The Beretta clattered to the floor.

I fumbled at the switch on the tank. The compressor kicked to life with a rumble: *thdr-thdr-thdr.*

Collington came at me, Colt in hand. "What the fuck's that!"

"A power stapler." I held it up close to his face. "Drop the gun and don't move. All I have to do is press it against your skull." But don't make me do it, I pleaded silently. Please don't make me do it.

"Brockway," I snapped. "Grab that gun you dropped. And find something to tie him up."

Leaning on his good arm, Brockway fought to push himself up. "I . . . please . . . no . . ."

Collington whirled and fired. Brockway crumpled. At the edge of my vision a bearded face flashed near the doorway. Kit? But what . . . ? From somewhere came the sound of a dog barking.

Collington jerked back toward me. The Colt was in my face. I thrust out with the stapler, trying to push the revolver away. My wrenched knee buckled. My feet tangled in the coils of the hose.

The *THWACK* of the staple gun was not quite drowned out by the explosion that sounded as Deborah's father fired again. Something hot seared my cheek. Then blood began spurting, red as a ruby, red as a flame, red as a child's crayon, from Brad Collington's eye.

THIRTY FOUR

Lemon yellow, soft aqua, seafoam green. *Seascape II.* I supposed it looked good, it and the others, hanging on the gallery wall.

"Very exciting work indeed." Muriel Gittelsohn, Hammerwood's owner, was elegant in rust-and-black silk, her iron-gray hair piled high on her head to make her look even taller and thinner than she was. "I'm proud and honored, having you in this show. It's such a privilege to be able to encourage a young artist like you, with such skill and clarity of vision."

"Thank you," I said flatly.

She patted my shoulder and moved on to make the same comments to Marise Krupinski about her crazy photo collages.

I turned away from my paintings. The colors were beginning to swim before my eyes. When I first looked at the work of my fellow artists in this show, I had instantly decided that mine was the worst. Then that it was the best. Then that it was the best and the worst at the same time.

I'd probably never be able to evaluate my own work accurately. There was nothing to do for it but go home and finish the painting on my easel. Then paint another one. And another one. And just keep painting.

It was late in the afternoon. The brie and bread and olives were almost gone, but there was still a good crowd of people sipping champagne and making that social buzz of conversation, polite and meaningless.

"Doesn't the show look great, Jess?" Darlene Chong was at my elbow, her sleek black curtain of hair gleaming. "I'm sorry you didn't get here this morning to help us hang it."

"Me too." While the others were having that pleasure, I had been still enduring a siege of questioning at the Hall of Justice.

"Muriel's really pleased. I'm glad I talked her into putting your paintings on this wall—it's the best angle in the gallery for showing things off."

"I'm sure it is." I tried to sound enthusiastic.

Darlene gave me an odd look. "What's the matter? Stage fright? Yesterday you seemed really excited about the show."

"I'm—yes, stage fright. I guess that's it."

The crowd included some familiar and welcome faces: Tyler, Lauren, Uncle Jack. Claudia had come earlier with an abundance of McFarlanes—sisters, brothers, cousins, her mom and dad. "Super stuff, Jess," she had bubbled. "Really fantastic. I couldn't wait to show off what extra-talented people I work with."

Roger and my little brothers were there. Keith regarded the proceedings with the disdain required by his new status as a fourteen-year-old, but Teddy seemed delighted. He announced he was going to be an artist too, although he was clearly more inspired by Ira Plotkin's rocket-ship sculptures than by my paintings. "This is wonderful, sweetheart," Roger had said, kissing my cheek. "Your mom would have been so proud."

I'd heard so many compliments that they'd begun to sound empty. Who was this great artist everyone was talking about? Nobody I knew.

What almost everyone had carefully refrained from mentioning were the shadows smudged under my eyes and the bandage where my cheek had been grazed by Collington's bullet. Those closest to me knew, but thank God, last night's events had come down too late to make the eleven o'clock news or the Sunday paper. Whenever some clown insisted on prying—"Hey, what happened to you? Get in a fight?"—I mumbled something noncommittal and turned away.

Kit Cormier came up and handed me a fresh glass of champagne. "Want to leave? You look tired. Gorgeous but tired."

I smiled at him. "Exhausted is the word. But let's stay until it's over. I hardly ever go to a gallery opening where I'm one of the stars. I'd better make the most of it."

Kit's eyes were soft, full of concern. And such a fantastic blue. "Thanks again for coming back last night," I said. "And for sticking it out at the Hall of Justice through that long ordeal."

"I was worried about you. But you didn't need me. By the time I got back to the theater it was all over."

"You're wrong. I do need you." It may have been the first time I'd said that to anyone.

He looked embarrassed though not displeased. "I'm glad I found Scruff in Collington's car. I'm surprised the creep didn't kill him."

"Some people think more highly of animals than they do of other human beings."

Darlene Chong appeared again. "Jess, there's a man looking for you." She pointed to a figure standing by one of the rocket ships: Nick Gardino, carrying a brown grocery bag.

I excused myself and went up to him. "Why, Inspector, I'm thrilled. I thought you'd be sick of my company after practically spending the night with me two nights in a row."

"Don't be flip, Jess. I thought you might like these." He handed me the paper bag.

Peeking in I saw a blazer and a pair of shoes—the ones I'd left behind on the *Esmeralda*. I looked inquiringly at Nick.

He shrugged. "Seems like the Brisbane police got an anonymous phone tip that they might find something interesting down at Heron Point Marina. When they reached the boat in question they found a guy nursing a knife wound. Odd wound, up through the armpit." He gave me a quizzical gaze. I said nothing.

"The guy had some outlandish tale and he was acting wild enough to make them suspicious. When they checked, sure enough, he was in the country illegally. They talked some judge into giving them a search warrant and found a lot of expensive white powder stashed in a locker under a bunk."

He nodded toward the bag. "They also found that stuff. I guess you left some details out of the story you told me last night. But I managed to put two and two together."

Apparently he wasn't going to press for the missing particulars. I was grateful. "Thanks for bringing this. How . . . how's Collington?"

"Touch and go. The eye's gone for sure. They don't know if he'll live, or if he does, whether his brain will be in good enough shape for him to stand trial."

My own hand—one little push on a power stapler. When I closed my eyes to quell the queasy feeling, my field of vision filled with red.

Nick pretended not to notice that I was trembling. "Brockway, on the other hand, is moaning and groaning. If there is a trial he'll be able to testify."

"What about Lucia Sanmarco?"

"A cousin turned up to take care of her. Poor woman." He nodded at *Mephistopheles.* "You do that?"

Involuntarily I tightened inside. "Yes."

"Not bad. That yours too?" He indicated *Seascape I.* "You know, your work's okay."

I wondered if he was referring to more than the paintings.

Gardino left, and I turned to look for Kit. Instead, I spotted another man standing just inside the gallery door. A tall man in his early fifties, with reddish hair and a hesitant expression, holding an overcoat and a flight bag.

I approached him slowly. He greeted me with a fleeting, cautious smile. We watched each other guardedly for a long moment before he spoke.

"I wanted to come and thank you," Allen Fraser said. He still had a pallor. The jail experience hung in his eyes like a ghost.

"Yes. Well, I'm glad we found out the truth." My throat was oddly dry. "I'm glad it wasn't you."

"I also wanted to say good-bye. I'm on my way to the airport."

"I see."

He shifted his coat and flight bag from one hand to the other. "There's a lot I have to do in New York now that Brad is—the business, of course. And someone should look after Braddy and Isabel."

"Yes. Well, have a good flight."

He cleared his throat. It sounded like a carefully rehearsed speech: "I've been thinking about what you said, Jessica—Jess—and you're right. I want to apologize. I am ashamed of what I did to your mother—and to you. I've changed since, I'm not the same person. But that doesn't undo the terrible things I did wrong. And I realize it's not fair to expect that you'd want to know me as a . . . a father . . . or even a friend. I thought it would be best if I just got out of your life again quickly."

A sudden hollow place opened inside me, one which wanted to fill with tears. Surely it was because of my lack of sleep. Because of yesterday's harrowing events.

For the briefest of moments his hand brushed my cheek, the edge of the bandage. "I hope you weren't hurt too badly."

I shook my head. I didn't trust myself to speak.

He offered a shy, fleeting smile. "Perhaps—if you agree—we could write once in a while? Exchange Christmas cards?"

"I . . . I think that could be arranged."

He looked away. His gaze traversed the room, turned inward for a second, returned to me. "Maybe, Jess—as long as I'm here—maybe you'd be willing to show me your paintings."

For a moment I stared at him—this man, no longer quite a stranger, who was my father. Red hair like mine. Tall and lean like me. His cheeks were wet.

I could sense Kit's presence just behind me, a sort of warmth. Tyler and Roger were watching, ready to step in at the least signal.

I slipped my arm through Allen's. "I'd be pleased to show them. And then . . . do you think . . . I mean, maybe you could postpone your flight for a couple of days? I'd like us to get to know each other."